"Let's get this out of the way."

Finn tangled his hands in Jessie's hair and lowered his face to hers in a kiss that had her heart stuttering. Instead of stepping back, he drew her even closer, until she could feel the heat of him along every line of her body.

The porch beneath her feet seemed to tilt and sway, and she reached out for his waist.

Lost in the kiss, he backed her up until she bumped into the back door, and still the kiss spun on and on until at last they were both gasping for breath as they reluctantly stepped apart.

"So much for professionalism." Finn quirked his lips, but then he was suddenly looking at her with such fierce concentration, she could feel the heat of it all the way to her toes. "All that proved was..." He abruptly yanked open the back door. "I think you'd better go inside."

RAVES FOR R. C. RYAN'S NOVELS

THE COWBOY NEXT DOOR

"Satisfying...This sweetly domestic story should win Ryan many new fans."

—*Publishers Weekly*

"*The Cowboy Next Door* is a work of art."

—Fresh Fiction

COWBOY ON MY MIND

"A strong, protective hero and an independent heroine fight for their future in this modern rough-and-tumble Western."

—*Library Journal*

"This talented writer...invites you to join a little journey that has you biting at the bit for more."

—Fresh Fiction

REED

"4 stars! Ryan's latest book in her Malloys of Montana series contains a heartwarming plot filled with down-to-earth cowboys and warm, memorable characters. Reed and Ally are engaging and endearing, and their sweet, fiery chemistry heats up the pages, which will leave readers' hearts melting...A delightful read."

—*RT Book Reviews*

LUKE

MATT

ALSO BY R. C. RYAN

BORN *to be a* COWBOY

R. C. RYAN

FOREVER

New York Boston

Copyright © 2019 by Ruth Ryan Langan

Cover photography by Rob Lang. Cover design by Elizabeth Turner Stokes. Cover copyright © 2019 by Hachette Book Group, Inc.

Forever
Hachette Book Group
1290 Avenue of the Americas, New York, NY 10104
read-forever.com
twitter.com/readforeverpub

First Edition: November 2019

Forever is an imprint of Grand Central Publishing. The Forever name and logo are trademarks of Hachette Book Group, Inc.

The publisher is not responsible for websites (or their content) that are not owned by the publisher.

The Hachette Speakers Bureau provides a wide range of authors for speaking events. To find out more, go to www.hachettespeakersbureau.com or call (866) 376-6591.

ISBNs: 978-1-5387-1119-4 (mass market), 978-1-5387-1121-7 (ebook)

Printed in the United States of America

OPM

10 9 8 7 6 5 4 3 2 1

To families, whether by birth or choice.
To my own crazy family, who make me
so very proud.
And of course, to Tom. Always to Tom,
the great love of my life.

BORN *to be a*
COWBOY

PROLOGUE

Haller Creek, Montana—Seventeen Years Ago

Stupid horse," ten-year-old Finn Monroe muttered after he was tossed from the saddle. He slumped in the tall grass by the edge of Haller Creek, his backside thoroughly bruised, his faded jeans soaked.

Free of its inexperienced rider, the roan gelding, Beau, stepped into the creek to drink.

Mackenzie Monroe, Finn's adoptive father, brought his own mare to a halt and dismounted. "Old Beau throw you again, son?"

"I'm not your son." Finn's knee-jerk response was spoken through clenched teeth.

His older brothers, Ben and Sam, might be fooled by this rancher's soft words and kind eyes, but Finn knew better. He'd been through enough foster homes to know that sooner or later every adult he trusted would eventually turn on him. If they weren't rationing food as punishment for some infraction of their cherished rules, they were writing scathing reports about his foul language, his unwillingness to handle the required chores, or his quick-trigger temper. And one, a hulk of a bully named Horace Fredlubber, had actually used his fists on him, leaving Finn so bloodied that he had vowed he would do whatever it took to escape that hellish existence.

And now here he was. In the middle of Nowhere, Montana, expected to muck stinky stalls and herd dumb cattle. Today he was being forced to ride to high country on the back of a horse that wouldn't follow behind the others and constantly veered off the path to make its own way. Finn had been slapped in the head with low-hanging branches, had nearly toppled headfirst down an embankment, and was now soaked clear through, while his brothers were far ahead, playing at being cowboys and laughing like loons.

Mac reached out. "Give me your hand, Finn."

"I don't need your help." Ignoring the outstretched hand, he got to his feet and let out a string of curses at the discomfort of waterlogged jeans weighing him down.

He enjoyed a moment of satisfaction at the frown that appeared on Mac's handsome face. His adoptive father had made it clear he wouldn't tolerate coarse language in his presence, and to reinforce the issue, saw to it that a chore was added each time one of the boys violated that rule.

"You'll take Sam's chore tomorrow. Mucking stalls."

"Yeah. Sure. Bring it on." Finn knew it wouldn't be long until this man would be like the others before him, resorting to physical punishment when he'd had enough.

Mac reached out and Finn ducked, only to realize the man was just taking hold of the horse's reins, which were dangling in the water.

Seeing the boy's reaction, Mac deliberately kept his tone easy. This wasn't the first time he'd seen Finn and his brothers brace themselves for physical punishment, something that was abhorrent to Mac.

"Beau's testing you, Finn. A horse can sense a novice rider. If you want him to do things your way, you need to learn how to be firm without yanking on the reins and hurting him. Each time you pull too hard, he'll go the other way just to show you he's bigger and, therefore, in charge."

"He's always going to be bigger than me. How can I ever take charge?"

"By learning patience. Try liking him. Animals respond to kindness. Then give him a chance to like you, too." Mac paused before adding, "I see something special in you, Finn."

"Yeah? What?"

"A bright, inquiring mind."

"I'd rather be as big as Ben, and as tough as Sam."

"Being smart is even better than being big and tough."

"Why?"

"Because a smart man can win every fight without resorting to violence. When you use that brain instead of your fists, you'll win every time. Just ask Zachariah York about the many battles he's won in the courtroom."

Finn thought about the lion of a man who lived with them and used big, fancy words that only a genius could understand. "That fussy old geezer?"

"That fussy old geezer is one of the most brilliant lawyers in the country. And he never had to resort to his fists to win a case."

Leading Beau to dry land, Mac surprised the boy by tethering the animal before choosing a sunny spot in the grass to sit, as though he had nothing more important to do than sit and talk.

Mac whipped off his wide-brimmed hat and wiped an arm across his forehead before glancing up. "A good day to ride. Look at that. Not a cloud in the sky." Mac waited until Finn followed his lead and settled in a warm, dry spot. "My wife, Rachel, used to say a day this perfect was proof that God's in His heaven and all's right with the world."

Finn shot him a quizzical look. "What the fu…" He caught himself in time to avoid another chore. "What's that supposed to mean?"

"I like to think it means that on a day this perfect, we can trust that there's a Higher Being watching out for us."

"Yeah?" Finn's scowl deepened. "Where was your Higher Being when horrible Horace Fredlubber was beating me senseless?"

Mac went very still, as he always did when one of his boys revealed a hint of the unbearable pain they'd endured before coming into his life. These three brothers usually guarded their secrets like hoarders, and Finn, the youngest, most of all.

Mac chose his words carefully. "I believe that even at our lowest point, when we feel we can't take anything more, goodness finds a way. Maybe it's just a hint of a smile when our eyes are filled with tears. Or maybe it's three ragged boys, bent on stealing, who showed a glimmer of light in the darkness."

Something in the way he spoke had Finn looking at him more closely. "Oh, man. Are you crying?"

"Even grown men cry, son." Mac swiped an arm across his eyes and got to his feet before offering a hand to Finn.

This time the boy accepted his help and stood quietly while Mac pulled himself into the saddle and led Beau toward Finn.

Without a word Finn mounted.

As he followed behind Mac's mare, Finn found himself comparing the life he had now with the life he'd lived before coming to this ranch. It was true that he and his brothers were expected to work alongside Mac and the three old men who lived here. Roscoe Flute was an ancient cowboy. He only had a couple of teeth, but he had a killer smile—and he seemed to always be smiling. Otis Green was a black man from the south side of Chicago, who should have been a fish out of water on a ranch in Montana but managed to fit right in, raising a variety of fruits and vegetables in his carefully tended garden behind the barns. And Zachariah York was a prim and proper retired lawyer who did most of the cooking, while the others handled the ranch chores. Mac called the old man brilliant. Finn decided to pay more attention to what he had to say.

Finn had to admit that here in this place he and his brothers routinely did things a city boy like him had only dreamed of doing. But they were constantly exposed to something else they'd never had before—books and respect. Teasing and laughter. So much laughter that sometimes Finn forgot for hours the miserable life he'd left behind. The laughter was contagious. He found himself wanting more of it.

As for the books, he often got lost in them, especially if Zachariah was the one reading aloud before bedtime.

There was a gentle kindness in this place. A special kind of respect for one another he'd never experienced before.

He was intrigued to learn that Mac thought he had
a good mind. Nobody had ever encouraged him to be
smart. Was it possible he could one day be as smart as
Zachariah?

Maybe, Finn thought as he caught up with his brothers,
he'd give his adoptive father and life as a rancher a
real chance.

Hell, what did he have to lose?

CHAPTER ONE

Haller Creek, Montana—Present Day

Finn Monroe unlocked the door to his law office and tossed his battered attaché case on the desk. He then removed his fringed buckskin jacket and draped it on the back of his chair. Both the attaché and the jacket had been gifts from his mentor, Zachariah York, when Finn had passed the bar. They'd been the old lawyer's trademark and were now Finn's daily uniform, as was his longer-than-typical hair. He figured if Zachariah could look like a lion in court, he could, too.

He'd begun his practice here in the little town of Haller Creek by accepting every legal request that came his way, from an arrest for impaired driving to settling neighbors' property disputes. Recently he'd snagged the attention of the national media by winning a case against the county for the largest monetary award ever, for a rancher who had suspected county officials were blocking his herd's access to his water supply. There was now talk of submitting Finn's name for a city office, even though he insisted it wasn't his dream.

Finn ignored all the background noise of politics and continued to go about his business.

Hearing the door open behind him, he glanced over his shoulder.

"Mr. Monroe?"

The feminine voice was soft, tentative.

He tried not to stare, but the women who usually came to his little office here in Haller Creek didn't look like corporate executives.

Instead of boots, denims, and a T-shirt, she wore heels, a sleek dress, and a matching jacket. Her blond-streaked hair fell in soft waves around a small, heart-shaped face. Except for the nerves that had her wringing her hands, she was almost too perfect to believe.

To put her at ease, Finn stepped around his desk to offer a handshake. "My friends call me Finn. Finn Monroe."

"Jessica Blair." She paused and tried to smile. It had her lips quivering. "My friends call me Jessie."

"Nice to meet you, Jessie. You're not from around here."

"I grew up in Arvid. It's a little town about a hundred miles from here."

He nodded. "I've heard of it. Lots of great cattle ranches. Did you grow up on a ranch?"

"Yes. My aunt Nola, Nolinda Blair, raised me on her ranch after my parents died when I was five. She's the only family I've ever had."

"You're lucky to have family willing to take you in. It sounds as though you love her a lot."

Her eyes filled, and Finn had to resist an unnatural urge to wrap his arms around her and offer her comfort.

Instead he indicated the chair facing his desk. "Why don't you sit and tell me why you're here."

As she sat, she said, "Please, give me a minute."

He rounded his desk and took a seat facing her. To give her time, he asked the first question that came to him. "Is your aunt's ranch big?"

Jessie nodded. "Big enough to provide a comfortable life for us, and for four previous generations of Blairs."

"I bet she and her husband needed a big family to keep it all going."

"Aunt Nola never married. There were just the two of us. And a team of loyal wranglers who'd been with her for years."

"So you worked the ranch with her?"

"I did until I left for college. And even then, I came back every chance I had, and every summer. I've always loved living on her ranch."

Seeing the glint of fresh tears, he gave her time to compose herself. "I know what you mean. My family has a ranch outside of town. When I'm not here, I'm at home on a tractor or riding in the high country with the herds."

Her eyes brightened. "You're a rancher? Then you understand how important the land is."

"I do." He folded his hands, hoping to ease her into the reason for her visit. "If you grew up in Arvid, why are you here?"

"When I went on the internet and researched the town of Haller Creek, yours was the only law office listed."

"Why Haller Creek?"

"My aunt mentioned it. She said that's where her new wrangler had once worked."

"Does your aunt want me to look into this wrangler's background?"

She shook her head. "I'm here because..." Again that threat of tears. When her lower lip quivered, she bit down before speaking. "I believe my aunt is in some sort of serious trouble. All because of a smooth-talking cowboy. She's disappeared without a trace."

Finn let out a slow breath. "So your aunt's missing?"

She nodded.

"And this wrangler...?"

"Wayne Stone." She lifted a handkerchief to her nose as if she'd just smelled something distasteful.

"Wayne Stone is the smooth-talking cowboy?"

Another nod while she twisted the handkerchief around and around her fingers.

"Have you gone to the police with your suspicions?"

"Yes." She lifted her head. "They looked into it. They said the marriage was valid, and there was no sign of foul play."

"Wait a minute." He held up a hand to stop her. "Marriage? When did your aunt marry him?"

"Two weeks ago. Even though she barely had time to get to know him."

"That must have been a surprise. Did she tell you about it before the wedding?"

"She called me the day they were getting married, on the way to town. She said after the wedding they were leaving for a honeymoon. And there hasn't been a word from her since."

"I'm guessing your feelings were hurt that she waited so long to let you know."

"This isn't about my hurt feelings." A big tear rolled down her cheek and she brushed it aside. "It isn't like Aunt Nola to do something like this. This is completely out of character."

"It may not be usual, but a woman has the right to share her life with someone. And going on a honeymoon isn't a crime."

"You don't understand. She couldn't bear to be away from the ranch for more than a few days at a time. And now she's been gone for two weeks without a word. I just know something's wrong."

Finn steepled his hands on the desk. "Miss Blair, you don't need a lawyer. If the police won't help, and you want to pursue this further, I'd suggest a private detective."

"I hired one." She dug into her pocket and held out a business card.

Finn took it and read the name. "Matthew Carver. Retired FBI agent." He looked over at her. "Are you happy with his work?"

She nodded. "He called to say he had some news. He sounded...agitated. We were supposed to meet yesterday."

"Let me guess." Finn sat back, folding his hands atop the desk. "He never showed up, and you realize he skipped town with your money."

"No." Another tear slipped out and she brushed it aside. "He was involved in an accident on the interstate. He's dead, and whatever information he had for me died with him."

Finn experienced a little tingling at the base of his spine—a sure sign that he was beginning to get sucked in. "A good investigator would have kept notes. Could you call his office and ask his assistant..."

"I called. Her name is Bev, and she's his wife. She was so grief-stricken she could barely speak, but she said when his belongings were returned to her, his briefcase containing all his notes was not among them."

The little tingling got stronger.

Finn sat staring at the woman across the desk, mulling the consequences of what he was about to do. If he took this case, he'd be up to his eyebrows in work that could keep him from helping friends and neighbors in need of legal counsel.

Still, there was that tingle.

And the fact that she was just about the prettiest woman he'd ever met.

He dismissed that out of hand. He wasn't stupid enough to let important work pile up while he pursued some ridiculous story for the sake of a pretty face.

Was he?

Yeah, maybe he was.

And right now, though he could think of all the reasons why he should send her packing, the only thing that mattered at the moment was getting a chance to know more about the fascinating Jessica Blair. And maybe, just maybe, he could help her.

"I'll need a lot more information than this." He lifted a packet of documents from his desk drawer and passed them to her. "I'd like you to fill these out. If I need more, where can I find you?"

She took in a deep breath. "I checked into the Dew Drop Inn on the interstate last night so I could find you first thing today."

"Okay." He shoved back his chair. "While you answer everything on these pages, I'll head on over to Dolly's Diner and bring back coffee. How do you take it?"

"Two sugars and two creams."

He grinned. "So you like a little coffee with your cream and sugar."

That remark brought a half smile to her lips.

As he started down the street, he was chuckling to himself. He'd figured that a woman with a figure like that would never let sugar past her lips.

His smile suddenly dissolved when he realized it may not be the only wrong impression he'd had. As he began to put time and distance between them on the walk to Dolly's and back, he began to question his rash decision to take this on.

Jessica Blair could turn out to be a jealous, vindictive relative who'd just discovered she'd been locked out of a hefty inheritance. And though her nerves looked real enough, she could be nothing more than a really good actress playing on his sympathy.

"Two creams. Two sugars." Finn set the lidded cup on his visitor's side of the desk before taking his chair and picking up the completed pages.

As he started to read, he looked up. "You're an accountant?"

"A certified public accountant with Ayers and Lanyer in Bozeman."

At the mention of one of the state's biggest firms, he lifted a brow. He would have pegged her for something in the public eye. Modeling. TV news.

"I've taken a leave of absence until my aunt is found. My boss isn't exactly happy about it."

Finn nodded. "Then there's no time to waste. I'll begin by running a check on Wayne Stone. If he worked on ranches in Haller Creek, he should be easy to find. From time to time I employ a detective, Basil Caldwell, also a retired FBI agent, and I trust him to be thorough and discreet. He should have something for me by the end of the day. Can you give me a number where I can reach you?"

She spoke the numbers, and he entered them in his cell phone before giving her his number as well.

"As soon as I hear from Basil, I'll call you with the information."

For the first time her smile wasn't forced or nervous. "Thank you, Finn. You don't know how much this means to me."

"Don't thank me yet. The police could prove to be right, and we'll find we don't even have a case."

She touched a hand to her heart. "I don't care what the police think. I know I'm right. And I know when your detective starts checking, he'll know it, too. I've lived with my aunt long enough to guarantee she would never willingly be gone from her ranch this long."

Finn watched her walk out the door before sitting down to continue reading through the papers she'd filled out. Her handwriting was easy to read. He wished he could say the same for the woman. He wouldn't be the first person to lose perspective because of a pretty face. But what he liked even more was that she had a good mind to go with the looks. Anyone working for Ayers and Lanyer had to be sharp. But that didn't mean she was to be trusted. He intended to reserve judgment until he found out more about Jessica Blair and her aunt.

If he'd learned one thing since going into this business, it was the fact that a good mind and a pretty face could mask a greedy heart.

CHAPTER TWO

Finn tossed his attaché case on the passenger side of his truck before heading back to his family's ranch.

The little town of Haller Creek was bustling with people happy to be outdoors. Winter in Montana was always blustery, but this particular year had been long and bitter. Now the hillsides, covered with snow just weeks ago, were showing signs of green. Cattle were being herded to higher elevations, where they could soon feast on lush grass. The wranglers who tended them had replaced their heavy parkas with rolled shirtsleeves.

Springtime was a season of hope, and nowhere more than here in Montana.

When he arrived home, he noted the line of vehicles parked alongside the back porch and found himself grinning. As always, his oldest brother, Ben, and his wife, Becca, had managed to make it out to the ranch for supper. And that was a good thing, especially since

Penny, his middle brother Sam's new bride, was just about the best cook in the entire state. Ben, Haller Creek's sheriff, was happy about that because Becca was taking cooking lessons from Penny. Ben claimed he didn't marry Becca for her cooking skills, and it was true that they were madly in love, but Finn figured good cooking couldn't hurt.

Ben and Becca were currently building a new home on a parcel of land on the family ranch. Until it was ready, they still lived in town in her rental house.

Sam and Penny were planning on doing the same, but they were still in the talking and planning stage, and still living in the main house.

The old red van parked alongside the barn belonged to Mary Pat Healy, and that meant she'd just returned from another road trip. Mary Pat, the county's social worker, nurse, and homeschool advisor, visited every isolated ranch in the district during the year, dispensing equal amounts of advice, comfort, and hugs to the many ranch families who held her in highest esteem. She'd been a friend to their family since before Finn and his brothers had come here to live as Mac's sons.

As Finn walked up the porch steps, he could smell the amazing scent of pot roast and cherry pie and was reminded once again of how happy he was that his brothers' wives enjoyed cooking. Though he had no intention of following their lead, the women who graced their family were much better cooks than Zachariah, who had formerly assumed most of the kitchen duties.

Now Zachariah could concentrate all his energy on assisting Finn whenever he had to prepare for a particularly challenging trial.

The first to greet Finn was Archie, Ben and Becca's

dog, wriggling with delight. Finn knelt to scratch behind the big brown mutt's ears and was rewarded with wet kisses.

"About time you got here." The shiny sheriff's badge on Ben's shirt winked in the light as he clapped a big hand on his brother's shoulder. "We're holding supper for you."

"Nice of you, bro." Finn tossed aside his attaché case bulging with papers and rolled the sleeves of his white shirt before accepting a longneck from Sam.

Otis Green and Roscoe Flute tramped into the mudroom and washed up at the big sink before strolling into the kitchen, to greet the others.

Archie rushed up to greet each member of the family as they entered, expecting to be petted. He wasn't disappointed. The entire family lavished him with love. He dashed over to Zachariah, whose lion's mane of white hair framed a handsome, weathered face.

"Welcome home, Finnian." Like the others, Zachariah paused and leaned down to run a hand over the dog's head as he stepped out of his room to join the group. "Good dog, Archibald, old boy."

Finn glanced around. "Where's Dad?"

Zachariah pointed. "Mackenzie is in the parlor, no doubt going through the mail as always, sorting the bills."

Finn strolled into the other room and found his father frowning over a letter in his hand, his pencil stuck behind his ear.

"Another bill?"

Mac Monroe looked up, his frown easing at the sight of his youngest son. "A legal document of some kind."

He handed it over.

Finn read through it. "This is from the county, ordering

you to remove stray cattle that have migrated onto the southern rangeland that's been declared off-limits, or the owner is threatening you with a stiff fine. Were you aware of any cattle straying from our property?"

Mac shrugged. "It's news to me. But I can't deny it until I check it out. If it's true, it can't be any significant number of cows. Most of the herd is still in the east meadow."

"But the county wouldn't issue an order like this unless there was a complaint. Who would complain about our cattle roaming on land that has been unused for two decades?"

Mac shook his head. "I don't know any more about this than you do, son. But I'm hoping you'll file an official legal response."

"You can count on it. There's nothing I like better than the chance for a good fight." Finn folded the document and dropped an arm around his father's shoulders. "Come on. Time to eat."

As they ambled into the kitchen, Mac managed a smile. "I was so caught up in that letter from the county I forgot to ask how your day was, Finn."

"It was . . . interesting."

His pause wasn't lost on the others.

Becca, Penny, and Mary Pat looked up from the stove, where they were busy stirring gravy, carving the roast, and lifting rolls from the oven.

"Okay." Ben, filling glasses from a pitcher of ice water, gave a grunt of laughter. "Now that you've got our attention, what's that supposed to mean?"

As they took their places around the table and began passing platters of roast beef and creamy mashed potatoes and a big bowl of fresh garden greens, Finn shrugged.

"I had a visit from a mystery woman who said her aunt has gone missing, and she fears for the old woman's safety at the hands of a smooth-talking cowboy."

Ben gave a grunt of laughter. "Shouldn't she be calling me?"

"Yeah. She said she'd already gone to her local police in Arvid, and they couldn't find any reason to investigate."

"Arvid?" Ben nodded. "I know the chief there. Frank Tyler. Isn't this woman a long way from home?"

"Yeah. This is where the cowboy claimed to have worked before meeting her aunt."

"So why hire a lawyer? Why not an investigator?"

Finn shrugged. "She hired a private investigator. He turned up dead in a one-car accident after phoning to say he had some news."

"One car?" Ben's law enforcement antenna went up a notch. "Was alcohol involved?"

"Apparently not. It was after midnight. He is suspected of falling asleep at the wheel."

"So the police won't bite, and a private investigator has an accident. And this woman's crying foul play?" Ben looked around at the others. "This sounds like the plot of one of those B movies. Are you sure you want to take her on? What if she turns out to be some crazy airhead hoping to become the next reality TV star?"

Sam was shaking his head and grinning. "Or a lunatic swearing that aliens abducted her poor old auntie."

Finn accepted a platter of beef and helped himself before passing it to his brother. "Or she could be afraid and in need of my help. At any rate, she got my attention. I contacted Basil Caldwell and asked him to see what information he could gather on a cowboy named Wayne

Stone." He glanced around the table. "Does that name ring a bell?"

The others shook their heads.

"Okay. Tell me, bro." Sam was grinning. "I'm going to ask the obvious question here. Is this woman good-looking?"she used

"Oh yeah."

At Finn's admission, he saw the looks being exchanged. "Okay. So she's better than good-looking. But there was just something about her story that got to me."

"I'm betting she shed a few tears." Ben shared a grin with his wife.

"And she had this little-bitty breathless voice that quivered with every sentence," Sam added.

When Finn's eyes narrowed slightly, the teasing ramped up.

"Oh, Finn. Please help me." Ben used his best falsetto.

"My hero." Sam put a hand to his heart, and then to Finn's forehead. "Hey, bro, I think you're running a fever. You're really hot for this girl."

Really getting into it now, Ben winked at Becca. "I'm thinking we should refer Finn to old Doc Higgins."

His mention of the town's ninety-year-old psychiatrist, who still showed up at eight thirty every morning at his office in the Haller Creek Medical Clinic, had the entire family joining him in laughter.

Even Finn couldn't help himself.

"I know." He shook his head. "I keep telling myself it's not that pretty face that had me volunteering to take this on. But she really did have the tears and the whispery voice and..." He shrugged. "I guess you had to be there."

"Good thing we weren't," Sam deadpanned. "Or

the whole bunch of us would be seeing Doc Higgins tomorrow."

Finn sat at the kitchen table with Zachariah, drinking his last cup of coffee and going over details of the day's strange meeting.

"There was just something about her that had me believing that her aunt really is in danger."

"You said yourself, Finnian, that you were dazzled by her."

"But I wasn't knocked unconscious."

The old lion merely smiled. "A woman like you describe has a way of stealing a man's mind. Even the most brilliant among us, my friend, who believe we're immune to such things."

"I know she could be a really good actress. But I had the feeling that what she most wanted was for someone to believe her, after the police were so quick to dismiss her claims."

"And then there's the private detective."

Finn nodded. "Dying in an accident right after calling to say he had news. She said he sounded excited." He lifted his hand, palm upward. "No. She used the term *agitated*. She said he sounded agitated." He turned to Zachariah. "That's when I knew I wanted to look into this a little more."

"I'll admit I'm intrigued along with you. I'm sure, if this wrangler was employed in any of the ranches around Haller Creek, Basil will have his records by morning."

"That's what I figure, too. As you told me when you first recommended him, when Basil Caldwell starts digging, there isn't a rock big enough to hide any dirty little secrets."

Zachariah smiled. "I've known Basil for more than thirty years. He's the best in the business." He pushed away from the table. "I'm heading off to bed now, Finnian. I look forward to hearing how your meeting goes with Basil." He paused. "I don't believe you told us the young lady's name."

"Jessie. Jessica Blair."

"Jessica Blair. A pretty name. Good night, Finnian."

"'Night, Zachariah."

As Finn made his way upstairs, he thought of Jessica Blair, probably already asleep in one of the dingy rooms of the Dew Drop Inn, the only motel within twenty miles of Haller Creek.

It was hard to imagine a smart, beautiful woman staying at the Dew Drop. But then, everything about Jessica Blair seemed improbable.

Like Sam had said over dinner, it was like the plot of a bad B movie that very quickly emptied the theater.

Except that, Finn thought with a grin, he'd already decided to stay until the closing credits rolled.

CHAPTER THREE

F_{inn} was fast asleep when the ringing of his phone broke the stillness of his room.

"Yeah?" Through a fog of sleep, he heard his brother's voice.

"Finn. Ben here. I'm at a motel on the interstate. The Dew Drop Inn. Know it?"

"Um."

"I hope that's a yes, because there's a woman here who asked me to call you."

It took Finn a moment before the words made sense. "Jessie? Jessica Blair?"

"That's the one. Your new client. There's been a fire."

"A fire in her room?"

"In the motel. Looks like the entire place is destroyed. The volunteer fire department is here now. An inspector will determine where and how the fire started. But for now, I have Jessie and a handful of cowboys who were lucky to make it out with the clothes on their backs. I'll be taking them to my office until they decide where to go."

Finn cradled his phone between his shoulder and chin while reaching for a pair of jeans. "I'll be there as soon as I can."

"Good." In an aside Ben added, "I can see why you went brain-dead. Even with soot on her face, she's a knockout. And if you tell Becca I said that, you'll be dog meat, bro."

The line went dead.

Finn swore as he dressed and raced down the stairs to his truck. He made it to town in half the time it usually took.

Jessie was sitting in Ben's office, wrapped in a blanket, hair wild and tucked behind her ears. She looked small, frightened, and alone, causing something in Finn's heart to twist.

"Hey." He stepped inside and tried for a smile. "You okay?"

"I've been better."

"Were you able to salvage anything?"

She held up her purse. "My phone, driver's license, credit cards. Only because they were under my pillow. I kept them close because the motel was . . . sort of creepy."

"Well, there you go. You followed your instincts. And the best thing of all, you're alive."

"Yeah." She hugged the blanket around her.

Ben stepped in, shaking his hat against his leg. "You made good time."

"Where are the cowboys?"

"I took them to the Fisher Ranch to be put up in the bunkhouse since they're scheduled to start later this week." He glanced toward Jessie. "I thought, since Miss

Blair's car burned, she might like to try that bed-and-breakfast out at the Potter place. Billy Joe and Frieda aren't open for business yet, but I know they've got the rooms finished."

"Maybe another time. I think for tonight I'll just take Jessie back to the ranch."

"Okay." Ben turned to Jessie. "Is that all right with you?"

She nodded as though speaking would be too much effort.

"You'll need clothes. The Haller Creek Aid Society keeps a supply on hand for emergencies." Ben nodded toward the door. "One of them is here now with a box of supplies."

He held the door as a tiny, birdlike woman stepped through the doorway. "'Morning, Mrs. Gaddy. Sorry to wake you."

"'Morning, Sheriff Monroe. You're not responsible for the time an emergency strikes." It appeared that she'd tossed a parka over her pajamas. Her feet were encased in work boots, and her bed-head hair and round glasses gave her a comical appearance. But there was no doubt she'd been through a situation like this before and was ready to take charge.

She glanced at Jessie. "You poor thing. Getting caught in a fire can leave a mind and body scrambled. You follow me."

As she led the way to the back room, Jessie meekly followed.

A short time later the two women were walking arm in arm, and Jessie was dressed in a simple denim shirt and jeans rolled to her ankles. On her feet were scuffed sneakers. In her hand was a heavy denim jacket.

Mrs. Gaddy paused at the door. "If you need anything at all, you call me. Our Haller Creek Aid Society is prepared for any emergency. Don't you be a stranger now, Jessie."

"Thank you, Flo. And be sure to thank the folks who donated all this, too."

When the older woman was gone, Ben turned to Jessie. "Are you all right with spending the night at our ranch?"

"Yes. That will be fine."

Ben nodded. "Well then, if you've got all you need, I'll swing by sometime tomorrow for your statement. For now, try to get some rest."

"Thank you, Sheriff."

Finn took Jessie's hand and led her from Ben's office to his truck, parked just outside the door.

Once inside, he cranked up the heat before starting along the main street.

"That had to be scary."

"Yes." Her voice was soft in the darkness.

"Did the smoke alarm wake you?"

"I guess. No. Wait. Maybe it was somebody pounding on my door." She took in a breath, as though it was too much effort to speak. "I'm not sure. One minute I was asleep, and the next I was awake and smelling smoke and seeing flames shooting through the ceiling. When I ran outside, my rental car was on fire. I'll have to call the rental agency in the morning."

"The most important thing is that you're okay." He reached over and put a hand on hers.

Very deliberately she pulled her hand away and clutched her hands together in her lap. In a very small voice she said, "This was no accident."

He looked over. "You're suggesting that someone would risk the lives of everyone in that motel just to scare you?"

"Maybe he doesn't want me scared. Maybe he wants me...dead, and doesn't care how many others are hurt along the way."

Finn thought about that and drove the rest of the way in silence, his eyes narrowed on the almost deserted highway.

Now that Jessie had said aloud what she was thinking, he couldn't dismiss it out of hand. A missing aunt who had always loved her ranch. A savvy private detective now dead. And a motel fire that almost killed many, including the frightened young woman who insisted that all of it was the result of foul play.

When they arrived at the ranch, Finn helped Jessie out of the truck while she clutched her purse, the only personal item left to her, like a lifeline.

Inside, though it was barely past dawn, the household was bustling with activity. Penny and Mary Pat were already cooking breakfast while the men were about to head toward the barn for morning chores.

When Finn and Jessie stepped into the kitchen, all conversation came to a screeching halt. All heads turned toward them.

Finn kept a hand on Jessie's arm. "Everybody, this is Jessica Blair. Jessie, this is my family. My father, Mac; my brother Sam; his wife, Penny; Mary Pat Healy; Zachariah York; Roscoe Flute; and Otis Green."

"Your...family?"

Sam, the family tease, was grinning. "Careful. There will be a test to see how many names you remember."

While the others chuckled, she managed a weak smile.

"I'm afraid Jessie's been through an…incident that left her pretty shaken."

As Finn explained about the motel fire, the two women gathered around her.

"Are you hurt?" Mary Pat asked gently.

"No, I'm fine."

"Thank heavens you were able to make it out safely. And with your things," Penny added.

Jessie glanced down at herself. "These aren't mine. Mrs. Gaddy from the Haller Creek Aid Society brought a box of clothes. I escaped in…" She paused, clearly embarrassed. "What I'd worn to bed."

"Oh, you poor thing." Penny turned to Mary Pat. "Why don't we take her up to the guest room and help her settle in?"

As they started away, Zachariah hurried to the stove and began stirring something so it wouldn't burn. One by one, the men made their way to the mudroom and pulled on old boots and jackets before heading out for barn chores.

When they'd gone, Zachariah poured a mug of coffee and handed it to Finn. "So this is your new client. I can see why you were dazzled, Finnian."

"I think she's feeling overwhelmed right now. I wasn't sure what to do, so I brought her here. I'm glad Penny and Mary Pat were here to lend a hand."

"It's always helpful to have a woman's touch in a crisis."

Finn stood, holding the cup but not drinking.

"What is it, Finnian?"

He seemed to shake himself out of a mood before looking over. "On the way here, Jessie said she believes the fire was intentional. And that she was the target."

"What do you think?"

Finn shrugged. "I guess we'll know soon enough. The fire department will ask an inspector to determine whether it was deliberate or accidental."

"That isn't what I asked. What do you think, Finnian?"

He took a long sip of coffee before saying, "I realize lightning can strike twice. Twice can be coincidental. But I don't like the odds of there being this many accidents happening to one person, unless it's by design."

Penny and Mary Pat led Jessie upstairs to the guest room.

Jessie stood in the doorway. "Whose room is this?"

"I used to be in here, before Sam and I married." Penny gazed fondly around at the big bed with a white down comforter and a salmon-colored throw at the foot, and the pretty rug in tones of pink and aqua. "I loved this big old room when I came here. I loved looking out that window at the hills filled with cattle." She held out a hand to Jessie. "The best thing about this room is that it has its own bathroom through that door."

Jessie brightened. "I could use a shower. I reek of smoke."

"Of course. You'll find everything you need in there. And in here..." Penny crossed the room and opened a closet door. Inside it was filled with feminine clothes. "Take whatever fits you."

"I couldn't..."

Penny caught her hand. "Sam and I have the room down the hall while we're having our new house built. I store all my clothes in here, and I can't possibly wear all of them. Please, I insist, take whatever fits you."

Jessie's eyes filled and she blinked hard. "Thank you." She turned to include Mary Pat. "Thank you both."

As the two women stepped from the room, Mary

Pat called, "When you've showered and dressed, come downstairs to the kitchen. As soon as the men finish their morning chores, we'll have breakfast."

Jessie managed a smile. "Thank you."

As soon as the door closed, she walked into the bathroom and shed her borrowed clothes before stepping into the shower.

She didn't know how long she stood under the warm spray, using soap and shampoo to wash away the acrid stench of smoke and fire.

Afterward she rummaged through Penny's closet and helped herself to a T-shirt and denims.

Finn's sister-in-law was close enough in size that Jessie was able to easily wear her clothes by rolling up the jeans to her ankles.

Feeling almost human, she stepped out of the bedroom and made her way down the stairs to the kitchen, where the wonderful fragrance of freshly ground coffee lifted her spirits even more.

CHAPTER FOUR

Jessie stood in the doorway, watching as Mary Pat and Penny filled platters with ham, eggs, and fried potatoes. Zachariah fed bread to a toaster until a basket was filled with toast.

Finn, freshly showered and dressed for a day at the office, was removing little pots of jam from the counter and setting them in the middle of the table.

It was a scene that brought a lump to her throat as she thought of the similar breakfasts at her aunt's ranch, except that it had always been just the two of them.

Oh, Aunt Nola. Where are you? What's happened to you? Are you safe? Hurt? Are you...?

She took in a breath, pushed aside her troubling thoughts, and started forward. "Let me help."

She lifted a pitcher of freshly squeezed orange juice and began filling tumblers before placing them on a tray.

"Thanks, Jessie."

At Mary Pat's words she looked over with a smile. "The juice was always my job at my aunt Nola's ranch. I'd bought her an electric juicer and she thought that was the greatest invention. Before that, she'd used one of those glass..." Her words died when she spotted the aged glass juice squeezer on a counter. "Oh, you have one just like Aunt Nola's."

The three women shared a laugh while Penny explained, "I found it in a cupboard, and Mac said it belonged to his mother. I've been using it ever since he insisted he wanted everything of hers to be enjoyed."

"That's sweet." Jessie circled the table and set a glass of orange juice in front of each setting.

When she paused beside Finn, he accepted a glass and gave her a smile. "Isn't it amazing what a shower and a change of clothes can do?"

"Yeah." She returned his smile. "I'm feeling almost human again."

"Well, you look great."

"Thanks." Jessie found herself stumbling over the word, which wasn't at all like her. But seeing Finn with his family, and glimpsing the warmth and humor and love among them, had just added a dimension to Finn she hadn't expected. She was glad to hear the bustle of the arriving family in the mudroom, giving her a chance to turn away, effectively hiding the heat that stole over her cheeks.

The men washed up at the big sink, then circled the table while Zachariah filled coffee mugs and the others carried platters of steaming food to the table. When all was ready, they took their places around the table and paused to join hands.

Jessie's hand was engulfed in Finn's and she glanced over in surprise.

He nodded toward Mary Pat, who said, "Bless this food and all who are gathered here, before we once more travel our many roads."

For some strange reason her words brought a lump to Jessie's throat and she ducked her head.

Beside her Finn said softly, "You okay?"

"Yeah. Fine." She turned away to accept a platter of scrambled eggs and was grateful to allow the conversation to flow around her.

Midway through breakfast Finn stepped away to take a call on his cell phone.

"Yeah, Basil. What do you have for me?"

"Sorry, Finn. After a thorough check of the county records, nobody by the name of Wayne Stone has a record of working any of the ranches in or near Haller Creek. Want me to move to neighboring counties?"

"No. Not yet. Maybe she got the name wrong. I'll see if my client has a photo of him."

"All right. I'll be glad to follow up on any further leads you get."

"Thanks, Basil." At a sudden thought Finn asked, "Did you happen to know a retired FBI agent named Matthew Carver, who was a private investigator in Arvid?"

"I didn't know him personally, but I knew of him. I heard he lost his life in an accident recently."

"Any chance it wasn't an accident?"

After a brief pause Basil said, "Not that I've heard, but I'll ask around."

"Thanks. I'll be in touch." Finn disconnected and returned to the kitchen in time to hear Sam agreeing to ride to the south pasture with Mac.

Mac turned to Finn. "As soon as Sam and I have a

chance to investigate whether or not any of our cattle have strayed onto the property, you can send off a response to that letter from the county."

Finn nodded. "I'll take care of it, Dad. But I can't see the harm in a few cattle straying onto land that hasn't once been used for rangeland in all the years I've been here."

Mac shrugged. "Maybe there's a county employee who gets paid to travel around and watch for strays encroaching on county property."

Finn's recent court battle against the county had opened his eyes to just how far public officials would go to retain the status quo. His voice rang with indignation. "Even so, this doesn't belong to the county. That southern land is privately owned by Ellen's widower."

"By a man nobody has ever seen," Sam added.

"Still." Mac's eyes took on a faraway stare. "It was my mother's wish that the land be set aside for any of Ellen's heirs."

In an aside, Finn said to Jessie, "Family business. I'll explain later."

She merely nodded.

Sam was the first to push away from the table. "Great breakfast, Money." He kissed his wife's cheek.

Jessie turned to Finn. "Money?"

"Penny's name before she married Sam was Penny Cash. The minute they met, he started calling her Money."

Jessie was smiling at the look of love that passed between Sam and Penny.

Sam started out the door. "Okay, Dad. Time to roll. Will we drive a truck, or take horses?"

Mac pulled himself back from his thoughts to say,

"Let's ride. It's been years since I've been on that southern strip of our old ranch. I'd like to see it close up."

"Horses it is." Sam started toward the mudroom. "I'll saddle them. You take your time."

Mac trailed behind. "I'm capable of saddling my own horse, son." He turned at the door. "I'll see you all at supper." His gaze settled on Mary Pat. "Will you be here?"

She nodded. "I won't be on the road for another day or two. I promised Penny I'd help with dinner again tonight."

"Good. Tonight, then." His smile bloomed as he turned away.

Finn suddenly turned to Jessie. "Do you have a photo of Wayne Stone?"

She shook her head. "No. I never had the chance to even meet him."

"Do you think your aunt would have any at her ranch?"

"She may. I couldn't say."

"How would you like to drive over there?"

"Today?"

He smiled. "Now. It shouldn't take us more than a couple of hours to drive over and back."

She got to her feet. "I'll get my purse."

When Jessie started toward the door, Finn turned to Mary Pat and Penny. "We'll still make it home in time for that special supper you're planning."

Penny looked up from the stove, where she'd retrieved the coffeepot. "Who says it's going to be special?"

"If you and Mary Pat are cooking, it's bound to be special."

She crossed the room and pressed a kiss to his cheek. "That just made you my favorite brother-in-law for the day."

He laughed as Mary Pat hurried over to give him a hug before saying, "You do know how to charm."

"I'm not the only one."

At her arched brow he leaned close to add in a stage whisper, "Don't think I haven't noticed the way Dad lights up whenever you're around."

"Does he now?" The older woman patted his cheek. "That just might earn you an extra dessert tonight."

Zachariah, Roscoe, and Otis, still seated at the table, burst into laughter.

It was Otis who said, "Leave it to the youngest to figure out the easiest way to get what he wants."

"I had very good teachers."

The three were still laughing as he walked from the kitchen.

A short time later he returned with his attaché case. Jessie followed, purse in hand, ready for a road trip.

As Finn drove, he picked up the thread of conversation left unexplained at the breakfast table.

"The family business I mentioned concerned my father's sister, Ellen. She was sixteen when she ran off with a wrangler on the family ranch. Her parents went through a range of emotions when their only daughter left without a word. They expected her to return any day, but when she didn't, her father disowned her. After he died, Mac's mother changed her will, deeding the southern portion of the ranch to her daughter or, in the event of her death, any heirs. Shortly after her death, a notice arrived from the county, advising that Shepherd Strump, Ellen's widower, was claiming the land and ordering Mac and his family to steer clear of it. And to this day, though nobody has ever showed up to work the land, Dad has abided by the county's order."

"Why didn't your grandmother leave any of the land to you and your brothers?"

Finn frowned. "I should explain. Ben, Sam, and I are adopted. We came along years after all this nasty family business."

"Adopted." She turned to look at him. "The three of you are so in tune with your father, I'd have never guessed."

"You should have seen us when we were new here."

"Were you scared?"

"We were angry, mean, foul-mouthed delinquents, ready to fight anybody who got in our way."

"You're kidding. How could mean, foul-mouthed troublemakers morph into a sheriff, a lawyer, and a rancher?"

"Through a lot of hard work on Mac's part. Looking back, I'm amazed by his patience and love. He and those three old guys probably had a lot of sleepless nights over the three hell-raisers living under their roof, but in the end, we all became family."

"I noticed. Despite the differences, you're all so relaxed and happy." Jessie sighed. "I had that with Aunt Nola. I really thought it was an unbreakable bond."

Finn couldn't resist reaching a hand to cover hers. It was cold, he noted, despite the sunshine streaming through the truck windows. But this time she didn't snatch it away.

"Maybe when we get to your aunt's ranch, you'll discover this was all some kind of mistake, and she'll be there, eager to tell you all about her honeymoon."

She gave a deep sigh. "Oh, Finn, I hope you're right. But she hasn't phoned me or answered my calls. Not once. Still, I want to believe I'm wrong. I wake up every morning thinking this will be the day she'll call and invite me over to meet her new husband." Her voice trembled slightly. "And we'll all live happily ever after."

CHAPTER FIVE

Jessie pointed. "You'll leave the interstate at that cross-roads up ahead. Turn left onto the asphalt road and follow it for a while."

Like every native of Montana, Finn knew that *a while* could mean a mile or more than twenty. It didn't matter. The area wasn't heavily populated, unless you counted the herds of cattle darkening the hills around them. The ranches here were few and far between, with vast range-land separating them.

After following the road for several miles, he could see a sprawling ranch house in the distance. Drawing closer, he could make out the barns and outbuildings, and a graceful white two-story house with a wide porch encircling two sides of the main portion of the house.

"Your aunt has a fine, sturdy house."

Jessie nodded. "My great-grandfather built it. Aunt Nola lived her entire life with her parents, caring for them in their old age, just as they'd cared for their parents. After they died, she cared for the ranch in the same way." She sighed. "She loved this place too much to ever leave it willingly."

"Hold on now. Let's not jump the gun."

Jessie nodded and leaned forward as Finn turned the truck into the long, circular driveway and came to a halt at the front door.

She didn't wait for him, but stepped out and headed toward the back porch. Over her shoulder she called, "We never used the front door except for company. That leads to a big parlor. This door leads to the heart of the house, the kitchen."

He trailed behind her and watched as she sailed up the back steps and twisted the door's handle.

The door didn't budge.

He saw her shoulders slump as she fished in her pocket for her key. A moment later she opened the door and stepped inside, with Finn behind her.

"Aunt Nola." Even while calling out her aunt's name, Jessie was shaking her head. "If she was here, the door would be unlocked. I've never known Aunt Nola to lock the door unless she was heading to town. And even then she left it unlocked more often than not."

As they walked through the rooms, Finn noted the bright, airy windows free of curtains or drapes, offering an unobstructed view of the rolling hills beyond. The furniture was old but elegant. In the parlor, two wing chairs sat on either side of a stone fireplace. A sofa had a handmade afghan draped over one arm. In the dining room an oak side table displayed fine china and crystal and an oak dining table big enough to seat a dozen guests.

As they climbed the stairs to the bedrooms, he noticed

the walls were decorated with a dozen or more framed photographs of ancestors, many of them bearing a resemblance to Jessie.

Finn paused. "Is this you?"

She turned back to study the framed picture of a little girl with golden curls and a missing front tooth, holding the hand of an auburn-haired woman wearing overalls and rubber boots.

"That was my first year here on the ranch." She pointed to a photograph above it, with a handsome man and a beautiful woman holding a baby between them. "And that's me with my parents."

Upstairs she showed Finn her old bedroom, where more photos covered the top of a six-drawer dresser. While he remained to study them, Jessie moved down the hall to her aunt's room.

A few minutes later he found her there, kneeling by the open closet door.

"What do you have there?"

She looked up. "Aunt Nola called this her treasure chest." She picked up a simple shoebox stored among a cluster of leather boots and similar boxes, before carrying it to the bed.

She removed the lid. Inside she found an old photo of her aunt, auburn-haired, green-eyed, and smiling for the camera.

After rummaging through the articles, she gave a sudden gasp. "This is new."

"How do you know?"

"Because I've never seen it before. And I've seen all my aunt's treasures."

She handed over the photograph and Finn studied the same woman as in the earlier photos. But this woman's hair was now threaded with gray. She wore simple denims and a plaid shirt, the sleeves rolled to her elbows. The man beside her was long-limbed in his faded jeans and cowboy hat. His arm was around her shoulders in a proprietary way. And though she was looking at him, he was staring straight into the camera, eyes narrowed in thought.

"Could this be Wayne Stone?"

Jessie gave a shrug of her shoulders. "I wish I knew. But I do know it wasn't here a month ago. On my last visit home Aunt Nola asked me to bring down her treasure chest. She had an old photo of my father—her brother— she wanted me to have. And I went through everything in this box until I found it. I know this picture wasn't among them."

"Good. We'll take it along. If we can identify him as Stone, maybe Basil can find someone in Haller Creek who will recognize him."

He motioned toward the wranglers who could be seen in the hills with the herds. "Why don't we talk to some of your aunt's old employees and see if they can shed any light on her disappearance."

Jessie replaced her aunt's shoebox in the closet and tucked the photo in her pocket before following Finn down the stairs.

Out in the barn they saddled two horses and headed toward the hills.

As they rode, Finn couldn't help noticing the sleek cattle, the well-maintained outbuildings.

"Your aunt took good care of her inheritance."

"She was a rancher to her core, and so proud of everything her family had worked for."

As they came up over a rise, they spotted a range shack and a cluster of wranglers on horseback.

Finn glanced at Jessie. "Do any of them look familiar?"

"No. But Hugh Jenkins, Aunt Nola's foreman, often takes on extra help in spring and again in the fall." She led the way toward the group of horsemen before dismounting. "Hello. I'm Nola Blair's niece, Jessie. Is Hugh inside?"

The wranglers glanced at one another before one of them said, "I don't know anyone named Hugh."

"Hugh Jenkins. He's ranch foreman here, and has been for the past twenty or more years."

"You'd want to talk to Ken Kyle. He's the one who hired me."

Another wrangler nodded. "Kyle hired me, too." He pointed. "He's up there with the herd."

Jessie pulled herself into the saddle and she and Finn rode in silence until they reached the top of the hill, where a flat meadow was crowded with cattle.

After inquiring about Ken Kyle, they were directed to the far side of the herd.

"Ken Kyle?"

At Jessie's question, one horseman separated himself from the others and lifted his wide-brimmed hat. "Yes, ma'am. I'm Ken Kyle. What can I do for you?"

"I'm looking for Hugh Jenkins, the longtime foreman here."

He shrugged. "Sorry. I just started here a couple of days ago. I don't know anyone by that name."

She glanced at Finn before saying, "Mr. Kyle, my name is Jessie Blair. I'm Nola Blair's niece."

He gave her a blank look.

She tried again. "Nola Blair owns this ranch."

He shook his head. "Sorry. I don't know anyone by that name. I was hired by a man named Wayne Stone, who said he was the owner of this place."

She slipped the photo from her pocket. "Is this Wayne Stone?"

He barely glanced at the photo. "Sorry. I never met my employer."

"Then how did he hire you?"

"Over the phone. He said he got my name from Ron Eberly, who just recently sold his ranch and was about to let all his wranglers go. His offer was too good to pass up."

Finn asked, "How are you and the wranglers paid?"

"We'll get a check in the mail. Instead of being paid once a month, like most ranchers do, Mr. Stone promised it will arrive every Friday. With a deal like that, it was easy for me to hire a slew of wranglers looking for work."

Finn took one look at Jessie's face and knew he needed to get her away from here before she broke down.

"Thanks, Ken." He offered a handshake. "I'd like to give you my card. If the new owner shows up, or his wife, would you give me a call?"

The cowboy shrugged and accepted the card. After reading it he looked over. "Why is a lawyer asking questions about the owner of this ranch? I hope we're not facing any legal troubles."

Finn gave him an easy smile. "Miss Blair here is worried about her aunt. She's been gone since her marriage to Wayne Stone. She'd really appreciate knowing whenever her aunt returns safely home."

"Sure thing." The cowboy tucked Finn's card into his shirt pocket before saying, "Nice meeting both of you."

"You, too, Ken. And thanks for the information."

Finn turned his mount toward the distant ranch house, and Jessie did the same.

They rode across the meadow in silence.

When they reached the barn, they unsaddled their horses and turned them into stalls, forking feed and pouring water into troughs before making their way to Finn's truck.

As he drove away, he saw the way Jessie turned her head, studying the house with a sadness she couldn't hide.

He reached over and took her hand. "I know this is all too much to process in one big gulp. But hang on, Jessie, and we'll sort through this."

She looked down at their joined hands before turning to look at him. "Do you really think so? Or are you just trying to humor me?"

"I'm a lawyer. My job is to weigh all the facts as I gather them, and try to make some sense of them. Right now, I'm as confused as you are. But I'm beginning to think there's something very wrong here. If you're willing to trust me, I'll walk with you through this maze and we'll come out the other side."

"But will we come out the other side whole? Or will I be forced to accept this . . . this stranger as the legal owner of my aunt's ranch?"

"That's the million-dollar question." He squeezed her hand. "I hope Wayne Stone finally shows his face. And I hope, when he does, your aunt has simply fallen hard for a good guy. But if he turns out to be a scam artist, or if she's been harmed in any way, you have my word I won't rest until he pays."

"But look how brazen he is. He just walked in and took over another person's lifelong property without a fight."

"Oh, he'll have a fight on his hands if he doesn't have the answers to your questions. I guarantee you that. Because there's nothing I like more than a good knock-down, drag-out brawl. I just happen to do my fighting in a courtroom."

She was silent for the longest time before saying softly, "Thank you."

"I haven't done anything yet."

"You believe me. You're the first to do that. You'll never know what it means just to have you on my side."

Finn stared straight ahead. "I guess I'd know a little about that. When I was a scared, angry kid, I thought the whole world was against me. Then I met Mac, and he let me know he would stand by me, no matter what. Knowing that changed my whole world."

He turned and met her direct gaze. "Everybody needs to know they have somebody on their side, Jessie."

He shot her one of those sexy smiles that did strange things to her heart. "So, my advice to you is"—his tone changed to a teasing drawl—"you stick with me, little lady, and we'll get to the bottom of this mystery."

She found herself laughing despite her worries. "That's really cheesy, Counselor."

"But it made you smile."

She nodded and turned to stare out the window. Finn looked over to see Jessie lean her head back and close her eyes.

It may have been the emotional toll she'd been enduring, or simply the soothing motion of the vehicle as it ate up the miles back toward Haller Creek, but he soon heard the sound of her soft, even breathing that told him she'd found some escape in sleep.

He took the opportunity to study her as she slept. Her hair fell over one eye, drifting like a cloud against her cheek.

It was true that his first impression of her had been that she was almost too pretty to believe. But it wasn't her physical beauty he was thinking about now. There was a sadness, a vulnerability in her that touched a chord deep inside.

He understood what it meant to need someone to believe in you. But more than that, he knew how lost a person could be without family. It had been the separation from his brothers all those years ago that had left the deepest scars. With Ben and Sam by his side, he could face anything. Without them, he'd felt the weight of the world on his young shoulders.

Such a heavy load for Jessie to carry on those slim shoulders, he thought as he studied her. And for some reason he didn't want to probe too deeply, he felt a real kinship with this woman who had burst into his life with a wild tale and sad, trusting eyes.

He knew there were those who would call him a fool for getting involved in this whole crazy story. After all, the authorities who dealt with such things on a regular basis had already discounted her fears. Still, he couldn't agree with them. In fact, the more he looked into this, the more he began to believe. Or was he talking himself into something because he really wanted to believe her? It was easy to care about Jessie. Despite the air of sophistication, there was a simple goodness in her that tugged at him.

Hearing alarm bells going off in his mind, he looked away from her and turned his attention to the road.

Time to remind himself of one more fact. He was a lawyer. She was his client. And he couldn't mix business and pleasure.

CHAPTER SIX

When Finn parked the truck, Jessie's head came up and she looked around, struggling to get her bearings.

"Where are we?"

"Back at my home." He pointed to the line of trucks alongside the back porch. "Looks like my brothers beat me to it again. Not that I'm surprised. They always seem to make it in time for supper."

He stepped out and circled around to open the passenger door.

As Jessie moved along beside him, she looked over. "You're lucky to have so much family."

"Yeah." He leaned close, like a conspirator. "But don't let them know I admitted that."

She was smiling as they climbed the steps and walked through the mudroom on their way to the kitchen.

The minute they entered the house, Archie raced toward them, tail wagging, tongue lolling.

Finn stooped. "Jessie, this is Archie. He was rescued by Ben and Becca, and has become another member of the family."

"Hi, Archie." She was instantly on her knees, accepting wet doggie kisses and laughing. "Oh, he's a sweetheart."

The chorus of voices and the sound of laughter greeted them, causing them to stand and pause in the doorway.

To Finn it was a familiar sight. Penny slicing something in a roaster. Becca lifting a pan of biscuits from the oven. Mary Pat tossing a salad. Zachariah filling glasses with water before placing them around the table. Otis and Roscoe, fresh from tending the herd in the hills, washing up at the big sink, while Ben and Sam and Mac stood together, sipping longnecks and sharing an amusing story about their day.

Ben was saying, "...threatened to sue the county if she couldn't find her false teeth after spending a night in jail drying out. And I told her she was so drunk the night before, she probably swallowed them. And wouldn't you know, she dropped to her knees and clutched her stomach, claiming she'd sue to have them surgically removed."

Mac and Sam were laughing so hard they had to wipe tears from their eyes.

Sam shook his head. "Only Minnie Purcell could be that gullible." He looked at his brother. "So, did you find her false teeth?"

Ben nodded. "On the floor under the bunk in cell two."

"So," Sam asked, "they fell out while she was asleep?"

"Looks like it. Of course, she was asleep in cell three. But she thinks she may have loaned them to old Titus McCool, who was sleeping off a drunk in cell two, and claimed he couldn't eat without his teeth."

Another round of laughter followed that statement.

Mac looked over. Seeing Finn and Jessie, he crossed the room. "I hope your trip to Arvid brought some answers."

Finn shook his head. "Just more questions."

Mac dropped an arm around Jessie's shoulders. "I'm sorry to hear that."

Finn could read the surprise in her eyes before she leaned into Mac for a moment before she straightened and pulled away. "At least I got a chance to show Finn my home."

"It's a nice place. You'd like it, Dad. Lots of hills covered with lots of cattle."

"With so many ranches failing these days, it always does my heart good to hear about one that's prospering."

Through her pain Jessie felt a glow of pride. "My aunt is a good caretaker of her family's treasure."

"That's really nice to hear."

"So you're Jessie." Becca crossed the room to offer her hand. "You've already met my husband, Ben. I'm his wife, Becca."

"Hi, Becca." Jessie nodded toward the wriggling dog. "Archie's mama."

Becca laughed. "That's me."

"He's so sweet."

"We think so, too."

They turned when Penny announced that supper was ready. As they took their places around the table and joined hands while Mary Pat intoned a prayer, Jessie glanced at Finn beside her. He winked, and she felt a tiny curl of heat dance along her spine.

All of this should be alien to her, and yet, for some strange reason, everything about this felt so right. Not just this large, noisy family, but this man. Maybe it was because he was the first to believe her. That meant so much more than she could say. Of course, it didn't hurt that he was just about the best-looking cowboy she'd ever met. He was fun to be around, and sexy as hell, even though he didn't seem to be trying to impress her. He was just being himself. Maybe, she thought, that's what was so appealing.

She shrugged aside her thoughts as they settled into their places and began passing platters of roast chicken, oven-roasted potatoes, tiny garden peas, salad, and rolls warm from the oven.

Archie crawled between their feet and settled under the table, hoping for scraps.

Everyone was talking at once, and blanketed by the blur of voices and laughter, Jessie sat a moment, taking it all in. Despite the nagging worry about her aunt's safety, despite the fear that everything familiar in her life was being threatened, she felt a tiny flicker of hope. There was just something about this loud, strange bunch of odd characters that Finn called family that put her at ease.

He leaned close to whisper, "You okay?"

She smiled. "Yeah. I'm fine."

"Good." Beneath the table he closed a hand over hers and again she didn't pull away. Instead she let the warmth of his touch, the strength of it, fill her with a quiet sense of peace.

Mary Pat was carving more chicken and passing it. "Will you be staying the night, Jessie?"

Finn answered for her. "I'm hoping to persuade her to become a longtime guest."

"Oh, I hope you will, Jessie. The more the merrier." Mary Pat looked across the table at Mac, who nodded in agreement.

Jessie's cheek dimpled. "Thank you so much for having me. I will, for now. I'll take it a day at a time."

"Good." Sam exchanged a grin with Ben. "And, as long as you're staying on, it's time you get initiated into the Monroe Doctrine."

"What's that?" Jessie looked from one brother to the other.

"Those who don't cook get to do the kitchen cleanup." Finn laughed. "Tonight that means just you and me."

She nodded. "I think that's only fair."

"Woo boy." Sam high-fived Ben. "You and I just found a willing kitchen cleaner to set us free."

"Not on your life." Becca nudged her husband. "We didn't get here until Penny had finished all the hard work. So we'll be lending a hand in the cleanup duties, too."

Sam drew an arm around Penny's shoulders. "Does this mean I get a pass because of your hard work?"

"Wrong, cowboy." She shared a laugh with Mary Pat. "Tonight we ladies will sit in the parlor drinking our coffee while you join the others in here."

Sam merely chuckled. "Your loss, Money. We'll be the ones having all the fun in here."

Sam was right, Jessie thought as she and Becca joined Ben, Sam, and Finn in cleanup duties. She couldn't remember having this much fun—and they were doing nothing more than clearing the table and washing dishes.

Between the rowdy jokes, the teasing, and the occasional splash of sudsy water when she least expected it, she'd never laughed this much.

Sam was a born tease, but Ben and Finn could hold their own against him. Becca had the look of a fragile doll, but when it came to interacting with Ben's brothers, she took a backseat to nobody. The more raucous their antics, the bolder Jessie became, until by the end of the evening she was trading mock insults with Sam while judging a contest between Ben and Finn to see who could stack the most plates and set them in the cupboard without dropping a single one.

Finn won, but only because Ben bobbled his stack and had to hurriedly set them down or risk dropping an entire armload.

Seeing the expression on his face, Jessie laughed so hard she had to grab on to Finn's arm.

"Oh, Ben." She took in a breath. "I wish you could have seen the fear in your eyes."

"I was wondering how I'd replace fifty-year-old dishes."

"And how you'd explain the mess to Dad," Finn added.

"Yeah. There's that, too." Ben wrapped an arm around Becca. "Okay, babe. Our work is done here. Time to get back to town."

They all trooped into the parlor to join the others, while Ben and Becca called their good nights before summoning Archie, who was calmly chewing a rawhide bone under the table.

When they were gone, Mary Pat turned to Jessie. "Things sounded pretty noisy in the kitchen. How was your introduction to the Monroe cleanup crew?"

"That was the most fun I've ever had washing dishes."

Sam tugged on a lock of Jessie's hair. "Wait until morning when you get to have even more fun doing laundry."

While the others laughed, Finn said, "Now he's really trying to test your limits." He gave her a long, steady look. "But if you're dying to do laundry..."

More laughter before Mary Pat held up a hand. "Don't

push your luck. Jessie was a good sport, but there's a limit."

"Spoil sport," Sam muttered before winking at his wife.

"Come on, Sam." Penny set aside her empty coffee mug and caught her husband's hand. "We've both put in a full day."

After calling good night, the two climbed the stairs together to Sam's room.

Otis and Roscoe had long ago left for the bunkhouse to continue their ongoing game of gin rummy.

Zachariah yawned. "Good night, Jessica. Finnian." With a courtly nod he made his way to his own room off the kitchen.

In an aside, Jessie asked, "Is he always so formal?"

"Yes. He can't help himself. But you'll get used to it." Finn saw Jessie glance toward the stairway. "Tired?"

She nodded.

"Me, too. I'll walk you upstairs."

"All right." She turned to Mac and Mary Pat, seated side by side in front of the fire. "Thank you for your hospitality. It means the world to me."

"You're welcome, Jessie. You're welcome here as long as you'd like." Mac smiled.

Mary Pat lifted a hand. "Good night, you two."

When they reached the top, Jessie turned to Finn. "You don't have to walk with me. I know the way."

"I know." He continued walking alongside her as she moved down the hallway.

At the guest room she paused. "Your family is amazing. I was feeling so sad, and then suddenly they had me laughing, and I forgot all my troubles."

"Good. That's the way they affect me, too. I can have the worst day, but once we get together, the bad things fall away and I forget why I was feeling so concerned."

"That's a wonderful gift, Finn."

He nodded. "And don't I know it." He paused. "You going to be all right all alone in here?"

"Finn, except for Aunt Nola, I've been alone most of my life."

"I know. It's just...I want to..."

She absorbed a lovely warm feeling along her spine. She could feel him staring at her mouth, before he abruptly turned away. "Good night, Jessie."

"Good night, Finn."

She opened the door and stepped inside before leaning against the closed door and taking a long, slow breath.

She touched a hand to her chest and could feel her heart racing.

Odd. She almost felt his mouth on hers as surely as if he'd actually kissed her. And then he'd turned away. Was that disappointment she'd felt?

She crossed the room and stood at the window, staring at the surrounding hills, dark with cattle. Such a familiar sight. And yet it all seemed new and fresh here in this place.

She undressed and slid into bed, her mind still whirling.

What was it about Finn's home and family? All those terrible troubling feelings that plagued her on the long ride back had dissolved the moment she'd stepped inside this place today.

These people, and this house filled with the most mismatched family she'd ever met, felt right somehow. The old cowboy, lacking teeth, with that wonderful smile. The sweet, courtly gardener, whose speech carried a hint of Chicago. The retired lawyer, who spoke as formally as though still in a courtroom. Ben, who adored his wife, Becca. Sam the tease and his wife, Penny, who cooked like a professional. Mary Pat, the wandering social worker beloved by everybody, according to Finn. And Mac, who had the kindest eyes she'd ever looked into. When he'd hugged her like a father, she'd wanted to melt into him.

And finally, Finn, who believed her when nobody else had.

Was that why she was so drawn to him? Or was there something else going on? Something she didn't want to explore too deeply?

It was the wrong time in her life to have these feelings. She needed to put all her energy into finding her aunt.

Just below her calm surface there was a bubbling cauldron of absolute terror that something evil was at work in her aunt's life and that if she didn't act—and soon—it would all end in disaster.

But for now, for tonight, she would just let go of all the fear and worry and tension and trust that here in this place she was safe, and that somehow tomorrow would be better.

Oh, sweet heaven, she prayed it was so.

It was her last thought before sleep took her.

CHAPTER SEVEN

Jessie descended the stairs. She'd heard Finn and Sam heading out to the barn earlier. Having grown up on a ranch, she knew chores started at dawn. From the kitchen came the wonderful aroma of freshly brewed coffee and the cheerful voices of Penny and Mary Pat as they started another round of cooking.

As she was about to pass through the parlor, she caught sight of Mac alone at his desk. The entire desktop was littered with bills, receipts, and assorted scraps of paper.

She paused. "End-of-the-month bookkeeping?"

He looked up with a frown that turned into a smile when he caught sight of her. "I'm afraid so. This paperwork is the bane of my existence."

"But a necessary part of running a business."

He nodded and tucked the pencil behind his ear. "It seemed simpler when I was younger. Then I just kept all my receipts in an envelope, and at the end of the year I added them up, deducted them from the sale of cattle, and paid taxes on the profits. Now there are so many rules and regulations about what is and isn't considered legal to claim on my taxes, the paperwork eats up half my time every month."

He stood, pressing a hand to the small of his back. "Sorry. I didn't mean to complain or bore you with this stuff. Let's go to the kitchen and grab some of that coffee I've been smelling for the past half hour. It's making my mouth water."

Jessie held back. "I'm never bored talking about numbers. It's how I earn my living. And more, it's my passion."

He looked at her as though she'd just spoken a foreign language. "You like talking numbers?"

"I'm an accountant. Actually a CPA with Ayers and Lanyer."

"I know of the company. I've heard they do a fine job for some of the mega-ranches owned by corporations."

"They do a fine job for anybody who hires them." She smiled. "Including family-owned ranches."

Mac shrugged. "Sorry. I just meant they're probably too rich for my blood."

"But I'm not. Would you like me to take a look at all this"—she swept her hand to include the paperwork spilling across his desk—"and see if I can ease your burden?"

"I couldn't…"

"If you're willing, it would also ease my conscience. I wouldn't have to feel that I'm accepting your hospitality without paying it back."

He gave her a long, steady look. "Let me get this

straight, Jessie. Are you saying you'd actually enjoy cleaning up this mess and making sense of it?"

"I'd love it. It's the perfect way to keep my mind off of everything else that's happening. Trust me, Mac. I would be really happy to lose myself in work I'm comfortable doing."

His smile spread slowly, crinkling his eyes and putting a twinkle in them. He glanced at his desk before turning back to her. "It's all yours. I certainly wouldn't want to keep you from having fun. But first…" He put a hand under her elbow. "Let's have some of that coffee."

They were both smiling as they walked into the kitchen.

Breakfast was the usual noisy affair, with Roscoe and Otis joining Sam and Finn in the mudroom, shedding boots and washing up at the sink before heading to the kitchen. Zachariah, always a slow starter in the morning, ambled out of his room and was handed a mug of coffee before he spoke a single word.

He drank. Sighed. Then smiled and called out a greeting to all of them as they trudged into the kitchen.

Penny and Mary Pat had prepared eggs scrambled with onions and red and yellow peppers and served with enough hot sauce to bring a smile to all their faces. There were thick slabs of fried ham, oven-roasted potatoes, and a stack of pancakes with maple syrup.

Having cleaned his plate twice, Sam leaned back and turned to Penny. "That was just what I needed, Money. Now I think I could go a round or two with those ornery cows up in the north pasture."

"If you're heading into the hills, I'll pack you a lunch."

He chuckled. "Right about now the last thing I'm thinking about is food."

"You'll thank me a few hours from now." She kissed his cheek and walked to the stove to retrieve the coffeepot.

Mac turned to Mary Pat. "What are your plans for the day?"

"Penny and I are going to drive to town with a list of supplies. We thought we'd see if Becca can join us for lunch." She turned to Jessie. "Want to join us?"

Jessie nodded. "I'd love to." She glanced down at her borrowed clothes. "I feel guilty wearing all your things, Penny."

Penny shook her head. "They're yours for as long as you need them."

"I know. And I'm so grateful. But it's time I bought some of my own."

"Great." Penny turned toward the sink. "Let's plan on leaving in an hour."

"That gives me time to take care of a little chore." Jessie shared a smile with Mac.

Penny shot them both a suspicious look. "Sounds like you two are planning some sort of conspiracy."

When neither of them said a word, Penny shrugged. "All right. I love little secrets." With a sly grin she circled the table, topping off their coffee.

Mac turned to Roscoe and Otis. "This looks like a good day to drive the equipment to the east meadow and start clearing the land."

"I thought you were planning on spending the day in the parlor with bookwork."

"That's all taken care of."

"Good." Roscoe smiled. "Then let's deal with the meadow. Best to get it done before the rains come."

The others nodded in agreement.

Finn excused himself and headed up the stairs to shower and dress for a day at the office.

A short time later he descended the stairs of the now-silent house and was surprised to find Jessie seated at his dad's desk, her fingers moving with lightning speed over a calculator.

He stopped dead in his tracks. "What are you doing?"

"Your father's dreaded paperwork."

"Yeah. I can see that. But why?"

"I offered, after seeing him working on it this morning. When I explained that I love this kind of thing, he was happy to turn me loose on what he calls 'the bane of his existence.'"

"I know how much he hates it." Finn leaned close to glance over her shoulder. "So that's the little secret you two shared. How bad of a mess is it?"

"It's fine. I've seen much worse. Your dad keeps really good records. Like so many ranchers, he's simply annoyed by the time all these little details take him away from ranch chores."

Finn looked at her much the way his father had earlier. "Are you sure you're okay with this?"

"Finn, it makes me happy. And, as I told your father, it eases my guilt at accepting all the wonderful hospitality your family is showing me. A room of my own, not to mention my own bathroom. And these amazing meals. This will make me feel like I'm contributing in my small way."

"Believe me, this isn't small. I know how much Dad hates doing this bookwork."

"Well, I'm in my glory."

He shook his head. "It takes all kinds."

She was grinning. "Yes, it does. And look at you."

She looked him up and down. "An hour ago you were a grubby ranch hand, mucking stalls. Now you're a slick lawyer."

"Maybe not so slick."

She shook her head. "Don't try to deny it, Counselor. Who wouldn't be dazzled by this handsome face?"

He wiggled his brows like a mock villain. "You think I'm handsome, little lady?"

"A momentary lapse." To cover, she added, " I've been meaning to ask you about this intriguing buckskin jacket." Without thinking, she lay a hand on his chest.

He closed his hand over hers and was pleased to see she didn't pull away. "You like it?"

"I do. Don't ask me why. It's outrageous and hokey, but I love it. I'm betting you're the only lawyer in the state of Montana who wears a fringed buckskin jacket to court."

"It was Zachariah's trademark uniform. If you have time later, ask him to show you some of the newspaper clippings of his glory days."

She brightened. "Thanks. I will."

"There's nothing Zachariah likes more than talking about his years as one of the most celebrated lawyers in the state of Montana." He started to turn away. "Okay. I'm off to work." He paused and continued holding her hand against his heart. "Maybe I'll see you in town later."

"Maybe. I'll leave that up to Penny and Mary Pat. They may want this to be a girls-only day."

"That will be good for you, after spending so much time with all of us."

"I love my time with all of you. You're surrounded by an amazing number of fascinating people, Finn Monroe."

"Yes, I am. And out of all of them, one is . . . even more

fascinating than the rest." Without warning he dipped his head and nearly kissed her before he realized what he'd almost done.

She may be beautiful and beguiling—and clearly intrigued by him as well—but she was also his client.

The first rule of law. Never, under any circumstances, behave in an unprofessional manner toward a client.

He felt her hand tighten in his, as though ready to draw him closer.

He held on for a fleeting moment, wondering at the way his heart jumped. He hadn't planned this. And now, he needed to step back or face the consequences.

"I almost crossed a line there. That was unprofessional of me. I'm sorry."

He saw the look of surprise that had her eyes going wide. And he saw something else before she ever-so-carefully leaned back. A hot blaze of passion in her eyes before she blinked the look away.

He managed a smile. "I'll see you at dinnertime."

As Finn sauntered away, Jessie sank back into Mac's leather desk chair and reminded herself to breathe. Minutes later she heard the back door open and close, and the sound of the truck's engine before it faded away.

And then there was silence.

She sat for the longest time, wondering at the way her heart had nearly exploded when she'd thought he was about to kiss her.

She'd wanted him to. Had actually invited it. And felt a real sense of loss when he'd stepped back.

What made Finn Monroe different from the other men who'd come and gone in her life? She couldn't say. Maybe it was the fact that he believed her when so many others hadn't. Maybe it was his simple kindness. He'd raced to her side from the comfort of his bed in the middle of the night after the motel fire, though he barely knew her. He'd driven her to her aunt's ranch, and had taken the time to check with the wranglers. And now he'd given her sanctuary here in his own family home.

Maybe her reaction to him was simply the result of all that was happening in her life, making her feel alone and vulnerable.

But maybe, she thought, she should stop looking for reasons and just admit to herself that Finn Monroe was one handsome, sexy cowboy.

A cowboy who really knew how to make a girl feel special.

The fact that he'd behaved like a courtly gentleman, refusing to give in to the opportunity to kiss her, just made him all the more tempting.

She took in a long breath and forced herself to finish tallying these numbers before joining the women for the drive to town.

CHAPTER EIGHT

Penny drove slowly along Main Street, pointing out the various stores and points of interest.

"Up on that hill is the church, and just over there the school where I'd hoped to teach."

Jessie swiveled her head to stare at her. "You're a teacher?"

Penny couldn't hide the look of pride that came over her. "I was offered a position in a nearby town, but it was too far. I asked for something here in Haller Creek. Right now I'm substitute teaching whenever they need me. And whenever one of the regular teachers is ready to take a leave, I'm at the head of the list as a full-time replacement."

"You'll be a great teacher, Penny."

"Thanks. It's my dream." She pointed. "This is the new Haller Creek Medical Clinic. We're all so glad to have it so close. And there's the hair and nail salon, and over there the bank. If you need clothes, you can find most things at the Family Store." She found a parking slot and pointed to the tidy shop between the hair salon and a gift shop.

Jessie stepped down and turned to the others. "Are you coming with me?"

Mary Pat nodded. "I need a few things myself." She turned. "Penny?"

Penny shook her head. "I'll drive to Hank Henderson's and leave the truck there so they can load the supplies in the back. Then Becca and I will walk back here to join you. I'm sure we'll both think of things we need to buy."

Mary Pat was laughing. "That's the thing about being in a store. You always seem to find things you never even knew you needed."

As Penny drove away, Jessie and Mary Pat walked into the shop.

Mary Pat called to the young woman behind the counter, "Ellen Carter, meet Jessie Blair."

"Hi, Jessie." The pretty redhead indicated the shelves and racks. "Help yourself to anything you need. The fitting rooms are in the back."

"Hi, Ellen. Thanks." Jessie followed Mary Pat's lead and began rummaging through racks and counters of women's clothing. Soon she was headed to the fitting room in the back of the store, her arms laden with jeans, tops, and underthings.

A short time later Mary Pat called out, "How're you doing in here, Jessie?"

"Fine. What do you think?" Jessie stepped out of a small room wearing work denims and a baggy shirt.

"Not bad. But I think you can do better than that."

Jessie chuckled. "Oh, I already have. These are just for doing chores in the barn and around the house."

While the two were still trying on clothes, they heard Becca and Penny chatting as they moved into the other fitting rooms.

Each time one of them found something they liked, they stepped out to model it for the others.

An hour later, wearing brand-new skinny jeans and a denim jacket, her feet encased in a pair of sturdy hiking boots, Jessie paused to model her new outfit for Mary Pat, Penny, and Becca, who murmured approval.

Ellen looked from behind the counter. "Will there be anything else?"

The women eyed the clutter of handled bags and shared a laugh. "Anything more and we'll need an army to haul them home." Jessie handed the girl her credit card. When everything was bagged, she turned away. "Now where are we headed?"

"Lunch," the others called in unison.

"Okay. Will I carry these with me?"

Mary Pat shook her head. "Can we leave them here until we're ready to head home, Ellen?"

The young woman smiled and nodded. "I was going to suggest that very thing."

"Thank you," Jessie called as she followed the others from the shop.

Outside, they paused as Becca asked, "Are we in the mood for Dolly's Diner or Horton Duke's chili over at the Hitching Post?"

Mary Pat chuckled. "What kind of welcome would we be giving if we didn't introduce Jessie to Dolly's home cooking?"

Jessie arched a brow. "I don't know. Chili sounds . . . interesting."

"If you have a cast-iron stomach." With a laugh Mary

Pat looped her arm through Jessie's, and Penny and Becca did the same as they headed toward the pretty little diner down the street.

"Is there any special dish I should consider?"

All three women replied, "Dolly's meat loaf."

"But be prepared," Mary Pat said in an aside. "Dolly makes it a point to learn all she can about everybody who sets foot in her diner."

"Should I answer her questions?"

At Jessie's worried look, the others burst into laughter.

"Jessie," Mary Pat said softly, "she won't need to ask. She'll tell you all about yourself, and add all the latest gossip about you and Finn while she's at it."

"So..." Nibbling Dolly's excellent meat loaf, Becca glanced across the table at Jessie. "Were we right about Dolly?"

Jessie chuckled. "She's just a walking encyclopedia. She even knew how many wranglers were involved in that motel fire."

"Told you." Becca's voice lowered. "Speaking of that fire...Jessie, how are you coping with everything? Especially your aunt's disappearance?"

Jessie sighed. "I feel so much better now that I have Finn and all of you on my side. Until Finn, I was feeling so alone. The authorities have absolutely refused to take this seriously." She began nervously tapping her fork on the tabletop. "I guess I don't blame them. I know I wasn't making a lot of sense, suggesting that my aunt couldn't possibly be happy on a honeymoon when she was so in love with her ranch. But that's the truth. I know in my heart Aunt Nola would never be gone this long unless there was something seriously wrong."

Seeing her agitation, Penny lay a hand on hers. "How are you and Finn getting along?"

Jessie took a sip of iced tea. "We're fine. I appreciate his help. Your brother-in-law is a good lawyer."

"I wasn't talking about professionally." Penny's lips curved and she shared a look with Becca. "I think the two of you make a cute couple."

"We're not a couple." Jessie turned to Mary Pat, hoping the older woman would save her from this discussion. "He's just...helping me."

"I'm glad you feel you can trust him." Mary Pat smiled at her across the table. "Finn has always been good at helping others."

Penny managed a straight face. "A regular Boy Scout."

That had Jessie glancing over at her before her laughter bubbled up. "Okay. I know what you want to know." She shrugged. "I wish I could give you an answer. But the truth is, I don't know what we are. One minute Finn looks like he's feeling all sweet and romantic, and the next he's turning away like I've got the flu and he doesn't want to come anywhere near me. He insists that it would be wrong to behave in a way that isn't"—she lifted her fingers to make air quotes—"professional."

"Ah." Mary Pat shared a look with the others. "That sounds so like Mac, doesn't it?"

Becca and Penny nodded.

She turned to Jessie. "Mac has spent a lifetime drumming into his sons' heads that they need to put aside their wild tendencies and behave like gentlemen. I see this as proof that what he once thought a hopeless goal has now become reality."

Jessie was staring at her with wide eyes.

She reached across the table to pat Jessie's hand. "I

believe Finn may like you a bit more than he'd intended. And that has a tug-of-war going on inside his mind."

"A tug-of-war." Jessie took another sip of tea before allowing a smile to blossom. "Now that's something I've never caused before. Do you think I should tug back? And if I do, I wonder which side will win?"

Penny's eyes twinkled with a spark of amusement. "Jessie, I was there when he first told us about your initial meeting. My money's on professionalism taking a backseat to liking you."

Around the table they shared matching smiles.

Later, after they gathered up their purchases at the Family Store and began the drive out of town, Jessie looked at the passing scenery before turning to the others. "I really like Haller Creek. It's just a sweet town, with sweet people."

Penny tipped down her sunglasses to peer over them at Jessie. "I know exactly what you mean. From the first day I came here, I felt as if I'd come home."

Home.

Jessie fell silent. It was true, she felt at home here… maybe even more so than at the family ranch she'd called home since she was five. But then, without Aunt Nola, that place was just another ranch.

At the first ring, Finn plucked his cell phone from his pocket and saw the caller ID. "What've you got for me, Basil?"

The private investigator was a no-nonsense, by-the-book man who wasted few words. "First, I checked the police records on the accident that took Matthew Carver's life. No hint of foul play. They've declared that he fell asleep at the wheel and closed the book on it."

Finn hissed out a breath. "Okay. Thanks for looking into it. Now what have you got on Wayne Stone?"

"Funny thing. The same people who didn't know Wayne Stone recognized the photo you sent me. About twenty years ago they knew the guy in the picture as Rogers Sutter."

"An alias?"

"Maybe. Owned a lot of real estate. Mostly ranches that went up for auction. Used to spend a lot of time at the county courthouse, according to my source. I thought I'd head up there and ask around."

Finn stopped him. "I can save you the trouble. I have to head there today to file some documents for my father. I'll see what I can find out. In the meantime, maybe you could check with your sources in the state offices and see if this guy could have any other alias we ought to know about."

"Will do. I'll get back to you."

Finn disconnected and sat a moment. It made no sense for a successful businessman to use an alias. Unless he wanted to avoid paying taxes. Or...Finn's legal mind made a leap from all the other reasons to the one that most intrigued him. Or this guy had resorted to illegal business practices to obtain some of that real estate and didn't want to leave a trail.

Finn completed the documents he was preparing for his father and placed them in his attaché case before heading to his truck. He wanted plenty of time to handle his business at the county courthouse before grabbing lunch with a colleague. And then, he thought, he'd be home for dinner.

Not that the meal mattered at the moment. All he could think about was Jessie, and that almost-kiss.

He was smiling as he started out of town and headed toward the interstate.

It had been a long morning at the county courthouse. Finn's first stop had been at the county clerk's office to ask who had issued the complaint about his family's cattle straying from their property. It had seemed to him to be a simple request. Still, after more than an hour, with three different employees in the office going through records and coming up empty, he'd been left with no answer.

Then he'd had to cool his heels before he managed to file the proper documents with the clerk. Documents that offered a rebuttal of the county's charge of animal trespass, to avoid paying a hefty fine.

At each stop along the way, Finn had shown the photo he had of Wayne Stone, or maybe Rogers Sutter, to as many officials as he could find.

Several of the longtime employees had studied the photograph for quite a while before shaking their heads. Once or twice Finn thought he'd detected a trace of recognition on their faces before each of them had firmly said they didn't know the man. Though he wanted to press, he didn't want to insult them. After all, he dealt with these people on a fairly regular basis whenever he had to present documents to the courts. The last thing he needed was someone who could delay or even deny a document filing. Other than the judges, these employees wielded a great deal of power.

In the end, he'd been forced to accept defeat in finding anyone who knew Wayne Stone, or whatever his name was. Finn hoped Basil was having more luck.

Over lunch with a colleague, Finn brought up the subject and wondered aloud why anyone used an alias.

"It's almost always because they're trying to circumvent the law." Cameron Colby Jr. had joined his father's prestigious law firm and was preparing to open a second office in Helena, the state's capital. He and Finn had attended the University of Michigan Law School together and, going to school so far from home, had formed a strong bond. Cameron had once again offered Finn a job with the firm. Finn had once again refused. It had become their private joke, though on Cameron's part, it was a serious offer.

"I get that an alias could help circumvent the law." Finn popped a chili fry in his mouth. "But if a man is a successful businessman, how can he hope to keep a second identity a secret for any length of time?"

"According to what you've heard from your investigator, he's already managed to keep it a secret for twenty years or more. That suggests that he has paid people to let him know whenever there's even a whisper about his secret."

Finn's eyes narrowed. "He has paid snitches?" He thought about it before nodding. "Yeah. It makes sense. He'd have to have eyes and ears, especially at the county level. Maybe at the state level, as well. If not employees, then friends of friends who could get information on a need-to-know basis."

Cameron signaled for the bill and was surprised when the waitress informed him it was already taken care of.

He looked across the table at Finn. "This lunch was on me. I was the one offering you the job."

"I already have a job. But you know I'm grateful for the offer. And thanks for your insight on this guy. I think I'm going to have to do a lot more digging."

"I wish I could stick around and help. It sounds like a challenge. You and I could make a great team, Finn."

Outside the restaurant the two old friends shook hands before going their separate ways.

As Finn made his way down the block, he had the oddest sensation that he was being followed. When he paused to open the door to his truck, he took a moment to look around. Seeing nothing unusual, he tossed in his attaché case and settled himself inside.

Minutes later he was driving back down the interstate, on his way to Haller Creek.

The closer he got, the more he began to relax. While he loved the challenge of dealing with the county courthouse officials, he loved the wide-open countryside and small-town living even more. He loved everything about his ranch—especially now that a certain pretty woman was staying there.

Maybe he'd just skip dinner altogether and go for dessert. But he knew he better keep his distance from Jessica Blair if he wanted to keep their relationship on a purely professional level.

Forbidden fruit. Always the sweetest.

Finn stepped into the kitchen to the sound of voices and laughter.

The entire family had already gathered around and was sipping lemonade or longnecks, looking relaxed and happy.

Finn's gaze was immediately drawn to Jessie, arranging rolls in a linen-lined basket. She was wearing new skinny jeans and a crisp cotton shirt, the sleeves rolled above her elbows. Her hair tumbled about her face in messy waves.

She was gorgeous without even trying.

She was laughing with Penny, as though they'd been friends forever. She looked up and smiled.

Just seeing her had Finn's cares of the day slipping away.

He accepted a longneck from Sam before saying, "I guess I don't need to ask how your girls' day went. I see you managed some shopping."

"I did. And lunch at Dolly's Diner. And..." She merely smiled. "Lots of girl talk."

"I guess I shouldn't ask."

"I'd never tell."

With a grin he walked over to his father. "How did your new accountant do?"

Mac looked more relaxed than he had in days. "I still can't believe what Jessie managed to do in a matter of hours. After shopping with the girls, she's managed to have everything cataloged, tallied, and filed. For the first time in weeks my desktop is clear. And she promised to show me a simple way to keep a handy file and do a weekly roundup of all the payments and inventory that will keep paperwork to a minimum."

"Sounds like you have an angel on your side, Dad."

"More like a genius." He glanced at Jessie before lowering his voice. "That sweet face hides quite a brain."

Finn was grinning as he stood there, letting the voices flow around him. He thought again about Cameron's offer today. Finn would be earning five times what he made in his little law office in Haller Creek. He could afford to live in one of the new mansions being built for Montana's movers and shakers. And he'd be spending his days in court as lead lawyer in high-profile cases that routinely made headlines.

But he'd be expected to relocate to Helena, more than a hundred miles from here. And after a day of fascinating courtroom drama, he would go home to empty rooms. No hum of voices. No easy laughter. No family to cheer on each success.

He tipped up his bottle and sipped his beer and realized he had no regrets about his decision. He enjoyed Cameron's friendship and was appreciative of the offer. But he loved his life just the way it was right here.

Penny called everyone to dinner, and the talk soon turned to the daily ebb and flow of ranch life in springtime. Calves being born, and new wranglers being hired to help guard the helpless newborns from predators attracted to easy prey. Fields requiring plowing and planting to take advantage of longer days and warmer nights.

Sam looked over at his brother. "You up for some fieldwork tomorrow?"

Finn shook his head. "Sorry. I won't be free until the weekend. Do you have enough hands?"

Sam nodded. "We hired six more a few days ago. Would you mind checking out their references?"

"I don't mind. Give me their names and Social Security numbers, and I'll handle it first thing in the morning. It's the least I can do, now that Ben and I are both leaving you with so much work."

Mac put a hand on Finn's shoulder. "Don't do that to yourself, son. As I reminded Ben when he accepted the job of sheriff in Haller Creek, I didn't take you three into my home and my life so I'd have free labor. I want all of you to be free to follow your hearts. The ranch will survive, no matter what."

"Besides," Sam added with a smug smile, "we all know I can work circles around both you and Ben, bro."

That brought a round of laughter.

"And we all know your biggest asset is your humility, *bro*." Finn's remark ramped up the laughter even more.

Sam chuckled and tipped up his longneck in a salute. "Just see that you're available for fieldwork this weekend. Wouldn't want my brilliant little brother to get soft hands."

"I've been dying to find out what you learned at the county offices today." With the rest of the family off to bed and darkness closing over the hills, Jessie settled herself on the porch swing beside Finn. "I didn't want to ask in front of your family. They have enough problems without hearing about mine."

"I wouldn't have kept you in suspense if I'd learned anything important." Finn looked up to follow the path of a shooting star. "Nobody recognized the man in the picture. But my private investigator found a few people who claimed to not know Wayne Stone but identified the guy in the picture as Rogers Sutter. Ring a bell?"

"No." Jessie huffed out a breath. "I wish Aunt Nola had written something on the back that could have identified him. But if it wasn't Wayne Stone, I can't think of anyone else who would have an arm around my aunt's shoulders like that. You saw the look on her face. She was staring at him like a teenaged girl with a crush, but he was just looking at the camera like a reluctant model." She sighed. "I can't help wondering who took that picture, unless..."

Finn turned to her. "Unless they used a camera with a timer, mounted on a tripod. Do you know if your aunt had such a thing?"

"She didn't. But I did." She clasped her hands together. "Aunt Nola bought it for me on my sixteenth birthday. I lugged it all over the ranch for the next couple of years, taking pictures of everything I loved. The cattle. The fields. The wranglers. Sunrises and sunsets. But when I went off to college, I left it behind. A camera, bags of lenses, and a tripod seemed like too much equipment to take, so I figured I'd just use it during summer breaks. Through the years Aunt Nola said she'd keep it for me until I got the itch to start capturing new photos." She looked over. "I'd forgotten all about it."

Finn smiled. "That may become the perfect excuse to visit the ranch again and do a search for your photographic equipment."

Jessie nodded. "Then you think we should go back?"

"I do. And maybe, if we're lucky, your aunt and her new husband might be there."

"If they ever return."

"Wayne Stone has already hired new wranglers. That tells you he's taking responsibility for the ranch and property."

"And neatly replacing my aunt as owner and operator of her own family property."

"Exactly. He's acting like a guy who has nothing to hide."

"Except that he may not even be who he claims to be." She stood and started pacing. "I feel like I should be doing more to find my aunt. It's been too long. I know in my heart something's terribly wrong."

Finn stood and put a hand on her arm to halt her movement. "You've gone to the police. You hired a detective. And now you have me. And I give you my word I won't quit until you have all your answers."

"Finn, I don't even know the questions to ask anymore." She looked up at him with a small smile. "But you're on my side. And that matters more than you'll ever know."

She touched a hand to his cheek. Just a touch, but she

felt him flinch and saw his eyes narrow on her with an intensity that had her heart leaping to her throat.

She lowered her hand. "Sorry. I didn't mean..." She started to step back. "I know you want to keep things between us professional, and even though I disagree, I'll respect..."

"You disagree?" He dragged her close. His eyes, moments earlier narrowed in thought, were now hot and fierce, and focused on hers. "You disagree?"

"What I mean is..." She swallowed. "Yes. I..."

"Okay." His voice was a low growl. "Let's get this out of the way."

He tangled his hands in her hair and lowered his face to hers in a kiss that had her heart stuttering. Instead of stepping back, he drew her even closer, until she could feel the heat of him along every line of her body.

The porch beneath her feet seemed to tilt and sway, and she reached out for his waist.

Lost in the kiss, he backed her up until she bumped into the back door, and still the kiss spun on and on until at last they were both gasping for breath as they reluctantly stepped apart.

"So much for professionalism." Finn quirked his lips, but then he was suddenly looking at her with such fierce concentration, she could feel the heat of it all the way to her toes. "All that proved was..." He abruptly yanked open the back door. "I think you'd better go inside."

"Inside?" She paused. "What about you?"

"I'll stay out here."

"I could stay out here with...Oh." Seeing the storm brewing in his eyes she let her protest die and stepped inside.

But before she headed to bed, she watched as he strode off into the darkness.

CHAPTER NINE

Jessie lay in the darkened room, listening to the sounds of the night. Somewhere a bird called and in the distance another answered. From up in the hills came the mournful howl of a coyote. And as always, the lowing of cattle in the background. Such familiar sounds, and yet tonight they all seemed new and exciting.

Because of that kiss.

She would like to think it was nothing more than a simple kiss, but there'd been nothing simple about it.

She couldn't begin to count the number of times she'd been kissed. But none had ever come close to Finn's.

Let's get this out of the way.

When Finn said that, she'd felt the same way. One kiss, and then they could get rid of this...curiosity, this sexual tension between them and concentrate on business. Except that, in an instant, everything changed. Instead of getting it out of the way, it had become this even greater firestorm that had her feeling so hungry, so needy, she couldn't seem to settle. It was like the edgy feeling she always got when a huge storm was blowing across the hills, causing the hair on her arms to rise, setting off alarm bells in the back of her mind.

The moment he'd kissed her, she'd been caught up in something so new, so primal, she'd been lost.

What bothered her the most was the fact that she didn't know how to handle this.

Finn had made it perfectly clear he wanted a strictly businesslike relationship.

That kiss had been as far from business as possible.

But what did she want?

She touched a finger to her lips, replaying that moment of pure magic.

She wasn't some teen with her first crush. But she had never before been thrust into a raging whirlpool with a single kiss.

In that moment she'd been in over her head and drowning. What's worse, she hadn't wanted to surface.

And unless she was mistaken, Finn had been as deeply affected as she.

She sighed. So, what did she want going forward?

She wanted what he wanted. A purely businesslike relationship.

She smiled in the darkness.

Liar.

She wanted more of what she'd felt tonight in Finn's arms. So much more.

Finn tossed aside his clothes and slipped into bed. He'd hoped a long walk around the barns would cool him off enough to settle, but the need was still churning inside.

He could have stepped away. That had been his plan. But no. He had to test himself. Get it out of the way, he'd said, as though somehow kissing Jessie would end the gnawing hunger.

Really dumb, he berated himself. It was like thinking he could eat a single potato chip, or take one lick of an ice cream cone.

Yeah right.

And look where it got him. Instead of behaving in a purely professional manner, he'd been so tangled up with need he'd wanted to tear off her clothes and take her right there on the back porch.

The image had him groaning.

If only she wasn't a client.

If only she wasn't staying here at his family ranch.

If only…

He needed to back off and hold firm to his original intentions. An honorable lawyer doesn't mess with a frightened client who comes to him with serious legal, and possibly criminal, issues. An honorable lawyer does his best to untangle the knots and find resolution. And do it all as professionally as possible.

He'd crossed a line, and now he needed to get back on track.

But he'd never before had a woman rock his world like this. Jessie was smart, independent, and fiercely protective of her aunt. And yet, beneath her strong image, there was this fragile, wounded bird who made him want to wrap his arms around her and keep her safe.

She was dangerous, uncharted territory, he realized.

He knew what his dad would advise. He could hear Mac's voice inside his head. That good, honorable man who'd taken in Finn and his brothers and turned them from dangerous delinquents to good men would counsel to always operate on the side of what they knew to be right.

With a deep sigh he knew what he had to do.

Tomorrow he would start over.

Jessie would be his client. He would be her lawyer.

Nothing more.

Finn paused in the doorway of the kitchen. Jessie was chatting happily with Penny and Mary Pat. She looked so fresh and pretty he wanted to cross the room and kiss her breathless. Instead, he stayed where he was. After the long night he'd put in, he didn't trust himself to get anywhere near her until he was in control of his feelings.

But all that tossing and turning hadn't been in vain. He'd had plenty of time to clear his mind, and he'd come to a decision.

As the men stomped in from the barns and began to wash in the mudroom, he accepted a cup of coffee from Penny.

She arched a brow. "You're not dressed for the office."

Finn saw the way Jessie paused to look over.

"I thought we'd take that drive to Arvid."

She set aside the platter of eggs and walked closer, to hear him above the chorus of men's voices. "Now?"

"We need to search for your old camera. Who knows? Maybe there's an SD card with all kinds of pictures your aunt took."

"Oh, Finn." She put a hand to her heart. "Wouldn't that be great?"

"Hey, now." Seeing her excitement, he gave a shake of his head. "It's just a thought. We may come up empty."

"But it's worth a try. Will we leave right after breakfast?"

"Yeah."

"I'll be ready."

He saw her smile of relief as she crossed the room and continued lending a hand with the meal.

Another reason to stay detached, he reminded himself. Putting a smile in her eyes was starting to mean way too much to him.

Jessie was animated as they drove through the countryside. The nearer they got to her aunt's ranch, the more excited she became.

"I didn't notice my camera in Aunt Nola's closet. I wonder if she stored it in my old room."

"Then we'll start there."

Finn saw the way her gaze swept the driveway as they pulled close. Her smile of anticipation faded into a frown.

She sighed. "No trace of a vehicle."

"That doesn't mean anything. Your aunt could be home, and her new husband out in the fields."

"Or not." She twisted her hands in her lap.

As soon as Finn brought the truck to a halt, she was out the door and heading toward the back porch. Finn followed more slowly, looking around for any sign of life.

Everything looked the way it had the last time they'd been here.

On a whim, he backtracked to the road and opened the mailbox, expecting to find it filled with mail.

The mailbox was empty.

By the time he returned to the ranch house, Jessie was nowhere to be found.

"Jessie." He paused at the foot of the stairs. "You up there?"

"Yes." She appeared at the head of the stairs. "Just as I thought. There's nobody here. I'm heading to my room."

He climbed the stairs and trailed behind her as she threw open a door and hurried inside.

The room was sparsely furnished. A bed, covered with a simple white down comforter. A desk and chair. A closet, with a few articles of clothing hanging inside. The big window was framed with white curtains and offered a spectacular view of the rolling fields beyond.

He grinned. "I was expecting some feminine frills."

"Sorry to disappoint you." She turned from the closet. "I took almost everything with me when I moved out. But I left a few things here that I could wear for ranch chores whenever I got a weekend home." She indicated worn, faded jeans and a few plaid shirts. "But my camera equipment isn't here."

"Can you think of anyplace else it might be?"

She shrugged. "I guess we could look in the basement."

"Let's go."

He followed her down the stairs, and then down a second flight to the basement. Like the rest of the house it was tidy, with a love seat and recliner facing a television hung above a fireplace. One entire wall was covered with bookcases filled to the brim, and below them, wooden cabinets.

"This was Aunt Nola's favorite spot. After supper she always came down here to read or watch TV." Jessie began opening the cabinet doors.

When she opened the last one, she gave a sigh of disgust. "No sign of my camera or tripod."

Finn pointed to a door. "What's in there?"

She shrugged. "A storage room. Most of the stuff stored

in there belonged to my grandparents. Things Aunt Nola couldn't bring herself to dispose of. She used to say she hoped I'd go through them one day and find something of theirs that I'd want to keep in their memory."

"That's nice." Finn tried the door. "It's locked."

Jessie looked around, before turning to the fireplace mantel with a smile. "There's the key."

She retrieved it and unlocked the door before turning on the light inside.

Unlike the rest of the house, the shelves in this room were bare. Boxes and packing materials were stacked in one corner next to an assortment of antique lamps, silverware, and glassware.

"I thought your aunt wanted to save these things for you."

Looking puzzled, Jessie nodded.

Walking closer, Finn knelt down. "These look like they're ready to be boxed up and shipped somewhere."

She studied the items carefully. "It's been a year or more since I was in here. But everything had been stored on these shelves."

"Why would your aunt sell these things?"

She shook her head. "I don't know. They all meant something to her."

Finn glanced beyond the boxes to a pile of broken things. "What's all this?"

With a gasp, Jessie knelt and began digging through the items until she held up a smashed camera.

Tears welled up. "I know Aunt Nola would never do a thing like this. She was so proud of that gift. And I was so thrilled she'd bought it for me."

As she got to her feet, her composure crumpled and the tears began to spill over.

The look of her, so defeated, had Finn gathering her close and pressing his mouth to a tangle of hair at her temple. "We'll get to the bottom of this, Jessie."

"But it's all so wrong." Her words, spoken against his throat, had his arms tightening around her.

She looked up, her face wet with tears. "I can't help thinking there's something evil happening here."

"If there is, we'll find out." Because he wanted to crush her against him, he took a step back and framed her face with his hands. "Why don't you see if the SD card is still inside?"

Jessie had to struggle to open the back of the camera, only to find it empty.

She set aside the smashed camera and stared around at the pile of broken items. "These may be inexpensive, but to my aunt they were family treasures. She never would have allowed this to happen."

Finn caught her hand and led her from the room. He locked the door and returned the key to the mantel before leading the way up the stairs and toward the back door.

He paused. "Want to look at anything else before we leave?"

Jessie shook her head.

"Okay then. We'll..." His voice trailed off as he caught the faintest glint of light above the kitchen door. Moving closer he studied the tiny pinpoint before saying, "Smile. We're being filmed."

She looked up. "A hidden camera?"

"A security camera. Did your aunt have it installed?"

Jessie gave a firm shake of her head. "Aunt Nola wouldn't dream of doing such a thing."

"Well, someone did." He opened the door and waited

until she'd stepped out onto the porch before following her.

Once in the truck Jessie looked slightly dazed. "A camera recording everyone who enters my aunt's house. Why?"

"Apparently, someone figures there's something worth guarding here."

"But what? You've seen the way we lived. Except for a few old things that belonged to my grandparents that have sentimental value, there's nothing of real value in there."

"What about the ranch itself? Wouldn't you say it's worth a great deal of money?"

"Of course. Especially one as well maintained as this."

As Finn drove away, his mind was working overtime. He no longer doubted that Jessie's aunt was in grave danger. The trouble was, they may already be too late. All indications pointed to someone who had already taken control of everything she'd ever valued.

Someone who wanted to make certain the plans already set into motion weren't thwarted by the ranch's owner, or a certain niece who could make waves.

CHAPTER TEN

Over dinner that evening, Jessie and Finn were uncharacteristically silent while the family replayed the events of their day.

Ben and Becca had made it to the ranch in time for supper. Archie lay at their feet, contentedly dozing after a run through the fields.

"I couldn't believe my mother's news." Becca's voice held a trace of excitement. "She and my dad are planning their first ever cruise."

"How lovely." Mary Pat looked over. "Where are they going?"

"The Virgin Islands." Becca and Ben shared a smile. "Mom really hoped to cruise to Greece, but Dad said they'd be away too long. He couldn't possibly leave the store for more than ten days. So they settled for this, and Dad has asked me to run his 'empire' while they're away."

Penny chuckled. "Does he really refer to his hardware store as his empire?"

Becca nodded. "And he never lets anyone forget that he's the supreme emperor."

That had everyone laughing. Becca's father, Hank Henderson, was well known around the town of Haller Creek as a man who insisted on having a hand in every aspect of his business. And until Becca had learned to assert herself, Hank had also tried to micromanage his daughter's life.

Still, as this first ever vacation for Hank and his wife proved, he was learning how to let go, at least in some small way.

Ben turned to Mary Pat. "I noticed some boxes in the back of your van. Does this mean you're getting ready for another road trip?"

She nodded. "I've allowed myself to be lazy long enough. Sometimes I worry that I'll get so comfortable here I'll start thinking about retiring. So it's time to head into the hills and make my rounds."

Mac's smile faltered. "You know how heavy the rains are in spring, especially the closer you get to the foothills of the Bitterroots."

Mary Pat merely smiled. "I know. But then, here in Montana, every season offers one challenge or another." She put a hand on his. "It's a trip I've been making now for more than thirty years. I'll be careful."

Remembering her perils from another trip, Sam couldn't help saying, "I hope you've packed plenty of kitty litter in case you get stuck in the mud."

With a laugh Mary Pat nodded. "It was the first item on my list."

"That's good. We wouldn't want you trapped out there

in snow or mud." He looked across the table at Otis and Roscoe. "Speaking of mud, I'm heading up to the hills tomorrow to help with the calving. Spring rains always bring new life. Want to go along?"

Roscoe grinned. "Wouldn't miss it."

Otis joined in. "Once those calves start coming, you'll need all the hands you can get."

Sam turned to his wife. "We may be up there awhile. Think you can rustle up enough food to keep us from starvation?"

Penny laughed. "I'm already on it." In an aside she added, "I wouldn't want my poor cowboy to starve."

He leaned close to press a kiss to her cheek. "That's my girl. I knew I could count on you, Money."

Since the day Penny had come into his life, he'd been a changed man. And the others around the table couldn't help smiling at the love that flowed between roughneck Sam and his sweet bride.

Long after Ben and Becca had called their good-byes, and the rest of the household had settled in for the night, Finn sat in front of the fireplace with Mac and Zachariah, heads bent close, filling them in on what he and Jessie had found at her aunt's home.

"She said the items in the basement storage room had belonged to her grandparents. Her aunt had kept them all these years so Jessie could take her time going through them and decide which of them she'd like to keep as family keepsakes. And now they're ready to be boxed and wrapped for shipping. Does that sound like something a woman would do after a hasty marriage?"

Mac chose his words carefully. "It sounds as though someone intends to clean house."

"Or clean up. There's a huge market for antiques. But there's more." Finn couldn't keep the thread of anger from his tone. "Jessie said her aunt would have never bought a security camera. She never even locked her doors. And now somebody feels the need to record every visitor that walks through the door."

"It sounds like someone wants to be in control."

"Exactly. What I wouldn't give to examine the recording from that security camera."

Zachariah's tone was stern. "I'll remind you, Finnian, that you're a lawyer, not a private investigator. If you were to be caught doing something like that in a private citizen's home, it could cost you your license to practice law."

Finn nodded gravely. "I get it."

"But," Zachariah added, "you may want to mention it to Basil. A man with his talents could no doubt transfer that security footage to your computer without leaving a trace of evidence."

Finn and Mac shared matching looks of surprise.

Finn had to bite down hard on the grin that tugged at his lips. "Why, you wily old fox. Who'd have ever guessed that such a paragon of virtue hid such a villainous heart?"

"Hardly villainous, Finnian. A man of the law does what he must for his client." Zachariah's blackbird eyes twinkled. "Especially if the client is a beautiful orphan standing alone in a raging storm."

Mac threw back his head and roared. "Are you writing a novel now, Zachariah?"

"Merely stating the facts, Mackenzie, my friend. Our Finnian has a duty to do everything in his power to see that the lovely Jessica not only endures, but wins out over evil."

Finn pounced on that phrase. "So, you believe, as I do, that she's caught up in something sinister?"

"I do. But the authorities cannot act unless they are given incontrovertible evidence that a crime has been committed. So far, all you have are the words of your client and your own suspicion. Now, in order for Jessica to see justice, you must uncover compelling facts that prove your theory."

Finn stood and offered a handshake. "Thanks, Zachariah. I'll call Basil first thing in the morning."

"You may want to phone him now. Judging by the speed with which this mystery man is working, there's no time to waste."

Finn nodded his agreement.

After saying good night to both men, Finn made his way up the stairs to his room and pressed the number for his private investigator. After giving him all the latest information, Finn hung up and stood staring out the window at the distant hills, wrapped in shadows.

That was how he saw Jessie's story. A mystery wrapped in layers of shadows.

Long after he'd slid into bed, his mind continued circling everything he'd uncovered so far.

Zachariah was right. This cowboy who'd taken over Nola's ranch was leaving little to chance. And he appeared to be a man in a hurry.

The clock was ticking. And now that he and Jessie were on that security footage, the mystery man would be feeling even more pressure to finish whatever evil he'd begun. And to eliminate anyone he saw as a threat to his plans.

Finn knew in his heart that unless he could persuade

the authorities that a crime had been committed, it could be too late to save Jessie's aunt.

If it wasn't already.

Finn woke up early and went out in the barn to muck stalls. He'd found through the years that he did his best thinking while doing mundane ranch chores. The hard, physical activity helped to sharpen his mind and keep him focused.

Sam stepped into the barn and stopped in his tracks. "Whoa. I didn't expect to find my brilliant brother the lawyer getting his hands dirty."

"Not to mention my boots," Finn said with a grin.

"Yeah. In order to clean stalls you have to step in a lot of..." Sam paused, laughing. "Got something on your mind, bro?"

"Too much. I thought this would help." Finn forked another load of straw and dung into a wagon.

"Anything you care to share?"

At Sam's invitation, Finn told him about the latest visit to Jessie's family ranch, and his suspicions about the danger he believed her aunt to be facing.

Sam leaned on the handle of his pitchfork. "Don't you think it's time to ask the police for help?"

"Jessie went to the police in Arvid first to ask their help. They checked out the ranch and said they found no sign of foul play. They reminded her that her aunt is of sound mind, and if she wants to throw her life away on some smooth-talking cowboy, their hands are tied."

Sam nodded. "I guess Ben would be forced to say the same thing. Lawmen have to play by the rules."

"Exactly. That's why I called my private investigator

last night and asked him to do a couple of things the law can't do."

Sam's eyes widened. "Are you saying my play-by-the-rules brother asked an employee to break those rules?"

Finn was grinning. "I assume you approve?"

"Hell yes." Sam slapped his brother's shoulder so hard, Finn nearly dropped his pitchfork. "Way to go, bro."

When the chores were finished, the two brothers marched toward the house with matching smiles.

Inside, the wonderful smells in the kitchen had them salivating. After washing up in the mudroom, they accepted mugs of steaming coffee before sitting down to a breakfast of steak, eggs, and potatoes fried with green pepper and onions. They passed around a basket of toast and another of cinnamon rolls fresh from the oven.

Sam leaned toward his wife. "Now this is what I call breakfast."

Penny ran a hand over the rough stubble on his chin. "I can't let my man go up into the hills without a reminder of what he's leaving."

He looked across the table at Mac. "See what a smart woman I married?"

"Smart and talented." Mac nodded toward the wrapped containers that lined the countertops. "I think Penny's sending along enough food for an army."

Otis spoke for all of them. "There can't be too much food for an army of wranglers who'll be dealing with ornery cows and newborn calves for the next few weeks."

"Don't I know it?" Penny looked around the table. "It may be springtime, but up in those hills, the weather is so unpredictable, I expect you could be dealing with snow squalls or freezing rain. I'll head up to the highlands by the end of the week with a fresh supply of food."

Mary Pat chewed her lip. "I wish I could stick around and lend you a hand."

Jessie, who'd been silent until now, spoke up. "I'd be happy to help, Penny."

"Thanks, Jessie." Penny's smile bloomed. "I just hope I don't work you so hard you regret the offer."

Jessica exchanged a look with Finn before saying, "I think hard work is just what I need right now. I'm grateful for anything that will be a distraction."

CHAPTER ELEVEN

At the sound of his office door opening, Finn looked up from his computer to see his investigator walking in.

"Hey, Basil." Finn stood and reached across his desk to offer a handshake. His palm was engulfed in a beefy hand strong enough to crush steel.

"Finn. Figured I'd stop by with a report on everything I have so far."

"Good." Finn indicated a chair across from his desk.

"After your call last night I decided to pay a visit to your client's ranch."

"In the middle of the night?"

Basil grinned. "Sometimes nighttime's the best time. The place was in darkness. Nobody around. I was careful to avoid being caught on camera, but I managed to find out quite a bit."

He dug a portable computer drive from his shirt pocket. "Here's everything captured on the security camera since it's been installed. Pretty boring stuff, except for the fact that both you and your client are on it, front and center during your recent visit."

"Yeah." Finn frowned. "By the time I noticed the camera, I figured it was too late to do anything about it. If our guy was watching in real time, he already knew he'd had visitors."

Basil tapped the device before handing it over. "I also photographed each box of family treasures, and found address labels ready to be applied once the boxes are sealed for shipment. They'll be heading to a collector in Connecticut with a shady reputation. I've already alerted the authorities there, who'll be more than happy to have a reason to pick him up once these boxes are delivered."

"And the name of our cowboy?"

Basil shrugged. "Still a mystery. No return address labels. And that raises the question. Since he's got all this down to a fine art, I have to believe he's done it before. A number of times. And yet, Wayne Stone, or Rogers Sutter, or whoever he is, doesn't exist in any of the files I've checked."

"So, he uses a different alias each time. Still, someone ought to be able to recognize him."

"Unless he drastically alters his appearance. Or he pays off a lot of people to keep his secret."

"Nobody has that much money."

Basil scratched his chin. "I don't know, Finn. You sell enough ranches, along with all the furniture, treasures, and livestock, you could amass quite a bank account." He stood and reached across the desk for another handshake. "I've still got several sources I want to check out. I'll stay on it and get back to you if I hear anything at all."

"Thanks, Basil."

When the investigator was gone, Finn watched out the window as he drove away. Then, inserting the drive into his computer, he skimmed through hours of film showing only a man who appeared to be in his late sixties, wearing denims and boots and a plaid shirt, coming and going through the door. It was the same man pictured with Jessie's Aunt Nola. There seemed to be nothing furtive or nervous about his behavior. He appeared to be a man completely at ease as he entered and exited in a loose, easy gait.

As if he had all the time in the world to go through someone else's home, examining and cataloging the items a family had accumulated over a lifetime.

As if he already owned it.

But if that were so, was his new wife alive? Or...?

Feeling restless, Finn tucked the drive in his shirt pocket and changed programs on his computer, losing himself in the tedious task of checking out the references of the wranglers Sam had recently hired to help with the herds and spring calving.

This was exactly what he needed to distract from the troubling questions that were churning in his mind.

Finn tossed his attaché case on the passenger seat of his truck and turned on the ignition.

As he headed out of town, he thought about the attrition rate of wranglers who could never finish a season on any given ranch. Most often it was because their former employers had to let them go for being drunk and disorderly, or for failing to perform simple ranch chores.

Sometimes their Social Security numbers didn't compute, which often meant they weren't in the country legally. And then there were the ones with criminal records. If they'd done their time and really wanted another chance, most ranchers were willing to give them a try, but a lot of ex-cons weren't willing to be honest about their past and resorted to false identities instead.

Out of the list Sam had given him, Finn had found only two cowboys with questionable backgrounds. Buck Hoyt and Clint Sawyer. Finn would turn their records over to his dad and Sam. Now that they had a lawman in the family, they would probably ask Ben to do a thorough check before making a final decision to keep them or let them go.

As he turned the truck onto a two-lane highway, Finn gave a sigh of pure pleasure.

As much as he loved his job, he was always happy to be headed home. But since Jessie's arrival, there was an added air of expectancy. He loved walking in and seeing her in the kitchen, helping Penny, or in the parlor seated at his dad's desk, going over the figures that Mac had always found so tedious.

Odd, how in just a matter of days, they had all begun seeing Jessie as part of the family.

It was true that his family had always made visitors feel welcome. It was a gift they had, and one that he found endearing. Still, this visit felt special because of Jessie. From the moment she'd stepped through the door, he'd watched her charm all of them, from tough old cowboy Roscoe to Archie, Ben and Becca's dog, who rushed to her side whenever he came for a visit. It was clear everyone, both human and animal, adored her.

She had time for each of them, as though she had nothing more pressing than to lavish them with her smile and all her attention. And they in turn responded to her in a special way.

Special. If Finn had to describe her in one word, it

would be that. Beyond her dazzling smile, beyond the gorgeous face, beyond the thoughtful attention, she had a special gift of heart.

He was grinning as he came up over a rise where the highway narrowed and there was only a metal guardrail separating the road from a boulder-strewn drop off.

As he reached the top of the rise and started down the other side, a gasoline truck in front of him began slowing down for the dangerous descent.

Reflexively, Finn put his foot on the brake.

His truck hurtled forward without a pause.

Annoyed, he pumped the brake. The truck continued on, gaining speed with every foot of the descent.

The realization that his brakes had gone out swept over him in an instant. Sweating now, he eased his truck into the oncoming lane far enough to see if any traffic was heading toward him. With any luck he could swing past the gasoline truck and get to a flat surface somewhere up ahead where he could slow his vehicle enough to bring it to a gradual halt.

He found himself staring at his worst nightmare. A cattle hauler was huffing its way up the incline toward him.

By now his truck, midway down the hill, was reaching a speed that would guarantee a fiery crash if he couldn't find a way to stop a rear-end collision with the gasoline truck.

He was forced to take a calculated risk. If the cattle hauler was loaded, its speed would be impeded, and he might be able to pass the gasoline truck and tuck back into his lane while dodging a horrible accident. If not, his truck, so much smaller and lighter than the cattle hauler, would be a tangled mass of flaming metal before being tossed over the guardrail and into the chasm below.

There was no time to debate. Worse, there was no other option on this narrow, twisted highway.

Gritting his teeth, Finn pressed the accelerator to the floor.

Though it seemed to take forever, his truck managed to pick up even more speed before it passed the gasoline truck as the cattle hauler raced toward him. As he swerved the wheel, he managed to tuck his vehicle in front of the gasoline truck just as the cattle hauler, its air horn booming, rushed past with such power, it rocked Finn's truck from side to side.

For the space of a heartbeat he was forced to fight the wheel and feared he might yet go over the embankment.

His truck continued speeding down the hill and careened around a curve, and then a second horseshoe curve, before slowing and finally coming to a gradual rolling stop by the side of a level stretch of road.

Finn sat, his hands locked on the wheel, his head bowed on his hands, while his entire body vibrated with the delayed reaction to what had just occurred.

Minutes later, when the gasoline truck rolled past, the driver laid on his horn and gave Finn the sort of gesture any sane man would give a fool who had passed in such a dangerous manner.

With a weak grin, Finn continued sitting there until his shakiness passed. Then, as his brain began to function, he phoned a friend in Haller Creek.

"Tony?"

He exhaled as the deep voice on the end of the line greeted him.

"Tony, I could use your help."

*   *   *

An hour and a half later the Haller Creek Gas and Garage tow truck rolled to a stop beside the back door of the ranch.

"Thanks, Tony." Finn stepped down, grateful that he'd had time to calm his nerves and walk without his legs turning to rubber. "Call me with what you find."

"Will do. And I sure hope your suspicions are wrong about your brakes being tampered with." Tony Russo drove the tow truck in a wide circle and headed back to town.

Finn took in a breath and pasted a smile on his face. No sense worrying his family until his suspicions were confirmed or denied.

"Hey." With a smile brighter than sunshine, Jessie looked over as he stepped into the kitchen. "Penny made lasagna. She said it's one of your favorites."

"Yeah." He stood a minute, taking in the sight of her in fresh denims and a pink shirt, the sleeves rolled to her elbows, her hair long and loose. "You're turning into a regular Rachael Ray."

That had her laughing. "In your dreams, cowboy. Penny does all the real work here. I just try to look like I know what I'm doing."

"Don't let her kid you," Penny called from across the room. "Today our domestic goddess baked buttermilk biscuits from scratch."

"Domestic goddess?" Finn's lips curved into a smile. "I'm betting you've never been called that before."

"You got that right." Jessie whisked a few more drops of olive oil into her dressing and tasted before looking over to see Finn heading toward the parlor. "Where are you going? Dinner's ready."

Finn started out of the room. "Just going to get comfortable. I'll be right back."

Upstairs he undressed and stepped under the shower, letting the warm spray play over his taut muscles. A short time later, dressed in jeans and a plaid shirt, he walked into the kitchen to find Ben and Becca talking with Mac and Zachariah.

"Hey, bro." Ben watched as Finn bent to ruffle Archie's furry neck before handing Finn a frosty longneck. "We passed Tony Russo on the way here. That looked like your truck he was towing."

Finn took the bottle from his brother and drank, feeling calm and steady once more. "Yeah. I had a little car trouble."

"You should've called me."

"I figured you were on duty chasing bad guys. Besides, Tony said he'll have it fixed by tomorrow."

"Okay." Ben shrugged and began talking about his day in town as they gathered around the table.

Though he knew he would share the information with his family, he wasn't ready to do it just yet. So while Finn listened to the family's conversation during dinner, and nodded in all the right places, his mind was still on that stretch of highway where he'd very nearly lost his life.

It was nearly midnight when the call came. Long after Ben and Becca had gone, and the family had retired for the night, Finn was still sitting in front of the fireplace, where the fire had burned to embers.

"Yeah, Tony."

"Like you asked, I paid particular attention to anything that looked out of place. Your brakes were deliberately tampered with."

"You're sure?"

"Positive, Finn. If you'd crashed, the evidence would

have been destroyed. But I know deliberate damage when I see it. This was no accident."

"Thanks, Tony. I want you to write this up in language a layman can understand. I may have to call on you as a witness in a trial one day. Would you be willing?"

"You bet. Anyone traveling that stretch of highway between Haller Creek and your ranch would understand just how deadly brake failure could be. Looks like you've got a dangerous enemy, my friend."

"Yeah."

When Finn hung up, he sat staring into the fireplace, feeling a blaze of red hot fury that matched the heat of the glowing embers.

His hunch had been correct. This had been a deliberate—and potentially deadly—act.

It would have been an easy matter for anyone monitoring the security camera to identify the visitors to Nola's ranch. Once someone had a name to go with the face, it would have been fairly simple to get his office address. But it would take time and talent to damage his brakes just enough to hold for a few miles, before failing on that particular stretch of highway.

How had someone managed enough time and privacy to do such a thing without drawing suspicion to himself?

Finn dialed Basil Caldwell's number and explained the situation. Before their conversation ended, Finn asked, "Did the police report on Matthew Carver's accident mention any tests done on his brakes?"

"Afraid not. But then, there was no reason to test what was left of his vehicle, since the police labeled it 'asleep at the wheel.'"

"Yeah. And I'm sure by now what was left of his car has been flattened for scrap metal. Thanks, Basil."

Knowing Ben was on duty, Finn phoned him. After telling his brother about the incident with his brakes and Tony's insistence that they'd been intentionally tampered with, he heard Ben's expletive before asking, "What can I do to help?"

Finn kept his tone low. "I trust Basil to gather whatever information possible. But even the best investigator can't guarantee that another incident won't occur. I realize you're the law in Haller Creek, and that Arvid isn't your jurisdiction, but I'm hoping you can persuade the authorities in Arvid to take another look at Jessie's aunt and her new husband."

"I'll definitely call the chief first thing in the morning and lay it all out. But unless there's proof of a crime being committed, their hands are tied."

"Yes, they'll want proof. And I'm doing my best to find it. I understand they have to play by the rules, Ben. Thanks."

As Finn made his way upstairs to bed, his mind was working overtime.

Proof of a crime.

He hoped it came soon.

How many times could he and Jessie hope to escape without a scratch?

Thinking about Jessie and the motel fire, the death of the private investigator she'd hired, and Finn's own incident today had him feeling a sense of urgency. Every day that the identity of her aunt's cowboy remained a mystery was another day that this smooth operator would have to strike out at him and Jessie—the only two people left who threatened his carefully planned scheme.

CHAPTER TWELVE

'Morning, Dad. Zachariah." Finn looked up from mucking stalls as Mac and the elderly lawyer stepped into the cavernous barn and walked toward him.

Mac leaned an arm atop the stall door. "What's up, son? Why the invitation to meet you out here instead of in the kitchen?"

"I have some things to tell you. I'm also asking for your help."

The two men listened in stunned silence as he related the event of the previous day.

Mac's big hands closed into fists. "Tony is absolutely certain your brakes were deliberately tampered with?"

Finn nodded. "We all know Tony is the best auto mechanic in the business. And he said he'd be willing to testify to it in court."

"Have you talked to your brother?"

Finn nodded. "I phoned Ben last night. He'll talk

to the authorities in Arvid and suggest they widen their investigation."

Zachariah pinned him with a look. "And Jessica?"

Finn took a breath. "She has a right to know. Especially in light of that motel fire. I'm more convinced than ever that it was arson. And that Jessie was the target. She's Nola Blair's only kin. If this wrangler hopes to take over Nola's ranch, he needs to eliminate her and anyone she may have confided in. That's where the two of you come in. With Sam, Otis, and Roscoe up in the hills, I need you to stay close to the ranch until this is resolved."

Mac nodded. "I understand, Finn."

Zachariah held up a hand. "Finnian, my boy, you need to warn Penny, as well. She and Jessica have been spending a lot of time together."

Finn sighed. "I know. I hate sounding an alarm like this, and adding to Jessie's worries. But someone capable of tampering with a truck's brakes, and possibly setting a motel fire, is capable of much worse."

"And what about you, son?" Mac turned a troubled look on Finn.

"Forewarned is forearmed. Now that I know, I'll be careful. Or as careful as I can be and still do my job."

As the three made their way to the house, they shared looks of grim determination.

Penny passed around a platter mounded with scrambled eggs. "Sorry. I'm so used to cooking for an army, I've forgotten how to cook for just a few."

Seeing Finn's plate nearly empty, she smiled. "Try to eat a bit more so all this won't go to waste."

Finn helped himself to seconds. "Good food could

never go to waste around here. Besides, I've worked up an appetite mucking stalls."

Just then Ben and Becca strode in, with Archie wiggling his way toward Jessie. With a laugh of delight she dropped to her knees and accepted several wet doggie kisses before offering him a treat.

Seeing her simple joy, Finn felt a stirring of anger that he would be the one to steal it from her when he had to warn her of further impending danger.

He turned to Ben. "You just get off duty?"

Ben nodded. "And it didn't take much persuasion to have Becca ready for the ride here, as long as she could count on a breakfast like this."

As they ate, the family managed to empty an entire pitcher of orange juice and a pot of steaming coffee, while devouring eggs and potatoes and lighter-than-air pancakes.

Finn waited until the meal was finished before bringing up the subject he'd been dreading.

After filling them in on the details, he turned to Jessie. To soften his words, he put a hand on hers. "Now that my friend Tony has confirmed that the brakes were tampered with, we have to face the fact that we're in the crosshairs of a dangerous man."

Jessie pulled her hand free and looked stricken. "Oh, Finn. This is all my fault."

Finn frowned. "Don't be sill—"

"Before, he just wanted to get rid of me. But now, after our visit to Aunt Nola's ranch, and that security camera he installed, he knows you're helping me."

"Jessie, don't..."

She shoved away from the table and stood wringing her hands. "Don't you see? I'm the reason you almost got killed on that highway yesterday. And you know it. That's why you waited until now to tell me what happened."

Finn stood to face her and put his hands on her shoulders. "Nobody forced me to take this on, Jessie. I volunteered. The only reason I waited until now to tell you is because I wanted to know if Tony confirmed my suspicions. And now that we know, we're going to see this through together." He looked around at the family gathered at the table. "All of us."

Ben scraped back his chair and crossed to them. "Finn's right, Jessie. We're all in this. And now that the authorities in Arvid have been alerted, we have even more help coming."

Jessie turned to Ben. "You've called the Arvid police?"

He nodded. "Chief Frank Tyler and I are acquainted. I've met him at various law-related functions. And after hearing the latest details, he told me he'd do everything he could to aid you, including initiating a search for your aunt."

Jessie's eyes filled, and she swiped at a tear that rolled down her cheek.

"Thank you, Ben."

"It's a start." Ben looked around at the others. "But it's a long way to go from searching for a missing woman to investigating these other crimes. Until the authorities confirm that the motel fire was arson, and until we can find out who messed with Finn's brakes, all we have are our suspicions. But at least we're all on the same page."

Finn could feel Jessie struggling to hold back her tears. Though he hated to add to her nerves, he knew this had to be said aloud. "I'm sorry, but I have to ask you a favor."

"Anything, Finn. After all..." She swallowed. "Since I brought this to you and your family, I'll do whatever I can to make it up to you."

Finn kept his hands on her shoulders, as much for his own needs as hers. His voice lowered, softened. "First, Jessie, you need to get over the fact that this is somehow your fault. You had no way of knowing you were being followed by this...scum who sweet-talked your aunt. But now..." He looked into her eyes. "Promise me that, until this guy is found, you're never alone. Wherever you go, whatever you do, you have someone with you whenever I'm not around."

Before she could issue a protest he added, "There's safety in numbers. I think we're dealing with a coward who doesn't want to have a fight on his hands. He's hoping to silence any protest by sneaking around to eliminate those who get in his way. That's how he torched the motel. It's how he messed with my brakes." He touched a hand to her cheek. "Just promise you won't be alone."

She sighed, and he could see how much it cost her to give a nod of her head. "I promise."

"Thank you, Jessie."

"Finn..."

She looked so serious.

"You know you had an angel on your shoulder yesterday."

"Is that what you think?"

She nodded. "That's what my aunt always said whenever something disastrous turned out all right. And it's true. How else can you explain the fact that you walked away from that nightmare completely unharmed?"

He squeezed her hand before heading for the doorway. "Time for me to shower and head to town. I'll call with any news."

* * *

Finn held the phone between his shoulder and ear as he spoke with Basil while making notes on his computer. "I've been thinking about something that I'd almost forgotten to mention to you." He described his visit to the county offices. "When I asked about someone named Wayne Stone or Rogers Sutter, I had the sense that some of the employees there knew more than they admitted to. They didn't really say anything, but it's just a feeling I had. I thought I could see signs of recognition in some of their eyes. You mentioned our guy could have a snitch on his payroll. Could it be someone with access to county records?"

Basil's tone was thoughtful. "That's a possibility, Finn. It could also be how this guy found your client's aunt. Having someone in county records who knows which ranches in the area are failing and which are showing a profit would be a real benefit to him. Especially if his snitch could also supply some personal information. A lonely, grieving widow, for instance. Or even better, a woman who has never married, with little or no family who could lay claim to her estate."

"Yeah." Finn felt a sudden tingle of memory. "Here's something else I almost forgot. That same day, after lunch with a buddy, I had the feeling that I was being watched or followed. But I didn't spot anyone or anything out of place. At the time I let it go. Now, after that incident on the highway, I'm having second thoughts. Maybe somebody wanted to know what kind of vehicle I drive. Or record the license number. Or am I letting my imagination get the best of me?"

"That's not such a stretch, Finn." Basil's tone lowered as he considered. "Why don't I head on over to the county offices and do a little sniffing around? Maybe I'll manage to find a skunk in the bushes."

That had Finn smiling for the first time in an hour. "Great. Thanks, Basil. I'd say this skunk will give off a real odor. Keep in touch."

"You can count on it."

When he set aside his phone, Finn made several more notes on his computer before sitting back to stare into space.

There was something he was forgetting. Something hovering on the edge of his mind, tantalizingly close, that he couldn't quite bring into focus. He decided that work was the best way to keep moving forward. Maybe poring over mundane documents would help him relax and allow his brain to focus on the missing pieces of this puzzle.

On the drive back to the ranch, Finn couldn't keep from testing the brakes several times, especially whenever he came up over a rise in the road. Just thinking about what nearly happened had his teeth clenching.

"You had an angel on your shoulder."

Jessie had been so somber. So serious. They never talked about what she would do if her aunt didn't survive. But knowing what the stranger was capable of, Jessie had to be keeping a lot of terrifying thoughts to herself. Could her belief in angels keep her steady when her world was collapsing?

Finn hoped so. She was so sweet and good, and so strong in the face of all this turmoil in her life.

When he'd first met her, he'd thought she was fragile. Now he was learning that there was nothing weak or delicate about her. She'd been through a lot in her life, and she was still standing strong.

CHAPTER THIRTEEN

Jessie sat at Mac's desk, her fingers tapping the keys of the computer as she recorded the expenses in a neat column. She was grateful for the opportunity to lose herself in this familiar routine. It was her escape from the dark, ominous thoughts that fought to push their way forward.

She paused, staring into space. Dear, sweet Aunt Nola was so much more to her than a beloved aunt. Throughout her life, Nola had been mother, father, protector, and mentor to a frightened, lonely little girl missing her parents. It was Nola who had insisted a grown-up Jessie go away to college and break the bonds of dependency, despite her own protests. Jessie claimed that all she'd ever wanted was to be a rancher like her aunt. But Nola insisted that she first had to taste the world beyond the ranch. To spread her wings and fly. And the experience had opened Jessie's eyes to so much she hadn't known. College had introduced her to not only science and math, but also the arts, politics, and young people who had never been on a ranch. Some of them, though very different in background and temperament, had become her friends.

As a girl she'd always loved the challenge of math. But she never would have known how much it satisfied her if she hadn't been encouraged to take advanced classes that forced her to grow and stretch and learn. And when the job offer had come from such a prestigious firm, it had been Nola who had insisted she give it a try.

The ranch will always be here, darling Jessie. After all, it's your inheritance. Your legacy. But think how much that fine education will enhance your skill as a rancher someday.

But it means leaving you alone again, Aunt Nola. I've been gone four years now. I miss you. I miss us.

No more than I miss you, darling Jessie. You're the light of my life. You always were. You always will be. But I want you to grow and live and taste all the things I never tried. And when I grow too old to handle all this, I'll be comforted by the knowledge that I gave you wings. Remember, I'm not going anywhere. I'll always be here. This land of my father, and this grand home he built, is the great love of my life. And I want it all to be yours when I'm gone.

Jessie felt the tracks of hot tears flowing down her cheeks. Surprised, she wiped them away with her thumbs and sat back as the knowledge filled her like sunlight on a dark day.

Nola had to be alive.

She knew it in the deepest recesses of her heart. If her aunt was dead, she would have felt it as surely as if a knife had pierced her own heart.

Her aunt was being held somewhere against her will,

until this madman could secure the rights to everything. The ranch. The herds. The house and all its possessions. And Nola's money.

The bank accounts! The thought slammed into her like a fist.

Of course. Why hadn't she remembered this earlier?

Jessie picked up her phone to call Finn. Before it could ring, she heard the crunch of a truck's wheels on the driveway and flew to the door.

"Finn." She dashed into his arms as he strode up the porch steps, nearly taking them both down in her haste.

"Well." With a rogue's grin he wrapped her close in his arms, loving the feel of her plastered against him. "Now that's what I call a warm welcome."

"No. It's not about..." She stopped, caught her breath, and tried again. "I mean, of course I'm happy to see you but..."

His smile did the strangest things to her heart. "Same goes, Jessie."

She pushed a little away, trying to get her bearings. "But I just thought of something important. I was about to call you when you drove up."

He continued holding her, reluctant to break this un-expected rush of heat. "Whatever it is, you're a whole lot happier than you were this morning."

"Yes. That's just it. I was feeling sorry for myself, and suddenly I realized that Aunt Nola can't be dead."

"And why is that?"

"Because I'd know it here." She put her hand over her heart. "She's always been the most important person in my life. Don't you see? If she died, I would feel it."

His look softened to concern. "Jessie, a lot of people lose loved ones without ever..."

"No. I understand that. I know what you're trying to say. But I'd know if she was no longer alive. Don't ask me why, but I just know."

"I hope you're right."

"There's more, Finn. I just remembered the most important thing. My aunt's bank accounts have my name on them, too. Aunt Nola wanted me to be able to access her money without having to jump through any hoops in the event she was incapable of taking care of herself."

Seeing the way Finn's eyes narrowed, her smile faded. "Isn't that a good thing?"

He nodded. "A very good thing. That means this guy can't seal the deal until he can get hold of her money. But it also means you're in even more danger than I thought. Don't you see?"

She swallowed. "Yes. I guess you're right. When he finds out that there's a second name on her accounts, he'll be furious."

"And twice as dangerous. Now he won't just want you out of the way. He'll want to find a way to force you to go with him to the bank before he disposes of both you and your aunt. That means we all have to take extra precautions to see that you're never alone."

"I understand. But still..." She tucked her arm through his as they walked into the house. "Finn, he needs to keep Aunt Nola alive until he can get everything to avoid probate, which can take months or years. That means it isn't too late. We need to find my aunt while she's still alive."

He nodded. "That's the plan. I want you to contact your local bank in Arvid and let them know that you want to be notified about anyone asking about your aunt's finances. I'm thinking that would have been one of his first steps after securing her name on the marriage certificate. In the meantime, I'm hoping the local police can come up with something we missed on our last visit to her ranch." As he tossed aside his attaché case, he turned to her. "Were there any special places your aunt loved to visit? A private, secluded spot she might have revealed to a new husband? The perfect place to keep her against her will without being found?"

Jessie gave a slow shake of her head. "There are none that I can think of. But maybe this cowboy has a place where he can hold her without raising suspicion." She clenched a fist. "If only we could find out who he really is and where he came from."

"I'm working on it."

Her eyes went wide. "Do you have any leads?"

"Not yet. But Basil was following up on something we talked about this morning. I should hear from him as soon as he has anything concrete."

"Oh, Finn." She pressed his hand between both of hers. "We have to find Aunt Nola. And soon."

"I know." He looked up as Zachariah stepped into the kitchen.

The two men exchanged a look before the old lawyer deftly began charming Jessie with a story about Finn and his brothers when they'd first arrived at the ranch.

Finn took that moment to slip upstairs and change. By the time he'd returned, dressed in faded denims and a plaid shirt, Jessie was sharing a laugh with Zachariah, Mac, and Penny.

She looked up as Finn stepped into the kitchen. "I find it hard to reconcile the man you've become with the hot-tempered delinquent who, along with Ben and Sam, created so much chaos when you first arrived here."

Finn chuckled. "We didn't so much arrive as storm the gates. In fact, when we broke into Mac's home, we were bent on stealing as much food and warm clothes as we could carry."

"Speaking of food…" Penny turned from the stove. "Dinner's ready."

Finn tipped up a longneck and took a long drink. "I think you'd better hold off for a few more minutes."

At Penny's arched brow, he grinned. "I suspect Ben and Becca will be rolling up any minute now. They seem to never miss one of your meals if they can help it."

The words were no sooner out of his mouth than they heard the sound of wheels crunching on gravel and a series of quick barks as Archie leapt from the SUV.

The others were sharing a conspiratorial smile as Ben and Becca stepped into the mudroom. Archie bounded into the kitchen and began wriggling around Jessie, hoping for his treat.

He wasn't disappointed.

Finn handed his brother a cold bottle before winking at Penny. "Now dinner's ready."

Amid much laughter, they gathered around the table.

After dinner and kitchen duty, the family ambled out to the big porch to watch a glorious sunset.

Penny stood on the porch steps, a hand shading the last of the sun's blinding rays from her eyes. "I know Sam is up in the hills watching this same sunset." She turned. "I love that we can be miles apart and still share the same view of the heavens. Knowing that, it doesn't feel as though he's so far away from me."

Mac and Zachariah settled into the big log chairs softened with red-checked cushions.

Mac nodded. "I know what you mean, Penny. I often find myself watching a sunset, or the moon rising, and hope Mary Pat is safely at someone's ranch, watching the same thing."

Zachariah sent his old friend a smile. "Mary Patricia will be back soon, Mackenzie. That fine woman knows her way around this state."

Ben and Becca sat close together on the log swing, and moved even closer to make room for Finn and Jessie.

Jessie leaned her head back to stare up as stars began winking in the sky. "Oh, this is nice. What a great spot to unwind."

"Yeah." Finn chuckled. "It's a whole lot nicer since Becca brought us all this furniture. Before that, we just sat on the steps, or on overturned buckets or bales of straw."

Jessie looked over. "Becca, where did you get all this?"

"An elderly rancher and his son make it. It's been their hobby during the winter months. They'd been giving it away to friends until I convinced them to let me try to sell some of their furniture at my garden shop. It's become my best-selling item. When I saw how empty this porch was, I decided it would make the perfect gift for Ben's family, to thank them for all they'd done for me."

"That doesn't come close to what you've done for me, Becca." Ben and his wife exchanged loving looks before he patted the sturdy log arm of the swing. "And look how well it ages. I expect it will be here for our grandchildren."

Becca squeezed his hand. "That's the plan."

Their smiles would rival the sun.

A short time later Ben whistled for Archie before

getting to his feet. "We need to head home. I'm on night duty."

As soon as the dog appeared out of the darkness, Ben and Becca called their good nights and left for town.

As darkness began settling over the countryside, Mac retreated to the parlor and Zachariah retired to his room and his shelves of legal journals.

Penny paused in the doorway. "I'll be hauling supplies up to the wranglers tomorrow, Jessie. Still want to lend a hand?"

Jessie nodded. "I wouldn't miss it."

When they were alone, Jessie turned to Finn. "Your family is so sweet and loving." She paused a beat before adding, "I know they're trying to distract me by talking about anything except my aunt. And I love them for it."

His lips curved. "And here they all thought they were being so clever."

"They were. It was nice to hear about something other than my troubles. And it worked. For a while I was able to forget." She sighed. "You're so lucky to have them."

"I know." His arm was around her shoulders. His fingers played with the ends of her hair. "We're both lucky to have people who matter to us."

"I love watching Ben and Becca together. The big, bad sheriff who goes all mushy whenever he looks at his wife."

Finn laughed. "Yeah. She's always had that effect on him. When we first came to Haller Creek, my big brother took one look at Becca Henderson and was hooked."

"That's sweet."

"That's not what her father thought. Hank Henderson was bound and determined to keep his daughter from marrying the guy he called the town's hell-raiser."

"Now that's just mean."

Finn gave a shake of his head. "When you get to know Hank, you'll understand. He's a straight-arrow, by-the-book guy who figured only a saint was good enough for his daughter. But now, he and Ben have found common ground."

"Because of Becca?"

"Because of Ben. He may be a tough cop, but he's got a heart of gold. He was willing to overlook everything Hank ever said or did, so Becca would never have to choose between her father and her husband."

"Smart man."

"Yeah." Finn felt a surge of pride. "That's my brother."

He stood and took her hand. "If you're heading to the hills tomorrow, you'd better get a good night's sleep. You could find yourself slogging through snowdrifts or mud holes."

"I remember springtime with the herds in Arvid. I always loved calving season. But thanks for the warning. I guess I'll remember to wear work boots from the mudroom instead of the fancy new boots I bought in town."

He shot her an admiring look. "I'm sure you'll manage to make them look sleek and sophisticated."

"Yeah. Right." She gave a soft laugh as they made their way inside and up the stairs.

At her door she paused and turned to him. "Have you heard from your detective?"

"Not yet. He won't call until he has something concrete."

"What about the Arvid police? Have they found anything?"

"If or when they do, I'll call you. I know how anxious

you are. And if there's no phone service in the hills, I'll personally deliver any information I have."

She reached over and squeezed his hand. "Thanks, Finn."

She glanced at their hands, then up to his face and waited for the space of a heartbeat, as though anticipating something more.

With his eyes on hers Finn lifted a hand to a strand of her hair that drifted across her cheek. It sifted through his fingers, softer than silk, and he tensed, reading the invitation in her eyes.

"I'm so glad I have you on my side, Finn. You and your family." Her warm breath whispered over his face.

"I'm glad, too." He could feel her in every pore of his body. Calling on all his willpower he reached around her and opened the door.

With a warm smile she turned away and stepped inside. "Good night, Finn."

"'Night."

Finn waited until the door closed before moving down the hall to his room. Once inside he crossed to the window to stare at the hills, black with cattle.

She'd made her feelings clear.

He could've kissed her.

Should've.

Would've, except…

There was that damnable lawyer's code of honor again.

There were times when he wished he'd never had to give up the old ways. The old Finn, the rough, loud, coarse tough guy who took what he wanted, when he wanted, would have said to hell with the rules.

He walked to the bed and sat on the edge while

nudging off his boots. After stripping, he climbed naked into bed and lay staring up at the ceiling.

That kid was dead and buried under years of learning the right way to live and work and love. If he wanted to be called Mackenzie Monroe's son, he would play by the rules.

Even if it killed him.

And dear God, this time, it just might.

CHAPTER FOURTEEN

The rain began shortly after midnight and continued into the morning. By midafternoon Finn decided to call it a day and leave his office to return to the ranch. On the long drive home he prayed Penny had been persuaded to wait until tomorrow to haul her supplies into the hills. If the highways and asphalt roads were covered with this much rain, it stood to reason the dirt trails leading to the herds would be ankle-deep in mud.

As he stepped into the mudroom, the silence of the house mocked him.

Zachariah walked out of his room holding a legal magazine. "You're home early, Finnian."

"I was hoping Penny would use common sense and wait another day."

"We talked about it. She knows the perils of this much rain, but she's missing her Samuel."

"She'll miss him a whole lot more if she gets buried in mud somewhere along the trail."

The old lion smiled. "Is it Penny you're worried about, Finnian? Or is it the pretty woman assisting her?"

"Both." Finn merely grinned. "Okay, I think you know." He turned away. "I'm going to change."

"And then?"

He paused in the doorway. "And then I guess I'll just have to head on up to the hills and make sure everybody's safe."

"A hero to the rescue." The old lawyer put the kettle on for tea. "Would you like me to pack you a lunch?"

Finn was halfway across the parlor. "No time. I'll eat something tonight with the wranglers."

"You'll be staying in the hills tonight?"

"With this rain, it looks like it."

Finn drove the all-terrain vehicle across a soggy meadow before beginning the ascent into the hills. A gusty wind made the torrent of rain feel like icy pellets against his face. Even his wide-brimmed hat was no match for the weather. He would have preferred the comfort of a truck, but he knew it could prove too heavy for the water-soaked ground.

The higher he drove, the heavier the rain fell, mixing with the melting snow atop the mountains and running in rivers that carved deep trenches into the soil.

As he rounded a curve, he came upon the ranch truck, its two front wheels buried in muck.

Seeing no sign of Jessie or Penny, he stepped from his ATV into knee-deep mud. The back of the truck had been carefully covered with a tarp. The trays of food were still inside, which told him the women had gone on ahead.

He climbed aboard his vehicle and started forward.

At the next bend in the trail he spotted both Penny and Jessie, slogging through the rain.

"Oh. Are we ever glad to see you." Penny threw her arms around her brother-in-law's neck and planted a kiss on his cheek.

"Not as glad as I am to see you." He grinned at Jessie, brushing damp hair from her eyes. "There's so much water, I was worried I might find the two of you swimming."

"It would have been a whole lot easier than walking in this." Jessie stepped closer. "Is there room on that thing for two more?"

"You bet." He glanced over his shoulder. "Hop on, both of you. Let's get going."

Jessie climbed on behind Finn, and Penny settled herself behind Jessie. Finn gunned the engine and they started a slow, steady climb until they reached a high meadow, black with cattle. Despite the rain, wranglers on horseback rode the perimeter while others walked among the cows, assisting in the calving, and often helping newborn calves to stand in the soggy, rain-drenched grass.

At first glance it appeared to be bedlam. But a closer look proved that every cowboy seemed to know exactly where he ought to be when he was needed.

Spotting them, Sam turned his gelding toward the ATV and slid from the saddle to gather Penny close. Afterward, he held her a little away to give her a long, steady look. "Were you engaging in a little mud wrestling, Money?"

She and Jessie shared a laugh. "Our truck got stuck and we were hoofing it when Finn came along."

Sam grinned at his brother. "Finn, the hero. Not that I'm surprised." Keeping his arm firmly around his wife's shoulders, he started toward the nearby range shack.

"Why don't you two lovely ladies go in there and get warm while Finn and I see about getting your truck up here?"

Penny and Jessie needed no coaxing to get out of the cold downpour. When they paused on the long, covered porch, Sam tied his horse to the hitching post and climbed aboard Finn's ATV.

With a wave, the two brothers took off, spewing a stream of mud behind.

"Ahh." Jessie sat on a wooden bench outside the door of the range shack and tugged off her soaked boots. As she tipped each one over, mud and water trickled out.

She peeled off her socks and wiggled her toes.

Beside her, Penny did the same.

The two young women were laughing as they stepped inside the cabin.

"Finally. Snug and dry," Jessie murmured.

"And soon it'll be warm." Penny crossed to the fireplace and held a match to kindling. Afterward she filled a blackened coffeepot with grounds and water and placed it over the fire.

As it brewed, the two women took turns showering, and before long the cabin was filled with the wonderful aroma of coffee and woodsmoke. Finally warm and cozy, they sat in front of a roaring fire and sipped strong, hot coffee.

Jessie rolled the cuffs of her denims before tucking her feet underneath her on a cushioned rocker. "Do you think Sam and Finn can get our truck out of the mud?"

"If they can't, they'll send for a couple more wranglers. After the hard work the crew has been putting in up here, they're not about to let all that food sit on the side of the hill." Penny laughed. "There's one sure thing that can turn a man into a superhero. And that's hunger. Whether the reward is food or good loving, a man will do whatever he has to."

Jessie shared her laughter. "I'll keep that in mind."

Penny studied her over the rim of her cup. "So. How about you and Finn? Are the two of you at that good loving stage yet?"

Jessie gave a shake of her head. "We're...attracted. But we haven't acted on the attraction."

Penny bit back a smile. "Your choice? Or Finn's?"

"Finn thinks we should keep our relationship on a purely professional level."

"Hmm." Penny arched a brow. "I'm not surprised."

"What does that mean?"

"Finn is the youngest, and he was separated from his older brothers at a very vulnerable age. So when they first came here to live with Mac, Finn wasn't ready to trust anybody or anything. From what I've heard, Mac had to work really hard to gain Finn's confidence. But once he did, Finn decided the sun rose and set on Mackenzie Monroe. I think he'd do anything to make his adoptive father proud. He certainly wouldn't want to violate a client-lawyer privilege just to satisfy his lust." Penny put a hand to her mouth to stifle the laugh. "Though I have to say, there's something awfully sexy about a guy who's trying to do the right thing, even if it kills him."

"You mean, even if it kills me." Jessie joined in her laughter.

Penny's eyes went wide. "Really?"

"Are you kidding?" Jessie put a hand to her heart. "I've never met a man like Finn. Besides being drop-dead handsome and sexy, he's smart. What a combination. And his loyalty toward his family really touches me. All he has to do is look at me, and I go all weak in the knees. There's just something about him…"

Her voice trailed off at the sound of vehicles approaching.

The two women flew to the door and watched as Sam drove the truck alongside the porch. Finn turned off the engine of his ATV directly behind the truck.

Both brothers, coated with mud from head to toe, were grinning like fools as they carried the trays of food to the door and handed them off to the women.

Sam started toward the distant herd, with Finn behind him. Over his shoulder he shouted, "Let us know when supper's ready."

Jessie called to Finn, "Don't you want to clean up first?"

"Why?" His smile widened. "I'll just get dirty again." He winked before walking away.

"Hey, Buck." Sam slapped a big hand on the shoulder of a grizzled cowboy. "Say hi to my brother Finn."

"Another brother?" The old man grinned, showing a gap in his mouth where teeth were missing. "I already met the one who's sheriff." He turned to Finn. "What do you do? When you're not birthing calves, that is."

The wranglers around them shared a laugh.

"Finn's a lawyer," Sam said. "But he's pretty good at calving, too."

"But not as good as Sam." Finn offered a handshake. "Nice to meet you, Buck."

Sam turned to another cowboy to say, "Clint Sawyer, this is my brother Finn."

Instead of calling out a greeting, the wrangler turned his back on them.

Finn shot a surprised look at his brother. "Friendly guy."

Before Sam could respond, the wrangler shoved his way through a cluster of bawling animals to assist an agitated cow struggling to give birth.

Sam remarked, "Reminds me of our introduction to the joys of being a rancher in springtime, our first year here."

"Yeah. Mud and blood and calves dropping all around us." Finn gave a shake of his head as he plowed ahead and assisted in another birth.

A short time later Finn looked up as Otis shouted to Sam, "One of our wranglers needs stitching up."

"What happened?" Sam peeled off his gloves and started toward the old man, with Finn trailing behind.

"Sawyer got his arm cut real bad on barbed wire. He's already headed toward the truck. I'm going to have to drive him to the clinic at Haller Creek."

"It'll take you hours to navigate all this mud," Finn called. "Maybe Roscoe could stitch him up here. He's stitched up plenty of cowboys and animals."

Otis shrugged. "Sawyer said he'll be needing a tetanus shot, too. Danged barbed wire was rusty as an old nail."

Sam nodded. "Okay. Just stay safe. And you may as well spend the night at the ranch. No sense trying to get back up here after dark."

When Otis nodded and walked away, Sam dropped an arm around Finn's shoulder. "Lucky you came up here today. With one of our new hired hands and Otis both out of commission, we can really use you."

"Glad to oblige." Finn was grinning. "Of course, I really came up here so I could enjoy Penny's good cooking."

"Tell that to somebody who doesn't know you like I know you, bro."

At Finn's questioning look, Sam gave him a level look. "What really brought you up in the hills today was Jessie. But I will say this. You've got good taste."

With wide grins, the two brothers dove into the thick of the herd and were soon swallowed up in the gritty task of calving.

CHAPTER FIFTEEN

Best food ever." Sam, freshly showered, set aside his plate and dropped an arm around Penny.

They were seated at a table that ran the length of the cabin's porch. Some of the wranglers sat with their backs to the wall, balancing their plates on their laps, while others had taken their plates inside, to eat in front of the fireplace.

Penny turned to Sam. "You ate so fast you barely had time to taste anything."

"Doesn't matter, I know you're an amazing cook." He drew her close to press a kiss to her cheek. "My stomach's full, my clothes are dry, and I'm with the prettiest girl in Montana. Life doesn't get much better."

Finn shared a grin with Jessie. "See what happens when Mr. Tough Guy gets walloped by Cupid's club?"

She arched a brow. "Don't you mean arrow?"

"The way Sam's talking, I'd say Cupid's arrow would have to pack a hell of a punch."

That had the others laughing.

Some of the wranglers were already pulling on their parkas and heading back to their horses to take the first watch of the night. The rest of the wranglers were eager to head inside the range shack to sip a longneck by the fire before crawling into their bunks.

Jessie looked across the table at Penny. "I guess we'd better start cleaning up and heading back to the ranch."

"Not tonight." Mac, who had ridden up early in the morning to lend a hand to the wranglers, gave a firm shake of his head. "There's no sense taking a risk on those trails. Morning's soon enough to head back."

Finn closed a hand over Jessie's. "I know it's not the most comfortable situation, but Dad's right. It's dangerous out there in this rain."

Jessie nodded. "I'm fine with it. Don't forget. This isn't my first rodeo, cowboy."

Finn chuckled. "I'm glad you grew up on a ranch. But I know you've been away from this kind of thing for years now."

She smiled. "I guess it's like riding a horse. You never forget."

"Good." He squeezed her hand, but didn't lift his away. "I'll give you a hand with the cleanup."

Her smile deepened. "Penny and I will take all the help we can get."

Clouds swept past a thin quarter moon in the night sky. The rain had finally blown over, leaving the stars to give off their dazzling display. The familiar lowing of cattle drifted on the still air.

Penny and Sam joined Jessie and Finn, seated on the

steps of the porch, their backs against the rail, sipping the last of the coffee.

Jessie had a blanket draped around her shoulders to ward off the chill left by the storm.

Mac opened the cabin door and stepped out. "All clear, ladies. The last of the wranglers is sleeping." He glanced at Sam and Penny. "I'm sorry to say there are only three empty bunks left. That means you two will have to double up."

Sam huffed out a dry laugh. "Gee. What a shame."

The others shared his laughter as he gave his wife a mock lecherous stare.

That had Penny touching a hand to his rough stubble of beard. "After the day you've put in, cowboy, I'll bet you ten dollars you're asleep as soon as your head hits the pillow."

"You're on." Sam grinned to the others. "Remember when Penny was so afraid of gambling, she figured I was doomed to hell? Now she's betting me."

Finn helped Jessie to her feet before clapping a hand on his brother's shoulder. "She's not gambling, bro. It's a sure thing. You're practically dead on your feet."

Sam shrugged. "There's always tomorrow."

"And the day after that," Penny said with a kiss to his cheek.

They all trooped inside and removed their boots before climbing fully dressed into their bunks.

Finn turned to Jessie. "Top or bottom bunk?"

"I'll take the top. That way, if it collapses in the night, I'll land on you."

He was grinning. "Now there's an image that might keep me awake all night."

He waited until she'd climbed the rough ladder before

settling into the lower bunk. As he lay in the darkness he listened to the sounds of Jessie moving from side to side, as she found her comfort zone.

Comfort zone.

He wished he knew of such a place. Right now, he was as far from comfortable as a man could be.

In the glow of firelight he glanced over at his brother, his arm draped possessively around Penny's waist, one leg thrown over hers, his breathing already slow and steady, attesting to the fact that he was sound asleep.

Growing up without an anchor of family, Finn had never understood how a man could make a commitment to one woman for the rest of his life. Had never really wanted that for himself. But right now, this minute, he envied Sam's contentment. He would gladly trade it for this aching, hungry yearning that twisted inside. There was a fierce need to toss aside all the good, decent rules he'd set for himself, and just take what he wanted.

And just what was it he wanted?

He wanted to take, to possess, to satisfy the need rising in him. To devour, to feast until he was sated. He wanted to make love with Jessie in every way he could imagine. And right now, his imagination was on fire.

Still, that wasn't love, he reminded himself. It was lust, pure and simple. But right now, with the fire burning inside him, it would be enough.

Beyond that, he didn't want to overthink the situation. Besides, he didn't know the first thing about love.

He closed his eyes, willing his mind to stop. But it was impossible, with Jessie asleep just out of reach.

And so he lay, fighting the jumbled images, the demons, that teased and taunted and drove him nearly mad with a hunger that couldn't be satisfied.

*   *   *

By morning the rain had blown over, and the hillsides had turned green overnight. Tiny shoots had broken through the warm, moist earth, with promises of wildflowers and lush range grass.

Just seeing the sunlight breaking through the last of the clouds seemed to give the wranglers a much-needed lift. As the first group finished their breakfast, they were replaced by a second wave of cowboys returning from night duty, riding the perimeter of the herd.

After changing into dry clothes they filled their plates with thick slices of ham, fried chicken, mounds of scrambled eggs, and Texas toast, and washed it down with gallons of coffee.

While they were eating, Otis returned, parked the ranch truck, and made his way to the cabin, where he accepted a plate from Penny with a smile of thanks.

Mac glanced around. "Where's our wrangler?"

"Doc gave him a hundred stitches or more. He said the cut was long and deep, and looked more like a knife wound than a tear by barbed wire. But just in case, he gave him a tetanus shot and said he can't do any heavy lifting until that cut has time to mend, or else he'll just tear it open and risk infection."

Sam frowned. "I'm sorry to hear that, but what good is a wrangler who can't do any heavy lifting?"

"That's what Sawyer said. So he decided to head on home to River Bend and recover. He said we can mail his final paycheck here." He handed Mac a slip of paper.

Mac studied the post office address before handing it over to Jessie. "As long as you and Penny are heading back to the ranch today, you may as well put this on my desk and make a note of how many hours Clint Sawyer worked. I'll mail his check when I get back to the ranch."

She nodded and tucked the scrawled note in her shirt pocket.

An hour later Mac and Otis and Roscoe were saddling their mounts for another day with the herd.

Sam gave a resigned sigh as he kissed his wife and headed toward the horses in the corral. Over his shoulder he called, "If I'm not back at the ranch by the end of the week, you'll know we've had a banner year for calves."

"As much as I'll miss you, I'm hoping for that banner year."

He shot Penny a grin. "Me too, babe. Me too. But not as much as I'm hoping to get back to you as soon as possible."

Finn loaded his ATV into the back of the truck before climbing up to the driver's side.

He turned to Jessie and Penny. "Got everything?"

"I hope so." Penny gave an anxious glance at the steep, narrow trail, where the runoff of snow from the higher elevations still formed overflowing streams on either side. "I wouldn't want to have to turn around in this mess when we're halfway down this mountain."

Finn chuckled. "Be warned. If you forgot anything, you'll have to do without it until the next time you drive up here."

"I just hope the ground has time to dry out before I make this trip again." Penny crossed her fingers.

The two women fastened their seat belts as they began the challenging descent.

When they were finally down the hill and at the ranch,

they all breathed a sigh of relief before they unloaded the truck and hauled the empty containers into the kitchen. Afterward they were only too happy to head upstairs for warm showers and fresh clothes, before tackling another round of chores.

In his room, Finn checked his cell phone, noting the calls he'd missed while up in the hills, where there was sporadic phone service.

The first call he returned was to his investigator, Basil Caldwell.

"Yeah, Basil? What've you got?"

He listened, then said, "I'll be in Haller Creek in an hour."

After a quick shower and shave, he dressed for work and headed downstairs.

In the kitchen, Penny and Jessie were seated at the table, sipping hot tea.

Seeing Finn's buckskin jacket, Jessie's eyes widened. "You're going to your office?"

He nodded. "I was hoping to give you two a hand with the chores. If I can't make it home for supper, I'll call." He paused a beat before glancing from Jessie to Penny. "You'll stay close?"

The two women shared a smile before Jessie batted her lashes and said, "Yes, sir. I wouldn't dream of leaving the safety of my guardian, sir."

"Good girl." Finn was laughing as he strode out the door to go meet Basil.

CHAPTER SIXTEEN

Jessie sat at Mac's desk in the parlor entering figures in his ledger in her neat, orderly fashion.

Every once in a while she would pause and sit back with a smile, reliving the previous day. It should have been a disaster. Heavy rains washing out the trail. The truck buried in mud. She and Penny trudging in ankle-deep muck, their hair plastered to their necks, wondering if they would ever be able to feel their cold toes again. And then along came Finn on his ATV, and the entire day seemed like a party. Riding behind him, sandwiched between Penny's arms and Finn's broad back. Feeding the wranglers, and watching the loving interaction between Penny and Sam. Even the kitchen duty and cleanup had been fun, thanks to Sam and Finn and their endless teasing. And sleeping in a bunk above Finn, warm and snug and content.

Heaven.

The only thing better would have been sharing his bed.

She forced herself back to the task at hand and flipped through the ledger searching for the hours Clint Sawyer had put in.

When she came to his name and read the notation alongside it, she realized he was one of the new hires flagged by Finn for questionable employment, since his Social Security number didn't compute. Clint Sawyer had been employed less than a week.

She tallied his hours and the pay due him before marking it in the ledger and leaving a note for Mac.

She found herself hoping Sawyer was able to mend quickly and find work soon. The money he had coming from the Monroe ranch would hardly pay the bills.

The ringing of her cell phone interrupted her thoughts.

Seeing Finn's name on the caller ID had her smiling.

"Hey, cowboy. I hope you're calling with good news. Or did you just want to tell me you miss me?"

Her eyes went wide before she managed to say, "Oh, Finn. Do you think this could be connected to my aunt's situation?"

She listened again before nodding. "I'll be ready."

She closed Mac's ledgers and flew to the kitchen to share her news with Penny.

"Now tell me everything Basil said." Jessie settled herself into Finn's truck and buckled her seat belt before turning to him.

His eyes were hidden behind mirrored sunglasses as he headed away from the ranch toward the distant highway.

"One of the avenues Basil has been pursuing is the deaths of women ranchers living alone. In each case, he followed up to see if any of them had married recently before their deaths. He's found several. All the deaths have been declared by the authorities to be of natural causes. No suspicion of foul play recorded."

"But why are we driving to this particular town? I've never heard of Harmony, Montana."

"Neither have I. I looked it up. A small ranching community, much like Haller Creek. It's a bit of a drive. We won't get back until well after midnight. But I think it's worth looking into. A widow named Evelyn Troop died there shortly after marrying one of her wranglers. After the marriage her longtime employees were terminated." Finn turned to Jessie. "Sound familiar?"

She nodded, too stunned to speak.

"There's more. Her new husband hasn't been seen since. But her estate was declared legally his, and since there is no family to protest, the fears of her longtime ranch foreman have gone ignored."

Seeing Jessie's hands clasped tightly in her lap, Finn reached over and placed his hand over hers. "It could be a coincidence. But I have a feeling about this, Jessie."

A lone tear squeezed from the corner of her eye. "I pray you're right, Finn. With each day that passes, my fears for my aunt grow. We have to find her before…"

"I know. But hold on. Basil's still chasing every lead he finds."

"I'm so grateful. To him and to you."

He gave her a gentle smile. "Just doing our best, ma'am."

She managed a smile. "Fingers crossed that we find some answers in Harmony."

* * *

"Chad Hill?" Finn approached the bewhiskered cowboy working in a cavernous barn.

"That's me." The man leaned on his pitchfork. "Are you Finn Monroe, the fellow who called me?"

"I am. And this is Jessica Blair."

"Ms. Blair." The old man whipped off a work glove to offer a handshake.

"We've been in town, talking to the sheriff and the town doctor. And now we were hoping you wouldn't mind telling us what you told the authorities about your former employer."

The wrangler nodded and set aside his pitchfork. "Let's talk outside."

They followed him out the door and took a seat on a wooden bench beside a corral teeming with horses.

"I worked for the Troops for twenty-three years. The last ten or so years I reported to Evelyn Troop after her husband, Oren, died. Mrs. Troop was no spring chicken. I guess none of us ever thought she'd marry again, but..." He shrugged. "It was quite a surprise when she up and married this new hire, Wyatt Seabold. He'd only been working with us about a month. The first time I introduced him to Mrs. Troop, she didn't even seem to notice him. A few weeks later, they're husband and wife." He gave a slow shake of his head. "How can a man sweet-talk a woman like that into marriage?"

At those words, Jessie glanced over at Finn, her eyes wide with questions.

"I mean..." Chad went on, needing to explain. "She hardly ever went into town. I know she never spent a Friday night at the bar, 'cause I'd have seen here there. She was just a simple, sweet, stay-at-home widow. And

Wyatt seemed to spend all his time with the cattle. How did he find time to court her?"

"Did you see her after their marriage?" Finn asked.

"Not once. Wyatt said they were on their honeymoon and would be back later. The next thing I knew, Ms. Troop was dead and my entire crew of wranglers was fired. None of it added up, so I went to the authorities with my suspicions."

"Did they investigate?"

"They did." He shrugged. "They said she died of natural causes. A heart attack, they said. Evelyn's heart was weak, and her physician attested to that fact. They told me I had nothing but a suspicious mind. And it isn't as though her ranch has been abandoned. There's still a crew of wranglers keeping things moving along smoothly, and they say her new husband keeps in touch and handles all the bills and such. Still…" Another shrug. "What do I know? The sheriff here in town echoed what her doctor said. Death by natural causes. No proof of any foul play. Still…" He chose his words carefully. "I have a bad feeling about it. It just didn't seem at all like Evelyn to up and marry so fast. And then to die…" His words trailed off.

"Have you ever been back to the Troop ranch?"

He met Finn's direct look. "I couldn't if I wanted to. The new wranglers were given orders to keep away any intruders and just do their jobs. At least that's the word around town." He stood suddenly, too agitated to sit. "I'm sure the authorities know what they're talking about. I'm just being jealous of somebody taking over my job. But I liked Oren Troop. A straight shooter. So was Evelyn. And I can't help thinking none of it adds up." He looked away. "I'm one of the lucky ones. I got this new job right away.

But some of my crew weren't so lucky. A lot of them had to head on up to Canada looking for work. I just don't think it's what Evelyn would have wanted."

He glanced at the storm clouds rolling in, darkening the sky. "I'd better get back to my chores."

Finn and Jessie got to their feet and offered handshakes. "I appreciate your time, Mr. Hill."

"Call me Chad."

Finn handed the cowboy a card. "This is my number, Chad. If you think of anything at all, give me a call."

The wrangler tucked it in his shirt pocket and walked with them as far as the door of the barn.

He stood watching as they made their way to their waiting truck.

As they drove away from the ranch, Finn glanced at the sky, growing darker by the minute as lightning flashed, followed by a loud rumble of thunder.

He fiddled with the radio and heard the severe storm warning being announced.

Jessie bit her lip. "Think we can make it back home before it hits?"

Finn shook his head. "Not a chance." He handed her his phone. "See if there's a motel nearby. The way those winds are rattling the windows, we need to find shelter, and fast."

Jessie scrolled through Finn's phone, checking for motels, and came up empty. Suddenly she paused.

"Here's a ranch that offers a bed and breakfast."

"How far?"

She studied the map. "Maybe half an hour."

He frowned. "I'm not sure we can outrun the storm, but we can try."

A half hour later they sped along a dirt road until they

came to a sprawling ranch in the middle of rolling meadows. The hills surrounding it were black with cattle.

With rain pelting the windshield, Finn left Jessie in the
truck and raced inside to see about rooms. Minutes later a
rancher climbed into a truck and Finn returned to put his
own truck in gear.

Jessie's face fell. "No rooms?"

"They don't rent rooms in their home." Before she
could say a word he shot her a grin. "But they have a
guest cabin."

As they followed the owner's truck, a bolt of lightning
lit up the sky, followed by a jolt of thunder that shook
the ground.

Jessie grabbed Finn's arm and held on.

He looked over. "You afraid of storms?"

She gave him a look of absolute panic. Her voice
trembled. "Of course not."

"So, you just wanted to get closer." He struggled to
hold back the grin that teased his lips as they followed a
narrow dirt trail for half a mile before coming to a halt in
front of a small, neat cabin.

The owner was already inside.

Finn and Jessie made a mad dash through the torrent
of rain. Once inside they watched as the owner coaxed a
cheery fire to kindling.

Turning, he pointed to a huge basket on the kitchen
table. "My wife always sends along supplies. There's
coffee and cocoa, bread, cheese, eggs, bacon, and fruit."

A series of lightning flashes nearly blinded them,
followed by a cannon of thunder.

Jessie latched on to Finn's arm.

The ranch owner studied the deer-in-headlights look
in Jessie's big eyes and gave her a reassuring smile. "And

for newlyweds, we always add a little extra." With a smile he pointed to the bottle of Champagne and two flutes. "If you folks need anything, just phone us. The number's here. Welcome to our honeymoon cottage." He placed a note on the table, tipped his hat, and was gone.

CHAPTER SEVENTEEN

Honeymoon cottage? Newlyweds?" When the door closed behind the rancher, Jessie gaped at Finn. "You told him we were married?"

"All I said was I had the most beautiful woman in the world in my truck who was terrified of storms and in need of shelter."

"Really?" The words she'd been about to hurl at him were suddenly forgotten. "You called me beautiful?"

"You can't blame a guy for telling the truth." Finn was grinning. "And he and his wife probably figured any cowboy with a beautiful woman for company would be a fool not to be married to her."

"Still, you didn't bother to ask for two rooms?"

"I asked if he had any rooms available." Finn's smile grew. "The way you were shaking in your boots, I'd have been grateful if he'd offered a stall in his barn. When he said all they have is the honeymoon cabin, I took it without question. And honestly, I can't see you being alone here while this storm is raging, although if you say the word, I'd be happy to sleep in my truck."

"Don't you dare." She reached out to grab his arm. "I was just thinking about your insistence on protecting our lawyer-client relationship."

He absorbed the warmth of her touch. "I thought about it. For a second. Then decided your comfort was more important than my scruples."

"Gee. Thanks, Counselor." Her teasing tone softened. "But you're absolutely right. I'd be terrified alone." Jessie looked around the tidy cabin, the sound of the rain drumming on the roof, barely muted by the hiss and snap of the fire. "I'm not complaining, Finn. Really. I'm so grateful to have a snug, warm shelter. And this is so much more than I'd hoped for."

"Good. I'm glad you approve." He shook the rain from his parka and hung it by the door before crossing to the fire. "Why don't you sit over here and I'll get the coffee brewing."

"Oh." She kicked off her wet shoes and settled into a cushioned rocker before draping an afghan over her lap and letting her head fall back with a sigh of relief. "Thanks. This is heavenly."

Less than a minute later there was another flash of lightning followed by a boom of thunder so loud, it jolted the little cabin as though it had taken a direct hit.

Jessie was out of her chair and across the room, both arms wrapped around Finn's waist, her face pressed to his back.

For long moments he closed his hands over hers, enjoying the press of her body to his. Then, feeling the tremors that rocketed through her, he turned and gathered her into his arms. "Try to think of this as just a lot of noise."

"Noise? It's a wicked storm, Finn. Strong enough to blow this cabin down. And it's erupting right over our heads."

"But only for a while. Before you know it, it'll blow over and let loose up in the hills."

Another bolt of lightning flashed, and she squeezed her eyes shut, waiting for the thunder. When it came, her fingers dug into his back, holding on for dear life.

He pressed his mouth to a tangle of hair at her temple. "Trust me. You're safe here, Jess."

She shivered and opened her eyes. "I know. At least I want to believe it, but..."

"Believe it." Hoping to soothe, he ran soft, feathery kisses from the corner of her eye to the tip of her nose, and from there to the corner of her mouth. "I won't let anything happen to you."

"Finn..."

"Shh." He found himself enthralled by her lips. The shape of them. The texture. The invitation.

He hadn't planned any of this, but she was so close, and soon his mouth was on hers, moving, tasting. Taking.

She sighed and relaxed against him, offering more.

And he took, no longer nibbling, but feasting.

Devouring.

"You're delicious." He paused to look at her as he rubbed a thumb over her mouth before dipping his head and kissing her again. "Absolutely delicious."

"And you're..." Her arms tightened around his neck and she poured herself into the kiss.

When they came up for air, his pulse rate had gone up several notches. "You're doing it again, Jess."

"Doing what?"

He ran his hands across her shoulders, down her sides. "Making me wish I didn't have to behave professionally."

The corners of her lips curved. "Sorry."

"No you're not. Judging by that impish grin, you're enjoying my discomfort."

She laughed. "You're right. I'm not sorry. Well, I am about the storm. But if I have to wait out a storm, I'm not sorry about having my very own big, strong cowboy here to help me get through it."

"And who's going to help me behave?"

"Who says you should? Maybe it's time to just ignore that Goody-Two-shoes conscience of yours and ravish me, Counselor."

Though he was smiling, his eyes narrowed on her with a look so fierce, she could feel the hunger, the heat pouring from him into her, inflaming them both.

"As long as you want this to happen, I don't see how I can resist any longer." He dragged her so close she could feel the thundering of his heart inside her own chest as he kissed her long and slow, taking her on a roller-coaster ride that had her world tilting at a crazy angle. And all the while his wonderful, work-roughened hands moved over her, inviting, seducing.

His thumbs followed the swell of her breasts, teasing her already taut nipples, despite the barrier of her clothes.

"Wait." Her breath caught in her throat.

"Too late." He flashed a devilish grin. "I'm enjoying myself way too much. How about you?"

"Umm." In answer she pulled his face down to hers and kissed him full on the mouth.

"I'll take that for a yes." His heart was pumping furiously as he reached for the buttons of her shirt.

He managed the first two before, on a wave of frustration, tearing the next ones in his haste to remove it from her.

She was laughing as she tugged his shirt over his head and let it fall to the floor. "Mmm." She ran her hands over his muscled chest and felt his quivering response to her touch.

He shucked his jeans and boots. "My turn." He unhooked the bit of lace, freeing her breasts and gave a sigh of pure pleasure. "God, Jess, you're beautiful."

He ran nibbling kisses down her throat, pausing at the sensitive little hollow between her neck and shoulder.

She arched her neck, loving the feel of his mouth on her skin. But when he began trailing kisses lower, then lower still, she forgot to breathe. And when he took one erect nipple into his mouth, she felt a spear of need so hot, so potent, she gave a guttural moan.

As the pleasure continued building, she clutched at him blindly. "Oh, Finn. I don't think I can wait."

He slid her jeans down. As she stepped out of them, he glanced at the tiny lace bikini panties she wore beneath. A slow smile spread across his face. "You do know how to feed my fantasies, Jess." As he slid them from her, he whispered, "I hope you have a whole lot more of these. I'd love seeing you every day in them. Or better, out of them."

At that, they came together, flesh to flesh as the heat rose up between them, fueling their needs.

His hands moved over her, lighting fires wherever he touched. And he was free now to touch her everywhere.

She could feel him in every part of her body, and still it wasn't enough.

Reading her mind he took her on a wild, dizzying ride,

taking her up to the very pinnacle, and then over. Giving her no time to recover, he continued an assault with teeth and tongue and fingertips until she managed to whisper, "The bed…"

"Too far. I'll never make it." He pressed her against the rough wall and lifted her.

In her frantic need she wrapped herself around him, framing his face with her hands. Her eyes were focused on his, loving the fact that she could see herself reflected in those dark depths.

His hands, those rough, calloused rancher's hands, were driving her mad with need.

"Please, Finn."

When he thrust inside her, she let out a cry, and for a moment he went very still. "God, Jess. I didn't want to hurt you."

"No. You didn't…you're not…" She sucked in a breath. "Whatever you do, just…don't…stop."

His eyes, so hot and fierce, softened with a smile. "Don't you worry, babe. I won't. Just hold on."

And then he began to move, to thrust. Slowly, deliberately, until she thought her body, already so highly sensitized, might explode with the fireworks rocketing through her. She could feel that same need pulsing through him as his movements became more urgent.

Heart racing, breath burning her lungs, she moved with him, climbed with him, higher, then higher still as she soared to the heavens, until she could feel herself flying free.

Her eyes closed against the blinding lights going off in her brain as, together, they reached a shuddering, shattering climax.

Like fragile crystal, she could feel herself splintering

into tiny pieces as she floated ever-so-gently back to earth.

It was the most amazing journey of her life.

Finn's face was buried against her throat. "Sorry." The word vibrated through her skin.

"Is this that old 'sorry I wasn't professional' hang-up?"

He chuckled, and she absorbed another vibration through her already highly charged body. "I meant, sorry I couldn't make it to the bed."

"Oh." She ran a hand through his hair before allowing it to drop limply. It was the only movement she could manage. "Maybe next time."

He lifted his head enough to look at her. "You want to go again?"

"Whenever you can manage it, Counselor."

He gave her a sexy grin. "I might need a few minutes."

"You're bragging. It isn't like you."

"Not bragging. Just fact. I'm ready any time you are."

She couldn't help laughing. "If you don't mind, just hold on to me for another minute or two. I'm not sure my legs will hold me."

"Weakling."

"All your fault. You wore me out. You were…really something."

"You think so?"

She wrapped her arms around his neck. "Now you're looking for compliments."

"Just the facts, ma'am."

"Okay. You're good."

"We're good. Together." He ran kisses from her earlobe to her throat. "I can do even better. Next time, I'll slow down. Promise."

"Finn, I needed fast. I was way too needy. But I like the way you think. I'll go for seconds when I build up my strength a little. Now let's see if I can stand on my own."

As he ever-so-gently eased her down until her feet touched the floor, she could feel his response to the intimate press of her body to his.

She arched a brow. "Why, Finn Monroe. You weren't kidding, were you? You're as good as your word. You really are ready for seconds."

He gave her that sexy smile that did such strange things to her heart.

With a laugh she caught his hand and led him across the room to the bed, just as a series of lightning strikes lit up the sky, followed by a long, low rumble of thunder. "I can't think of a better way to help me forget my fears of the storm."

He wiggled his brows like a mock villain. "Thank heaven for Mother Nature and her violent temper tantrums. Without that, I may have never had the opportunity to violate my code of ethics."

Laughing, they came together in a storm of their own as the wind and rain raged beyond the walls of the little cabin.

This time Finn showed her, with soft, easy touches and slow, drawn-out kisses, with whispered words and gentle sighs, another side to his lovemaking.

CHAPTER EIGHTEEN

At a distant rumble of thunder, Jessica automatically reached out in her sleep, only to find the bed empty beside her. She was fully awake at once.

Sitting up, she shoved her hair from her eyes and looked around the darkened cabin, illuminated only by the glowing embers on the hearth.

The mattress sagged as Finn sat on the edge of the bed holding two Champagne flutes.

Her smile bloomed. "I guess I fell asleep."

"Me, too. We wore each other out." He handed her a glass. "This ought to restore our energy."

She lifted the glass. "What'll we drink to?"

He touched the rim of his flute to hers. "How about to timely storms?"

"To storms." She was laughing as she took a sip. "I'll probably think of you every time I hear the rumble of thunder."

"And I'll see you in every lightning bolt." He drank before setting aside his glass and slipping into bed beside her. "And I'll always see you like this." He took the glass from her hand and set it beside his before gathering her close. Against her temple he whispered, "Naked. Gorgeous. And mine."

"I'm all yours." She offered her lips and he took them with a sort of reverence.

"Now, Counselor," she murmured against his mouth before twining her arms around his neck, "since I'm awake anyway, I believe I'll let you have your way with me."

His dragged her close, his tone gruff with passion. "Woman, you do know how to make me lose control."

She gave a husky laugh. "Promise?"

And then there were no words as they tumbled headlong into the eye of yet another storm.

"It sounds like your childhood with your aunt was a happy one." Finn lay back against the pillows, his fingers tangled with Jessie's, the other hand behind his head.

It wasn't yet dawn, and they'd spent the most incredible night loving, dozing, and then waking to love again. Once they'd opened the floodgates, they couldn't seem to get enough of the passion they'd worked so hard to deny.

"Looking back, my childhood was so happy. And surprisingly normal."

He chuckled. "What's surprising about being normal?"

She shook her head in wonder. "I remember being so afraid when my parents died, and I realized they weren't coming back. I didn't really understand death. But through it all there was Aunt Nola, taking me to her ranch, feeding me, sitting with me at night until I fell asleep. At first the ranch seemed so big and terrifying, but as the days went by, I started to lose my fear and enjoy the fact that it was so different from my life before. My aunt was up at dawn, and she always took me with her to the herds up in the hills, or to the barns for chores. One of her wranglers, old Billy..." Her voice lowered. "He's dead now, but he was so good to me, and he was always doing special things, like making me miniature tools. A pitchfork, a rake, so I could work alongside Aunt Nola. And when I wanted to ride, he brought me a pony and walked it around and around the corral until Aunt Nola agreed I was ready to ride with her." Jessie smiled, remembering. "And no matter how hard the work, she always managed to find time to talk, to listen, to answer my questions. Looking back, I marvel that a woman with no husband or children of her own could instinctively know how to make me feel safe and loved."

Finn squeezed her hand. "I can see why you love her so much."

Jessie nodded. "She became my whole life. All the love a little girl could have for her parents was transferred to Aunt Nola. I find myself wondering what sort of life I'd have had without her."

She turned to Finn. "I guess you'd know a little about that. What about your childhood?"

He shrugged, and she could feel a subtle shift in his emotions. As though trying to decide how much he could comfortably reveal without exposing too much.

To fill the silence she said, "Zachariah told me you and your brothers were hellions when you first came to the ranch."

He managed a quick grin. "Yeah. Total juvenile delinquents. We couldn't say a single sentence without swearing. It was the only way we knew how to communicate."

Again the silence stretched out, and Jessie worried that she'd overstepped her bounds. "I'm sorry, Finn." She sandwiched his hand between both of hers. "You don't have to talk about it if you don't want to. It's really none of my business."

"It's all right." He moved his hand from beneath his head and closed it over hers, as though needing that connection. "I'm not used to talking about the life I had before Mac. It's not something I like to remember. It wasn't pretty."

She could feel the tension in him as he began to speak haltingly.

"Like you, I was too young to realize what was happening. One day I was part of a happy family, with a father and mother and two older brothers. Then one day my parents were gone and we were taken from the only home we'd ever known to live with an uncle we'd never met."

Finn paused before saying, "He was the meanest man I've ever known, and I've known my share. Ben said he was our mother's brother, but they'd had a falling-out years before she married. Looking back, I realize he resented having to take in her kids. And he let us know, every day that we lived with him, just how much he resented us. He withheld food for the slightest infraction of his rules. And he had a wide leather belt he enjoyed using on us. One night when we were sent to bed without supper, Ben stole a box of cereal from the cupboard and sneaked it up to our bedroom. When our uncle walked in and found us eating, he brought out that belt and I swear I thought he wouldn't stop until we were all dead."

"Oh, Finn." Jessica couldn't hide the horror she felt.

"I warned you it wasn't pretty." Finn squeezed her hands. "Maybe that was our first salvation. When Ben's teacher saw his welts and bruises, we were taken away from our uncle. At first we were so glad. But then our initial joy turned to despair when we found ourselves in the system. Because we'd already become mean and defensive, the authorities separated us and sent us to different foster homes. I'm sure no family would take in three tough kids like us. I didn't see my brothers again for nearly six months, and then it was only for a supervised visit before we were separated again."

"You were all so young. And you'd already lost your parents. I can't imagine being separated from your brothers. That's too cruel for anyone to endure."

Finn nodded. "It was rough. I could tolerate most of the rules set by all the different foster parents in the following months and years. Some allowed only three stingy meals a day and no snacks. Some ordered all chores completed before school, which meant getting up at dawn. I could even take the bullying and the occasional beating from the worst of them…"

Jessica interrupted. "You were bullied and beaten?"

He took a minute before answering. "Yes. And hungry a lot. And teased at school when I had a black eye. There was also the time I showed up with a dislocated shoulder and the school nurse called in the authorities to have me removed from a particularly cruel rancher who wouldn't even take me to a clinic after shoving me against the barn wall so hard it broke some boards. He knew if a doctor saw the evidence of his brutality, I'd be removed from his care, and he'd lose his chance at having free help around his place."

"That's just despicable."

"The physical abuse toughened me up fast. I had to learn how to fight back, or I never would have survived. My brothers were the same. We were tough as nails, always ready to defend ourselves without fear. But the one thing I couldn't handle was the threat of never seeing my brothers again. And one day, during a supervised visit, I discovered that they felt the same way. So we made a pact to run and never look back. That's how we landed at the Monroe ranch in the middle of a blizzard."

"And found sanctuary."

He managed a smile. "Yeah. A haven. To kids like us it felt like heaven. But we weren't ready to trust Mac. I'm afraid my brothers and I put him and those sweet old men through hell before we were willing to believe Mac wasn't going to use us either as free labor or as a punching bag. Or else send us back when he'd had enough of our smart-ass attitude. We had a lot of anger stored up, and we didn't trust any adults." His tone softened. "Then one day we went to court with Mary Pat and Zachariah, Roscoe and Otis, and right up to the last minute, I figured it was all a setup and we'd be sent back to juvenile detention. Then a judge declared us legally sons of Mackenzie Monroe, and Mac gave us his word that there was nothing we could ever do that would cause him to stop believing in us."

Finn sighed. "It's not something I'll ever forget. It ties with the day I called him Dad for the first time."

Jessie felt tears flood her eyes but refused to pull her hands free of his, leaving the tears spilling unchecked down her cheeks.

He leaned over. "Hey. What's this? Babe, I didn't want to make you cry."

"I can't help it. Now I understand why you were so

determined to do the right thing about our lawyer-client relationship. You just needed to make Mac proud."

"Guilty." He shook his head. "I'd take a bullet before I'd bring him any shame. The man is a stickler for rules of conduct. At first I thought he was just trying to make our lives miserable. All those times he gave us chores because we swore or used our fists instead of our brains. But in time I realized he was doing it for our sake. Poor Dad had an uphill battle getting three lost boys on track to do the right thing and make their lives count for something. But no matter how many times we slipped back into our old ways of doing things, he never gave up on us."

"What an amazing journey you and your brothers have traveled."

"I'll say. From the depths of hell to the heights of heaven. I guess we've been through it all."

"I wish I could erase all the pain of those early years for you."

"Trust me, Jess. You've already helped more than you know." He lifted a hand to wipe the tears from her cheeks. And then, as softly as the patter of raindrops on the cabin roof, he brushed his mouth over hers.

He moved back a fraction, his hands framing her face as he stared into her eyes.

His voice was thick with emotion. "All that stuff I just told you. I've never shared any of that with another person, Jess. You're the first."

"Thank you for trusting me enough to share it, Finn."

"You're easy to talk to."

"And you're the most remarkable man I've ever…"

His mouth covered her in a kiss so filled with need, she forgot what she'd been about to say.

He dragged her against him and they came together

in a fierce effort to offer comfort in the only way they knew how.

And as they moved together, and clung together, they could feel all the old empty places inside their hearts being filled with a rare sort of peace.

"Champagne for breakfast?" Jessica sat up in bed as Finn settled on the edge of the mattress and handed her a fluted glass.

"A mimosa. Champagne and orange juice. A very respectable breakfast drink."

"Of course. Doesn't everyone enjoy this with their eggs and toast?"

Laughing, they sipped.

"Speaking of which…" Finn handed her a plate. "I've made bacon and eggs. We need fuel for the drive home."

They took turns eating from the same plate.

Jessica studied the glass in her hand. "I wish we could just stay here and hide away for a little while longer."

"Me, too." Finn took her hand in his. "I actually prayed for more rain."

"So did I."

At her admission, they both smiled.

Finn leaned close. "This time with you has been amazing."

She looked up at him with a smile. "For me, too."

"But since the storm's blown over and the roads are dry, I'm afraid we have no choice but to head back."

Jessie finished her mimosa and set the flute on the bedside table, next to the empty plate.

Finn put his glass beside hers and helped her to her feet before kissing her.

He took a last turn around the little cabin, checking to be certain the fire had burned out and there were no hot embers to cause an accidental fire.

Spying the little handwritten note atop the basket on the table, he arched a brow.

Jessie was smiling. "Just a little thank-you from the satisfied newlyweds."

"Aren't you the clever one?"

She laughed. "Well, the satisfied part is true."

He drew her close for a long, slow kiss. "More than."

They both looked up at a soft knock on the door. When Finn opened it, the owner was standing there. In his hand was an instant camera.

"The wife and I always offer to take a picture of the happy couple for your memory book. Would you folks like one?"

Finn turned to Jessie, who smiled and nodded.

The stood together, looking into one another's eyes as the light flashed.

The rancher nodded. "I always enjoy taking these. I sure hope, fifty years from now, you both look at each other just that way."

He waited until a second light flashed on the camera, before removing it and handing the photo to Finn.

"You folks come back any time you're in our town."

When he left, Finn paused in the doorway, looking around with a smile. "I won't soon forget this little cabin in the woods. Our very own private paradise."

Hand in hand he and Jessie walked to his truck and settled inside for the long drive back to the Monroe ranch.

"Look." Jessie pointed to the hills around them, washed clean by the rains and beginning to bloom with wildflowers.

Finn closed a hand over hers. "Mother Nature celebrating with us."

Jessie shivered. "I like her celebrations better than her temper tantrums."

Finn chuckled. "Oh, I don't know about that. I'm grateful to her for that full-blown storm last night. Without it, we'd have missed out on a really special time-out from the world."

Jessie looked over. "It was special, wasn't it?"

"You bet."

They were both smiling as the truck ate up the miles back to the ranch.

CHAPTER NINETEEN

Finn looked up from his desk as his investigator walked into his office.

"You look like the cat that swallowed the canary, Basil. What did you find?"

"I befriended a woman who works in the county clerk's office. Ida Hunt has been there for more than thirty years. She's getting ready to retire."

Finn gave him a knowing smile. "I guess that old charm of yours is still working."

Basil was grinning. "What can I say? I've always had a weakness for sweet old women."

"Apparently, so has our mystery man."

Basil nodded. "I've been going through the records of female ranchers who died within a short time of their marriage. Ida was giving me a hand with the records, when she said something that had me going in a different direction."

"What did she say?"

"If this was all done by the same guy, he'd have to be wealthy by now, and he'd be easy to spot by checking the tax rolls."

Finn eyes went wide. "Unless, of course, he's operating under a variety of aliases."

"Yeah. There's that. But Ida may have inadvertently put me onto something else. She introduced me to a woman in the property tax division named Sonya Park. When Ida told her what I wanted to research, I sensed a sudden coolness in Sonya's demeanor. At first I thought she just didn't like Ida moving in on her territory. After all, Ida is county census. You know, births and deaths and such, while Sonya is property taxes. Since I've always trusted my instincts, I decided to see if there could be more to her attitude than simple jealousy. So I thanked Ida and sent her away, saying I could do the rest by myself. But as I started going through the tax rolls, I couldn't help but notice how hard Sonya worked to stick close. At one point she was looking over my shoulder as I opened a file."

Finn arched a brow. "You think she has more than a passing interest in what you're up to?"

Basil nodded. "What if Sonya Park gets a bonus in her hands if she alerts someone to the fact that he's being investigated?"

"Interesting. I have a different thought. What if she gets a bonus to pass along the names of wealthy female ranchers?"

Basil's eyes narrowed. "Now we're on the same wavelength. She'd be in the perfect position to assist a guy bent on taking advantage of vulnerable women."

"What have you learned so far?"

"Not enough before the offices closed. But I intend

to return as often as needed, and I hope to get plenty of information in the coming days. I'll make a list of anyone who has doubled or tripled his properties in the past couple of years, while also working with Ida to come up with even more women who died shortly after getting married. If I can connect the dots, we just may find our sweet-talking cowboy."

Finn came around his desk to shake Basil's hand. "Good work. I think you're onto something."

"Me, too. As soon as I have enough information, I'll get back to you."

Finn watched through his office window as Basil climbed into his car and drove away.

It may take longer than he wished, but they were definitely making progress.

Now if only Nola's new husband kept her alive until he could take over her entire estate.

"Finn." Jessie's voice sounded breathless.

"Yeah, babe." He pushed aside his paperwork and leaned back in his chair. "I was just thinking about you." He glanced at the clock on the wall of his office. "I'll be home in plenty of time for dinner."

"Finn, I just heard from my aunt's bank in Arvid."

He tensed and sat forward. "What did they want?"

"They received a letter signed by Aunt Nola, asking them to mail her whatever forms she needs to fill out in order to add her husband's name to all her accounts." She took in a breath before adding, "The bank manager, Michael Dumont, said that he wanted me to know that he has no authority to prevent her from doing this. Nola has the right to assign her funds to anyone of her choosing. But because of my concerns for her safety, he responded to her letter with one from his office stating that such a change could only be made if the owner or co-owner named on the accounts could provide proper identification."

"Perfect." Finn's mind was already racing ahead. "The letter will slow down the process. Our cowboy won't be happy about this, but he'll have to comply with the bank's rules if he wants to get his hands on Nola's money. I'm sure he's an expert at forging documents, but it's just one more annoying detail he has to deal with before heading to the bank. I want you to call Michael Dumont back and ask if he will contact you the minute this guy shows up."

"I've already asked that of him. But, Finn, Arvid is more than an hour away. How can we possibly get there in time to catch this guy whenever he decides to pay a call?"

"We can't, but I'm sure my brother Ben can arrange with the police in Arvid to do that for us."

"Oh, thank you, Finn." Her tone changed from one of worry to one of relief. "And thank heavens for Ben's connections."

"Yeah. The town's bad boy has come a long way." He paused, and there was laughter lurking in his tone. "I'll be home soon if you'd like to thank me in any...special way."

"Men. Always thinking." She was laughing as she added, "I'm sure I'll think of something."

"I'm counting on it." He disconnected and sat smiling at the thoughts filling his mind.

Finn enjoyed the quick rush he always experienced whenever he parked his truck outside the back door of his home.

Home. For a kid who had been denied one, it was the closest thing to heaven.

He was smiling before he even stepped out of his truck.

He walked in to find everyone in the kitchen working on lunch. Though he took in all of them at a single glance, his gaze quickly zeroed in on Jessie.

She dried her hands on a towel and walked to the refrigerator to retrieve a frosty longneck.

"You look like you could use this."

"Thanks." He took her hand in his and just held it for a moment until he realized the others were watching.

Both he and Jessie pulled apart and knelt down to scratch behind Archie's ears, and they were rewarded with wet doggie kisses.

As Finn straightened, he caught sight of Mary Pat. He walked toward her and pressed a kiss to her cheek. "It's good to see you. We all missed you." He glanced at Mac. "And one in particular was getting anxious."

She merely grinned. "I'm glad to hear it. For a woman alone, it's nice to know someone misses me."

Sam turned toward them and motioned toward her old red van parked by the barn. "I'm amazed you made it back in that."

"Don't knock it," she said, laughing. "It's like an old trusty steed. I just turn it in this direction and it gets me here."

"Until it gives up." A frown of concern furrowed Mac's brow. "You know you're pushing your luck with that old thing."

"Hey. Stop worrying. I made it, didn't I?" She touched the tip of her beer bottle to his.

His features relaxed into a smile. "And we're glad you did."

"Lunch is ready." Penny set a platter of steaks in the middle of the big table, along with twice-baked potatoes and a salad with oil and balsamic vinegar.

There were rolls warm from the oven and a bowl of steamed early garden peas.

Everyone took their places around the table and joined hands as Mary Pat offered a blessing.

"Each time I return to this place I'm reminded how fortunate I am to be in the company of such dear friends. Bless those of us gathered here, and the many paths we take."

Talking, laughing, they sat and began passing the platters. And then, as they dug into the meal, their voices stilled as they simply savored the good food and the company of such good friends and family.

As usual, after their meal, the six young people washed the dishes and tidied the kitchen while the others took their coffee in the parlor. The sounds of teasing and laughter echoed from the kitchen all the way to the parlor.

With the chores completed, Sam removed a rolled piece of paper from a cardboard tube and began smoothing it on the kitchen table before calling, "Anybody interested in seeing the blueprints for our house?"

The entire family gathered around as he and Penny began pointing out the grand house they were planning on their plot of ranchland in the hills.

Jessie's eyes widened. "You don't plan on living here?"

Penny shared a look with Sam before smiling. "Don't worry. We won't be too far away. I'm sure we'll all still have dinners together. But as soon as Ben and Becca's house is finished, their builder, Conway Miller, said he'd start on ours."

They all turned to Ben, who was smiling broadly. "Conway is keeping his crew on track. Right now, barring any problems, he thinks we'll be able to move in by the end of summer."

Becca nodded. "Why don't we all ride up there right now and you can see the progress they've made."

Sam and Finn turned to Penny and Jessie. Seeing their smiles, they nodded in agreement.

"You can go without us," Otis called as he and Roscoe started toward the back door to continue their gin rummy game in the bunkhouse.

"Too far for me. I'm off to my room," Zachariah called before turning away.

Mary Pat gave a shake of her head. "As much as I'd love to see your house, it will have to wait for another day when I'm not so tired from a trip."

Mac was smiling. "I'll stay here and keep you company."

The six young people trooped out to the barn to saddle their horses and head up to the hills while the sun was still shining.

Along the way, their laughter and words of excitement drifted on the spring breeze.

"Oh, Becca." Jessie trailed the others through the half-finished house, admiring the master bedroom with its attached bathroom and walk-in closet, and the lovely fireplace in the great room. "It's all so beautiful."

"Yeah." Ben put an arm around his wife before pointing out the window. "But that's the prettiest thing of all."

They all turned.

"The view. The town way down there, and all around us, hills and cattle and wide-open spaces."

Sam nodded. "I feel the same way about the place we're planning. It's in the middle of nowhere. Not a neighbor in sight. And it's all ours."

As they walked to their tethered horses, Finn caught Jessie's hand.

"We've got a little more daylight. Want to take a ride?"

"Okay. Where to?"

"I'd rather show you than tell you."

To the others he called, "We'll be along in a while."

While his brothers and their wives called their good-byes and rode off, Finn turned his mount in the opposite direction.

Curious, Jessie rode along beside him.

As they continued to climb, they came to a high meadow abloom with wildflowers and ringed by a forest of trees. As they approached, a small herd of mustangs slipped away into the shelter of the forest.

Jessie's voice was barely more than a whisper. "Were those wild horses? Or did I imagine them?"

Finn nodded. "Mustangs. This is their turf. Whenever I'm here, I watch for them." His voice lowered with passion. "The first time I ever came here, I spotted them and knew."

"Knew what?"

"That this would be my place."

Puzzled, she glanced around at the flowers, the trees, the mustangs blending into the shadows of the forest like ghosts. "What do you mean?"

He slid from the saddle and helped her dismount.

"When Dad adopted us, he told us that each of us should pick out a plot of land that called to us and he would see that it became legally ours. Our very own piece of land that nobody could ever take away from us."

"Oh, Finn." She looped her arm through his. "What a special man your father is."

"Yeah. It meant so much to us. He not only took in three delinquents and promised to love us no matter how badly we behaved, but he gave us his name and his home and a future here on the land he loves."

She turned to him with shining eyes, blinking back tears.

Seeing them, he framed her face with his big hands. "Jessica Blair, did anyone ever tell you that you have a very tender heart?"

He lowered his head, pouring himself into the kiss.

He lifted his head to look at her. "Are you in a hurry to get back to the ranch?"

"Not particularly." She wrapped her arms around his neck and gave him a lazy smile. "Do you have something in mind?"

"Yeah." He kissed her again, this time with a flash of fire that had her blood heating, her bones turning to melted wax.

Against her lips he breathed, "Oh, yeah. I have... something in mind."

And then there were no words needed as they came together to feed a hunger in their hearts.

CHAPTER TWENTY

Ben parked his official police vehicle outside Finn's office. Minutes later Finn stepped out and settled himself in the passenger side.

As he fastened the seat belt, he glanced around. "Pretty fancy, bro. It's hard to imagine the two of us riding in this and neither of us is going to jail."

"Those were the bad old days." Ben put the SUV in gear.

The two brothers shared a grin as they headed out of town.

Ben adjusted his mirrored sunglasses before looking at Finn. "You tell Jessie what we're up to?"

Finn shook his head. "Nothing to tell yet. I don't want to get her hopes up and then have them dashed. The worry is eating at her. She wakes in the night in a sweat from a recurring bad dream."

"And you know this because...?"

Finn gave Ben the finger. "None of your business."

"Hey. I'm not asking for details of your love life. You're the one who just ran his mouth." Ben turned the car onto the interstate. "You want to be careful. Jessie's your client and she's going through a lot of trauma. That makes her vulnerable."

Finn hissed a breath. "You're a little late, Ben. I've been having that argument with myself since I first met her. And now I'm in too deep."

Ben gave a shake of his head. "I know the feeling. It happens to the best of us."

Ben and Finn sat facing Frank Tyler, Arvid's police chief, as they filled him in on the little they knew about Nola Blair's new husband.

He listened politely before frowning. "If, as you suggest, he's done this sort of thing before, why isn't he behind bars?"

Ben shrugged. "All we have at this point are theories. One is that he's using a different alias for each incident. And we suspect he has inside information, maybe at the county level. Tax rolls. Obituaries. Finn has an operative checking that out. But we believe he's now getting desperate to get his hands on Nola Blair's money. We think the letter to her bank may have been forged, and that's where you come in."

He turned to Finn. "My brother found this photograph."

Finn opened a manila envelope and held out the picture Jessie had found in her aunt's box of treasures. "Though we can't be certain this is Nola's new husband, her niece, Jessica, said she's never seen it before, which leads us to believe it was taken just prior to their wedding."

Chief Tyler frowned. "Or it could be just another wrangler who worked for Nola Blair."

Finn arched a brow. "This man has his arm around Nola's shoulders. That's not what you'd expect from an employee. And see the way she's looking at him? Like a woman looks at a lover."

Frank Tyler smiled. "All right. A lover. That's not enough to incriminate a man."

Finn nodded. "I agree. And we have no proof this is her mysterious husband. But we're grasping at straws, hoping to find Nola before her new husband is able to get his hands on her bank records."

The chief picked up the photo. "I'll make a copy for the bank manager and his employees. And I'll ask my men to familiarize themselves with this face, as well. If or when this guy shows up, I'll notify you. But beyond that, my hands are tied. As I told Jessica Blair when she initially reported her concerns, I can't arrest a man without a single shred of evidence of foul play. And I certainly can't arrest him for following proper banking procedures."

"But you'll call if this man is spotted in your town?"

The police chief nodded before getting to his feet.

"Thanks, Frank." Ben shook the chief's hand.

Finn did the same before adding, "Thank you, Chief. My client is absolutely convinced that her aunt is in grave danger."

"And if I understand correctly, once her aunt's new husband signs the necessary paperwork, your client will be in danger, too."

At Finn's questioning look he added, "In danger of no longer having access to her aunt's considerable estate."

Finn's tone hardened at the sarcasm in the chief's voice. "I'm sure you've seen plenty of such cases, but I can assure you this isn't one of them."

The chief frowned. "Money can drive otherwise normal

people to do some really strange things. I understand from your brother that you had no long-term relationship with the Blair family. Yet this young woman sought you out, a lawyer in a town a hundred miles from here, with a wild story of her aunt having been sweet-talked into a hasty marriage with a no-good wrangler."

Finn's eyes narrowed. "Look, I know what you're suggesting."

"She didn't hire a lawyer here in Arvid. She went out of her way to hire a stranger."

"She came to Haller Creek because her aunt said her husband used to work there."

"And you claim to have found no record of his employment in your town."

"That's correct. But we think he may have used another identity."

"Or it simply never happened the way she told you. This wouldn't be the first time a greedy young person with dreams of an easy life sees it slipping away and concocts a story out of desperation."

Finn banked his rising anger and fought to keep his tone professional. "I understand your concerns, Chief. I felt the same way when I first met Jessica Blair and heard her story. But now I believe my client beyond a shadow of a doubt."

"Of course you do, Counselor." Frank Tyler gave a low rumble of laughter. "That's your job. Even if your client was standing over a bloody corpse holding a smoking gun, I would expect you to vigorously defend your client in court."

To hide his annoyance, Finn started to turn away.

Still laughing, the chief added, "And as I recall from my first meeting with her, your client is a pretty young thing who could turn heads just by walking into a room. It's clear she's got you hooked, young man."

Knowing it was useless to argue his case, Finn stalked from the chief's office.

Ben trailed more slowly.

Once in the car, he laid a hand on his brother's arm. "Don't take it personally, bro. After years in this line of work, I'm sure Chief Tyler has seen his share of dysfunctional family situations. He's just calling it like he sees it."

"And he sees Nola's new husband as a decent, law-abiding citizen, and Jessie as a money-hungry liar." Finn swore, loudly, fiercely, before turning to stare morosely out the window.

"You said yourself that you'd had doubts about her at first." Ben maneuvered the vehicle along the main street's cars and trucks and pedestrians, a worried frown creasing his forehead.

They drove out of town and along the interstate for miles before Ben broke the silence.

"We're going to find this guy, Finn. And Jessie's going to be reunited with her aunt."

"You don't know that. Every day brings us closer to disaster."

"What I know is this. You've told me that Jessie feels an unbreakable bond with the woman who raised her. She's absolutely convinced Nola is still alive. And that's good enough for me. I intend to do everything within the limits of the law to save Jessie's aunt. And if that's not enough, I'll just have to uncover some hidden super-powers to match the superpowers of my little brother, the best damned lawyer I know." He reached a hand out to Finn. "Deal?"

After a moment Finn nodded and gave him a fist bump. "Deal."

Back at his office, Finn sat back, wishing he had some hopeful news for Jessie. He felt as though they were crawling through the middle of a marathon, while Nola's mysterious husband had breezed past them and was now miles ahead.

Finn kept thinking there were things he'd missed along the way, but he was so caught up in the big picture, the little things were falling by the wayside.

Like Jessie, he was desperate to find some trace of Nola. The longer she was missing, the more dire her circumstances. If her new groom followed his usual pattern, he could have already put into motion the next logical step in his plan for her "natural" death.

Finn's head came up, wondering if Nola Blair had any medical conditions that only her doctor would know about. Wouldn't that be something she would share with a new husband, especially if he was really good at gaining a woman's confidence?

There was more. Finn's mind was racing. What if Nola has a fondness for doing something risky? Something that could be considered the perfect way for a murderer to make her death look accidental.

He ran a hand through his hair before picking up his phone and calling Jessie. Though he knew it would cause her fresh pain, the questions needed to be asked. And she was the only one who could answer them.

"Jessie." Finn's voice took on a tenderness that he wasn't even aware of. "Did your aunt give you her medical power of attorney?"

She hesitated. "Have you heard something, Finn?"

"No." He was quick to ease the sudden air of expectancy in her tone. He hated lifting her hopes so often, only to dash them just as suddenly. "I'm thinking that we need to talk to Nola's doctor to see if she had any health issues her new husband could use against her. But unless you have her medical power of attorney, a trip to Arvid to talk to her doctor would be a waste of time."

"Before I went off to college she asked me to sign a number of documents. One of them was her medical power of attorney. But I have no way of knowing if that's been changed after all these years."

"We'll just have to take a chance. First thing tomorrow, let's plan on driving to Arvid." As an afterthought he added, "And maybe, if we're lucky, we'll run into another storm and have to spend the night at some remote little cabin."

The sound of her soft laughter lightened his heart. "Are you sure you can spare the time away, Counselor?"

He assumed a slow, easy drawl. "Little lady, it would be a supreme sacrifice. But your comfort is my main concern." He paused. "I'm sure you know by now I'm just a guy who's always willing to go the extra mile for his clients."

She laughed. "Bless you. Now you'll have me watching the weather reports with fingers crossed."

He disconnected and sat back with a smile. If only he could always make Jessie laugh with a few simple words.

He picked up a notebook and began jotting down questions he wanted to ask Nola's doctor tomorrow.

CHAPTER TWENTY-ONE

An hour after speaking with Finn, Jessie tallied a column of numbers and was jotting down the total when her cell phone rang.

The moment she saw the caller ID she felt all her breath leave her lungs. Her throat got so tight she could barely get a word out.

"Aunt Nola? Is it really you?"

"Jess...i...ca."

"Oh, Aunt Nola. I've been so worried about you! Are you all right?"

"Fine." There was a long pause before she added, "Just a little weak from a virus I must have picked up."

"Oh, that's awful. Where are you? Have you seen a doctor?"

"No need."

Again a pause, causing Jessie to say quickly, "Tell me where you are and I'll come get you. You sound weak, Aunt Nola. I'll drive you to Arvid to see your doctor."

"This call is not about me. Now listen to me, Jessica. I have important business to discuss. I want you to meet my husband, Wayne, at the bank in Arvid to sign whatever documents are necessary to remove your name from my bank accounts, to be replaced with his name. Now that we're husband and wife, it is only proper that we do so."

"Of course, Aunt Nola." Jessie struggled to make her mind work. Was this a setup? After all these days of constant worry, this was the last thing she'd expected to hear. Jessie had to swallow hard before saying, "If this is what you really want, I'm happy to do whatever you ask. Would you like to put Wayne on the phone and we'll arrange a day and time to meet?"

Another pause before Nola's staccato words came out almost like hiccups. "He's leaving now. You're to meet him at the bank as soon as you get to town."

"Today? Now? But I..." Jessie bit back the protest that bubbled up. She took a breath and softened her voice. "Are you all right, Aunt Nola?"

"Enough of that. Stop your fussing and get going."

"This is all so sudden. Your marriage. And not returning to your ranch. I want you to know I went there looking for you. I'm worried about you. I hope you know how much I miss you, Aunt Nola."

The older woman's voice became instantly animated. This was the voice Jessie recognized from her childhood. "I miss you too, Jessie darling. I hope you always remember how much I love..."

When the line went dead, Jessie hugged the phone to her heart and allowed the tears to fall unchecked.

Her aunt was alive.

Nothing else mattered.

She punched in Finn's number on her cell phone before racing up the stairs to find her purse and keys.

When he answered, she nearly shouted. "Finn. My aunt just called me." Breathless, she snatched up her purse and barreled down the stairs toward the back door. "Of course I'm sure it was Aunt Nola. Nobody could fake that voice."

She snatched a set of keys from a hook by the back door. "I hope your family won't mind if I take one of the ranch trucks." As she hurried toward the barn, she explained in a rush, "This is all so sudden. I can't think. Aunt Nola's been sick with a virus."

At Finn's question she paused before climbing into a truck. "No, I don't know where she called from. I should have insisted, but I was so surprised to hear from her, I couldn't seem to make my brain work. But I'll ask her husband when I get to Arvid."

She paused at the rush of questions he began hurling at her. "No, I didn't speak to him. She said he's already on his way to Arvid, and wants me to meet him at the bank. Can you meet me there and together we can persuade him to let us follow him to wherever my aunt is staying?"

Finn's tone was edged with frustration. "I'm not at my office in Haller Creek. I've just arrived at the county offices. Even if I drop everything and head out now, I'd never make it in time. Jessie, I don't want you to go alone."

"I have to." Her eyes filled and she blinked away the tears. "Finn, I've been desperate to hear from my aunt. I'm willing to do whatever she asks."

"None of this rings true, Jess. None of it. You're being set up."

Jessie sighed, trying to clear her mind. "I know it's

sudden. But it's my first contact with Aunt Nola since her wedding." She thought a minute. "What about the police chief? Do you think if you called him he could meet us at the bank? That way, if there are any questions about this stranger's honesty, I won't be alone."

She could hear the relief in his tone. "Good thinking. I'll call him now."

She smiled. "Oh, that's good. All right, Finn. When I meet with Wayne Stone at the bank, I'll try to get as much information about my aunt as possible. I'll make certain to ask where she is, how she is, and when they plan on returning to her ranch. I'll ask everything in front of the bank manager and police chief. And I'll stick like glue to the police chief and let him decide whether or not to trust this man. If he or the bank manager expresses any concerns about Wayne Stone, I'll ask for a delay until Aunt Nola is well enough to accompany him to town."

Finn's voice sounded pleased. "All right. I'll try to reach Ben and see if he can head over to Arvid as well. I'd feel a lot better having Ben alongside you. As for me, I'm already heading to my truck. I'll get to Arvid as fast as humanly possible."

"Thanks, Finn. Drive safely. If you're not there in time, I'll call you as soon as our meeting ends and give you all the information I have."

Jessie put the truck in reverse and backed out of the barn before driving along the gravel driveway as fast as the vehicle would allow.

Alive.

Alive.

Aunt Nola is alive.

The words were a litany of joy singing through her mind.

She clung to that thought, hugging it to her heart.

Just the sound of her aunt's frail, tired voice had given her such renewed hope.

Halfway to Arvid, Jessie pulled the truck over on the side of the highway.

She was so nervous her hands were shaking. Soon she would confront the man who'd sweet-talked her aunt.

How she prayed he was good and decent and someone worthy of Aunt Nola. The fact that her aunt was trusting him with her money meant she had no regrets about her hasty marriage to him.

Oh please, she whispered. *Just let all my wild fears be groundless.*

More than anything in this world, her dear aunt deserved happiness. And if this man could give Nola real joy in her life, Jessie would embrace him, despite the unorthodox way he'd swept her aunt off her feet.

Taking a deep breath, she pulled back onto the highway. As she passed another mile marker on the interstate, she could feel her heart pounding.

She was in such a state of high anxiety, she wondered how she would survive the next leg of her journey.

Her moods alternated with each passing mile. She was in a wild state of euphoria to know that her aunt was still alive. After all the fears, all the nightmares, Aunt Nola was alive.

Just as suddenly she thought about all the unexplained mysteries since her aunt's marriage. The new team of wranglers. The empty ranch house. The security camera. The family treasures boxed for shipment.

Wayne Stone had a lot of explaining to do. And she wanted him to explain in front of the police chief and the bank manager. She wanted witnesses to his deception, if that's indeed what he was guilty of. And if by chance her aunt was actually happy and safe, she wanted proof of that, as well.

Oh, how she hoped and prayed that this had all been some terrible misunderstanding.

She wanted, more than anything in this world, to see her aunt. To hug her. To hear from her own lips that all was well.

She needed to stop somewhere and get her emotions in check. And maybe delay her meeting enough that Finn would have time to get to Arvid.

She pulled off the interstate and followed the signs to a small diner.

Inside she ordered coffee and sipped it slowly, her mind on overdrive as she thought about how tantalizingly close she was to finding her aunt.

With Ben and the police chief of Arvid to bolster her courage, she would push until she got the answers to all her questions.

And then she would have a grand reunion with her sweet aunt, who had been mother, father, and mentor to her for all these long years.

She owed it to Nola to get to the bottom of this.

CHAPTER TWENTY-TWO

Jessie drove through the little town of Arvid without really seeing it. She passed the residential areas, as well as Hal's Grocery and Vern's Drugstore, though they held no interest for her today.

She drove past the elementary school and playground, with its chorus of children's voices at play, and the new high school, where a group of student athletes snaked along the track. She passed the old stone church with its shiny steeple reflecting the afternoon sun. She paused at the medical clinic to allow an ambulance to turn in front of her before turning into Arvid Bank, with its drive-through window and parking lot on the opposite side.

By the time she exited the truck and walked to the door of the bank, her heart was beating a tattoo in her chest, and she wondered how she would ever be able to keep breathing.

Once inside, she took several deep breaths before looking around.

In the far corner of the bank, behind a wall of glass, she saw the manager, Michael Dumont, at his desk. She recognized Chief Frank Tyler, in his crisp uniform and shiny badge, seated across from him. When she'd first approached Chief Tyler with her suspicions about the danger her aunt was in, he'd listened attentively and promised to look into it. But a day later, after investigating, he'd found no evidence of foul play. Though he'd remained polite, she'd sensed the change in his attitude. She'd had the distinct impression that he thought she was some sort of hysterical female who was wasting his time. She hoped to heaven he'd softened his attitude toward her.

She took a moment to breathe before stepping into the manager's office.

When both men turned to look at her, she realized there was a third man, seated beside the chief. Her view of him had been blocked by the bulky figure of Frank Tyler.

"Ah. Here you are." The stranger was smiling warmly as he shoved away from his chair to step close and take her hands in his. "I was just telling Mike and Frank here how eager I was to finally meet Nolinda's niece."

Jessie knew her jaw had dropped. This wasn't the man in the photo. In fact, this portly man, with his white hair and rimless glasses, his dark suit and conservative blue tie, shoes polished to a high shine, looked for all the world like someone's grandfather.

He turned to the bank manager and police chief. "If she isn't the spitting image of her aunt. I can see why Nolinda loves her so much."

"You call my aunt Nolinda?"

"That's her name, and I much prefer it to Nola, though

I know that's what you and most folks around here call her." He blushed slightly. "I hope you won't hold my little eccentricity against me. A woman as lovely as my Nolinda deserves a lovely name."

The bank manager's smile grew. "Spoken like a man in love."

"That I am. And proud of it." In a courtly manner, Wayne kept Jessie's hand in his as he led her across the room. He held a chair and waited until she was seated before taking the seat beside her.

"I'm so sorry your aunt couldn't come with me. She's been dying to see you, Jessica. But she's fighting a virus, and I don't want her lifting a finger until she's feeling stronger." He looked beyond her to the police chief. "I contacted her doctor, and he said with a virus there's no need for medicine. He advised rest, plenty of fluids, and more rest. And that's what my sweet Nolinda is doing. I told her she'll be so rested when this virus runs its course, she'll probably insist on joining her wranglers up in the hills with the herd."

At the mention of that, Jessie's head came up. "When I went to the ranch, I learned you'd fired her wranglers."

"Indeed. And I'd do it again." He took Jessie's hand before directing his words to the police chief. "There wasn't enough proof to file a police report, but Nolinda found little things that didn't add up. Items missing from the house while we were away. Rumors of the herd being abandoned after dark while the wranglers spent time in town at the bar. You know what they say." He winked to the two men. "When the cat's away, the mice will play."

Both the police chief and the bank managed nodded in agreement.

Wayne smiled. "So the first thing I did was install a security camera at the house so Nolinda would know if anyone violated her privacy. Then I hired a new crew. A crew, I might add, that came with excellent recommendations."

He caught Jessie's other hand, forcing her to meet his eyes. His tone softened. A grandfather speaking gently to a grandchild. "As you are aware, your aunt has always worked hard. It's all she knows. She told me how shocked and saddened she was at the death of her brother and his wife, and how she raised you. As she told the story, she never once complained about doing a job she was totally unprepared for. She generously put you through school and college, without ever taking time for herself. Isn't that so?"

Jessie nodded, feeling her eyes fill before she blinked several times to keep from embarrassing herself. The mere thought of her sweet, generous aunt making so many sacrifices on her behalf had her feeling weepy.

Wayne's tone sharpened. "But you're all grown up now, and your dear aunt saw to it that you have all the tools needed to make your own way in the world. I want you to know, Jessica, that your aunt and I will always be here for you should you require our help. But if I have my way, your aunt is going to slow down and become a lady of leisure. I don't care how many people I have to hire to keep her place running, as long as my Nolinda learns to let go and enjoy her new life as my wife. As I told her, she was a mother before ever becoming a wife. Now that she has me to share the load, I want nothing more than her happiness. She's never been anywhere but here in Montana. My hopes for a long, lazy honeymoon had to change when she became ill. As soon as she's strong enough, I intend to take Nolinda on an extended honeymoon around the world."

The bank manager gave Jessica a long look. "It sounds like your aunt is one lucky lady."

He turned to Wayne. "I'll need to see some identification, Mr. Stone."

"Mike, call me Wayne." He released Jessie's hands from his grasp and indicated a manila folder atop the manager's desk. "You'll find my passport and birth certificate in there. I had to travel to Europe recently on business. And I have my driver's license right here."

He pulled out his wallet and removed his license before handing it over.

As the bank managed reached for the documents, he asked, "What business are you in, Wayne?"

"I own WS Industries. My firm conducts scientific research on improving animal feed. Nolinda and I are hoping to isolate a small herd of her cattle and chart their growth and overall health while they're fed a special grain my scientists have been testing over the past several years. Nolinda shares my enthusiasm for this project. This final field test will hopefully revolutionize the animal feed industry, and provide hundreds of jobs for the good folks of Arvid and the surrounding towns."

"You don't say?" The bank manager exchanged an excited glance with the police chief. "That would be a godsend for a lot of struggling ranchers who have to work a second and sometimes even a third job in order to survive."

Jessie folded her hands tightly in her lap, while the police chief and the bank manager looked over the various pieces of identification.

Minutes later, satisfied with what they'd seen, the

manager withdrew several documents from a desk drawer and turned them toward Wayne. "I'll need your signature here..." He indicated the line and watched as Wayne signed with a flourish. "And here."

A second document was signed and dated.

After reading both documents and checking the signatures with those on the passport and license, the bank manager smiled.

"I'd say everything is now in order, Wayne." He turned to Jessie. "I'll need you to sign off on these earlier documents, just to attest that you understand that you are no longer a valid co-signer on your aunt's bank accounts."

Jessie glanced toward the police chief, who was smiling and nodding.

She peered through the glass enclosure, wishing with all her heart that Finn would come walking in. But there was no sign of him or his brother Ben.

Though the meeting had gone smoothly enough, and Wayne had answered all the questions to the satisfaction of both the bank manager and the police chief, she had the oddest sensation that she was a bit player in a grand drama; and this was all some sort of carefully rehearsed presentation.

All her instincts were screaming for more time. She struggled to think of a way to slow things down.

As she picked up the pen, she turned to Wayne, determined to stick to her decision to challenge him in front of witnesses. "I'm hoping you'll allow me to follow you to the place where you're keeping my aunt."

"Keeping her?" His smile was benevolent. "She's the one who's been keeping me. Keeping me so happy, our days seem to blend together into one long dazzling haze of love."

The bank manager and the police chief chuckled.

Jessie fought to keep her tone friendly. "It isn't my intention to intrude on your privacy, but I've missed my aunt, Wayne. It would give me such pleasure to see her, and to know that she's recovering from her virus."

"Are you willing to risk catching that virus, too?"

"I'd risk anything. I need to see Aunt Nola. Just to be assured that she's all right."

"Well then, taking you to see her will be my pleasure, Jessica. Although I should warn you, we're still on our honeymoon. But then," he added with a wink to the two men, "I intend to see that Nolinda and I remain on our honeymoon for the rest of our days."

Jessie was grasping at straws. "Where have the two of you been staying?"

His smile beamed. "I have a comfortable little place off the beaten track, nestled in the hills about an hour or so from town. It's proving to be the perfect spot for Nolinda to rest. No neighbors to come calling and tire her out. No church ladies bringing her homemade soup at all hours, and wanting to stay and gossip. And especially none of the wranglers bringing her their troubles with the herd. I've made that my responsibility until my Nolinda is strong enough to resume taking charge."

He touched a hand to her arm. "But just so you can satisfy your concerns, I'll be happy to take you there as soon as we're finished with our business in town."

Jessie released a little sigh, hoping with all her heart that Finn or Ben would arrive any minute now and join her. "Thank you. I'd appreciate that."

"Well then." Wayne sat back, and carefully folded his hands.

The bank manager leaned across his desk to point to the document still in front of Jessie, unsigned.

Sensing his impatience, Jessie struggled to come up with a reason to delay further. After a few more seconds, she wrote her name where indicated, and sat back as he signed the documents and added his notary public seal. How she wished Finn had been here. Maybe, if he had, he could have come up with something more to ask. As for her, she was fresh out of ideas. This entire meeting had gone in a direction she had never anticipated.

And grandfatherly Wayne Stone had been the biggest surprise of all.

While the manager opened a folder and filed the documents, Wayne stood and offered a hand to both the manager and the police chief.

"A pleasure to meet you, Mike. And you, Frank."

The two men were effusive in their praise of how efficiently the meeting had gone.

The police chief turned to Jessie. "I hope you have a pleasant visit with your aunt, young lady."

Young lady, indeed. What he meant, she realized, was young troublemaker. He'd already made up his mind about this. Wayne was the good guy, looking out for his lady love, and she was being overly dramatic, looking for trouble where none existed.

His voice, she noted, had lost the warmth he'd extended to Wayne Stone. Again, he was putting her on notice that he would tolerate no further waste of his precious time.

"Thank you, Chief Tyler." She turned to the bank manager. "Mr. Dumont."

As she followed Wayne from the bank, she glanced around the parking lot, hoping to see Finn or Ben.

Before she could turn to her truck, Wayne had his

hand beneath her elbow, steering her toward her aunt's ranch truck.

She tried to pull free. "I'd prefer to follow you in my own vehicle, Wayne."

With the police chief close enough to hear, Wayne upped the wattage of his smile.

"Knowing your aunt, you were raised to respect the value of a dollar saved. If she were here, Nolinda would insist that there's no reason to waste gas on two vehicles when one will do. I'll take you for a visit, and when you're ready to leave, I'll bring you back here."

"But then you'd have to leave my aunt alone again. I'll take my own vehicle."

"You'll do no such thing. I insist."

Jessie glanced helplessly at the police chief, but he had his hands on his hips, nodding in agreement.

Wayne helped Jessie into the truck before circling around to climb into the driver's side. As they pulled away from the bank, he lowered the window and waved to the police chief. "You have a good day now, Frank."

"You, too, Wayne. It was a pleasure to meet you. I look forward to seeing you often here in Arvid. I'm sure the citizens of our town will be grateful for the jobs you bring."

"With good folks like you and Mike, I have no doubt it will be a long and profitable collaboration."

With another wave, he closed the window and maneuvered the truck around the few vehicles in the parking lot.

CHAPTER TWENTY-THREE

Wayne was humming a little tune as he drove away from the bank, in the opposite direction from the interstate.

Jessie looked around. "Where are we headed?"

His smile grew. "Nolinda described you as a curious child. Even when you first came to live with her, you wanted to know everything. The why and how of things. How everything worked. How they were fixed. Are we there yet? Why? Why not?"

She blew out a breath. "I guess I'm still that curious girl. Where are we headed?"

"To my place. I'm afraid it's not part of a town, but rather a bit isolated. You can imagine how much your dear aunt loves it. She's always liked keeping to herself."

"You seem to know a lot about her."

"That's a husband's job. The more I know, the more I can please her."

"How did you two meet?"

He chuckled. "There you go again. How? Where? Why? I'll leave all that to Nolinda. She can tell you as much or as little as she pleases. Maybe, like me, she'd rather keep some personal secrets locked away in her heart."

The more Jessie peppered Wayne with questions, the more he favored her with that bemused smile. "Nolinda warned me you were impatient." He patted her hand. "You'll have the answers to all your questions soon enough."

Jessie watched as the familiar landmarks of Arvid slipped away as they followed a country road, and found herself questioning all the things she'd been so certain of.

The man beside her was no handsome, smooth-talking cowboy, capable of sweeping lonely women off their feet. Instead, this courtly grandfather had been a perfect gentleman throughout their introduction. In truth, he was the exact opposite of what she'd expected. If she were being honest with herself, she would have to admit that he was the type of man she would have chosen to be her dear aunt's companion for the rest of her days. Successful without boasting. Cheerful even when being challenged. And quietly capable of shouldering irksome responsibilities that could prove draining for her aunt alone.

Still, Jessie couldn't shake the unsettling feeling that Wayne Stone was almost too perfect to be true. And there was this strange feeling she had in his presence. Fingers of ice along her spine. Little prickles of unease that she couldn't dispel.

She sat back and took a deep breath, before plucking her cell phone from her pocket.

She needed to fill Finn in on all that had happened, and let him know where she was headed. If she was lucky, he was close enough to bypass the town and head directly to the back roads they were now traveling.

Distracted, Jessie's head came up sharply as the truck screeched to a stop so abruptly it caused her to be thrust forward, straining her seat belt and causing her to drop her phone. It clattered to the floor of the truck and slid toward Wayne.

In one smooth motion he scooped it up.

Jessie turned slightly, her hand extended, expecting him to return her phone. Her smile faded when he tossed it out the window.

Jessie was outraged. "What do you think you're doing?"

"I'm keeping you from passing information to your lawyer."

"My... lawyer?"

"Finn Monroe. Or has he become more than your legal counsel now that you're living with him and his family?"

"How would you know...?"

"I know everything about you, little troublemaker."

"How dare..." Whatever words she'd been about to say died in her throat as he backhanded her, causing her head to snap back. Blood trickled from the corner of her mouth.

Before she could recover he reached beneath his seat and straightened.

She stared with a look of horror at the object in his hand.

He was holding a gun, pointed directly at her head.

Finn pulled into the bank's parking lot and felt a wild sense of relief when he spotted the ranch truck parked among several vehicles. He dialed Jessie's phone and waited as it rang and rang before going to voice mail. Frustrated, he disconnected.

When Ben had phoned to say that he was busy delivering a prisoner to the state police offices and would hurry over as soon as possible, Finn had driven like a madman, determined to stand beside Jessie when she confronted Wayne Stone. The last thing he wanted was for her to face her aunt's tormentor alone.

He walked into the bank and headed directly toward the manager's office. A family photo on the desk showed the heavyset man and his wife with their toddler between them.

Finding the room empty, Finn crossed the lobby to ask a bank teller where the manager was.

She looked up from her ledger. "I believe he left for lunch after ending his meeting."

"Was there a young woman at the meeting?"

She nodded. "Yes. And the police chief and an older gentleman."

"How long ago did the meeting end?"

She shrugged. "I'm not sure. Maybe fifteen minutes or more. Can I help you?"

Finn nodded. "Do you know if the woman went to lunch with your manager?"

She shook her head. "I'm sorry. I was busy with a customer, and didn't see any of their party leave."

"Where does the manager usually eat lunch?"

"There are only two lunchrooms in town. Annie's, just up the street, and the All Day Pancake Place on Second."

"Thanks." Finn stalked up the street and was relieved to see the man in the photo seated inside the little diner. Disappointment washed over him when he saw no sign of Jessie.

As he approached the manager's table, a waitress cleared the remnants of lunch and placed a slice of mile-high coconut cream pie in front of him before topping off his coffee.

"Michael Dumont?" Finn stuck out his hand, forcing the man to set down his fork.

"That's me. And you are...?"

"I'm Finn Monroe, Jessica Blair's lawyer."

"Chief Tyler told me about you."

Finn nodded toward the dessert. "Sorry to bother you at lunch, but I'd hoped to be with Jessie when she met in your office. I see her truck in the parking lot. I thought she might be having lunch with you. Do you know where she is?"

"Having a nice visit with her aunt, I guess."

"She's gone to her aunt's place? Why did she leave her truck?"

The manager shrugged. "She went in Wayne Stone's truck."

"You're certain?"

Michael Dumont nodded. "I was watching from my office when she and Wayne and Chief Tyler parted in the parking lot." He chuckled. "Your client was pretty insistent upon seeing her aunt. I'm afraid Wayne felt obligated to take her with him."

"The documents naming him co-signer on Nola Blair's accounts have been signed and notarized?"

The manager gave him a pleased smile. "I saw to them myself."

"Despite our suspicions about the man in that photo we gave you?"

The bank manager eyed the slice of pie before saying tiredly, "Chief Tyler told me all about your conspiracy theory. Believe me, Wayne Stone doesn't look anything like the man in that photo."

Seeing Finn's look of surprise, he went on smoothly, "The elderly gentleman who came to my office today was a great guy. Both the chief and I were impressed with his credentials."

"His credentials?"

"He's a wealthy businessman. Owner of WS Industries, employing scientists working on improving animal feed. He's about to provide jobs for hundreds of our citizens. I'd call those pretty impressive credentials. And now..." He picked up his fork. "I'd like to finish my lunch before I return to work."

Finn knew he was being abruptly dismissed, and would get no further answers from this man. "Thanks for your time."

He turned away and hurried out of the diner before heading toward the police station.

When he arrived, Ben was just pulling up. Finn quickly filled him in and they stepped inside and crossed to the chief's office.

Though it took only seconds, to Finn it seemed an eternity.

Frank Tyler confirmed what the bank manager had already said. "Miss Blair left with Wayne Stone to visit her aunt."

Frustrated, Finn pressed him. "Do you know for a fact that she went willingly?"

"Do you think I'd have let her go if he'd tried to force her?" The chief's ruddy face darkened like a thundercloud. "The stranger I met today was a perfect gentleman, who is about to improve the quality of life for many of our people right here in Arvid. What's more, he's legally married to Miss Blair's aunt. It's obvious that your client feels resentful about his intrusion into her well-ordered life. After all, this marriage has effectively cut her out of her inheritance. But I'll say it again. The Wayne Stone I met today was a perfect gentleman. And after Miss Blair pestered him to see for herself that her aunt was recovering from a virus, the poor man had no choice but to take her with him. I'm sure he'd have rather returned to his bride alone."

"Do you know where they've gone?"

"He said he has a quiet place in the hills where he can take care of his wife without tedious visits from well-meaning neighbors and friends."

"Sounds like the perfect place to keep her isolated."

At Finn's words the chief held up a hand. "Now I'll tell you, Mr. Monroe, just what I think about this whole conspiracy theory of yours. Wayne Stone had all the proper documents needed. Furthermore, he answered all Miss Blair's questions and remained open and friendly, even though your client was obviously agitated and spoiling for an argument. I certainly hope, after a visit with her aunt, Jessica Blair will be ready to accept the fact that her aunt has moved on with her life. Something her niece, now a grown woman, ought to do, as well."

Before Finn could respond, Ben shook the chief's hand. "Thanks, Chief Tyler. My brother and I appreciate everything you've done. We'll be in touch."

With a firm grasp on Finn's arm, Ben smoothly turned him toward the door and steered him outside.

As the door closed behind them, Finn wrenched his arm free. "What the hell...?"

"I have no jurisdiction in Arvid. This is Frank Tyler's town, and you can see that he's already made up his mind about this. But you know I always have your back, bro. Come on." He led the way to his police car and drove Finn to the bank to retrieve his truck.

As he drove, Ben's eyes narrowed in thought. "As a police officer, I have no choice but to work through proper channels. I'll contact the state police and ask them to give me everything they've uncovered about Wayne Stone. And I'll request a copy of the bank's security video, so we can see for ourselves what this guy looks like. I would have requested it from Chief Tyler, but I could see that he wasn't about to cooperate. He won't have a choice if the state police make a formal request."

Finn's temper was on a short fuse. "And in the meantime, we have to waste time going through proper channels. You may be bound by the rules, but I'm not."

"You bend the rules too far, you could end up losing your license to practice law. Is that what you want?"

"My law practice doesn't mean a thing if Jessie is in danger. I won't rest until I find her, Ben."

When Ben's police car stopped in the bank's parking lot, he reached across the seat to grab Finn's arm before he could step out. "I hear what you're saying. Just remember. You're not alone, bro. We've always had each other's backs. My being a cop doesn't change that. See to it that you keep all of us in the loop. You hear me?"

"I hear you. And I heard what the bank manager and police chief think about this guy. They think he's the salt of the earth." Finn's jaw was clamped so tightly his words were a hiss of fury. "I'm not buying any of it. My gut tells me Jessie's in trouble." He shot his brother a fierce look. "Ben, I have to find her."

Ben nodded. "On the off chance that we're wrong

about all this, I'll ask the bank managed to notify me if Jessie returns here to pick up the truck."

"Thanks." Finn slammed the door of brother's police car and climbed into his truck.

He dialed Jessie's number again, and after several rings it went to voice mail. He had to fight to keep a note of desperation from his tone. "Call me when you get this, Jess."

He tucked his phone into his pocket and took off in a cloud of dust, his mind turning over every tiny detail he could think of.

He had no idea where he was going. But he knew he couldn't sit idly by and wait for a phone call from Jessie that might never come.

He'd move heaven and earth if necessary. He wouldn't stop until he found the woman he loved.

The thought had him gripping the steering wheel until his knuckles whitened. Why had it taken him so long to admit the truth?

He'd known, almost from the first time he'd met Jessie, that she was different from every woman he'd ever known. Despite her wild story and the fact that nobody had wanted to take her seriously, he'd been drawn into her troubles and had never looked back.

So much had happened since their introduction. The motel fire, causing him to believe it may be set in order to frighten her off. The abrupt changes at her aunt's ranch. A security camera to record anyone who entered. The loyal wranglers fired, and a new, unknown crew hired with orders to keep strangers away. The valuables boxed for shipping out of town. And Basil's suspicion that a woman in the county offices may be an accomplice willing to pass along information to someone paying her.

The county offices.

Finn thought about the horrifying moment when his brakes failed, and Tony Russo, owner of the Haller Creek Gas and Garage, confirmed that they'd been tampered with.

Why hadn't he connected all the dots before? Maybe because so many other incidents had crowded it out of his mind.

Or...

He slammed a hand against the steering wheel. Because it had been aimed at him and not Jessie. And he'd foolishly assumed that the only ones in danger were Jessie and her aunt.

For the first time he realized just how well-informed Wayne Stone was. This was no simple cowboy out to snag a lonely woman's property. It was a carefully planned operation that he'd probably perfected over the years. This con artist had been miles ahead of all of them. While they were still trying to figure out who he was, Wayne had already been following Jessie, hoping to eliminate her before she spoiled all his plans. He would have known about the private investigator she'd hired and had him eliminated. He'd have seen Jessie go to Finn's office. Maybe that was when he decided he needed to eliminate her quickly. When she'd managed to survive the motel fire, he could have been watching. Had he seen her go home with Finn? Had he actually followed them to the ranch?

Had Wayne been watching them ever since? With his spy in the county offices, Wayne could have learned that Finn was getting too close. But in order to tamper with his brakes, Wayne would have needed private access to his truck.

A thought had Finn's blood running cold. Was it possible that Wayne Stone had been on their ranch?

The wranglers. The ones with questionable references.

He snatched up his cell phone and punched in a number.

When he heard Basil's voice, he told him where he was and what he suspected. Minutes later, he tucked his phone into his pocket and stared at the expanse of highway to his left and the looming country road to his right.

Somewhere out there Jessie was riding into danger.

Chief Tyler had said Wayne Stone had a secluded place in the hills.

Finn decided to take a calculated risk and try the country road, praying it would lead him to Jessie.

Was she a willing passenger? Or had Wayne Stone already let it be known that she was now his prisoner and that she would never be coming back?

CHAPTER TWENTY-FOUR

Ben watched as Finn drove away before entering the bank and asking a favor of the manager. He'd been assured that he would be notified when Jessie returned for her truck. Then he began making phone calls, first to the state police, and then to his family, to alert them of all that had happened.

He may be bound by the rules of law, but that wouldn't stop him from finding ways to ease Finn's burden.

He touched a hand to the badge on his shirt. He wore it proudly and would never do anything to betray the code of honor. But he knew intimately the pain his brother was feeling.

If they all worked together, even without the help of Chief Tyler and the Arvid authorities, they could crack this crazy case.

They had to. From the look of abject misery in Finn's eyes, Ben knew with certainty that Jessie owned his brother's heart. If Wayne Stone managed to hurt her, Finn would never be the same.

At Ben's urging, Mac put his cell phone on speaker and signaled the family to gather around.

In a few words Ben told them about the meeting Jessie had in the bank manager's office. "Chief Tyler said Wayne Stone wasn't at all like the smooth operator Jessie had described. Instead, he was a successful business owner who promised plenty of jobs for the people of Arvid, and was a genial, grandfatherly type. In his words, a perfect gentleman."

Zachariah interrupted. "How did our Finnian take that news?"

"Badly. What's worse, Jessie left her truck at the bank and is traveling with Wayne Stone to see her aunt."

It was Sam who asked, "Do you know if Stone forced her to go along with him?"

"According to Chief Tyler, Jessie pestered Wayne Stone until he felt he had no choice but to allow her to see for herself that her aunt was fine."

Mac exchanged a look with Mary Pat before asking softly, "What's your take, Ben?"

There was a pause before Ben's voice came over the speaker. "I'm with Finn on this, Dad. My gut feeling is Jessie and her aunt are in trouble, and this con artist is so convincing, we're the only ones willing to believe they're in danger. There have been too many incidents to think they're mere accidents."

Mac's voice remained soft, but now there was a thread of steel in each word. "When someone threatens one of us, he'd better be ready to deal with all of us. Tell us what you want us to do, Ben, and we're on it."

"I'm awaiting word from the state boys and Basil. As soon as I have the information I've asked for, I'll let you know. In the meantime, you might want to head on over toward Arvid. I've asked the state police to track Jessie's cell phone. Once we have an approximate location, we can fan out and try to locate this isolated home Wayne Stone boasted of."

"You're still in Arvid? Didn't you say you have no jurisdiction there?"

"I don't. But the state police do, and they've asked me to join their team as they investigate. That gives me the power of the law anywhere in the state."

Mac nodded his approval. "Good work, son. Keep us posted."

Mac trailed behind the others out the door, where they divided their party into two vehicles.

Zachariah, Penny, and Becca settled into the first truck, with Sam at the wheel.

Mary Pat, Otis, and Roscoe climbed into the second truck, with Mac driving.

All of them wore tight, grim looks of concentration as they began the long ride away from their ranch.

They'd been through so many painful experiences in the past and knew that there was no promise of a happy ending. The most carefully planned strategies in the world could unravel in an instant.

Still, they clung to the hope that if they all stuck together, willing to do whatever it took to save Jessie and Nola, they could work a miracle.

Jessie was no stranger to guns. They'd been a natural part of her life on her aunt's ranch. But she'd never before had one pointed at her, and it was such close quarters.

There was no way he could miss if he decided to shoot. Her initial reaction was absolute terror. Seeing the feral look in Wayne's eyes, she had no doubt he could kill her without remorse.

He leaned close and pressed the muzzle to her temple.

The mere act of swallowing sounded overloud in her ears.

In one smooth motion he snapped a handcuff to his right wrist, before snagging her hand. She watched in silence as he snapped the other cuff to her left wrist.

"Just in case you were thinking of bailing on me." He winked, and for a moment he was that courtly gentleman in the bank manager's office. Then his tone hardened, and he was instantly transformed into a monster to be feared. "If you try it, I'll just handcuff you to the truck and drag you along the road until you beg me to put you out of your misery."

He put the truck in gear and sent her an icy sneer. "All the way to Arvid I kept wondering how I was going to get you away from town without causing a scene." He gave a low laugh. "And then you made it all so easy, practically begging me to take you to see your dear old auntie."

As he turned his truck onto a dirt trail, spewing a cloud of dust, Jessie stared around, struggling to detect any landmarks. With her cell phone gone and no way to contact Finn, she would have to depend on herself to lead her aunt to safety.

That is, she thought with a gnawing fear, if Aunt Nola was still alive when they arrived at their destination.

Ben's voice was calm, deliberate. The voice of a police professional as he reported to his family over the phone.

"The state police have tracked Jessie's phone. It's

stationary. No movement, which says to them that it's probably been tossed. But at least it gives us a starting point. It's just a few miles outside Arvid, in an isolated area of high country. No ranches that they know of. There's some weather coming in, but once it clears they hope to send up a helicopter crew."

Ben felt Mary Pat's hand close over his arm. "Have you told Finn?"

"Yes, Dad. He's not far from there. He's driving the back roads, hoping to see anything that might indicate a cabin hidden in the hills."

"Let him know we're on our way, Ben."

"I will. Is Sam there with you?"

"He's driving a second truck, with Penny, Zachariah, and Becca."

Ben's voice sharpened. "Becca? What's my wife doing there?"

"She was having a cooking lesson with Penny, and refused to be left behind." Mac cleared his throat. "We'll keep her close to us. I have Mary Pat, Otis, and Roscoe with me."

Ben's voice softened. "Thanks. Stay safe, Dad. And tell Sam the same. I'm on my way, and should meet up with you in the next hour."

"I'll tell him, son." Mac paused. "And, Ben?"

"Yes, sir?"

"I know you're doing all you can. But there's something we can all do together."

"What's that?"

Mac glanced at Mary Pat, who nodded her approval. "Pray."

"Right. I will, Dad."

The line went dead.

*   *   *

Wayne's truck followed a dirt trail that climbed into the heavily wooded hills for several miles. Suddenly he veered off, driving between two towering evergreens and into a dense forest.

Jessie peered through the tangle of branches, hoping to find some landmark to note for possible escape. She could see nothing except woods.

It wasn't until the truck halted that she could make out a small cabin, nearly invisible because of the trees that surrounded it.

Wayne suddenly opened the driver's door and dragged her across the seat with such force, she fell to her knees.

"Get up." He yanked on the handcuff, forcing her to her feet. "And be quick about it."

In order to keep from falling again she had to run to keep up with his long strides.

He shoved open a door before calling, "Honey, I'm home." He chuckled at his little joke.

As Jessie's eyes adjusted to the gloomy interior, she could make out the figure of her aunt, lying unmoving on the floor across the room.

For a moment Jessie's heart nearly stopped.

But then Nola's eyes widened, a sign that she was alive.

Seeing it, Jessie felt a wave of gratitude. Her aunt was alive. But her mouth was covered with a filthy rag, and as Jessie was hauled closer, she could see that Nola's hands and feet were bound.

Jessie's moment of relief turned to horror as Wayne reached out and stripped away the gag before saying, "Look who came to call."

Nola's face revealed her terror. "You gave me your

word you wouldn't hurt her. You know I only cooperated in order to spare my niece."

"Lesson learned, Nolinda." Wayne sounded positively cheerful. "Never trust the words of the world's best con artist."

When Nola broke into tears, Jessie felt her own heart break. In her lifetime she had never seen her strong, brave aunt cry.

Wayne's voice turned to a snarl. "Shut up or I swear I'll give you something to really make you cry. I'll be happy to kill your niece right now and make you watch."

Jessie had to stand by helplessly as her aunt struggled to stem the tears.

Wayne leaned down and cut the ties binding Nola's wrists. Before she could rub the feeling into them he removed the cuff from his own wrist and snapped it onto Nola's, binding Nola and Jessie together.

Jessie dropped to her knees on the dirty rug that cushioned her aunt's body and gathered her close, feeling the tremors coursing through Nola's body.

"Aww. Hugs." Wayne's voice rose on a note of sarcasm. "I've got no time for this." He gave Jessie a rough shove and she fell forward, nearly crushing her aunt.

Wayne grabbed her feet and twisted her until her body was beside Nola's. Then he bound Jessie's ankles in the same way Nola's were bound.

Nola lifted her hand and stared at the cuffs that bound the two women together. "Oh, Jessie. There was no way to warn you. Wayne was holding a gun to my head when we talked. I never meant for you to be caught up in this, honey. I tried so hard, but..."

"Shh." Jessie glared at the monster who hovered over the two of them, laughing at their pain. "Don't you know that anything that affects you affects me, too? We're family, Aunt Nola. You've been so good to me my whole life. Our lives are intertwined. How could I not be involved?"

"And now you'll suffer the same fate as…"

Jessie closed her free hand over her aunt's and whispered, "As long as we're alive and together, there's hope."

Wayne's voice, as cold as steel, broke in. "Sorry to break up this little love fest. Enjoy what time you have left. As soon as I tie up some loose ends here, you'll have an eternity to be together."

CHAPTER TWENTY-FIVE

Finn answered Ben's call on the first ring. "What've you got for me, Ben?"

Ben's voice was quietly confident. "The state police ordered the bank manager to transmit the security footage of Wayne Stone. They ran his image through their system and have found a match. Only the name in their records is Clint Sawyer. When I checked with your operative, Basil told me that name matched one that he found in his search of wealthy widows who died shortly after marrying. Now the state police are putting the full force of their security team on this case."

"That's good news. I only hope it isn't too little too late."

"Finn, it's only a matter of time before they crack this."

"We don't have the luxury of time, Ben. This guy has been one step ahead of us all the way. Now that he has control of Nola's bank accounts, he doesn't need Nola or

Jessie. There's nothing to stop him from getting them out of the way."

Recognizing his brother's note of despair, Ben chose his words carefully. "We've come so far, Finn. We can't let this guy win."

"Don't you think I know that?" After a moment of silence, Finn added, "I know one thing. I intend to find Jessie, or I'm going to die trying."

Jessie lay beside her aunt, absorbing the tremors that rocked the older woman.

She looked at Nola with concern. "Wayne said you've been fighting a virus."

Nola glanced at the man seated at a table in the far corner of the room, poring over dozens of pages of documents, before whispering, "He gave me something that made me sick to my stomach."

"He said he spoke to your doctor."

Nola nodded. "He wanted it on the record that the doctor said the only thing he recommended for a virus was rest and plenty of fluids."

"On the record?"

"So that the authorities wouldn't question him later about why he never took me for medical treatment. He could say he was simply following doctor's orders."

"Aunt Nola, are you feeling any better at all?"

Nola shook her head. "If anything, I'm growing weaker. But I don't know if it's what he's giving me to drink, or from a lack of exercise. I've been bound and gagged and confined to this bed since he brought me here."

"Does Wayne feed you?"

"Only liquids, which he forces down my throat. And

though I'm terrified that he's poisoning me, I've grown too weak to fight him."

Jessie looked around the sparse cabin. "I don't see a bathroom."

"There's an ancient outhouse in back of this shack. Even there, Wayne gives me no privacy. He insists on keeping the door open, even though I'm so weak, I'd probably fall before I managed even a few steps."

A tear slid from the corner of Nola's eye and rolled down her cheek. "I've been such a fool. I swallowed every line he used on me, like a lovesick teen. And even when he insisted that we keep our wedding a secret, I agreed, until we were on our way, and I realized I needed to share my happiness with you. Later, when the marriage documents were signed and we were alone, I had the first taste of his temper. He became another person. One to be feared. And now you'll suffer the same fate as..."

With her free hand Jessie wiped away her aunt's tears and grasped her shoulder. "We're not going to let him win, Aunt Nola. We're going to find a way to get free."

"Oh, honey, I'm so sorry I brought you into this horrible nightmare."

"You didn't bring me. I forced my way in. And I'm not going to rest until I find a way out for both of us."

"You don't understand just how vicious he is, Jessie. Once I became his prisoner, he openly boasted of the valuable land and ranches he's accumulated, thanks to the vulnerable women he calls stupid, lovesick old cows."

Jessie sucked in a breath at the desolation in her aunt's tone.

"In truth, Jessie, I've become resigned to the fact that I'm never going to leave this place. And maybe Wayne is right. I deserve to die after falling for the lies of a monster like him."

Jessie lay beside her aunt, feeling the way Nola's frail body shook with quiet sobs. And all Jessie could do was press her hand over Nola's, willing her aunt her strength.

The hopelessness of their situation weighed heavily on Jessie's mind. If only she'd fought against getting into Wayne's truck. But she'd already felt the sting of Chief Tyler's disapproval, and knew she would only add to his belief that she was a greedy ingrate if she'd resisted.

None of this had gone as she'd hoped. She'd had visions of Finn arriving in Arvid, only to find the police chief and bank manager proudly proclaiming how foolish she'd been for suspecting a fine, upstanding citizen like Wayne Stone. A successful businessman who was going to provide jobs for the needy ranchers in the area. Those two men had been practically drooling over the thought of Wayne's wealth being spread around their town. Was Finn being subjected to a lecture by Chief Tyler? Was he, even now, waiting patiently for her to call? Or worse, had he been persuaded that this had all been overblown and returned to his office in Haller Creek?

She closed her eyes, fighting a wave of absolute terror at the thought that she and her aunt might be alone in this nightmare, while Finn was blissfully unaware of the truth.

If that was the case, she knew she would have to be strong enough for both of them. No matter how desperate the odds against them, she had to be ready to fight to the death for Aunt Nola. She owed her life to this good woman. She wouldn't go down without a struggle.

*   *   *

Mac turned his cell phone on speaker as Ben's voice flooded the interior of the truck.

"The state crime team has come up with more on Wayne Stone. This is apparently one of many aliases he's used over the years. But the photographs in their file are all different. They have an expert going over the photos now, to see if they're all the same man, or if he has accomplices."

"What about Finn?" Mac asked. "Where is he now?"

"Finn's in a pretty desolate area of high country. Dense woods, and no sign of civilization. So far he's found no trace of Wayne Stone's truck, and hasn't spotted any deserted cabins."

Mac sighed. "For all we know, this Wayne Stone, or whoever he really is, could be taking Jessie miles away in another direction. Does Finn have any sense that he's getting close?"

Ben's voice revealed his frustration. "I think Finn's running on pure adrenaline. And if he doesn't soon find some trace of Jessie, he'll go a little crazy."

"Finn needs to know we're all with him." Mac shared a glance with Otis and Roscoe in his rearview mirror, and saw the two old men nod their heads. "I've tried calling him and get no service. When you talk to Finn again, let him know we're almost there."

Thunder rumbled overhead, and Finn found himself thinking about the storm that had driven him and Jessie to seek shelter, only to spend the most memorable night of his life in her arms. A little cabin in the woods had become their heaven on earth.

How ironic that even now she could be imprisoned in similar woods, in a house of horrors.

He'd been driving for what felt like endless hours, back and forth through a forest crisscrossed with tracks that ambled over hills and through streams, but led nowhere. All of them so far had taken him back to where he'd started.

According to Ben, the vicious storm that was now breaking overhead had been the cause of the state police helicopters being grounded. And now, though they were probably cleared for takeoff in their part of the state, this area would be off-limits until the worst of the storm blew over.

As he followed yet another dirt trail, a blinding flash of lightning knifed the sky, illuminating something in the distance.

A light?

The reflection of lightning on glass?

Finn turned off the truck lights and slowed his vehicle to a crawl just as the skies opened up with a torrent of rain.

Maybe, he thought, the rain was a good thing. The sound of it would mask his truck's engine.

While Wayne read the documents before him and scratched notes on a sheet of paper, Jessie used the time to study the little cabin. As far as she could tell, other than the door they'd used to enter, there was no other way in or out of this place.

That meant that unless she found a way to overpower Wayne, she would never be able to get her aunt, weakened by such cruel treatment, safely out of here.

She looked around for anything she could use as

a weapon. Except for the filthy rug and the scarred wooden chair and table Wayne was using, the shack was empty.

They were so far from civilization, nobody would ever come here. Cobwebs hung from the ceiling. The remains of dead animals littered one corner. This had no doubt been a deserted shack until Wayne had come upon it. It was the perfect place to carry out his evil deeds knowing nobody would pay a surprise visit.

When Wayne began folding the documents into a manila envelope, Jessie experienced a moment of sheer panic.

Hadn't he said that when he finished his business here he would be done with them, as well?

She reached over with her free hand to touch her aunt's face. "Do you know how much I love you, Aunt Nola?"

"Not nearly as much as I love you, Jessie, darling. You filled my life with such joy."

Jessie had a sudden thought. "Tell Wayne you want to use the outhouse."

Nola's eyes widened with absolute terror. "What are you planning?"

"I have no plan. But we have nothing to lose by trying something. Whatever I do, just agree with me and follow my lead." She squeezed her aunt's hand. "Promise?"

Nola gave a barely perceptible nod of her head. "Promise."

The older woman gathered her strength before giving a loud moan.

Wayne turned toward them with a dark look.

Nola's voice was barely more than a croak. "I need to use the bathroom. Now."

He swore as he picked up the manila envelope and

turned toward the rug. "Woman, you're more bother than you're worth."

"I've been on this dirty rug for hours."

His sly grin was quick. "Soon you'll be there for an eternity. I think I'll just let you lie there in your own filth."

"Please, Wayne."

"Please?" His lips turned into a chilling smile. "I see you're finally giving me a little respect."

He drew a knife and walked closer. In that moment Jessie had to swallow back a knot of fear that he intended to kill them now. He stooped and drew the blade through the bindings at their ankles before yanking Nola roughly to her feet, knowing that Jessie, still bound to her aunt by the handcuffs, would be forced to keep up with them.

Wayne opened the cabin door and continued holding on to Nola as they walked through the pouring rain to the tiny outhouse behind the cabin. The little structure tilted at an angle, and the door swung back and forth in the wind and rain.

As the two women stepped inside, Jessie reached for the door.

Wayne's hand was there ahead of hers.

"Uh-uh. We don't bother with privacy here." He gave a cruel laugh. "This door stays open. Don't even think about trying anything stupid."

"Go ahead, Aunt Nola." Jessie made a great show of shielding his view of the older woman by standing in front of her. With her back to Wayne, she mouthed the words *scream as loud as you can*.

When Nola let out a piercing scream, Wayne made a move to shove Jessie aside.

In that instant Jessie kicked him in the groin with all her strength.

With a grunt of pain he fell backward and Jessie, with Nola cuffed to her, was on him, pounding him about the head and face with their handcuffs.

With her free hand Jessie managed to wrestle the gun from him and fired off a shot.

Now it was Wayne's turn to scream as the bullet grazed his arm. But as his outrage and adrenaline kicked in, he swept his hand in a wide arc and dislodged the gun from Jessie's hand.

Seeing him rummaging about in the wet grass for his pistol, Jessie pulled her aunt to her feet and began dragging her along, hoping to escape.

Nola, too weak to keep up, stumbled, pulling Jessie down with her.

Wayne was on them like a dog, venting his fury by kicking them both as they lay in the mud.

Taking aim with his gun, his words were a hiss of supreme confidence. "Now you two fools are going to pay for all the grief you've given me."

CHAPTER TWENTY-SIX

Finn was speaking to Ben on his cell phone when he caught another flash of light and saw, through the thick brush, the outline of a shack looming up before him.

"This has to be it." Adrenaline kicked in and he wasn't even aware of stashing his phone in his pocket.

He grabbed his rifle and was out of his truck in an instant.

Despite the rain battering the trees and pounding the earth, he could make out the rumble of a man's voice somewhere nearby.

Moving quickly through the tangle of tree branches, he caught sight of shadowy figures disappearing behind the shack.

Before he could reach them he heard a woman's scream, and then a man's grunt of pain. As he began running toward them, the unmistakable sound of a gunshot reverberated through the night.

Finn's heart stopped, and for a moment he nearly went down on his knees with the realization of what he'd heard. He was too late.

In his mind he could see the monster, Wayne Stone, shooting Jessie and her aunt, and throwing their bodies in a shallow grave.

Just then Jessie's voice rang out, urging her aunt to run.

A feeling of relief poured through Finn. He'd been given another chance. And then a wave of anger, so deep, so dark, took over his mind. His blood froze to ice in his veins, and he knew what he had to do. If necessary he would sacrifice his own life for Jessie.

His heart was pounding as he rounded the back of the shack and took in the terrifying scene.

Jessie and her aunt were lying in the wet grass. A man stood over them, taking aim with a pistol.

Jessie was alive. The knowledge that he was so close gave him a surge of confidence.

"Drop the gun, Stone."

Wayne's head whipped around, his eyes wide with surprise.

Instead of doing as he'd ordered, Wayne merely stood his ground. "You picked the wrong time to be out riding, cowboy. I give the orders around here. And unless you drop that rifle and kick it over here right this minute, I'll pull the trigger. I may not be able to kill both of these whiny little troublemakers, but you can bet one of them will be dead before you can get off a single shot."

"Don't listen to him, Finn." Jessie's voice came out in a sob.

"Finn?" Wayne blinked against the pouring rain. "Oh, this is too good." He waved his pistol. "One of the Monroe brothers decided to be a hero?"

His tone suddenly changed to a hiss of absolute fury. "Now you listen, hero. I'll only say this one time. Do as I say or your pretty little lover won't be so pretty with a bullet in her head. Drop your weapon now, and kick it over here."

While Jessie and Nola watched with matching looks of despair, Finn did as Wayne ordered, tossing down his rifle and kicking it toward Wayne, who scooped it up before taking aim with his pistol.

Wayne's face contorted in rage. And then he pulled the trigger.

Finn was too shocked to react, and suddenly he felt his arm drop uselessly to his side as a spurt of blood gushed from the bullet wound, staining his shirt in ever-widening circles. As the bullet slammed into him, he gave a hiss of pain and pressed his hand to his bicep, hoping to stem the flow of blood.

"Now you know I mean business. That little gunshot is in retaliation for what your stupid lover did to me. Only she wasn't aiming for my arm. She was hoping to kill me, but she's a lousy shot."

Finn absorbed a quick jolt of pride at Jessie's determination. She wasn't about to go down without a fight.

And neither was he.

Wayne waved his pistol. "Walk ahead of us, Monroe."

Struggling against the pain, Finn's eyes narrowed on the man. "Where to?"

"To my mansion." Wayne kicked Jessie. "Get up, woman. That little trick you tried to pull will cost you." He waited until Jessie, tethered to her aunt, helped Nola to her feet. As the two women followed Finn toward the door of the shack, Wayne trailed behind, his pistol aimed and ready.

Once inside he ordered Finn to lie on the floor, where, ignoring the blood streaming from his own wound, he bound Finn's wrists and ankles.

Next he dragged the two women across the room, pushing them down on the filthy rug before binding their ankles.

When Wayne had assured himself that all three were rendered incapable of escaping, he pulled a handkerchief from his pocket and tied it around his arm to staunch the blood. And all the while he cursed Jessie for causing him so much pain.

"I should have known you'd try something stupid." He glared at the two women. "But now, I'll have my revenge."

He walked outside and returned carrying a container of gasoline.

The sight of it had Nola gasping aloud.

Hearing it, Wayne's eyes narrowed on her. "I'd planned a slow death for you by poison, Nolinda. But the meddling of your tiresome niece has me changing my plans."

While his three prisoners watched helplessly, he circled the room pouring gasoline along all four walls.

He began to chuckle. "Now the fun begins."

He removed the handcuffs from Nola and Jessie and bound them together with rope.

"Wouldn't want to waste a good pair of cuffs," he muttered. "Besides, years from now, when some cowboy stumbles on your ashes, there won't be any suggestion of foul play. The authorities will just figure some hikers, or some down-and-out trail bums got caught in a storm, and a fire caused by lightning took them out of this world. With any luck, it could be years before anybody comes this way. In the meantime the authorities will give up the search for you, and you'll become just another cold case."

"How will you explain the loss of your wife without a body?" Jessie cried.

He merely smiled. "You heard me tell my new best friends, Police Chief Frank and bank manager Mike that the little woman and I would be going off for an extended honeymoon around the world. By the time I return, Nolinda will have taken sick in some faraway land, and I'll be a broken-hearted widower."

Finn spoke up. "Even if it's in another country, when you return, the authorities will want proof of your wife's death."

Wayne threw back his head and laughed. "I've got friends who can give me whatever documents I want, including a death certificate. That's how I've been able to live in comfort all these years, thanks to the goodness of all my poor, deceased wives. And it will be time for me to begin another identity."

For good measure he tossed the last of the gasoline around the door before stepping out into the night.

"Sorry I can't stick around to watch the fireworks. But I can guarantee that you three will have a hot time tonight."

Laughing at his little joke, he tossed a match and watched as a trail of flame began licking its way along the wall.

He slammed the door shut.

Inside the cabin they could hear the growling of Wayne's truck, overloud at first, then growing softer as he made his escape into the depths of the forest.

And then, with the storm breaking overhead, all they could hear was the sound of the flames and the smell of gasoline as the fire began to feed on the rotten wood of the old cabin. Even the rain battering the roof couldn't douse the flames inside the cabin as the fire began to burn out of control.

Ben spoke into his cell phone. "Dad, I'm turning on my flashers so you and the others can spot my vehicle in this rain. I'm on a dirt trail on the northernmost edge of these woods. That's where Finn said he was before his phone suddenly went silent."

Mac slowed his truck and signaled for his passengers to keep an eye out. Within minutes Roscoe pointed, and Mac said, "We're coming up behind you, son."

"What about Sam?" Ben asked.

A truck's lights could be seen deep in the woods. "He's just south of us. I'll let him know where we are."

"I'll call him." Mary Pat was already dialing on her phone.

Hearing the sound of a helicopter overhead, Mac said, "I thought the state police copter was grounded."

"It was, during the worst of the storm. Once it blew over their area, they were airborne." Ben glanced skyward and could make out the sweep of light as the police used powerful searchlights to scan the forest.

Ben continued, "Since I don't have any better information, I say we try to find where Finn went."

Spotting Sam's headlights breaking free of the woods and coming up behind him, Mac called, "All right, Ben. We're all here now. You lead the way and we'll follow."

As their convoy began to move carefully through the dense forest, hoping to spot Finn's tracks, they heard the sound of an explosion so powerful, the earth trembled beneath their vehicles.

"Thunder?" Mary Pat asked.

Just then the night sky lit up with a fireball that could be seen for miles.

"Not thunder." Mac's voice was tight with the horror of what they could all see. "God in heaven. An explosion."

"Finn." Jessie's voice was choked. "I want you to know how sorry I am that I brought you into this."

"I don't understand." Her aunt's voice was rough and scratchy from the smoke. "Who is Finn?"

"My lawyer." Jessie felt tears well up and spill over. "At least that's all he was when I first hired him. But now he's the love of my life."

"Love?" Nola struggled to see the stranger who would have her niece saying such a thing.

Finn gritted his teeth against the pain of the bullet wound. "You need to know that my only regret is that I couldn't save you, Jessie. But I'd have gladly given my life in exchange for yours. I love you, baby."

The cabin was enveloped in a cloud of smoke so thick it was impossible to see across the room.

The earth shuddered beneath them, and they were tossed about like rag dolls.

Finn, his eyes glazed with pain, managed to push himself close enough to the women to see them struggling to free themselves.

Jessie gave a cry of helpless fury. "It's no use. I can't budge these ropes."

"Maybe I can." Forcing himself to endure the intense heat, Finn dug in his heels and backed up to the wall, gritting his teeth as the flames burned through the bindings, scorching his flesh with pain so deep it had him nearly losing consciousness. But he knew that their only salvation now was to escape before this old cabin collapsed in on itself. Already the flames were licking up the wall and quickly consuming the roof.

Flaming timbers began falling around them.

With his wrists free, Finn grabbed a burning piece of wood and, ignoring the pain to his hands, used it to free his ankles before turning to the women.

As he tore away the ropes binding their wrists and ankles, a portion of the roof collapsed, sending up a spray of embers as the fire raged out of control.

Finn grabbed Jessie's arm. "Can you stand?"

With his help she got to her feet and reached for her aunt. "She's too weak to walk, Finn. I'm not leaving without her."

"Run. I'll carry her." Finn bent and gathered Nola into his arms.

Seeing his pain as blood flowed from the bullet wound, Jessie wrapped an arm around his waist to lend him her strength. "I'm not going anywhere without the two of you."

Just then the flames reached the door of the cabin; the entire wall and door burst into an impenetrable firewall.

They turned, hoping for another avenue of escape, but the cabin was now consumed with flames and collapsing all around them.

Jessie's eyes widened with a look of absolute terror. "There's no way out of this, Finn."

"We've come this far. We're not turning back now." With a final burst of adrenaline, Finn was able to rise above the excruciating pain from the bullet in his arm and the burns to his flesh. With Nola in his arms he quickly had Jessie wrap and lock her arms around his waist.

When she stumbled, he paused. "Hold on, baby. No matter what, don't let go."

She got to her feet and held tightly to him as they made a final dash to freedom through the wall of flames and burning door, while timbers crashed and embers singed their hair and clothes.

As soon as they were a dozen yards away, they dropped to the wet grass. As remnants of adrenaline rushed through their veins, they lay, faces lifted to the rain, coughing and choking from the smoke they'd inhaled.

Finn turned and gathered Jessie close and held her as shudders tore through her body.

"Hang on, babe. We made it."

"Are we truly safe, Finn?"

His arms tightened around her. He didn't think he'd ever be able to let go.

"We're safe, Jessie. Safe and together."

He wasn't certain if it was the rain, or the tears from Jessie's eyes that were running down his face. He knew only that Jessie was alive.

Alive.

And for that, he would have a lifetime of gratitude.

CHAPTER TWENTY-SEVEN

The convoy of vehicles raced toward the fireball lighting up the sky.

Finn's family feared the worst as they watched the remnants of a small building collapse to a pile of rubble.

They jumped out of their trucks and raced toward the blaze. When they caught sight of the figures in the grass, they gathered around, stunned into silence by the realization that Finn, Jessie, and her aunt had made it safely out of that horrible inferno.

"Mac, there's so much blood." Mary Pat was already slipping out of her rain poncho to wrap it around Nola, whose teeth were chattering.

"Shock is setting in on Nola." With quiet competence Ben tied a tourniquet around Finn's bloody arm. "Looks like you took a bullet, bro."

Finn hissed in pain and nodded.

Ben turned to Jessie. "Were you or your aunt shot?"

"No." She was holding tightly to both Finn and Nola, as though afraid to let go or they'd disappear. "But Aunt Nola is very weak from her confinement and because of the poison she was forced to ingest."

"Poison? You know that for a fact?" Ben's hand was at Nola's forehead, searching for signs of a fever. "Are you certain Wayne Stone was poisoning her?"

"He admitted it before he left us to burn to death."

The family gave a collective gasp of alarm.

"He did this? Has he escaped, or is he in…there?" Ben's gaze scanned the fiery remains.

"We heard him leave. If it hadn't been for Finn, my aunt and I would already be dead." The minute the words were out of her mouth, the enormity of what they'd just come through began to set in, and Jessie couldn't stop her body from trembling. "Finn was so brave. Even after Wayne shot him, he kept on fighting for us."

"Don't listen to her." Through clenched teeth Finn caught his brother's arm. "I never would have found this shack if Jessie hadn't made a courageous attempt to escape with her aunt."

"You did?" Becca and Penny knelt on either side of Jessie and her aunt, while Penny wrapped Jessie in her jacket.

"I was desperate. That monster had weakened Aunt Nola until it was impossible for her to get away from him."

Nola looked up at the others, her voice rough from smoke and weakness. "Jessie was so brave. But then, that's always been her way. My wonderful Jessie is a scrapper."

The two women fell into one another's arms and began weeping softly.

Finn touched a hand to Jessie's wet cheek, his voice revealing his pride. "Yeah. A scrapper."

A line of trucks and police vehicles raced through the woods and came to a shuddering halt.

As the officers walked toward them, Finn caught sight of Wayne in their midst. But instead of white hair, he now had a shaved head. And the glasses were missing, as well. But it was, without a doubt, the man they'd known as Wayne Stone. The same clothes. The same fierce scowl. This was the man they'd seen in the photo in Nola's box of treasures. No wonder he'd taken such pains to destroy both the camera and the film.

"You caught him. We were afraid he'd get clean away."

A state police trooper looked confused. "This man is not under arrest. We found him driving in the forest, and he said he'd spotted a fire and was racing to the spot. He's done nothing wrong."

"Nothing wrong?" With a burst of strength that had everyone watching in stunned surprise, Finn was on his feet, crossing the distance that separated them. "You expected to be home free when your police escort found us all dead, didn't you, Stone?"

He landed a blow to Wayne's face that had blood spurting from his nose like a fountain.

With a howl of pain Wayne cupped his hands to his face shouting, "This crazy fool broke my nose. I'll sue all of you. You have a duty to protect me."

When one of the troopers wrapped his beefy arms around Finn, pulling him aside, Sam stepped up to finish what Finn had started. "You tried to kill my brother, you son of a..." He landed a blow to Wayne's midsection, dropping him to his knees with a grunt of pain.

The trooper in charge gave a signal, and two of his officers subdued Sam.

The trooper turned to Ben. "You need to control these people, Chief Monroe, or we could be in trouble."

"These 'people' are my brothers."

"Then be aware. Your brothers just assaulted a man under our protection. This man hasn't been charged with any crime."

"He soon will be." Ben turned to the two women lying in the grass. "Is this the man who poisoned you, Miss Blair?"

Nola nodded. "He is. He's altered his appearance, but I'd know him anywhere."

Satisfied, Ben went on to ask, "This is, without a doubt, the man who imprisoned you, and set fire to this cabin before trying to escape?"

Nola was crying now. "He's the one."

"They're crazy as loons," Wayne said. "I know my rights. It's their word against mine."

"And my word, too." Finn shrugged off the restraining arms of the trooper. "Check his truck. I'm sure you'll find a white wig there, unless he tossed it out the window. You should find handcuffs as well. And an empty gasoline can."

The officer turned to Wayne. "Because of the allegations made, we have to search your truck. Do we have your permission?"

Wayne gave one last attempt. "No, you do not! Do you know who I am? I'm one of the richest landowners in Montana."

"Well, based on these allegations, we can get a search warrant, so either way we'll be searching your truck. It will be easier if you give your permission now, sir."

Wayne took in the many police officers surrounding him, and reluctantly nodded his head. The state police chief dispatched two officers to Wayne's truck. A short time later they returned, carrying the incriminating evidence.

Finn's family formed a protective circle around Finn, Jessie, and Nola.

Wayne turned to the state police officers. "I'll see all of you in court. For false arrest. For allowing these hell-raisers to attack me while under your protection. You're not going to get away with this. I know all about Mackenzie Monroe and his so-called family. A pack of misfits. All of them. Once you find out just how much influence I have in this state, you'll be begging me not to take away your badges."

As the officers led Wayne to their police van, Mac watched with a puzzled frown. Wayne Stone's words had made this sound like a personal vendetta.

Before he could ask any questions, they heard the whirr of a police helicopter directly overhead. They watched as it landed in a nearby clearing.

Ben hurried to direct a group of police medics to the spot where Finn, Jessie, and Nola still huddled in the rain. "We need medical assistance here. A bullet wound. A victim of poison. Smoke inhalation. And I'm sure you'll find burns on all of them, as well."

As they began assessing the wounds, Ben turned to his father. "The medics will fly them to the clinic, Dad. You'll want to go with them."

Mac cleared his throat. "I can drive myself to town, son."

Mary Pat gave a firm shake of her head. "You'll fly with them. I'll drive your truck. We can be there in a few hours."

Mac opened his mouth to protest, but she put a finger on his lips to silence him. "Those hours will feel like an eternity, Mac. I know you. You're suffering right along with Finn. You're going with him."

He gave a grateful nod.

As Finn, Jessie, and Nola were strapped onto gurneys for the flight to Haller Creek, Ben leaned close to his brother. "Don't worry. We'll take care of everything."

Finn, already beginning to slip into a pain-killing haze, gave his brother a thumbs-up.

As Mac walked beside the gurneys, the rest of the family made their way to their vehicles, eager to leave this scene of so much pain and anguish behind.

It was Sam who said what all of them were thinking.

"Wayne Stone had better hope they never let him out on bail before his trial." His hands fisted at his sides. "If I get another chance at him, prison will seem like a day at the spa."

Finn awoke to the sound of beeping and whooshing as machines monitored his heart rate and blood pressure.

The minute he opened his eyes, his family gathered around the bedside.

"How're you doing, son?"

Finn tried to smile, but it was too much effort. "You tell me, Dad."

"You're doing fine." Mac nodded toward the others. "You've had a lot of people pulling for you, Finn."

"Thanks." He felt the familiar, calloused hands grip his shoulders as Otis and Roscoe bent over the bed to lend their support.

Zachariah looked properly solemn. "You gave us a scare, Finnian. When we heard that explosion and saw that fireball light up the sky, we weren't certain just what we'd find."

"But we were all praying," Mary Pat added.

The others nodded.

Mac's tone softened. "There's someone here who hasn't left your side. But she stepped back to make room for all of us."

He wrapped an arm around Jessie's shoulders and drew her toward the bed.

As soon as he caught sight of her, Finn managed a smile.

"Where . . . ?" Finn's lips moved, but only a single word came out.

Jessie leaned close. "You're in recovery. The doctor removed the bullet."

"What . . . ?" He held up his hands, covered in thick dressings.

"Both your hands are badly burned. The doctors gave you something for pain. It's strong enough that you'll be in and out for the next few days."

He digested that before trying again. "Nola?"

"The clinic wants her flown to a hospital in Bozeman for testing. They're preparing her for the flight now."

"And you?"

Jessie brushed a kiss over his mouth. "I'm alive, thanks to you, Finn."

"Jess . . ." He absorbed the warmth of her mouth on his, and knew there was something he wanted to tell her. Something so important, it didn't matter that they had an audience. But the pain medicine was playing with his brain.

"Yes?" She touched a hand to his cheek.

"I . . . lov . . ." He wanted to close his hand over hers, but he didn't have the strength to move.

In slow motion his eyes closed.

Drained, he slept.

Pain woke Finn. His eyes opened, and he was forced to blink against the blinding sunlight streaming through the window. His eyes felt as gritty as sandpaper.

He looked around to get his bearings.

Beside his bed was a row of monitoring equipment. On the other side of his bed was a reclining chair. Beneath a blanket, his father lay snoring softly.

He felt a momentary stab of disappointment. He'd hoped to see...

"Well." Jenny Turnbull, the pretty nurse at the Haller Creek Medical Clinic, breezed into the room. "I see you're awake. Dr. Clark asked me to check on you. On a scale of one to ten, ten being the worst, what's your level of pain?"

Her voice had Mac sitting up. "You okay, son?"

Finn managed a nod. "I'm good, Dad. You should have gone home with the others."

"There's plenty of time for that." Mac watched while Jenny took Finn's temperature and made notes. "What about that pain?"

Finn tried to evade. "Where's Jessie?"

"In Bozeman with her aunt. She called last night to say that since she's the only family Nola has, she'll have to remain there until her aunt is discharged."

Jenny Turnbull hovered beside Finn's bed with a packet of pills and a glass of water. "Your pain?"

At the news that Jessie wasn't here, he could feel the pain in every pore of his body. "I guess it's a ten."

"I thought as much." She handed him the pills and he popped them into his mouth before drinking the water.

She turned to Mac. "Your son is going to sleep for a couple of hours, Mr. Monroe. That'll give you plenty of time to head to your ranch and shower and shave. Finn will probably be coherent by late this afternoon."

He nodded before putting a big hand on Finn's shoulder. "Think you can sleep, son?"

Finn lied. "You go ahead, Dad. I'm already groggy."

When he was alone, he stared at the ceiling, wishing with all his might that Jessie was here with him. He knew it was selfish of him. He understood her need to be with her aunt. They were family. And he was...

What was he?

Her lawyer.

Her protector.

But that was before. When she'd needed a lawyer and someone to protect her from a monster who wanted her dead.

Now, with Wayne Stone locked up, and her aunt safely in a hospital where they could do all kinds of sophisticated tests to make her well, Jessie had no need of a lawyer or a protector.

What about him?

He loved her. With every fiber of his being. He had no doubt that she loved him, too. And now, with their long siege ended, they could talk about a future.

He could feel his brain shutting down. Against his will his eyes closed. Even while he cursed the effects of the pills, he slipped into a long, painless sleep.

CHAPTER TWENTY-EIGHT

Three weeks later the little plane put down on the tiny airstrip outside of Arvid. As Jessie helped her very healthy-looking aunt down the steps, Finn stepped out of his truck and hurried over.

For nearly a full minute the two of them simply stared, while Nola watched. Aware of her scrutiny, Finn smiled in greeting.

It was Jessie who spoke first. "I was told we would have transportation back to the ranch. I didn't realize it would be you. You look..." She swallowed. "Good as new."

She took one of Finn's hands, experiencing a sudden rush of heat. With an effort she ignored the thrill that shot along her spine and turned his hand palm up, staring at it to avoid looking into his eyes. "The burns seem to have healed nicely. How about your arm? Any permanent damage from the bullet?"

"Some pain. A little stiff. The doctor said it'll ease off."

"Well…" Jessie glanced at her aunt. "I know you're still feeling weak, Aunt Nola. Let's get you home."

With Finn on one side and Jessie on the other, they walked Nola toward the truck.

Helping her into the backseat, Jessie fastened her aunt's seat belt before shutting the door and stepping down.

Before Jessie could climb into the passenger side Finn gathered her close. "Oh, babe, I've missed you."

"Finn." She breathed his name on a sigh and touched a hand to his face. "I've missed you, too. So much."

"Thank heaven. I thought for a moment there you'd forgotten all about me." He lowered his head and kissed her with a sense of urgency. He raised his lips to her temple. "You've been gone too long. Despite the phone calls, I was starting to worry."

"The doctors wanted to keep an eye on my aunt until they were satisfied there would be no lingering effects of the poison."

"So she's good now?"

"She's not back to full speed yet, but she's doing fine."

"I'm glad." Finn kissed her again for good measure, before helping her into the truck.

After circling around to the driver side, he fastened his seat belt and drove toward Nola's ranch.

When they turned into the driveway, the older woman let out a long, slow sigh. "Do you know how many times I feared I'd never see this place again?"

Jessie's eyes filled as she heard the tremor in her aunt's voice. Ever since she found Aunt Nola, Jessie had become an emotional wreck, crying at the slightest thought of what she'd almost lost.

As she and Finn helped Nola from the truck, the older woman made a sound of impatience. "I hate how weak

I still am. I've always been able to take care of my own needs."

Jessie's tone softened, hoping to soothe her aunt's frustration. "It isn't just physical, Aunt Nola. It's a mind-body thing. The doctors warned that you've suffered a traumatic experience that won't leave you just because you're now safe. They've arranged for an experienced counselor to visit as often as you feel the need to talk this out."

Nola hugged her niece. "That will help. But the best medicine of all is being back here, and having you with me, just as we were for all these years."

Jessie shot a pained glance at Finn before leading her aunt to the door.

Once inside, Jessie helped her aunt to a comfortable chair in the parlor before heading to the kitchen to make tea.

Finn followed her.

When the door closed, he gathered her into his arms and pressed his mouth to her temple. "Oh, how I've missed this. Just let me hold you, Jess."

"Finn..." With a deep sigh she pushed a little away. "We need to talk."

He shot her a sexy grin. "I was hoping we could talk later. In your bed or mine."

"Oh, if only." She turned and set a kettle on the stove before saying, "In the hospital, Aunt Nola told me some things. The doctors on staff encouraged me to engage her as much as possible, to let her get it all out. During one of our midnight talks, when the staff made only an occasional visit to her room, she admitted that she'd fallen for Wayne's blatant lies because she was feeling old and lonely and abandoned, and he made her feel important."

Finn shrugged. "There's no need for her to feel ashamed. A guy like that has had a lot of experience conning his way into the lives of lonely women. He researched every one of his victims, and knew exactly what they needed to hear."

"I realize that. But I realize something else, too. It isn't Aunt Nola's shame. It's mine."

"What are you talking about?" He curled his fingers around her wrist, to draw her near. "Jessie…"

She held up a hand and stepped back. "This is all my fault. Wayne was right when he said that my aunt sacrificed her entire life for me. After my parents died, she took me in and devoted herself to me. And how did I thank her? By going off to college, and getting a big, important job in Bozeman instead of being here with the woman who raised me."

"That's what adult children do, Jessie." Ignoring her protest, he wrapped his arms around her, pulling her close. "They grow up and make lives for themselves."

"No." She pushed free of his arms. "You're not hearing me. I selfishly walked away and never looked back. My visits to the ranch became less and less frequent. And because of that, my aunt nearly died at the hands of a smooth-talking con who recognized what I was too blind to see. My aunt was lonely, and I wasn't here for her. Well, that's about to change. I've already phoned my boss to let him know I'm not coming back."

"You quit your job?"

"My life is here now."

"Jessie…"

As the kettle began its shrill whistle, she lifted it from the stove and filled a teapot. With quick, efficient movements she arranged teacups, cream, and sugar on a tray and picked it up.

Finn followed slowly behind her to the parlor.

Nola was asleep in the chair.

Jessie set the tray aside and started for the door, motioning for Finn to follow. She left the door open so she could hear if her aunt needed her.

Out on the porch, when Finn opened his arms, she stepped back. "I need to say this, Finn. And you need to hear me. My aunt and I owe you our lives. You saved us both from that monster, and I'll never forget it." Her tone lowered. "Just as I'll never forget you."

He gave her a long, probing look. "This sounds a lot like good-bye, Jessie."

She swallowed hard before lifting her chin. "I guess it is."

He shot her a puzzled frown. "Why?"

"Because my aunt needs me. And as long as she does, I need to be here for her."

"What about what you and I need?"

"It's not the same. I hope you can understand. We're young and strong and healthy. I'll always be grateful for what you did for us but..."

"I don't want your gratitude." The words were harsher than he'd intended, but the frustration he was feeling was obvious in his tone. "Jessie, we have something special. I meant what I said when we were facing certain death. I love you."

"I know." She felt her lip quiver and bit down hard. "I can't afford to think about that now. All I know is this. If it takes me the rest of my life, I'll make it up to Aunt Nola for what I put her through. Nothing else matters to me except her welfare."

"Not even the fact that we found a very special love?"

She backed up, afraid to touch him. Afraid if she did, she would lose what little determination she had left.

"I know what we found. And I know I'll never have the chance for that kind of feeling again with anyone else. But I have to be strong, not only for my aunt, but for myself. I'm sorry, Finn, but this is good-bye. Please know that I'll always love you."

Feeling the torrent of tears erupting, she spun on her heels and closed the door.

When she disappeared inside the house, Finn stood rooted to the spot, fighting a fierce desire to kick in the door.

And then what? he asked himself. Did he think he could simply carry Jessie off?

She had every right to worry about her aunt. Nola had been through hell and back. As the doctors had warned, it would likely have lasting consequences on both her mind and body.

He walked slowly to his truck, his mind in turmoil, his heart like a stone in his chest.

In his broken childhood, he'd had no loving role models. But later, living with Mac, he'd seen love at its finest. Finn knew what Mac would say about this. Jessie needed time and space to figure out her future. If he loved Jessie, truly loved her, he needed to do whatever it took, sacrifice whatever he had to, for the sake of her peace of mind.

He'd watched his brother Ben suffer the prejudice of preconceived notions from Becca's father. It had taken an iron will on his brother's part to finally win the love he and Becca so richly deserved.

He'd seen his brother Sam step back from declaring his feelings for Penny, so that she could be free to accept an offer of her dream job that had finally come her way. Fortunately for Sam, Penny's love for him was stronger than any other dream.

But he'd seen enough messy divorces in his law practice to know that love didn't always live up to the promise.

Finn sat in his truck, staring at the ranch house, willing the door to open and praying Jessie would come running toward him, saying she'd made a terrible mistake.

The door remained closed, and as he backed out of the driveway and started along the dirt road, he could feel his heart shattering into a million pieces.

He tried to imagine his life without Jessie. It simply wasn't possible.

As before, he would have his family, and his work. And though he loved both, they couldn't possibly fill all the empty places inside him the way Jessie's love had.

His future loomed before him, cold and empty and meaningless.

This pain was far worse than the bullet he'd taken, or the burns he'd endured.

Though his body would suffer only a few scars, he knew his poor heart would never heal.

Finn looked up from his computer when the door to his office opened. His father stepped inside.

"Ben called and asked us to come over." Mac indicated the rest of the family standing just outside Finn's office.

Finn lifted a hand in greeting before turning to his father.

Mac cleared his throat. "You've been spending a lot of time away from the ranch. It's been almost three weeks now, son."

"Yeah. Sorry about that." Finn fiddled with a pen on

his desk. "I figured it was time I tackled all the work that had piled up here in the office while I was..." He shrugged. "Otherwise occupied."

"I hope you can spare some time. Ben wants all of us together while he gives us the latest on Wayne Stone."

"Of course I can go with you." Finn shut down his computer and shoved away from the desk.

Outside, he joined his family to walk along Main Street until they came to the sheriff's office.

Inside, Ben was waiting, along with Basil Caldwell.

Ben's office was littered with enough chairs to accommodate all of them. As they took their places, Finn noted two additional chairs. Before he could comment, the door opened and Jessie and her aunt stepped into the room.

While the family members greeted Jessie and Nola, Finn stood back, studying Jessie with a look of naked hunger.

When she'd greeted all the others, she turned to Finn almost reluctantly. "Hello, Finn. How are your wounds?"

"All healed." A lie, he thought. His heart had taken a fatal hit. But at least nobody could see it. "And you?"

She managed a half-hearted smile. "I'm fine. And the doctors are really happy with the way Aunt Nola is healing."

The older woman walked to Finn and pressed a kiss to his cheek. "Thanks to you, Finn." She paused. "I was too exhausted and too overcome when I first returned home to say what I was feeling. I want you to know that what you did was truly heroic. Jessie fought hard to save me, but I was like a dead weight. If you hadn't found us in time, I know what our fate would have been."

He shook his head. "We were all in it together. I'm just glad we came through it alive."

As the others took their seats, Nola patted the chair beside hers. "Jessie, honey, you sit here."

Jessie took the seat her aunt indicated, effectively sandwiched between Nola and Finn. The chairs were so close, she could hear every breath he took. And with each breath, she could feel her heart hitching.

When all were seated, Ben began.

"Both Basil and the state police team are still digging up facts about the man we know as Wayne Stone. So far, the list of his crimes and victims are as long as my arm. But this is what we've learned so far. We've uncovered six aliases. Besides Wayne Stone, he's called himself Rogers Sutter, Clint Sawyer, Bill Seiver, Gene Struthers, and Wyatt Seabold."

Ben looked over at his family. "Are you seeing a pattern here?"

Puzzled, they merely stared.

He gave them a smile. "Maybe you need to see it on paper. He chose the first names of famous cowboys. And the last names all started with an *S*. The police profile team report that most of these serial criminals have these odd little idiosyncrasies. Wayne was really obsessed with cowboys and with his own genius. He honestly believed he was bulletproof and that the authorities would never touch him."

Ben turned to Basil. "Why don't you tell them what else you've uncovered?"

The detective held up his notes. "Those names were used by our guy while he conned the six women we know about so far. We expect we'll turn up more as we dig deeper. Miss Blair, you're the only one of his victims who managed to survive."

At Nola's little gasp, Jessie caught her aunt's hand and squeezed.

Basil continued. "The police are seeking court orders to exhume the bodies of all his known victims, to see if we can match the toxins that were in your blood to theirs. We believe once he successfully killed his first victim with no questions asked by the authorities, he saw no reason to change his mode of operation."

"There's more," Ben added. "The arson department confirmed that the motel fire that nearly killed Jessie was definitely arson. They're working to determine if Wayne Stone was caught on any security cameras in the area. Of course, he was so good at altering his appearance, he may not be recognizable. They feel this proves that Stone had targeted Jessie from the beginning, hoping to eliminate anyone who could be a threat."

Ben glanced at his brother. "And the brakes on your truck were deliberately tampered with. We now believe Wayne was watching Jessie, and when he learned of your involvement, knew he had to eliminate you, as well. He had himself hired as a wrangler to gain access to the ranch in order to set that little accident into motion and then, when you showed up in the hills, deliberately cut himself with barbed wire in order to leave without suspicion."

Sam swore under his breath. "Yeah. Clint Sawyer. And we actually paid him."

Mac's eyes narrowed. "I thought, for a moment in the woods, that I recognized him. And then discarded the notion. He's certainly a master of disguise."

Ben nodded. "This guy figured all the angles."

Basil flipped his notebook. "Although the authorities closed the book on the accident of Matthew Carver, the retired FBI agent Jessie hired, and his car is no longer available for testing, we believe his death was also deliberate." He paused. "We have the name of the woman

Wayne Stone was paying in the county offices to give him information on single women and the amount of taxes they were paying on their property. That gave our guy a long list of potential victims."

Ben added, "Ida Hunt was arrested and charged with aiding and abetting. Because of the number of victims, she was looking at a long prison sentence. When the state police told her how many years she would likely spend in jail, Ida agreed to be a witness against him in exchange for leniency."

Nola spoke up. "Is my marriage to this monster considered valid?"

Ben shook his head. "Because he used false information, the courts consider the marriage invalid. We've already asked for documentation to aid you in getting back any money or properties he may have already claimed while holding you hostage."

She gave a deep sigh of relief.

Ben explained, "It may take a lawyer to sort out all the legalities, since your signature appears on a lot of documents." He shot a grin in Finn's direction. "If you'd like, I could recommend a very good lawyer."

The sound of chuckling was a welcome relief from the tension in the room.

Ben looked around. "I know this doesn't answer every question, but Basil and the state team are working together, sharing information and hoping to put this to rest soon. From what we know so far, Wayne Stone, or whatever his real name is, has been working scams his entire adult life. He's a man with absolutely no conscience. And he has left a string of deaths and broken families across Montana, and possibly other states, as well. If he hadn't been stopped, we have no doubt he would have continued on this crime spree without a pause, adding more victims to his long list. Thankfully, the judge has refused to allow him to post bail, so he won't be a threat anytime soon."

As the family got to their feet to thank Ben and Basil, Finn stood back, watching as Nola crossed the room.

"Thank you, Chief Monroe." Nola's handshake was firm.

"You're welcome. And, Miss Blair, it's Ben."

"And I'm just plain Nola." She smiled. "I know you're Finn's oldest brother." She turned to Jessie. "I asked my niece to help me sort out the various family members."

She turned to Mac. "I understand you opened your home to Jessie while she was searching for me. I'll never be able to thank you enough, Mr. Monroe."

"It's Mac. And there's no need to thank me. That's what family does."

"Jessie has told me about your amazing family, Mac." She turned to include Mary Pat and the others. "I was alone until I took in Jessie after the death of my brother and his wife. I know some folks thought a single woman with no children of her own didn't have the proper tools to raise a child, but I was determined to do whatever I could to make up for the loss of her parents. If anybody had told me all those years ago that I would be the one getting so much more than I gave, I'd have never believed them. But it's true. Having Jessie has filled my life with such joy."

Mac nodded. "I know what you mean, Nola. Every person in this room has given me more than I could ever give back."

"Well." Nola turned toward the door. "I hope you will all agree to come to dinner one night soon, so I can thank all of you." She chuckled. "I'm not much of a cook, but

I learned how to roast a turkey just so Jessie could enjoy Thanksgiving every year."

Sam couldn't help boasting. "My wife, Penny, is the best cook in the county. Maybe in the entire state of Montana."

Penny flushed with pleasure. "Sorry, Nola. Sam likes to brag about me. But if you wouldn't mind a change of plans, why don't you and Jessie come to dinner at our ranch?" She looked at the others for confirmation before adding, "How about Saturday night?"

Nola beamed with pleasure. "I'd like that. I'm sure Jessie knows the way."

She glanced around and caught sight of Jessie and Finn standing awkwardly on the fringes of the family.

When they realized she was staring, they looked away. But not before she'd caught the yearning in both their eyes.

She reached out a hand to her niece, and Jessie hurried to her side to offer her arm.

As they started out the door, she called to the others, "Jessie and I will see you Saturday."

Long after the rest of his family had left for the ranch, Finn returned to his office and tackled a mountain of paperwork, determined to keep his mind off what he and Jessie had once had. It was the only way he could keep from going slowly mad.

CHAPTER TWENTY-NINE

Jessie pulled up to the Monroe ranch and parked her aunt's truck behind a string of vehicles near the back door before turning to her aunt.

"The red van belongs to Mary Pat."

"From what you've told me about her, she sounds like an amazing woman."

"She's been serving the families around here for a long time. Everything from visiting nurse to teacher to counselor. She's improved the lives of so many people, they ought to award her a medal."

Jessie pointed. "That tricked-out police SUV belongs to Ben. Finn said he and Sam still can't believe their older brother in on the right side of the law for a change."

"He was there when we needed him, and that makes him a hero in my book."

Jessie nodded. "The rest of the trucks belong to the Monroe ranch."

She circled around to help her aunt from the passenger

side, but Nola was already out of their truck and climbing the steps. Jessie had to hurry to catch up.

She noted the gift bag on her aunt's arm. "A hostess gift?"

Before Nola could respond, the door was opened and the Monroe family began spilling onto the back porch to welcome their guests.

Leading the way was Archie, tongue lolling, tail thumping with joy.

"Who's this?" Nola bent down to scratch behind the dog's ears and he rewarded her with wet kisses.

"This is Archie." Becca stepped out beside her husband, Ben. "We found him at the Haller Creek Dog Rescue. But we've decided Archie rescued us."

"Hello, Archie." Nola greeted the young couple. "Lucky dog."

"And lucky us," Ben added. "We can't imagine our lives without him."

Mac and Mary Pat warmly embraced both Nola and Jessie before stepping back to allow the others to lend their greetings.

Otis and Roscoe, just walking up from the bunkhouse, shook hands with the two women, saving their brightest smiles for Jessie.

Zachariah added a bit of formality. "Jessica, it is good having you back. And Miss Nolinda, welcome."

Nola smiled. "Your use of my formal name helps me like it. For a while, I thought I might never want to hear it again." She touched a hand to Zachariah's. "Thank you."

Sam and Penny stepped out to greet them before leading the way inside, through the big mudroom and into the kitchen, perfumed with the most amazing scents.

Nola breathed deeply. "Is that bread baking?"

Mac nodded. "Ever since Penny joined our family, she's been spoiling us."

Nola smiled at Penny. "I remember that smell from my childhood. My mother and grandmother always baked bread. I'm ashamed to admit that I didn't inherit their cooking gene."

Penny chuckled. "I didn't think I had, either. But with three hungry brothers, I had no choice but to learn how to keep them well fed."

While Penny turned to see to something in the oven, Sam passed around chilled longnecks and glasses of wine.

Penny pointed to a pretty tray of cheese and crackers. "Please help yourselves."

While the others laughed and chatted and moved about the room, Jessie felt her spirits plummet. Everyone was here. Except Finn.

Becca handed her a glass of pale wine. "I've missed you, Jessie. We all have."

"I've missed all of you, too, but I've been reluctant to leave my aunt alone." Jessie sipped, avoiding Becca's eyes. "I see Finn isn't here."

"He's been putting in a lot of hours at his office in town. He told us he didn't think he could make it."

"On a Saturday night?"

Becca touched a hand to Jessie's arm. "I wish I could say he'd be here. But lately he seems to be avoiding everyone."

Hearing the sound of another vehicle, both women fell silent.

Minutes later, as the rest of the family laughed and chatted, Jessie's heart started pounding the minute Finn stepped into the kitchen.

He tossed his attaché case on a side table before greeting everyone.

"Jessie." He nodded from across the room before accepting a longneck from Sam.

His formal, almost chilly greeting had her heart falling to her toes. "Finn."

Following his lead, she stayed where she was, aware that he was deliberately keeping the width of the room between them.

Maybe it was best this way. At least, as long as he kept his distance, and she was surrounded by so many people, she could get through this night without embarrassing herself. But try as she might, she couldn't keep from staring at him. He was so handsome. So strong and self-assured. She felt achingly miserable. He looked so cool and aloof, as though he'd already made his peace with a life apart from her.

"So, Mac." Nola had been eating nonstop since Penny first set her famous prime rib on a platter in the middle of the table. Along with it she'd made garlic mashed potatoes, a salad of greens and sweet peppers from Otis's garden out back, and a loaf of crusty bread warm from the oven, drizzled with olive oil and sun-dried tomatoes. "Have you ever leased cattle haulers from Miller and Company in Arvid?"

Mac shook his head. "I've been using MacMillan and Sons for years. I knew Fred MacMillan when I was a boy, and he and his sons have a fine reputation."

"That's good to know. I've been hearing rumors that Miller and Company may be going out of business." Nola helped herself to another slice of prime rib. "I'll be calling you for the number for MacMillan."

Mac nodded. "I'm happy to recommend them. How about your wranglers? Are you sticking with the ones Wayne hired?"

She gave a firm shake of her head. "I have no intention of trusting anyone connected with that monster. My old crew is back, including my longtime foreman, Hugh Jenkins, and they have things running smoothly. I'm eager to get back in the saddle and run the show the way I always did. The doctors have said I should be able to ride again soon."

For dessert Penny set a five-tier chocolate torte in the center of the table and began slicing it onto plates and adding scoops of chocolate-chip ice cream before passing them around.

Sam circled the table with cups of coffee. He'd appointed himself Penny's assistant for the evening and was doing a fine job of it.

For a short time conversation ceased as everyone hummed with pleasure while devouring the confection and happily sipping their drinks.

Seeing Finn at the far end of the table, Nola turned to Zachariah. "I'm told you've been Finn's mentor through the years."

The old lion smiled. "I like to think I had a hand in Finnian's desire to be a lawyer."

"I remember reading about you years ago. You've handled some pretty famous cases."

"I've been very fortunate in my career."

Nola chuckled. "Now you're being modest. Everyone of a certain age knows your name. You're one of Montana's shining lights."

Pleased, he gave a slight bow of his head. "That's kind of you to say."

Nola turned to Otis. "Penny said these salad greens and vegetables came from your garden."

He gave her a wide smile. "It relaxes me to dig in the dirt after finishing ranch chores."

"I feel the same way." Nola held up a hand, the nails short and blunt. "In my entire life I've never bothered with a manicure, because it would be money and time wasted. When I'm not up in the hills with the herd, or mucking stalls, I'd rather get down and dirty in my garden. Like you, gardening relaxes me." She touched a hand to his arm. "Becca told me you grow pumpkins. I'd like to know your secret."

"No secret." He shared a conspiratorial smile. "I swear, I just drop a few seeds in the ground, and dozens of pumpkins appear magically. For years, after we grew tired of pumpkin pie and the first snowfall, I used to scatter a hundred or more pumpkins in the fields for the deer and mustangs, figuring that's all they were good for. That is, until Miss Becca started selling them in her garden shop in town."

"Speaking of your garden shop." Nola smiled at Becca. "It's delightful. On the way here my niece took me on a tour of the town. First we stopped at Florence Gaddy's place to give her a donation for the Haller Creek Aid Society."

Mary Pat gave her a wide smile. "I bet Flo was grateful for the donation."

"Not as grateful as Jessie and I are for the care she showed after that awful motel fire."

Nola patted her niece's arm before turning to Becca. "I intend to return to Haller Creek another day and browse your shop to my heart's content."

Becca dimpled as Nola turned to Roscoe. "Jessie

told me you're the artist who made that beautiful arch announcing Becca's Garden."

"Yes, ma'am." Roscoe blushed.

"Roscoe, I don't care how much you charge, I just have to have one for the entrance to my ranch. Do you think you could do it?"

His color deepened. "I'd be happy to, ma'am."

"Oh, thank you." She laughed like a young girl. "I can already see it in my mind. A pretty wrought-iron arch proclaiming the Blair Ranch since 1870."

"What did I tell you, Roscoe?" Becca was all smiles. "Everybody who sees that piece of art wants one like it."

Nola turned to Sam. "I'm told you're the one who most enjoys ranching like your father."

Sam was grinning from ear to ear. "I do love it. Of course, when I first got here, I'd have been the last one to believe that. I thought the barns smelled. The cattle smelled. The whole life of a rancher smelled. And now I wouldn't trade it for any other life."

"I feel the same way." Nola shared his smile. "No matter how hard the work is, it satisfies my soul."

She turned to Ben. "Jessie tells me that you and your wife are building a home in the hills. I can't say I blame you for wanting a retreat from the crime you're forced to deal with on a daily basis."

Ben touched a hand to the badge over his heart. "I love my work, no matter how tough it is. But the new house isn't so much a retreat as a dream I've had since I was a kid. A place to call my own that nobody can ever take away." He looked over at Mac. "When my brothers and I came to live here, Mac invited each of us to pick a spot that called to us, and he would see that it was all ours. To kids without roots, that sounded like heaven."

"You're a generous man, Mac."

Mac shook his head firmly. "I'm just a lucky man, Nola. These three have given me so much more than I could ever give them." He put a hand over Mary Pat's. "And I've been lucky in the friends I have. Mary Pat and Zachariah made it possible for these three to become my sons. Roscoe and Otis had the patience of saints through the years as three rough-and-tumble boys learned how to be respectful men." He looked around. "I hate to think what my life would have been like without all of these good people to share it."

Nola nodded her head and glanced at Jessie. "I know what you mean, Mac. My niece has filled my life with such joy."

Jessie blushed and lowered her head.

Nola turned to Penny. "This was the most amazing dinner ever. If all of you had come to dinner at my place, it would have been a far cry from this. Thank you so much, Penny."

The young woman pushed away from the table and looped her arm through Nola's as she led the way to the parlor. "You're welcome, Nola. We're all so happy that you and Jessie could be here with us tonight."

As they gathered around the fireplace, Nola turned to Finn with a sly smile. "It seems I've talked to everyone here about the things they love. I know you love being a lawyer. And I'm told you're a good one. But there's something else I'd rather talk to you about."

He arched a brow. "What's that?"

"Love and marriage."

He went very still. "You've got me confused with my brothers. That's not something I have any experience with."

"You could say the same about me." She gave a self-deprecating smile. "After all, my only experience at love and marriage was a disaster. But I know how much I love my niece. That should count for something." She paused before issuing her challenge. "If not marriage, can you talk to me about love, Finn?"

Finn's eyes narrowed slightly. "What game are you playing, Miss Blair?"

"Now I'm Miss Blair?" She arched a brow. "I prefer Nola."

When Finn held his silence she reached for the fancy bag she'd brought. "This is for you, Finn. My little gift to thank you for saving my life."

"I appreciate the thought. But a gift isn't necessary." He eyed the bag with a wary look.

Her smile widened. "Go ahead and open it. It won't bite."

He reached in and removed tissue from a framed photograph of Jessie as a child, sad-faced and too shy to look directly at the camera.

To the others Nola said, "This was Jessie at the age of five, when she'd just lost her parents and had come to live with me on my ranch." Nola chuckled as Finn held it up for the others to see. "I can't tell you how terrified I was that I would make things worse for that shy, frightened, wounded little mouse you see in that photograph. But as the years flew by, she blossomed into this smart, self-assured young woman, ready to go off and conquer the world."

Nola pointed to the bag. "There's more."

Finn removed another tissue-wrapped package to reveal a framed photograph of Ben, Sam, and Finn, taken shortly after arriving at Mac's ranch, at the ages of ten, eleven, and twelve. They were sullen and defiant, dressed in hand-me-down jeans and torn T-shirts, their hair badly in need of cutting, showing the camera identical menacing scowls.

Finn looked over. Before he could ask, Nola explained, "Mary Pat was kind enough to lend me that old photo, which I had copied and enlarged before framing it."

As Finn held it up for the others to see, there were bursts of raucous laughter around the room.

"Look at us," Sam called. "We were the baddest of the bad."

"Hey." Ben dropped an arm around his wife and pressed a kiss to her cheek. "We still are."

"Yes, dear." Becca patted his arm. "Only now, thank heaven, you're on the right side of the law. You'll never know how happy that makes my parents."

That brought another round of laughter.

"There's one more." Nola watched as Finn removed a third tissue-wrapped photo.

It was a copy of the Polaroid photograph the rancher had taken of Finn and Jessie at the little cabin they'd shared during that memorable storm. Now, enlarged and framed, it revealed in vivid detail the joy radiating from the two of them. It was apparent to everyone how vibrant, how alive, how obviously in love these two people were.

Nola looked around with a sheepish smile. "I happened to see this in Jessie's room." She turned to her niece. "I hope you don't mind. I had it copied and enlarged before framing it."

To the others she said, "Anyone who can transform from this"—she pointed to the childhood photos—"to this"—she pointed to the smiling couple in the other photo—"has learned a great deal about love. Love of family can transform a shy girl into a self-assured career woman. Love of family can turn even the toughest little delinquent into a man of honor. But the love of a good man and woman..." Her smile grew. "Now there's the most amazing transformation of all."

In the silence that followed, Nola cleared her throat. "I didn't raise Jessie to be a slave to me in my old age. I raised her to be a strong, independent woman who would be free to follow her heart, no matter where it takes her."

Jessie started toward her aunt. "But I..."

Nola lifted a hand to stop her. "I know you think you're being noble, and giving me what I need. I overheard you that day you brought me home from the hospital. You were prepared to sacrifice the rest of your life to keep me from being lonely." Her smile softened, as did her words. "No matter where you go or what you do, we'll always be a part of one another's lives. That's what family is. And we'll get together often, to celebrate good times and bad. But my greatest joy in this world will be to watch my wonderful niece loving, and being loved by, a good man, and building a future with him."

She turned to Finn. "Now, would you like to talk to me about love?"

He was staring at Jessie.

And though Jessie tried to look away, she couldn't.

They were completely unaware of anyone else in the room. The look of hunger in their eyes was almost blinding in its intensity.

Finn reached out a hand and Jessie crossed the room to take it.

As they started out of the parlor, Nola called, "About that talk..."

"I owe you big-time, Nola." Finn speared her a glance. "We'll talk. Soon. I promise. But right now..."

Finn and Jessie stepped into the kitchen. Before the door even closed they came together in a fierce embrace.

Finn breathed her in, loving the way she fit so perfectly in his arms. "Oh, babe, I've been so miserable without you."

"So have I. You'll never know how many times I started to call you. But what was there to say? I thought I was doing the right thing by telling you good-bye. But oh, how it hurt. I love you, Finn Monroe."

"I love you more, Jessie Blair." He kissed her until they were both breathless. When he came up for air he whispered, "I didn't know how I was going to live without you, but I was determined to try. And now..." He framed her face with his hands, pressing butterfly kisses over the corner of her mouth, her cheek, the tip of her nose. "Thanks to that smart woman who raised you, I get a second chance. Will you marry me, Jessie, and spend the rest of your life making me the happiest man in the world?"

She wrapped her arms around his waist and held on as her whole world began to tilt and shift. "Yes, yes, yes! Oh, Finn, I thought we'd lost our chance for happiness."

The door opened and the entire family spilled into the kitchen, laughing, shouting, and offering congratulations to the happy couple.

"About time," Ben called as he slapped Finn on the back.

Becca hugged Jessie before stepping away to allow Penny to do the same.

Sam was busy teasing his brother. "How the mighty have fallen, bro. Didn't you once say you'd never fall into the marriage trap?"

"Did I?" Finn was too happy to think about a clever retort. Instead, he turned away to accept hugs from Nola and Mary Pat, and handshakes from Otis and Roscoe.

Zachariah solemnly shook his hand. "I do believe you've just been through your most earth-shattering trial of all, Finnian."

"Yeah. How'd I do?"

"You've made your old mentor proud."

Mac, who had stood back until everyone else had offered their congratulations, stepped up to clap a big hand on Finn's shoulder. "I'm happy for you, son."

"Thanks, Dad. I know I've been hard to live with these last few weeks."

Mac smiled. "Love is messy. But when it's between two good people, it's still the very best thing in the world."

Jessie walked up and said shyly, "I know this is sudden."

Mac couldn't hold back his laughter. "Jessie, the only ones who didn't see this coming were you and Finn. The rest of us wondered why it took you so long."

"Really?"

He kissed her cheek. "Welcome to the family."

And then, as they gathered around the table, passing out longnecks and glasses of wine to celebrate their good news, talking and laughing and making plans, Finn caught Jessie's hand and led her into the parlor.

With the joyful sounds of their family in the background, they stood together, locked in an embrace, filled with joy.

CHAPTER THIRTY

After a long day of chores, the family was gathered in the kitchen, sipping longnecks as they all helped put the finishing touches on dinner.

When Jessie and Finn walked in, Archie was the first to greet them, wriggling with delight.

"Hello, you sweet thing." Jessie stooped to scratch behind his ears while Finn tossed his attaché case aside and shed his cowhide jacket.

"Well?" Mary Pat paused in her work. "How did that office work out for you, Jessie?"

The young woman gave her a wide smile. "It's perfect. Just enough room for a desk and chair and a few filing cabinets, and possibly a second desk if I ever get enough clients to need an assistant."

Finn dropped an arm around her shoulders. "And since it's next door to my office, we can sneak in a few visits between clients."

Mary Pat laughed. "Best of all, the little town of Haller Creek will finally get its very own CPA. One of the complaints I hear from ranchers around here is that they have nobody to answer their hundreds of questions about filing their quarterly and annual taxes. I predict, Jessie dear, that you're about to become their best friend, and you'll soon have more business than you can handle."

Jessie put a hand to her heart. "From your lips, Mary Pat."

She and Finn accepted longnecks from Sam.

"Dinner is ready," Penny announced as she set a platter filled with thick slices of meat loaf in the middle of the table.

Roscoe breathed deeply as they took their places. "I've been thinking about this food for the past hour."

"Then you can start." Mary Pat handed him the platter and he helped himself before holding it out to Otis, who did the same before passing it on.

With Mary Pat leading, they joined hands and offered a blessing.

Around the table, the family spent a leisurely hour catching up on one another's day.

Becca shared a smile with Ben. "Wait until you see the house. It's already starting to look like a home."

"That's good news." Sam helped himself to seconds. "Because as soon as Conway Miller finishes with your place, he promised to have his crew start on ours."

Penny nodded. "The first crew has already roughed in the shell. The walls are up, and they promised to have the roof on next week."

Finn squeezed Jessie's hand. "We drove up in the hills before coming here. We've been looking over plans, and we think we know which one we'd like to build. As soon as Conway can fit us into his schedule."

He turned to Mac. "You've invited us to stay here until after the wedding, but I'm thinking it might be easier for us to get a small apartment in town until our house is built. That way we can both just walk to our offices."

Becca and Ben shared a knowing look before Ben said, "Since we're ready to move into our new house, why not rent Becca's little house in town? You can still walk to work, and it has everything you'd need."

Jessie's eyes widened. "You wouldn't mind, Becca?"

"Mind? I'd love knowing you and Finn were there."

Finn and Jessie turned to one another with matching smiles.

In unison they said, "Thank you."

When Ben's cell phone rang he stepped away from the table and walked into the parlor. A short time later he returned, just as Penny was passing around slices of carrot cake mounded with vanilla ice cream.

"If you don't mind, I invited Basil Caldwell to stop by. He and the state police have been compiling a list of Wayne Stone's past criminal activities, and he wants to bring us up to date."

Mac set aside his empty coffee cup. "Shouldn't Jessie's aunt be here, as well?"

Jessie smiled. "Aunt Nola is up in the hills with the herd. She'd never get cell service up there."

Ben nodded. "It's just as well. Basil doesn't think Stone's past crimes would impact Nola one way or the other. She has an airtight case against him."

Mac shrugged. "All right. Whatever you say, son."

When they'd polished off their dessert, Mac, Mary Pat, Roscoe, Otis, and Zachariah made their way to the parlor, where they settled into comfortable chairs in front of a roaring fire.

In the kitchen Ben and Becca, Sam and Penny, and Finn and Jessie tackled the cleanup. The sounds of teasing and laughter could be heard throughout the house.

Mary Pat reached over to put a hand on Mac's. "I'll never grow tired of hearing that."

He nodded. "I was just thinking the same."

"They won't be that far away, Mac."

He met her gaze. "I know. Like Nola, I've always known the day would come when all my chicks would fly. I guess we're never really prepared for it, though."

The crunch of wheels on gravel announced the arrival of Basil Caldwell.

Minutes later he stepped into the parlor, followed by the others, who sat crowded around the fire as he stood before them, reading from his notes.

"We've uncovered more details about Wayne Stone's early years. His legal name is Milton Morley. The youngest of six boys, he grew up on a farm in Minnesota. Two of his siblings still live there and work the farm. Their parents were hard-drinking and hardworking, and died years ago. Milton dropped out of school at sixteen and was never seen again. His brothers called him a chameleon. He could change in the blink of an eye from mild-mannered one minute to a tough, no-nonsense bully who had to be in control. They were glad to be rid of him."

Basil paused and cleared his throat. "Milton's first alias is believed to have been Shepherd Strump."

There was an audible gasp as the family heard the name of the cowboy who had lured Mac's teenaged sister away from her family when Mac was just a boy.

Everyone turned toward Mac, who looked thunder-struck.

Gradually, as the news sank in, Mac found his voice. "Was Ellen his first victim?"

"We believe so." Basil nodded. "I'm sorry to break this to you, Mac, but the authorities have found where she was buried. They're testing for toxins. They'd be willing to return her remains to you, if you'd like."

Mac's hands clenched in his lap. "Yes. Of course. She can be buried alongside our parents."

"There's more, Mac."

Mac blinked. "What more could there be?"

"Milton had a history of seeing to it that there were no loose ends. What he wanted from the beginning was to acquire as much land as possible. He saw himself as some sort of Old West cattle baron."

"And my mother made that happen by willing Ellen or her heirs the south pasture."

Basil nodded. "And he was happy to lay claim to it. But when you were notified that an heir had come forward, though you accepted it, your wife, Rachel, decided to investigate further. She went to the county seat to see if she could learn the name and address of the heir, so that she could surprise you with a reunion." Basil's voice lowered. "What she didn't know was that Milton, or Strump as he was calling himself, was paying someone in the records department to notify him if anyone should ever poke around his business. The authorities now have reason to believe that the accident that claimed the life of your wife, Rachel, and son, Robbie, was not an accident, but may have been a deliberate attempt to eliminate any further questions about Milton's claim. He made a mistake, of course. He thought you would be in that truck as well. But it seems that once the collision was deemed an accident by the authorities, he saw that your grief overtook you and figured it would keep you out of his business, and he decided he wouldn't pursue it further."

Mac's face had lost all its color. Seeing it, his three sons gathered around to stand behind his chair, their hands at his back and shoulders. Mary Pat clasped his hand in hers, noting that it was cold as ice.

He could barely speak. "Rachel and Robbie were... murdered?"

Basil nodded.

"And I should have died with them."

Zachariah looked at the three handsome men who stood like fierce protectors behind their adoptive father.

He used his best courtroom voice. "Apparently it wasn't your time, Mackenzie. As you can see, you still had work to do on this earth."

Basil set a clutch of documents on the mantel. "You'll want to look these over at some other time, when your mind isn't troubled. For now, that's all the information I have. If there's more, I'll notify you." Quietly he added, "I'll let myself out."

Ben trailed the detective to the back door and shook his hand before returning to the parlor.

Sensing Mac's need to be alone to digest such shocking information, Otis and Roscoe said their good nights and made their way to the bunkhouse.

Ben and Becca kissed Mac before leashing Archie and leading him from his warm spot in front of the fire.

Finn and Jessie kissed Mac before leaving on the long drive back to Nola's ranch, where Jessie was staying until the wedding.

Sam and Penny kissed Mac before heading up the stairs.

Zachariah shook his old friend's hand before going to his room off the kitchen.

Only Mary Pat remained, sitting silently beside Mac, staring into the flames.

When at last he spoke, his voice was raspy, as though speaking had become an effort. "I never dreamed..." He tried again. "They had planned a surprise for me, and instead..." Moments later he whispered, "I should have been with them. Maybe I could have..." He shook his head, finding it impossible to put into words the depth of his shock and grief.

Mary Pat put a hand over his. Over the years she had seen the guilt suffered by survivors of tragedies. She'd counseled the grief-stricken, the lonely, the lost. She knew all the right words. But for now, she chose to remain silent and just be here, hoping her presence would be enough to get this good man through this sudden, shocking revelation.

As the fire burned low, and the embers sent sparks up the chimney, they sat side by side, contemplating the mysteries of life.

Ever so slowly, as night faded and the first faint stirrings of dawn colored the horizon, a feeling of peace and acceptance began seeping into Mac's poor, battered heart.

He squeezed Mary Pat's hand and got stiffly to his feet. Helping her up, he lifted her hands to his lips.

"Thank you, my friend, for seeing me through this storm."

"Have the clouds lifted?"

He gave her a long, thoughtful look. "Maybe not all of them. But the thunder and lightning are behind me now."

She climbed the stairs beside him, until they reached the upper floor.

She touched a hand to his arm. "You and I have lived long enough to know that sunshine always follows a storm. Maybe by midmorning we'll see the clouds part."

He closed a hand over hers. "I'm counting on it."

He turned toward his room, then paused outside his door to wait until she stepped into the guest room down the hall.

When her door closed he remained a moment longer, deep in thought, before heading off to bed.

EPILOGUE

Monroe Ranch—Two Months Later

If springtime in Montana is a season of hope, summer is that lazy, hazy, crazy time to enjoy the many fruits of a rancher's labors.

The hills around the Monroe ranch were a riot of color, from deepest green to the brightest oranges and yellows to deepest blue and purple.

Bawling calves, delivered in muddy fields, in grassy meadows, and sometimes on barren hillsides, were now grazing happily on hillsides.

Heavy parkas and wool sweaters were forgotten as cowboys sought the cool waters of lakes and mountain streams in the midday sun.

At the Monroe ranch, love was in the air.

Penny, Becca, and Mary Pat, assisted by Zachariah, Otis, and Roscoe, were busy transforming the back porch and yard into a proper place for a wedding.

The big log table under the tree had been covered by a white lace cloth, anchored by low bowls of pink and white roses. Penny was busy frosting the five-tier cake with mounds of whipped frosting. Each tier was a different flavor, to satisfy the tastes of so many family members. A layer of chocolate followed by a layer of carrot cake, a layer of lemon butter, a layer of strawberry, and finally a layer of white cake dotted with cherries. The figures atop the cake were a man in a fringed cowhide jacket, carrying an attaché case, and a woman in a sleek business suit, holding a calculator in her hand. The sight of it had everyone smiling.

Sam stepped in from the porch, where he'd been helping to hang strings of twinkling lights.

He paused to kiss his wife's cheek. "You really managed to make them look like my brother and his bride, Penny."

She laughed in delight. "I think they may be my best ever."

Sam sniffed the air. "Do I smell barbeque?"

She nodded. "Ribs and chicken. Both the bride and groom requested it for their wedding supper."

Sam gave a nod of approval. "I'm glad my brother has such good taste."

"In food or in women?" Becca asked.

"Both. But don't tell him I said that." Sam looked up. "Speaking of the bride and groom..."

Dust rose up as a ranch truck arrived with Finn at the wheel. Seated beside him was Jessie, with her aunt in the backseat.

Finn parked the truck before circling around to assist the two women. Jessie was carrying a long zippered bag over her arm. Behind her, Nola carried a similar bag.

They climbed the steps and walked through the mudroom to the kitchen, where the family was gathered.

"Oh, my. Don't you look handsome." Mary Pat touched a hand to her heart at the sight of Finn, wearing a starched white shirt, string tie, denims, and cowboy boots polished to a high shine. Over it all was his ever-present buckskin jacket.

Zachariah looked on approvingly. "That jacket has started looking better on you than it ever looked on me, Finnian."

"Thanks, Zachariah. I only hope it continues to bring me the same good luck in the courtroom."

"I have nary a doubt."

Mary Pat led Nola and Jessie up the stairs to the big bedroom where they would dress for the wedding.

Inside she paused. "Do you two need any help?"

Nola nodded. "I'll be needing help with the zipper on this dress." She chuckled. "I haven't worn many dresses in my day. I'm much more comfortable in jeans and boots."

Mary Pat joined in the laughter. "I know what you mean. My lifestyle doesn't lend itself to dresses. But," she said to Jessie, "don't you worry. I bought a dress for this occasion."

"I wouldn't care if everybody wore boots and denim to the wedding, as long as all of you were here on this special day."

Nola kissed her cheek. "It is special, Jessie honey. I wouldn't have missed this day for anything." She paused. "And to think I almost did."

Jessie wrapped her arms around her aunt. "We won't talk about that. Remember. It's behind us now, and we can all look forward to a bright, happy future."

"Oh, honey." Nola wiped a tear from her eye before turning away to unzip the bag holding her dress.

The door opened and Becca and Penny stepped inside.

Soon the sounds of feminine voices and laughter drifted down the stairs as the five women helped one another with hair and makeup.

Downstairs, Otis and Roscoe hurried off to the bunkhouse to change.

Zachariah slipped away to his room to do the same.

Ben in his crisp uniform and Sam in his best denims and vest walked outside to fill a cooler with longnecks and a bottle of Champagne for the wedding toast.

Finn was alone in the parlor when Mac walked down the stairs looking rugged and handsome in his best Western suit. Father and son both paused before breaking into smiles.

"You ready for this day, son?"

Finn nodded. "You bet. How about you, Dad?"

"I guess I'll never be ready to see the last of my boys start a new life. But I'm happy for you. And so proud of the man you've become."

"Thanks, Dad." The two men enjoyed a bear hug before stepping apart.

Finn said, "While Jessie and I are away, Zachariah offered to look over the documents of your mother's will. As soon as I get back, I'll start the process of regaining your rights to the south pasture." He paused. "Do you have a copy of the will?"

Mac nodded. "I do. I appreciate this, Finn." He crossed the room and retrieved a ring of keys from his desk drawer. Holding up a smaller key he handed it over to Finn. "This will unlock a cabinet in my closet, where I stored a lot of family documents years ago. The folders are all labeled. I'm sure you'll be able to figure out the ones you need."

A short time later he heard the sound of footsteps on the stairs and turned as Finn walked toward him.

Instead of documents, Finn was holding a bottle of whiskey and a bottle of pills.

For a moment Mac merely stared at his son. Then, as the realization dawned, he gave a deep sigh.

"The only time I've ever seen you drink whiskey is to celebrate something memorable. And then only as a toast. But I've never seen you drink cheap whiskey, Dad."

Mac shook his head. "I don't."

"The date on this bottle of pills is exactly the same date that Ben and Sam and I broke into your house. I know it's none of my business, Dad, but would you care to explain?"

Mac paused for a long moment before saying softly, "That night you boys broke in, I was in a deep depression over the death of Rachel and Robbie. I'd gone someplace very dark in my mind, and couldn't seem to find a way out. So I went to town to get a prescription for sleeping pills from the doctor, and then I'd stopped to buy that bottle of cheap liquor."

Finn's eyes narrowed as the truth dawned. "You were going to end it?"

"I . . ." Mac stopped, then silently nodded.

"What stopped you?"

Mac lifted his head and fixed Finn with a look. "You and your brothers. All that pent-up anger and rebellion. I understood it. And I realized that you needed somebody to help you get your lives back." He clenched his hands at his sides. "As much as I wanted release from my pain, I figured your need was greater than mine. I thought I'd put my plans on hold for a while, and tend to the three of you."

"So while you were busy saving our lives..."

Mac finished, "You three were saving mine."

"Oh, God, Dad." Finn gathered his father into his arms and hugged him fiercely.

Mac's arms tightened around Finn, absorbing the quiet strength and the unconditional love he could feel.

They remained that way for long, silent minutes.

Finally, as they stepped apart, Finn nodded toward the stairs. "I'll just put these back where I found them, if that's all right with you."

Mac nodded. "I'll dispose of them later. Right now, we've got a wedding to celebrate."

When Finn disappeared up the stairs, Mac turned away to stare into the flames of the fire.

Hearing a sound, he turned to see Mary Pat standing in the shadows.

For a moment all he could do was stare. Finally he found his voice. "You heard?"

She walked closer. "I'm sorry, Mac. There was nowhere to go. I couldn't interrupt you and Finn at such a time."

She paused, choosing her words carefully. "I knew you were troubled by the deaths of Rachel and Robbie. But I had no idea the depth of your pain."

He took her hand. "It's not something I could bring myself to talk about. But I'm glad you know. I'll be forever grateful for those three hell-raisers, who completely changed the course of my life."

He caught her other hand and drew her closer. "You've changed my life, too, Mary Pat. You've been here for me through the worst and the best."

"That's what friends do."

"We are friends. You're my dearest, my best friend. But I've been thinking I'd like us to be more."

It was her turn to fall silent, as though unable to take it all in. Finally she looked at him. "Are you talking... commitment? Marriage?"

"I am. Does that make me a foolish old man?"

"Mackenzie Monroe, you will never be foolish in my eyes." She gave him a steady look. "Why now, Mac?"

"Maybe because, though it's summer, it's the autumn of our lives. We've wasted so many years."

"They weren't wasted. We had work to do."

"That we did. You, especially." He nodded. "I know you so well. You're probably getting that old familiar wanderlust, and planning your next trip into the wild."

"Would you mind?"

He shook his head. "Not at all. You have to live your life, just as I have to live mine. But I'd like to think— I fervently hope—that when you grow weary of the travels, you'll always come home to me."

"Home to me." She sighed and squeezed his hands. "Do you know how very special those words are? I've never had a home. Nor a love to come home to."

"Then let me be your first." He gathered her into his arms and kissed her.

"My first. My only," she whispered against his mouth.

As the doors opened upstairs, and footsteps sounded on the stairs, they stepped apart, wearing matching looks of happiness.

"Come on, Finn." Ben stood in the parlor and called up the stairs.

Finn hurried down. "Is Reverend Grayson here already?"

"Not yet. But Dad sent me. He wants us to join him and the others."

Finn didn't need to ask what this was about. For as long as he could remember, whenever they were planning a celebration, it would begin up the hill at the graves of Mac's family. Inside a wrought-iron fence lay the graves of his father and mother, and his wife and son, who had been taken from him far too soon.

And now, thanks to the diligence of the state police, Mac's sister, Ellen, was buried in the little plot of land as well.

As he and Ben climbed the hill, Finn thought about what he'd learned today. He was certain none of the others knew Mac's secret. He was determined that none of them would ever hear it from his lips. It was Mac's story to share or keep to himself.

When Ben and Finn stepped into the small enclosure, Sam began filling tumblers with good Irish whiskey.

Mac lifted his glass. "To Rachel and Robbie, to my parents, and sister, Ellen, home at last, where she belongs, in this circle of love."

Solemnly they all drank.

Zachariah lifted his glass. "To you, Mackenzie, for providing a loving home to all of us."

Otis and Roscoe nodded and smiled before drinking.

Ben grinned at Sam. "To our little brother, Finn, for his brilliant choice of bride. Since our wives already love her, he'd have found himself in a whole lot of trouble if he hadn't persuaded her to marry him."

Finn laughed. "We can thank Jessie's aunt for that. I'm so glad she decided to meddle."

At the sound of an approaching vehicle, they turned to watch as the minister parked alongside a row of ranch trucks and stepped out of his car.

Sam put an arm around Finn's shoulders. "Showtime, little bro. Let's go get you and Jessie married."

As the others trailed down the hill, Mac remained alone at the grave site. For long minutes he ran a hand over the smooth granite headstones of his wife and son, tracing their names with his fingers, before pausing alongside the marble urn containing the remains of his long-dead sister, Ellen.

"I'm glad you're finally all here together, where you belong."

As he turned away, he thought about all the events that had brought him to this day. He'd watched as the uncertainty of Ellen's sudden departure from their lives had torn his parents apart. The pain of losing Rachel and Robbie had driven him to deep despair that had almost cost him his life.

Three angry delinquents had filled his home with chaos, and so much love.

And now, with the sweet love he and Mary Pat felt for one another, everything had changed yet again. The pain of loss had been replaced with a sense of quiet peace.

In the house upstairs, Penny and Becca finished Jessie's hair and makeup, and began helping her into her gown. At her insistence, it was sleek and simple. A long column of white silk that ended mid-calf. On her feet, white sandals. In her hair, a mother-of-pearl comb holding a sprig of baby's breath.

The effect was breathtaking.

"Oh, Jessie." Nola, seated beside Mary Pat, wiped tears from her eyes.

"Don't cry, Aunt Nola." Jessie hurried across the room to hug her.

"I have a right to cry. I love you like a daughter."

"And I love you like a mother. That's why I bought you this." Jessie handed her aunt a white satin box.

Inside was a locket. Nola opened it to reveal a photo of Jessie and Nola on one side, and Jessie with her mother and father on the other. She turned it over to read the words engraved there. YOU DIDN'T CARRY ME BENEATH YOUR HEART, BUT I KNOW YOU CARRY ME ALWAYS IN IT.

That brought a fresh round of tears from Nola.

Jessie handed Mary Pat a white satin box containing a similar locket. Inside was a picture of Finn, Sam, and Ben on one side, and the three brothers with Mac, Mary Pat, Zachariah, Otis, and Roscoe on the other. Engraved on the back were the words FAMILY FOREVER.

Now it was Mary Pat's turn to weep.

Jessie handed Becca and Penny larger white boxes. Inside were double strands of pearls with jeweled clasps. The minute she'd fastened them around their necks, the two young women were hugging her and laughing together.

A knock sounded on the door and their voices stilled as they all looked up.

Finn's voice announced, "Reverend Grayson is here. Where are you hiding my wife?"

With a laugh the door was opened and the women came spilling out. As each one passed him, they paused to kiss his cheek.

When they were gone he stepped inside and brought his hand from behind his back, where he'd been hiding a nosegay of pink and white roses.

Before he could offer them to Jessie he paused and simply stared.

"Cat got your tongue, cowboy?"

He swallowed. "Jessie, you're so beautiful. You take my breath away."

"Good. I hope I always have that effect on you."

"You can count on it, babe." He stepped closer and held out the flowers.

She took them and lifted them to her face, breathing in their perfume. "They're beautiful."

"Not nearly as beautiful as the woman holding them." He framed her face with his hands and brushed a soft kiss over her mouth.

At a shout from downstairs, she caught his hand. "Come on, Finn. Let's do this."

As she took a step, he held up a hand. "Wait."

She arched a brow. "Having a change of heart?"

"Never. I just want..." He gathered her close and kissed her, lingering over her lips until they were both sighing.

He gave her that sexy grin that did such strange things to her heart.

"Okay. That'll hold me until we're alone." He caught her hand and they started down the stairs and out onto the porch, where the minister and their family stood waiting.

As they stood before Reverend Grayson and spoke their vows, with Ben, Becca, Sam, and Penny as their witnesses, Finn noticed Zachariah nodding as each word was spoken. Otis and Roscoe were smiling from ear to ear. Nola was wiping tears. And out of the corner of his eye, he saw Mary Pat tuck her hand in Mac's.

And then he was looking at Jessie, eyes shining, and his heart swelled with such love.

Life, he thought, didn't get better than this.

* * *

The wedding supper was, like their lives had always been, raucous and filled with laughter.

There was Penny's amazing barbecue. Ribs and chicken and steak, with slow-baked beans and oven-roasted potatoes and Texas toast. There were Champagne toasts, and slices of six-tier cake that had everybody raving.

Mac made a little speech about the joy he felt at seeing his sons settling down with such good women.

Nola managed a few words about how happy she was to see her Jessie find the love of her life.

Even Zachariah offered a few words about his student and fellow lawyer, and how satisfying it was to see Finn finally find love.

Through it all, Archie, wearing a white bow tied to his collar, wiggled his way under the table, catching any scraps that fell. A number of hands disappeared beneath the table, holding out bits of chicken and steak.

When Finn and Jessie disappeared inside and returned dressed in boots and denims, carrying overnight bags, the family gathered around to bid them good-bye as they left for their honeymoon.

Ben made a final attempt to find out where they were headed. "Just in case I need to get hold of you, Finn."

"You have my cell phone number, bro." Finn was grinning as he helped Jessie into the truck.

They were both laughing as they continued waving while they drove along the gravel driveway.

Jessie turned to Finn. "It wouldn't hurt to tell them where we're going."

"Knowing my brothers, if they knew, they'd be pounding on the door at midnight. Or dropping by for breakfast."

"I wouldn't mind."

He winked. "I would. The last time we stayed at that cabin, we only had a night."

"As I recall, it was a perfect night."

"It was storming. We couldn't even go outside."

It was Jessie's turn to wink. "I don't recall hearing you complain."

The two of them shared a laugh before Finn pulled over to the side of the road.

She looked surprised. "Did you forget something?"

"Just this." He drew her close and kissed her long and slow, then kissed her again. "Do you know how happy you've made me, Jess?"

"Not nearly as happy as you've made me." She wrapped her arms around his neck and offered her lips. "Now kiss me again, cowboy. We're on our honeymoon, remember?"

"How could I forget?"

As they came together, Jessie thought about how far she'd come. She'd been a stranger in a strange town, telling a story that nobody would believe. Nobody but Finn.

And because of Finn, she'd found a safe haven, a family that loved and accepted her, and the great love of a lifetime.

Life with this good man, she realized, was just the beginning.

Whatever came along, she would face it without fear, as long as she had Finn beside her.

In this big, crazy world, two kids who'd been dealt a tough hand in their childhoods had found one another. And with the help of generous souls who'd opened their hearts, they'd found all they needed to give and receive the greatest gift of all—love.

DOLLY'S DINER
FAMOUS MEAT LOAF

Ingredients

- ½ cup milk
- 1 cup soft bread crumbs
- 2 pounds ground chuck
- 1½ teaspoons salt
- Freshly ground black pepper, to taste
- 2 eggs, slightly beaten
- 3 tablespoons steak sauce
- 1 onion, finely chopped
- ½ cup finely diced green bell pepper (optional)
- ½ cup ketchup

Preheat the oven to 350°F.

Combine the milk and bread crumbs in a bowl and allow to soften (about 5 minutes).

In a mixing bowl, combine the ground chuck, salt, pepper, eggs, steak sauce, onions, green pepper (if using), and ketchup. Add the bread crumb mixture and combine.

Pat the mixture into a loaf pan and bake for 1 hour or until done. Allow to stand 5 minutes before slicing.

Enjoy.

ABOUT THE AUTHOR

New York Times bestselling author **R. C. Ryan** has written more than a hundred novels, both contemporary and historical—quite an accomplishment for someone who, after her fifth child started school, gave herself the gift of an hour a day to follow her dream to become a writer.

In a career spanning more than thirty years, Ms. Ryan has given dozens of radio, television, and print interviews across the country and Canada, and has been quoted in such diverse publications as the *Wall Street Journal* and *Cosmopolitan*. She has also appeared on CNN News and *Good Morning America*.

You can learn more about R. C. Ryan—and her alter ego Ruth Ryan Langan—at:

RyanLangan.com
Twitter @RuthRyanLangan
Facebook.com/RuthRyanLangan

For a bonus story from another
author you may love,
please turn the page to read

COWBOY TO THE
RESCUE

by A.J. Pine.

FOREVER
YOURS

*For those who go above and beyond to
keep the rest of us safe.*

CHAPTER ONE

Ivy Serrano smelled smoke.

Not the *Ooh! Someone must be having a bonfire* kind of smoke or the *Mmm! Someone is grilling up burgers* kind of smoke. She smelled the *Shoot! Something's burning* kind of smoke right here, in her new shop, on the day of her grand opening.

She glanced around the small boutique, brows knitted together. She'd been about to flip the CLOSED sign to OPEN for the very first time when it hit her. Something was burning.

After two years of putting her life on hold due to a family tragedy from which she thought she'd never recover, here she was, back home, starting over. And of all things, she smelled *smoke*.

It didn't take long for the smell to be accompanied by sound, the high-pitched wail of a top-of-the-line smoke detector. Although, if anyone was keeping score, *she'd* noticed first. One point for the Ivy, zero for technology.

Except then she remembered that each detector was wired to the next, which meant that in five, four, three, two, one...a chorus of digital, earsplitting screams filled eight hundred square feet of space.

Her senses were keen enough, though, that it only took a second to register that the first alarm came from the back office.

Her design sketches! And samples! And *Oh no!* It was opening day!

She sprinted through the door that separated the shop from her office and storage. The only appliance she had back there was a mini refrigerator, because every now and then a girl needed a cold beverage and maybe even a healthy snack and *ohmygod* this was *not* happening.

She gasped when she saw the charred cord and the licking flames dancing up the wall from the outlet. Items on her desk were turning to kindling as the fire reached paper. She grabbed the extinguisher from its prominent space on the wall and, amid the incessant shrieking, snuffed out the fire in a matter of seconds. She yanked on the part of the cord that hadn't been completely cooked and unplugged the appliance.

Problem solved.

Except the design drawing on her desk, the one she'd been working on for the past week, was partially burned and now covered in foam.

No big deal. She'd simply start over—on the first piece she'd been brave enough to attempt that reminded her of Charlie. And now she had to muster that courage again after—of all things—a fire.

Or it would be, once she remembered how to turn the alarms off. Did she rip the battery out of the first one and all the rest would follow? Or did she have to somehow reset each and every one? She spun in a circle, panic only now setting in, because she knew what happened once the first alarm triggered the rest.

She ran back to the front of the shop and pushed through the door and out onto First Street. Sure enough, an emergency vehicle had already pulled out of the fire station's lot, siren blazing.

She dropped onto the public bench in front of her store and waited the fifteen seconds it took for the truck to roll down the street.

"It would have been faster if you all had walked," she mumbled.

Four figures hopped out of the truck in full gear. One whom she recognized as her best friend Casey's younger sister, Jessie, started to unfurl the hose while another—yep, that was Wyatt O'Brien—went to open the nearby hydrant. The third was Wyatt's younger brother Shane.

Ivy stood and crossed her arms. "Fire's out already."

The last one—the one she hadn't recognized yet—strode toward her, his eyes narrowed as he took her in.

"Sorry, miss. But we still need to go inside and assess the situation, figure out what type of fire it was, and if you're still at any sort of risk."

She shrugged and cleared her throat, trying to force the tremble out of her voice. "It was an electrical fire. Probably caused by faulty wiring in a mini fridge cord because I had this place inspected a dozen times and know it was up to code. Used a class C extinguisher. I have smart detectors, though. Couldn't get the fire out before you guys were automatically called. Sorry to waste your time."

The fire was out. That wasn't the issue. Fire didn't scare her after the fact, especially now that she was so prepared. It was—*them.* She didn't want them here, didn't need them here, and certainly didn't require anyone's assistance. Just seeing their uniforms made it hard for her to breathe, made it impossible not to think of how Charlie wearing the uniform had cost him his life.

The man in front of her took off his firefighter helmet and ran a hand through a mop of overgrown dark auburn hair. If he weren't wearing the uniform, he'd have been quite handsome. She knew it was backward, that most women found men in uniforms sexy. But there was nothing sexy about a man who risked his life for a living. Noble? Absolutely. That didn't mean she had to find him attractive.

There was something familiar about him, though, even though she swore she'd never met him. Ivy knew just about everyone in town, especially those who worked at the fire station. So who the heck was this stranger?

"You still need to let us inside," he said. "We're not permitted to accept civilian confirmation of fire containment."

Ivy scoffed. "Just tell Chief Burnett it was Ivy's place and that I said everything is fine. He knows me well enough, so that should suffice."

The stranger grinned, but Ivy got the feeling it wasn't because he was happy.

"Chief Burnett is also my new boss, and I don't think he'd take kindly to me slacking off on my first call. But, hey, appreciate the heads-up and the unneeded paperwork I'll have to file when I get back to the station."

Definitely not a happy smile. Well, that made two of them. He wasn't happy to be here, and she wasn't happy to have him here.

He pushed past her and through the front entrance of the store—aptly called Ivy's—while two of his crew assessed the outside of the building's facade and the fourth jogged down to the end of the street and disappeared behind the row of stores that included her own.

"I really do have things under control in here," she called over the continued screech of the multiple alarms. When she received no response, she followed into the back office, where Needed-a-Haircut Man was inspecting the charred cord from the mini fridge and the blackened outlet.

"Don't you turn those off or something?" she yelled, barely able to hear her own voice.

The firefighter stood, pulled off his glove, and climbed onto her office chair. He reached for the smoke detector on the ceiling and pulled it out of its holster. Then he pressed a button, and it and all other alarms ceased.

"Thought you had things under control in here," he said with a self-satisfied grin as he hopped down to the floor, his boots hitting the linoleum tile with a thud.

Her mouth hung open for a second before she regained control.

"I did. I mean, I *do*. The detectors are new. This is the first time I've had to use them." *And I grew up in a firefighter household, thank you very much. So who are you to question what I do and do not have under control?* Of course, she kept all that to herself because her family was her business, but still—this guy had a lot of nerve.

He pointed to a button on the device marked with the word RESET.

"All you have to do is press and hold for five seconds, and they all turn off. But, if you accidentally do the same thing with the TEST button, all alarms will sound for half a minute. So I don't recommend doing that during business hours. Might scare customers away."

Ivy rolled her eyes. "I can read, but thanks for the warning."

"My pleasure," he said, smiling. "I'm gonna grab the rest of the crew so we can do a full assessment on the outlet, check your circuit breaker. Glad to see you're not using power strips."

"It was the *fridge*. I'm sure of it." That was the last time she took a hand-me-down appliance even if it was still under warranty. "Look, Mr...."

"*Lieutenant* Bowen," he said.

Her eyes widened. "What happened to Lieutenants Russo and Heinz?"

"Nothing. Lieutenant Heinz runs his team, and I run mine. Russo's wife got a really great job in Seattle. They're moving at the end of the month. I'm taking over his team. You new in town?"

She scoffed and smoothed out her A-line blue sundress, then straightened the shoulder straps made of small embroidered daisies she had painstakingly created on her sewing machine. It was one of the few items in the shop that was an Ivy Serrano original. Part of her wanted him to notice. The other part called her out on even considering flirting with him. Firefighters were not her type, yet today she seemed to need extra reminders.

"*No*," she said, indignant. "I was born and raised in Meadow Valley, California. Been here all my life. Mostly. But I can't believe I didn't know Jason and Angie were leaving town." She'd been in her own little world the past couple of months getting the shop ready to open. Had she really been so wrapped up in her own life that she'd missed everything happening around her?

"I might be a little out of touch," she admitted. "But I know *you're* not from Meadow Valley."

He chuckled. Even though it was a small smile, this one was genuine, going all the way to the crinkle of his blue eyes. *Not* that she was noticing his eyes. Or how his broad shoulders shook when he laughed. "Just got here last week from Houston. You're very perceptive, Ms...."

She could hear his light accent now. "Serrano," she said. "Ivy Serrano."

He raised a brow. "Any relation to Captain Emilio Serrano, who practically ran the Meadow Valley Fire Station up until a few years go?"

Ivy swallowed and her eyes burned. "Guess you did your homework. Captain Serrano is my father."

The playfulness left the lieutenant's eyes, but his gaze didn't falter. "I'm sorry to hear about your brother. From what I've been told, he was a hell of a lieutenant himself."

"Thank you." It had been two years since Charlie died in the line of duty, but it still felt like she'd found out only five minutes ago. She cleared her throat. "You were saying something about inspecting the outlet?" She was 99 percent sure the outlet was fine, but right now she'd let him and his crew tear apart the drywall if it meant this conversation would end.

"Right," he said. He pressed a button on a small radio clipped to his collar and called for the other three firefighters. "We should be out of here in less than an hour."

She nodded. "Can I still open the store? Today was supposed to be my first day."

"That'll depend on what we figure out after a short investigation," he said.

The three firefighters she knew poured into her office from the back door.

"Hey, Wyatt," she said.

Wyatt O'Brien, always the gentleman, tipped his helmet. "Hey there, Ivy." Then he turned to Lieutenant Bowen. "All clear out back, sir."

The lieutenant nodded. "Thanks, O'Brien."

"This was a waste of time," Shane said, storming past them all and back out front. That was pretty accurate. Wyatt's younger brother always had a bitterness about him that clung tight. Looked like not much had changed.

The lieutenant's jaw tightened, but he didn't say anything.

"Hi, Ivy," Jessie said.

Ivy forced a smile. She'd known Jessie all the young woman's life. But all she could hope when she saw her in uniform was that Casey would never have to go through what Ivy and her family did.

"Heard you're working the front desk at the guest ranch on your off days," Ivy said. *It's safer there. Maybe you'll like it and sign on full-time.*

Jessie nodded. "Those school loans aren't going to pay themselves off." She looked nervously at the lieutenant. "I'll go check on Shane." And she hurried after him.

Ivy pressed her lips together and forced a smile. "Thanks, gentlemen," she said to the two remaining men. "I guess I'll just wait up front and let you do your job."

She blew out a shaky breath and headed back into her unopened shop—past the checkout counter and the table of baked goods and refreshments she'd set up for her very first customers.

All she'd wanted was to start fresh and instead she'd started with a damned fire and four firefighters bursting her bubble of safety.

A small crowd had gathered outside the store, which meant the gossip mill was in full effect.

She knew to fight an electrical fire with a type C extinguisher. But the only way to fight small town gossip was to shift the focus. The last thing she needed was every person in Meadow Valley talking about poor Ivy and how fire had brought tragedy into her life again.

She squared her shoulders and fluffed out her brunette waves, then pushed through the door and out onto the street.

"Nothing to see here, folks! Just a quick inspection before Ivy's doors are officially open."

"I heard sirens!" a man shouted, and Ivy recognized Lonny Tate, the owner of Meadow Valley's Everything Store. Most small towns had a general store or a small supermarket, but not Meadow Valley. Lonny Tate prided himself on carrying everything from toilet plungers to the occasional bottle of Coco Chanel. The only problem was that because the place was a quarter of the size of the Target the next town over, you never knew for sure if what you needed was in stock.

"Was there a fire?" a woman cried. It was Mrs. Davis from the bookstore. "Oh, poor Ivy. Not another fire."

"I'm fine, Mrs. Davis," Ivy said. "Promise."

"If you're fine, then you'll call me Trudy like I've been asking you to do for decades," the woman said with mild exasperation. "The only Mr. Davis I know is my father."

Mrs. Davis—*Trudy*—was practically family to Ivy, so she understood the worry and wanted to put the woman's mind at ease. But *Poor Ivy*? The whole town would be calling her that before long if she didn't set the record straight.

She kicked off her wedge sandals and climbed onto the bench. A hush fell over the growing crowd of Meadow

Valley residents. The town was still abuzz after the annual Fourth of July festival. Ivy had hoped to open up shop before then to capitalize on the event, which was one of their biggest tourist attractions, but—as her good friend irony would have it—her electrical inspection hadn't yet gone through.

"There's no fire," she lied. "Everything is fine. Just a misunderstanding. The store will be open soon. But in the meantime…" She held a hand to one side of her mouth like she was telling them all a secret. "How about that dude ranch on the outskirts of town? I hear we got ourselves some real live cowboys over there."

"Oh!" Mrs. Davis exclaimed. "And I hear they hired that good-looking new fire lieutenant to give some trail tours. Turns out he's a bit of a cowboy himself!"

Suddenly the mumblings changed from the likes of *Poor Ivy* to things like "I've always had a thing for redheads" and "There's nothing sexier than a man on a horse," along with "You mean a redheaded firefighter on a horse."

Funny. Ivy thought the lieutenant's hair was more of a brown with a hint of red. And maybe there was something *slightly* sexy about a rancher on a horse, but not when fighting fires was in the mix. Fire was dangerous. Fire took lives. For the bulk of hers, her family had always worried about her father. But once he hit fifty and still hadn't let any blaze get the best of him, they'd all been lulled into a false sense of security, one that let Ivy and her family believe that Charlie, her brother, would also be immune.

They'd been wrong.

The throng of locals *Oohed*, snapping her back to the present. They weren't looking at her, though. They were looking past her. So she gazed over her shoulder to find the supposed sexy redhead striding through her shop door and out onto the sidewalk, his three cohorts following close behind. While the other firefighters pushed through the crowd and headed back to the truck, Lieutenant Bowen did no such thing.

When he saw her standing on the bench, he crossed his arms and grinned.

"Are you gonna sing or something?" he asked. "And if so, are you taking requests?"

She rolled her eyes.

He thought he was so charming with those blue eyes and that one dimple that made his smile look a little crooked but at the same time really adorable.

Again, all of the *nopes*. Men who played with fire were far from adorable.

"Am I open?" she asked. *Please say yes and then go away.*

"Open for business, Ms. Serrano. Though I think you'll need to retire that pesky appliance of yours."

"You heard the man!" Ivy said. "We are open for business!"

She hopped off the bench, slid back into her shoes, and held open the door, ushering much of the crowd inside.

"So," she said. "I was right?"

He nodded once. "You were right. But it's still my job to make sure."

"And it's *my* job to sell the stuff in there, so I better head back inside," she said. "Thank you, by the way. I know what you do is important. I just wish I could have caught the alarm before you all had to gear up and head over here."

He shrugged. "Beats pulling kittens from trees."

She laughed. He was funny. If he weren't wearing all that gear and the uniform underneath...But he was.

"You obviously haven't met Mrs. Davis yet," Ivy said. "She fosters kittens when she's not at the bookshop. And she's got a big old oak in front of her house. I'm sure you'll hear from her sooner rather than later."

"I'll consider myself warned." He glanced up and down the street, then back at her. "So what do people do around here for fun?"

Her brows furrowed. "I hear there's a new firefighter in town who leads trail rides at the guest ranch. Maybe you can look into that."

He chuckled. "Checking up on me already, are you?"

She brushed her hands off on her skirt. "Not sure how much you know about small towns, Lieutenant, but around here we don't need to check up. Information is pretty easy to come by, especially when someone new takes up residence."

"Okay, then. When I'm not riding trails or saving kittens, what do you suggest? What are *you* doing tonight?"

She shook her head. "Oh no. I don't date firefighters."

He leaned in close and whispered in her ear, "I wasn't asking for a date, Serrano. Tonight's my first night off since I got to town. Just figured if you were going out, it might mean you knew a thing or two about where someone might let off a little steam."

His warm breath tickled her ear, and a chill ran down her spine.

"Midtown Tavern," she said. "It's the only place open after eight o'clock."

She didn't wait for a response. Instead she headed into the safety of her shop and headed straight for the thermostat.

It was getting hot in here.

CHAPTER TWO

Even though he'd technically had a few nights off in his first week in town, as a new lieutenant—who'd beat someone on his team for the job—he wanted to hang around the station, get the lay of the land, and hopefully ingratiate himself to those who saw him as an interloper. Chief Burnett wanted to keep it under wraps who it was that lost the position to Carter. Regardless, things were tense. And it was never easy being the odd man out.

He'd had a good job back home at the Houston Fire Department. It was the *home* part of the equation that made leaving so easy. There was nothing like a father who disapproved of your life choices. Carter's solution? He left when opportunity presented itself.

Now here he was, a stranger in a strange land who didn't even have a place to live, which meant the firehouse bunk room was the closest thing to home for the time being.

He checked his watch. It was six o'clock on a Saturday evening, and aside from a trail ride he was leading at the Meadow Valley Ranch tomorrow morning, he had the next forty-eight hours off.

"Hey," he said to Wyatt and Shane, the two guys on his team. "What's the best place to go around here to get a burger and a beer?"

"Midtown Tavern," the two said in unison as they stared at the rec room television watching a baseball game that was *not* the Astros, so he didn't care what it was. But it looked like the consensus was in on nightlife in Meadow Valley. He nodded his thanks to the other two men, whose gazes stayed glued to the screen.

He shrugged, assumed the T-shirt and jeans he'd changed into was proper attire, and headed for the station's front door.

The sun shone over First Street like it was still high noon, which made it easy to spot his destination—right in the middle of the main block. He laughed. *Midtown Tavern* was quite literally *mid* town.

He crossed the street and strolled past the inn. Pearl, the owner—and Carter's great-aunt—had offered him a room when he'd first arrived in town, but he'd preferred the station. She was the reason he was here—the reason he'd learned about an opening for a new lieutenant and possibly part of the reason the chief had even considered an outsider, but both Carter and Pearl were doing their best to keep that under wraps until his one-month trial period was over.

"Secrets don't stay buried for too long around here," Pearl had told him. "So make sure they all realize how good you are at doing what you do before they have a chance to claim favoritism."

Carter knew he was good at his job. Damn good. *That* was why the chief had brought him in and why he was in the running—along with the other lieutenant— to be the next captain when the chief retired in a couple of years. This was it. One false move, and he would have to start from square one again at another station. He couldn't go back to his job in Houston. And truth be told, he needed this distance from home. Going back wasn't an option.

So he was bent on proving himself to everyone at the station, which meant no mistakes, no distractions, and no reason for anyone to say he got the job because of who he knew rather than because of his long list of qualifications.

He passed the Everything Store and chuckled at the signs advertising a flash sale on vegetable peelers in one corner of the window and the release of a romance novel in the other corner.

He sure wasn't in Houston anymore.

It might have looked like noon outside, but when he stepped through the doors of Meadow Valley's Midtown Tavern, it was officially Saturday night.

He grinned at the dark wooden tables and booths that framed a square bar in the center of the space. *This* was what he needed. A place to unwind and mix with the residents of what he hoped to be his new hometown.

He grabbed an empty stool at the bar and cleared his throat to get the attention of the woman behind it. Her back was to him as she typed something into a cash register, so all he could see was the dark ponytail that swished across the back of a black T-shirt that said MIDTOWN SLUGGERS in a baseball-style yellow font. The pockets of her jeans were painted with what looked like pink lily flowers. *Not* that he was paying special attention to the pocket area of her clothing. The vibrant art simply drew his eyes.

His eyes widened when she turned to face him, a receipt and a few bills in her hand.

"Serrano," he said. "And here I thought you owned a clothing store."

She smiled, not at him but at the older man on the stool next to him. "Here's your change, Lonny."

The man waved her off. "Keep it, Ivy. Put it toward repairing the damage from the fire." He shook his head. "Such a shame something like that had to happen on opening day."

Ivy leaned over the bar. "*Nothing* happened, Lonny. The shop opened. I sold a bunch of stuff. There's nothing to repair, but I *will* accept your tip because I was an excellent server."

She brushed off her hands and turned her attention to Carter.

"Evening, Lieutenant. Yes, I do own a clothing store. But sometimes I help out around here."

"You got a thing for flowers?" he asked, remembering the dress she was wearing earlier that day, the straps made of daisies. Or maybe it was *she* who stood out in his mind's eye, and the memory of what she wore simply followed.

Another woman sidled up to Ivy before she could answer, nudging her out of the way with her hip so she could get to the beer tap. "This is the new guy?" she said to Ivy while looking straight at Carter.

"Sure is," Ivy said.

"You're right," the other woman said, blowing blue-streaked bangs out of her eyes. "Totally not as sexy as everyone keeps saying."

Ivy backhanded the other woman on the shoulder. "*Casey!*"

Casey laughed. "Thanks for covering for me while I took that call. I'm good here, so you can—you know—punch out or whatever."

"You don't *pay* me," Ivy said, rolling her eyes.

Casey finished pouring the beer and winked. "Yeah, but I let you drink for free. And I'll add a bonus. You can take *Dreamboat's* order." Then she disappeared around the corner to deliver the drink to a patron on the other side of the bar.

Ivy's jaw tightened, and then she smiled what Carter guessed was her patented customer-service smile. "Yes, I like flowers," she said matter-of-factly. "What can I get for you, Lieutenant?"

"I'm off duty," he said. "You can call me Carter."

"Sure," she said. "Now, what can I get you, *Lieutenant?*"

He laughed. She sure was determined *not* to like him, which was fine by him. It didn't matter that he'd been attracted to her the second he'd hopped out of the truck in front of her store. He could have a drink, blow off a little steam, but that was it. No other distractions.

"I'll have whatever's on tap," he said. "How about you choose?"

She grabbed a beer and filled it with a dark wheat beer, then slid it across the bar to him.

"I didn't call you a dreamboat," she said. "Just for the record."

He nodded. "But there was talk of my sexiness, or I guess lack thereof?"

She shook her head and gave him a haughty lift of her chin. "*No.* I mean, I just don't get what all the fuss is about. So you're cute in a uniform and can supposedly hold your own on a horse. It's not like it's newsworthy." She looked around the bar and rolled her eyes. "Although not much happens in Meadow Valley, so I guess around here it is."

She poured another beer, then took a sip before setting it down. She glanced down each side of the bar, pursing her lips at the occupied stools.

Carter cleared his throat. "There's an empty stool right here." He nodded to the vacant seat on his left. They could sit next to each other and have an innocent beer, right?

She blew out a breath. "Yeah, I know, but—"

"But there's an empty stool. You obviously need a place to sit. You don't even have to talk to me." He took another pull of his beer. "I'm perfectly happy to drink alone."

Ivy groaned, set her beer down next to his, then disappeared the same way Casey had gone. A few seconds later she appeared next to him, hopped on the stool, and took a good long swig from her own mug as she stared straight ahead, not sparing him a glance.

"This is good," she said more to herself than anyone else. "Drinking alone, just me and my thoughts." She sighed. "Me and *my*self."

Carter stifled a laugh. "You don't do alone, do you?" he asked.

She finally shifted her gaze to him. "I do alone just fine. Quiet, though. Quiet isn't my thing."

He laughed out loud this time. "You're in a noisy tavern."

She threw up her hands. "I'm a talker, okay? An extrovert. I get energized by being around others, by interacting with them. If I were sitting over there?" She pointed to the side of the bar on Carter's right. "Lonny and his fishing buddies would be telling me all about what they caught today, and I'd tell them how the highlight of my day was *not*, in fact, the fire but the grand opening of my very own store." She directed him to the row of patrons on the side to their left, a group of women who looked to be about the same age as his mom. "If I were hanging with the knitting guild, we could talk design and what kind of pieces I'm thinking of making for the store when the colder months roll in."

"But instead you're stuck next to me," he said matter-of-factly.

"Exactly." She gasped, her hand covering her mouth. "I didn't mean it like *that*."

But she did, didn't she? And he should be relieved she wanted nothing to do with him, but instead he was— disappointed.

"So you think I'm cute in my uniform?" he asked, brow raised. What was he doing? He wasn't sure, but the urge to flirt with her just sort of took over.

"Of course not," she insisted.

"Like, kitten-hanging-from-a-branch-in-Mrs. Davis's-tree cute?" he added.

"No one is *that* cute." She snorted and took another sip of her beer. "By the way, I'm simply enjoying a drink after a long day. I know you weren't asking me out earlier. This doesn't mean anything. You just happen to be sitting next to the only free seat. So let's just forget whatever this is." She motioned between them.

So they were in agreement. There was *something* between them. Something neither of them wanted, but something nonetheless.

He laughed. "Wow. And here I thought your sunny disposition meant you were a people person." He threw back the rest of his drink.

"I *am* sunny... with the right company."

She buried her face in her mug, catching up with him.

"Yeah," he said with a laugh. "About as sunny as a box of kittens."

"You really have a thing for kittens, don't you?" she asked.

"Actually, I'm allergic. You were saying?"

"I wasn't saying *anything*, just that this isn't anything more than two locals drinking a beer at a pub. My opinion of you in your uniform is irrelevant, as is what you think of me. Not that I'm assuming you think anything of me at all or that you're any more or less attracted to me than I am to you. I'm not—by the way—attracted to you." She rolled her eyes, but it seemed more at herself than at him.

"Oh, I'm attracted to *you*, Ivy Serrano," he admitted. "But I don't want to date you."

Her mouth fell open, but she didn't get a chance to respond. A second later, Casey appeared from around the corner carrying a liquor bottle and three shot glasses.

"You know if I comply with your request, I'm enabling you, right?" Casey said.

Ivy nodded. "But a *fire* on grand opening day. Of all things. It destroyed more than my fridge. Got my latest sketches too."

"The ones with the—"

Ivy interrupted Casey's question with another nod. The two women had a language all their own—an immediate understanding between two people who knew each other better than anyone else. He'd had a friend like that once. He also knew loss not unlike Ivy's. How similar they were. If they'd met under any other circumstances... But they hadn't. There was also the issue of her not exactly supporting his career. That was an automatic deal breaker no matter how attractive she was.

Casey blew out a breath, lined up the three shot glasses, and filled them all with a light brown liquid.

Carter lifted his glass and sniffed. "That is *not* whiskey."

Casey shook her head. "No, Lieutenant, it is *not*. It's Ivy's favorite, apple pie liqueur." She groaned, then stared at her friend. "You know it actually pains me to say liqu*eur* instead of liquor, right?"

Ivy smiled. "I know. But it's also how I know you love me." She lifted her glass, her big brown eyes softening as they fixed on Carter's. "You know who my family is, which means you also know I have nothing but respect and admiration for what you and everyone else in that firehouse does. You save kittens and you save lives, and that's a really big thing. But you also risk your own lives, and I've already lost enough for this lifetime."

Casey grimaced at her shot glass. "She, Charlie, and I used to sneak this crap from her parents' liquor cabinet when we were teens. *My* tastes matured. Hers have not."

"To Charlie," Ivy said, and Carter guessed her brother was exactly the reason why she still drank the stuff he couldn't believe he was about to drink. Despite bad timing and the surety that nothing could happen between him and Ivy Serrano, he couldn't ignore the warmth that spread through him at being included in such an intimate act—toasting a loved one who'd been lost in the line of duty.

"To Charlie," he and Casey said together. Then all three of them drank.

The gravity of the moment was quickly lost once his taste buds caught on to what was happening.

"That was *terrible*," Carter said.

"I know," Casey replied.

"One more!" Ivy exclaimed.

Casey shook her head but poured her friend another. Ivy quickly threw back the shot, narrowed her eyes at the almost-empty bottle, then snatched it from her friend.

"Serrano...," Casey said with brows raised.

Ivy looked at her imploringly, her brown eyes wide and her lips pressed together in an exaggerated frown.

Casey relented, and Ivy poured and drank the remaining shot.

"Something stronger for you?" Casey asked him. "She doesn't usually drink like this," she whisper-shouted with one hand covering her mouth.

"I don't usually drink like this," Ivy parroted, her eyes narrowed at her friend. "But today kinda caught me off guard." She turned her attention to Carter. "Anyway, three is good luck, right?"

He held his hand over the top of his shot glass and shook his head in response to Casey's question. "It's my first full day on the ranch tomorrow. How about a burger," he said. "Hear they're pretty good around here."

Casey shrugged. "Probably because it's the only place to get one around here. You want something a little more gourmet—and I stress the *little*—head on over to Pearl's inn. Otherwise, I got you covered."

He laughed and guessed there was some friendly competition between the two main eateries in town. Because if there was one thing he knew for sure, his great-aunt's recipes were a force to be reckoned with. But he was steering clear of Pearl's during the busy hours, and a burger sure did sound good.

"Then I'll have a burger with everything and fries." He nodded toward Ivy. "She should probably eat something, too." He knew a thing or two about some days catching you off guard. Life was funny that way. It never waited for you to prepare for the worst before the worst got handed to you on a silver platter.

"This isn't a date, by the way," she told her friend as she pointed at Carter and then herself. "He finds me attractive but doesn't want to date me, and *I* don't date firefighters, so we have an accord." She hiccupped.

Casey raised her eyebrows. "An accord? Did you two write a treaty or something when I wasn't looking?"

"I'll have my usual, please," Ivy said, ignoring her friend's ribbing.

Casey winked. "A burger and fries for the gentleman and fried pickles for the lady who are on an *accord* and not a date."

She reached behind the bar and grabbed a tumbler glass, then used the soda gun to fill it with water. "In the meantime, drink this." She set the water down in front of Ivy, who pouted but did as she was told. Then Casey headed out from behind the bar and back toward the kitchen.

"You okay?" he asked.

She nodded, then swayed in her seat.

"Whoa," he said, catching her before she toppled off the side of the stool. "Maybe we should switch to a booth so we don't have another emergency today."

She nodded again, then let him help her down. She wasn't quite steady on her feet either, so he wrapped an arm around her torso and carried her water in his free hand as they made their way to an empty booth. She didn't object but instead responded by wrapping her arm around him.

His palm rested on her hip, and he had the distinct urge

to rub his thumb along the curve of her waist. He didn't act on it. But holy hell he wanted to.

Once she was situated in the booth, he slid into the seat across from her. Then he nodded at her half-empty glass.

"Drink more of that." He ran a hand through his hair. He really needed a cut. "You eat anything at all today?"

She drank, both hands wrapped around the glass, and shook her head. When she'd drained the contents, she set the glass down and swiped her forearm across her water mustache.

Damn she was cute. There was nothing wrong with thinking that or wanting to sober her up so he could keep her sitting across from him for as long as this night went on, was there? It was nothing more than two strangers getting to know each other, and where was the harm in that?

"The day just sort of got away from me," she said. "The fridge fire, the first day of the store being open—I kind of forgot to schedule myself a lunch break. I might need to hire on an assistant or something, but the store has to make some money first."

Carter caught Casey looking for them at the bar and waved her over to their booth.

"Pickles were up first," she said. "Figured you wouldn't want me to wait."

Ivy's brown eyes lit up. "Did I ever tell you you're my bestest friend in the whole wide world?"

Casey nodded. "Once or twice."

Ivy pointed at her friend but looked at Carter. "Isn't she beautiful? She broke *all* the hearts in high school, especially Boone Murphy's. Do you know they almost got married?"

For a second Casey looked stricken, but then she laughed. "And now he's getting married, so everything worked out for the best. Speaking of work, I'm closing, which means I need some backup in the friend department." She glanced at Carter. "Can you make sure she gets home okay? It's a short walk from here, ten minutes tops."

Carter nodded. "I'm on it."

Ivy dipped a fried pickle slice into a small bowl of ranch, took a bite, and sighed.

"See?" she said, chewing. "Now I have my best friend and my new friend. Today wasn't so bad after all."

"Atta girl," Casey said, patting her friend on the top of her head. "Also, nothing other than water for you for the rest of the night. You're supposed to open at noon tomorrow, and you don't want to miss the Sunday out-of-towners who want to go home with an Ivy original."

Ivy gave Casey a salute then went back to her pickles.

"Be back with your burger in a minute," she told Carter. "Want another beer?"

He leaned back in his booth and shook his head. "Just a soda," he said. "Coke or Pepsi. Whatever you got."

A second later it was only the two of them again.

"I don't have much of a tolerance," Ivy said.

Carter laughed. "Yeah. I sort of figured that out."

"Thanks for walking me to the table," she added.

"Mind if I try one of those?" he asked, eyeing her food. "If you're looking for a way to repay me, food always works."

Ivy shook her head. "I guess I can spare one. You did keep me from butt-planting or face-planting at the bar. Not sure which it would have been."

He snagged a pickle disk, dipped it in the ranch, and popped it in his mouth.

"Mmm," he said. "Those aren't half bad. And it would have been a butt-plant, judging from the angle of your sway."

Ivy blew out a breath, and a rogue lock of hair that had fallen out of her ponytail blew with it. "I'm not usually half in the bag before seven o'clock," she said. "Today was just—"

"One of those days," he said, finishing her sentence. "I get it. No need to explain. And the pickles and water seem to be helping you crawl back out of that bag, so no worries."

She smiled, and he was sure in that instant that Casey wasn't the only one breaking hearts when they were teens. He'd bet the last fried pickle that her smile alone had devastated a heart or two along the way.

"Food and water," she said with a shrug. "Who knew they were so much better for you than three shots and a beer?"

Casey took a break for dinner and ate with them. When they finished their food and Casey headed back behind the bar, Ivy insisted they head back as well.

"I don't want to hold up a four-top when there's only two of us," she said.

But he knew the truth. She didn't want to be alone with him because that would have been like a date, even if it wasn't. And though he knew that was the right thing to do—to keep Casey as their buffer—he'd have stayed at that table alone with her if she'd wanted. He'd have stayed until the tavern closed, if only to avoid the inevitable for as long as possible—saying good night to Ivy Serrano and good morning to a reality that didn't include terrible liquor or fried pickles or the woman he hadn't stopped thinking about since walking through her shop door that morning. She was beautiful, yes. But she was also strong-willed and funny. What it boiled down to, though, was that simply being in her presence made him forget the stress of the job, of being a new person in an unfamiliar place he hoped to call his permanent home.

He was in big trouble.

Carter had played with fire plenty in his line of work, but never had he felt more in danger of getting burned.

CHAPTER THREE

The sun had finally dipped below the horizon when they left the tavern two hours later. While country music blared inside the bar, as soon as the door closed behind them, all Ivy could hear was the buzz of the cicadas and the occasional chirp of a cricket.

"Wow," Carter said, looking up and down the street. "This place really does shut down at night, doesn't it?"

"Did you live in Houston proper?" she asked. "I imagine this is a far cry from city life. Spent some time in Boston when Charlie and Allison first had the baby and then again after he…" She cut herself off and shook her head.

Charlie had thought their parents would flip when he told them he was moving to the East Coast to be near Allison's family. Instead they'd seen it as an adventure—a reason to travel more—especially with their father nearing retirement. Ivy hadn't expected them to move there permanently, but then no one expected Charlie to die. After that, her parents couldn't leave the place where their son was buried, and Ivy couldn't blame them. "It's like it's happening for the first time every time I think of it. I wonder if it will ever get any easier."

They walked slowly, Carter seemingly careful to keep his hands in his pockets, which she appreciated. If his pinky accidentally brushed hers, she might do something stupid, like hook her finger around his.

Why had it been so easy to mention Charlie's name with a man who was a stranger before this morning? To share a sacred shot of apple pie liqueur and even her fried pickles? Opening day was a success, but she couldn't get past how it had started, with a fire and the reminder of what she'd lost. And here was this man who was the embodiment of that loss, and he'd somehow made it better.

"Couldn't you have been a jerk instead of a perfect gentleman?" she mumbled.

"Did you say something?" he asked.

She turned her head toward him, her eyes wide. "What? *No.* Cicadas," she said, protesting a bit too much.

"Cicadas," he mused. "Sure thing, Serrano."

She shifted her gaze back to the sidewalk and tried to ignore the charming lilt of his accent. They ambled along the sidewalk to where it looked like the street hit a dead end at the trees, but she kept on to the right and led him to a small residential area where most of the Meadow Valley locals lived if they weren't farmers or ranchers.

"It'll always hurt," he said as they slowed around the curve. "But after a while the hurt has a harder time clawing its way to the surface. It gets covered up by the good memories of the person you lost and eventually by new joy you let into your life—when you're ready, of course."

She stopped, shoved her hands in the back pockets of her own jeans, and turned to face him.

She stared at him for several long seconds. They were the only two people outside at the moment, but the way he looked at her made it feel like the quiet street was their own little world. If he were anyone else—if he *did* anything else for a living other than risking his life—she would... What would she do? The only relationship Ivy'd had for the past two years was with her own grief. She still wrapped it around herself like a blanket—a reminder to protect her heart from ever having to go through that again.

"You ever lose someone close to you?" she finally asked.

He nodded once but hesitated before saying more.

"It's okay," she said, breaking the silence. "You don't have to tell me. It helps enough simply knowing when people understand."

He cleared his throat. "We already shared my first emergency since coming to town, my first taste of fried pickles, and my first and *last* shot of apple pie liqueur. Why not share personal loss as well?"

His attempt at humor would have sounded callous if she couldn't tell it was a defense mechanism. She was an expert there.

"I'm all ears," she said.

He shrugged. "I was an idiot kid who got in the car after a party with a buddy who shouldn't have been driving. But because I'd been drinking, too, I believed him when he said he was okay to drive. Made it all the way to my street before he lost control and wrapped the car around a light post. Front end caught fire. I got out—and he didn't."

He said the words so quickly and matter-of-factly, like it was the only way he could get them out. It didn't stop her heart from aching, or the tears from pooling in her eyes. He more than understood what she'd been through yet hadn't said a word all night while she'd cocooned herself in her grief blanket tighter than she had in months.

She reached for him but pulled her hand away before making contact. This was too much. Their connection kept getting harder to ignore. She had to make a concerted effort to keep him at arm's length.

"I'm so sorry, Carter. I—you—this whole night you were so nice to me, and I had no idea that—"

There were no right words for wanting to wrap him in her arms while also wanting to run as far from him as possible.

"Hey there," he said, resting a palm on her cheek and wiping away a tear with his thumb.

She shook her head and stepped back, hating herself for doing it. But all she had left was self-preservation, and Lieutenant Carter Bowen was the biggest threat to it.

He cleared his throat, taking a step back himself. "It was more than a decade ago. And I meant what I said. It does get easier. I can talk about Mason now—remember how he was the best at making people laugh, even our teachers. He kicked the winning field goal at our homecoming game junior year. And he had a real future planned, you know? Football was going to take him to college, but he wanted to be a doctor. A pediatrician, actually." Carter laughed. "*He* was the one on the straight and narrow path while I cut class more often than I went."

Her eyes widened. "I don't believe that for a second."

He forced a smile.

"It's true. I never cut for the sake of cutting. It was always for work. My brothers and I knew from the time we were young that our future was already mapped out. After graduation, my two older brothers went to work at my old man's auto body shop. I was supposed to do the same. It wasn't like there was money for college for three kids, least of all the youngest." He shrugged. "I accepted my fate like my brothers had—until Mason died."

Ivy crossed her arms tight over her chest, the urge to touch him—to comfort him—almost more than she could bear. "You changed direction after the accident," she said. It wasn't a question. She knew.

He nodded. "Much to my father's dissatisfaction, but I was done letting others make decisions for me, especially when I know better than anyone else what's right for me."

"What about your mom?" she asked, tentatively.

"She was sort of caught in the middle. She understood us both but wasn't about to take sides. So I got my grades up senior year. Did two years at community college, got my EMT certification, then took out a loan so I could finish my bachelor's in fire science."

"So fighting fires is your penance for surviving when Mason didn't?"

He shook his head. "Maybe it started that way, but the more I learned, the more I realized I could help people in all sorts of capacities. Even did some presentations at local schools about my firsthand experience being in the car with someone under the influence. I hope to set up a similar program in Meadow Valley and neighboring areas."

She let out a shaky breath. "You're a good man, Carter.

Your father should be proud of you. I hope he comes around someday." Ivy dropped her hands to her sides. "I'm only a few more minutes this way. You can head back if you want."

He glanced up at the star-studded sky, then back at her. "Don't really have anywhere to be. Plus, I promised Casey, and I don't want to get on the bad side of the person who runs the one nighttime establishment around here."

She shrugged. "Suit yourself."

But she smiled softly as she turned away from him and strode toward the bend in the road. The safest thing she could do was put as much distance between herself and Carter Bowen as possible, but a few more minutes with him by her side wouldn't hurt anyone.

He didn't say anything for the rest of walk, letting her silently lead him to her porch, where she stopped short of the front door and pivoted to face him once again.

"Can I ask you something?" he finally said.

"Okay," she answered.

He scratched the back of his neck, avoiding her eyes for a moment, then squared his shoulders and set his blue-eyed gaze right at her.

"I've dated plenty. Some relationships got more serious than others, but I've never told a woman about Mason until tonight, and it hasn't even been twelve hours since I met you, Ivy Serrano. Why do you suppose that is?"

Because, Lieutenant, there's an undeniable connection between us.

Because, Lieutenant, if I believed in such a thing, I'd say we were kindred spirits.

Because, Lieutenant, it feels like it's been more than twelve hours. If it didn't sound so crazy, I'd say I felt like I've known you all my life.

But it wouldn't help either of them to say any of that. So she swallowed the knot in her throat. "Because, Lieutenant, I'm simply a good listener. It's my blessing—and maybe my curse. People like to tell me things they wouldn't tell anyone else. I guess I just have one of those faces." She shrugged, hoping it would sell the lie. "I wouldn't read any more into it than that."

Except that I'm a liar, and I want to kiss you, and you scare me, Lieutenant.

She finally gave in and skimmed her fingers along the hair at his temples and where it curled up above his ear. She couldn't let the night end without any sort of contact, hoping he understood this was the most she could allow herself to give.

"You need a trim," she said. "I could do it. Casey went to cosmetology school right after high school. She used to practice on Charlie, even taught me how to do a simple cut."

He laughed. "And here I thought you were going to break your own rules and do something crazy."

"Like what?" she asked, but she knew. She wouldn't be the one to say it, though. *She* wouldn't break the rules.

"Like kiss me," he said. And even though he was teasing her, hearing the words out loud made her realize how much she wanted them to be true.

Her cheeks flushed. "I don't date firefighters, Lieutenant. And you made it very clear that you don't want to date me."

"Good. Then we're both on the same page. I can't let anything get in the way of work right now. My future rides on everything that happens in the next month. Plus, I've already dated a woman or two who either couldn't handle the hours I worked or the risks I took. I won't change who I am, not for my father and not for any woman, even if it means missing out on something great. On *someone* great. No matter how much you bat those big brown eyes at me."

"I do *not* bat my lashes," she insisted. "Wait, what did you just say?"

She stood there, eyes wide, for a long moment as everything he said registered. Then she held out her right hand.

"Friends, then?" she said, the word leaving a bitter taste in her mouth. But it was all she could offer and all that it seemed he'd be willing to take.

He wrapped his hand around hers, his calloused palm sending a shock of electricity up her arm as he shook.

"Friends it is."

"Well then," she said. "I'm around after five tomorrow if you want that haircut. No charge, of course. Just a favor from one friend to another."

He nodded once, then let her hand go. "Appreciate the offer. I'll get back to you on that. Good night, Ms. Serrano."

"Good night, Lieutenant."

He flashed her a grin, spun on his heel, and then headed off the way he had come.

Ivy leaned against her door and let out a long, shaky breath.

"Friends," she said to herself. "*Friends*."

If she said it enough, she *might* even it believe it was true.

CHAPTER FOUR

Ivy went through the store, checking all outlets. even though she hadn't used any up front. You never could be too careful. Then she went to the back office, where she checked on her new battery-powered mini fridge and powered down and unplugged her laptop. She went to her design table, where she'd been trying out a new pattern, hated.it, and went at it with the seam ripper, then unplugged the sewing machine as well. Then she scanned the small space twice, made sure the circuit breaker looked up to snuff, and locked the back door. Once over the threshold and into the store, she doubled back one more time to make extra sure she hadn't left an unknown fire hazard behind.

It was a quarter past five. She remembered her offer to Carter the night before. It had been in the back of her mind the entire day. One minute she hoped she'd make it home to find him waiting on her doorstep while the next minute she prayed he'd forgotten the whole thing.

Why had she even put the offer out there? A hair-cut, one-on-one? It was almost as intimate as kissing. It wasn't like she could blame it on the alcohol. By the time he'd walked her home, she was as sober as could be. But the things she'd confided in him about losing Charlie—and what he'd told her about Mason? She'd connected with him in a way she hadn't anticipated.

Shake it off and move on, she said to herself as she turned off all the lights in the shop. *You get close to someone like that and you'll never find peace.* It was why she'd established her rule. And it wasn't just firefighters but police officers, too. She had the utmost admiration for those who put their lives before others, but she couldn't fall for someone like that. No way. No how.

When she'd finally satisfied herself that the shop was safe to leave for the night, she hoisted her bag over her shoulder and slipped out the front door and locked it behind her. After spinning toward the sidewalk to walk home, she gasped to find Carter Bowen leaning against a dusty, beat-up red Ford F-250.

"Evening, Ivy," he said. "Didn't mean to scare you."

She shook her head, half hoping she simply needed to clear her vision and it would be Shane or Wyatt or any other guy she didn't think about kissing the second she saw them. But nope, it was Carter Bowen all right. *Lieutenant* Carter Bowen. And tonight he was wearing a blue-and-white-plaid shirt rolled to the elbows, jeans that looked about as old as his truck, and dirt-caked work boots.

Shoot. He looked as good in clothes that should probably be marched straight to the washer as he did in his uniform. He'd have to take said dirty clothes off, and she'd bet he also looked pretty darn good—

Stop it, Ivy. You aren't doing yourself any favors letting your mind go there.

"Ivy?" Carter said, and she realized she had not offered him any sort of verbal response yet.

"Lieutenant. Hi. What are you doing here?"

He crossed his arms. "First, when I'm not in uniform, Carter will do just fine. Second, are we going to do that thing where we act like you didn't invite me around last night for something as innocent as a haircut?" He ran a hand across the stubble on his jaw. "Could probably use a shave, too. Don't suppose that's included with the cut?"

She swallowed, her throat suddenly dry. "I'm not pretending anything," she said. "Guess I was expecting you at my house, though, rather than outside my shop. My trimmer and barber shears are back at home."

He shrugged. "It's early yet. Sun won't go down for another few hours. Figured we could take a ride first, show you the trail I rode with some ranch guests earlier today. It's real pretty, and there's a great view when you get to the hill. Though I have to admit the view's pretty good right where I am now."

She rolled her eyes and fidgeted with the messy bun on top of her head. Today she wore a chambray linen tunic that had wrinkled the second she'd put it on, but she loved it anyway. It was so comfortable and looked great with her floral leggings and black moto boots. Comfort all around. Maybe she'd been sober when she'd gotten home last night, but that didn't mean waking up this morning was easy after putting away four drinks the evening before. She hadn't had it in her to wear wedges today.

"With corny pickup lines like that, it's a wonder you're still single. Wait, you are single, right? Not that it matters. I mean it might matter to *other* women, but not to *me*."

She winced. She was about as smooth as sandpaper.

Carter grinned. "I'm single. Not that it *matters*, since we are just friends. Is that a yes to the ride, then?"

She opened her mouth, then closed it.

"Everything okay?" he asked. "You said you were free after five. It's after five. It's not too hot, now that the sun is headed west…"

Not too hot. Ha. He was funny. Carter Bowen was an actual riot. Had he looked in a mirror? He was hot on a stick dipped in hot sauce. That was part of the problem. His overall charm didn't help either.

She rolled her eyes again and groaned.

"Okay now I feel like I missed a whole conversation," he said.

She laughed. "Only what's going on in my head. And trust me, you do not want access to what's in there."

He pushed off the side of the truck and took a step toward her. "May I?" he asked, lifting her bag off her shoulder.

"Um, sure," she said.

Now that he had her stuff, she guessed she had no choice but to go with him. Her house keys were in that bag, which meant she was practically stranded. That was sound logic, wasn't it?

He opened the passenger door and held out a hand to help her climb in. She plopped down onto a black leather seat with a stitched-up tear down the middle. The interior was clean as could be, but the dashboard looked like something out of an old movie. There was no USB port and a very minimal digital display for the radio.

When Carter climbed into the driver's seat and pulled his door shut, she gasped.

"Is that a tape deck?" she asked.

He nodded. "Works, too."

"Wait a minute," she said, brushing a hand over the dashboard. "Does this thing even have airbags? Because I'm not sure if you remember my safety setup in the shop, but I don't do risk."

He laughed. "The truck's old, but it's not ancient. Twenty years never looked so good on another vehicle."

She put one hand on the door handle, threatening to get out. "You didn't answer my question, Lieutenant."

He cocked a brow. "I'm not in uniform, Ivy. See how easily I bypassed the Ms. Serrano? I bet you can do it, too."

She sighed. "I can call you by your name." Except that meant they were dispensing with formalities, which also meant they were—what? They'd agreed on friends, but this little after-work activity already felt like something more.

"That's funny," he said. "Because I didn't hear you say it."

"Please, *Carter*, can you confirm that this vehicle is safe by today's standards?" She smirked.

He laughed. "*Yes*. There are airbags. It has four-wheel drive if we ever get stuck in the mud or—highly unlikely for this time of year—snow. Hell, it even has working seat belts. You forget I'm the son of a mechanic. I know a thing or two about maintaining a vehicle."

She pulled her seat belt over her shoulder and clicked it into place, then crossed her arms over her chest. "Tease me all you want, but there's no reason to ride in a death trap when I can walk almost anywhere I need to go around here. Plus, it's enough that you do what you do for a living. The least I can do is make sure you're cruising around town in something safe."

He laughed harder this time. "*Cruising*? Darlin', you

don't cruise in a machine like this. You ride, drive, and sometimes even tow, but wherever you're going, it's always with a purpose. Cruising is aimless, and I am anything but."

Damn he was sure of himself. In any other man, that quality would be sexy as all get-out. But she didn't want Carter Bowen to be sexy as anything.

He put the key in the ignition and shifted the truck into drive. She expected the tailpipe to backfire or the car to lurch forward, but the engine purred quietly as Carter maneuvered smoothly onto the street.

"It's been a few years since I've been on a horse," she said, her heart rate increasing. It wasn't because she was afraid of riding, though. It was being next to him, the thrum of anticipation, but of what she couldn't say. If he'd have kept to the plan and come over for a haircut, she'd have been in control. But Carter Bowen was literally at the wheel, and Ivy had no idea what came next. "Used to ride every summer at sleepaway camp," she continued. With her big brother, Charlie. There he was again, creeping into her thoughts and reminding her of what unbearable loss felt like. Her throat grew tight, and she hoped Carter would fill the silence while she pushed the hurt back into its hiding space.

"Well," he said with a grin. "This is your lucky day. Because in addition to this morning, I've been riding my whole life. My father may be all about cars, but my mother is a rancher's daughter. We spent a lot of time on my grandad's ranch growing up, and our mama made sure we could all handle ourselves on the back of a horse."

This made her smile, the thought of a young Carter and his big brothers, ribbing each other like brothers do, riding around a ranch.

"Sounds like you and your family were really close growing up," she said.

He nodded. "My father always preferred four wheels to four legs, but he managed." His jaw tightened, and his smile faded.

"I feel like there's another *but* in there somewhere," she said.

He blew out a long breath. "He makes a good enough living doing what he does. My brothers do, too. And for a long time I was fine with following along." He shrugged. "Meant I didn't have to take school too seriously and it meant my parents weren't breathing down my neck about grades and stuff like that as long as I was serious about the auto shop. And I was."

She laid a hand on his forearm and gave him a gentle squeeze. "But it wasn't important to you."

He shook his head. "I'd trade everything to have Mason back, even if it meant fixing cars the rest of my life. But I know now that something would have always felt like it was missing if that was the path I took. I wish I'd figured out what I was meant to do in a different way, you know? But I'm happy where I am now. What I do means something to me, just like I'm sure what you do means something to you."

Her hand slid off his arm and back into her lap. "I have a degree in fashion design," she said. "The stuff I sell in the shop comes from a lot of local designers. But—some of it's mine, too." Her cheeks heated. She was proud of the few pieces she had in the shop and would be even prouder when she sold them. But after growing up with a firefighter for a father and watching her brother follow in his footsteps, it was still scary to share her creative side, to run the risk of someone not liking a design or thinking her work wasn't as important, even when it was to her. "It's not saving lives," she blurted. "But it means something to me."

He rounded a corner and came to a halt at a four-way stop sign on a rural road outside the main part of town. She could see the sign up ahead welcoming her to Meadow Valley Ranch, but Carter put the truck in park.

"What are you doing?" she asked.

He turned to face her, one arm resting on top of the steering wheel.

"I'm making sure you can see the truth in my eyes when I say what I'm gonna say so you don't think I'm blowing smoke."

"Okaaay," she said, drawing out the word with a nervous laugh.

"Is making clothes your passion, the one thing in your life you can't live without? Filling your bucket and whatever other mumbo jumbo means you've found your calling?"

She nodded slowly, his ocean blue eyes holding her prisoner so that even if she wanted to look away, she couldn't.

"Then don't ever sound apologetic about it," he said, his face serious. "Because you're never going to change the minds of the naysayers, if there are any. And worrying about what other people think of what you do? All it does is rob you of some of the joy you're due."

He stared at her long and hard until she nodded her understanding, though she knew he was likely trying to convince himself even more than convince her. Still, the power of those words and the intensity in his gaze? No one had ever looked at her like that.

Once he got his response from her, he turned back to the wheel, put the car in drive, and drove them the final thirty seconds to the ranch.

After that speech and the way his eyes had bored into hers, she'd held her breath, thinking he might do something crazy like lean across the center console and kiss her right there. Only when they rolled to a stop in front of a stable and riding arena did she realize she hadn't yet exhaled. Or how much she wished he *had* planted one on her right at the four-way stop.

"You ready?" he asked.

To ride a horse? To find herself even more attracted to him by the day's end? To wonder if he *did* want to kiss her and what she'd do if it happened? Or how in the heck she was going to get this little crush out of her system once and for all? Because Carter Bowen could and *would* break her heart eventually. So no, she wasn't ready for any of it. Not one little bit.

"As I'll ever be," she said instead, and Carter flashed her a smile that knocked the wind straight out of her lungs.

Honey, you are in trouble, she said to herself as he rounded the back of the truck and opened her door.

"Did you say something?" he asked, offering her a hand to help her down. He had a pack over his shoulder he must have grabbed from the bed of the truck.

"Just how much I'm looking forward to an evening ride," she said.

Lies, lies, lies. Her words were nothing but lies. Only the flutter in her belly when her palm touched his spoke the truth. So she pushed it down deep, hiding it where she'd tried to hide her grief for two long years.

"Me, too," he said. Then he laced his fingers with hers and led her toward the stable doors.

And just like that, butterflies clawed their way to the surface without any warning at all.

Trouble with a capital *T*.

CHAPTER FIVE

Carter held the door for Ivy as they entered the stable. Sam Callahan—one of the ranch owners and also a recent transplant to Meadow Valley—greeted them inside.

"Ivy Serrano, this is Sam Callahan. Not sure if you've met him or his brother Ben yet. Or Colt, the third owner of the ranch."

Ivy shook her head and also shook the other man's hand. "I've seen you about town but don't believe I've officially made your acquaintance, Mr. Callahan. It's nice to meet you."

"It's just Sam," he said. "I'm not big on formalities, Ms.—*Ivy*," he said, grinning and catching his own error.

Sam, Ben, and Colt were young transplants to Meadow Valley, just like Carter. When it felt like he didn't yet fit in, which was most days, he at least had them as allies—and a horse to ride if he needed a quick escape.

"Ranch is officially open for business?" Ivy asked Sam.

"Sure is. It's a slow start, but we hope to get things off and rolling in the next several months. First year in a new business is the most important. Keep your fingers crossed we start drawing more folks into the area."

She smiled. "I'll cross all my fingers and toes that you have a great first year. Business for you means more business for the town, so it sounds like a win-win to me."

Sam shook Carter's hand as well. "Glad to have you back. You did a heck of a job this morning, even if we only have ten total guests at the moment."

Carter laughed. "Yeah, but those ten will tell ten more about it, and then *those* ten will tell ten more. You see where I'm going here?"

Sam shook his head ruefully, then waved his index finger at Carter. "I sure hope so. Building a new business in a new town isn't as easy as I'd hoped."

Carter shrugged. "If your mare treats Ivy well enough, she may just be the person to start spreading the news in town. Heck, when that happens and you're booking my riding services on the regular, I'll lower my commission from fifteen percent to ten."

Sam clapped Carter on the shoulder. "I sure met you at the right time. Someday I may really be able to pay you."

"As long as you let me ride the trails, consider me paid," Carter said.

Sam grabbed a straw cowboy hat off a bale of hay and tossed it on his head. "Have a nice ride, you two. Ace and Barbara Ann are all ready to go. You're welcome to stop by the dining hall when you get back, but I'm guessing by the saddle pack that you might have things under control."

Carter nodded. "Thanks for the offer all the same."

Sam turned back to Ivy. "It was nice to officially meet you. I'm sure we'll run into each other again sooner or later." And with that he strode out of the stable.

Ivy stared after him as he left. And then she stared some more. If Carter were the jealous type, he'd be—well—jealous. But how could he envy a man who caught her attention when she was nothing more than a friend? Pretty easily, it turned out.

Carter cleared his throat. "Not that it matters, but if I *were* trying to properly court you, would I have just introduced you to my competition?"

She spun to face him, cheeks aflame. "What? No. I mean—competition for what?"

He laughed. "I'm just wondering—and this is only a hypothetical, because this is in no way a courting situation—if I'd have shot myself in the foot by introducing you to someone who not only doesn't fight fires for a living but also must be pretty easy on the eyes for someone such as yourself."

Her throat bobbed as she swallowed, and her blush deepened.

"I'll admit that if anyone ever needed a visual display of what tall, dark, and handsome was supposed to be, it's the cowboy who just strode out those stable doors. And he has a brother? My oh my," she said, fanning herself.

He'd been teasing her initially, but now his confidence began to waiver.

"*But,*" she added, "there's one big problem with all of that."

Her tone encouraged him, so he took a step closer, even had the audacity to skim his fingers across her temple. "What's the problem, darlin'?"

She blew out a breath. "It's this other cowboy. One

who, after barely knowing me, helped sober me up after a bad day and even made sure I got home safely. He also *donates* his free time to lead trail rides at a new ranch in town. And truth be told, I prefer something closer to a redhead than a brunette. In fact, if this particular cowboy didn't risk his life for a living, I might very well be developing a little crush on him, which *would* make this a courting situation. But it's not, correct?"

It wasn't, as much as he wanted it to be. He'd thought about her the whole walk home last night, about what it would have been like to kiss her if she could only see him differently. Maybe that was what he hoped to accomplish by taking her out on the trail. All he knew was that sharing the view with ranch patrons earlier that day had been fun, but sharing it with Ivy would be something else. He hoped by the time they made it to the trail's end he'd figure out what that something else was.

He dipped his head, his lips a breath away from her ear. She smelled like the lavender fields from the farm that bordered his granddaddy's ranch, and he breathed her in, this intoxicating scent of home.

"No," he whispered. "It's not." Because a new job in a new town was tough enough. He was being tested by the chief, his captain, and everyone in his company. If he lost focus and slipped up, then where would he go? But the real issue was her. If he lost focus while falling for someone who, in the end, couldn't handle what he did for a living, then he wasn't simply putting his career on the line but his heart, too. He understood that Ivy's fear was based in reality, that she'd experienced a heartbreaking loss. And while he'd never push her into something she didn't want, it was impossible to deny this thing between them.

"Courting you, Ivy, would eventually mean kissing you. And I'm not sure you could handle my kissin'."

"Why's that?" she asked, her voice cracking.

"Because," he said softly, "I'd leave your lips swollen and your brain so foggy you won't remember your own name." Yet he wouldn't push her too far too fast. She had to choose him. Because despite bad timing and he being the type of guy she swore she'd avoid, a part of him had already chosen her.

She sucked in a breath, and it took every ounce of his resolve to straighten and take a step back when all he wanted to do was exactly what he'd said.

"Then I guess we're on the same page," she said, but he could hear the slight tremble in her voice. It matched his quickened pulse and the irregular beat of his heart.

He nodded. "I'll just throw my pack on Ace's saddle, and we'll be good to go." He glanced down at her boots. They weren't riding boots, but they looked sturdy enough for a motorcycle, which meant they were sturdy enough for a horse.

His gaze trailed up her toned legs. He could see every curve of muscle, her round and perfect backside, in those form-fitting pants.

"See something you like?" she teased, having regained her composure.

Good Lord did he ever.

How the heck was he supposed to read that? He wanted something other than friendship from her but only under the right circumstances. But after all her protesting—was Ivy flirting back?

"Just making sure you had proper boots for riding. Those will do," he said coolly, doing his best to maintain control.

He got Ace ready to go, then introduced Ivy to Barbara Ann and helped her into the saddle. At least, he *tried* to help her, offering to give her a boost, but she stuck one foot in the mare's stirrup and hoisted herself into the saddle like she'd done it every day of her life.

She shrugged and stroked the horse's mane. "Guess it's like riding a bike. You never really forget." She pulled her sunglasses from the collar of her shirt, batted her big brown eyes at him, and then covered them up. "I'm just waiting on you, cowboy."

He crossed his arms and stared up at her. "You want to take her for a lap or two in the arena before we hit the trail to make sure you've got the hang of it?"

"Sure," she said. "Meet you out there."

He stepped aside, and Ivy led Barbara Ann out of her stall and into the arena with ease.

He laughed and shook his head. She could make clothes, cut hair, put out her own fires, and hop onto the back of a horse like she grew up on a ranch herself. She also seemed to be able to make him forget that there was no room in his life for romance right now, especially with a woman who couldn't support what he did for a living.

He strode to a shelf right inside the stable's entrance and grabbed the cowboy hat he kept in there for his trail rides, then headed back to Ace's stall and mounted his own trusty steed. When they trotted into the arena, Ivy and Barbara Ann were galloping around the track. Damn she looked good on the back of a horse. Maybe this was their common ground. Back in town she was a woman still grieving an incomparable loss, and he was the man who—by the simple nature of his profession—reminded her of it. Maybe out here on the ranch for one perfect evening they could just be Carter and Ivy.

She rounded a turn and pulled on Barbara Ann's reins so she came to a halt beside him and Ace.

"Color me impressed, Ms. Serrano," he said. "You're a natural."

She beamed. "That. Was. Amazing! I've never felt so—so—"

"Alive?" he asked.

She shook her head. "Free. Free of all the worry swirling around my head, you know? Will the shop do well? Will my own designs sell? And everything else that gets me all twisted up in knots." She blew out a breath. "*Thank* you for bringing me here. I don't know if you knew it was what I needed or not, but wow. This is the perfect end to a stressful opening weekend."

"Now you know why I help Sam and the boys out for free. Ain't nothing like being on top of a horse and leaving the rest of the world behind every now and then." He nodded toward a gate on the other side of the arena and a path that eventually forked into three different directions. "You ready? We're going to do the open trail to the right."

"Ready," she said.

And they hit the trail.

* * *

How was it that Ivy had grown up in this town but had never seen these rolling green hills? It probably had something to do with there not having been a Meadow Valley Ranch or a stable full of horses until now. Maybe, though, the town wasn't the only thing she was looking at from a different perspective.

She tugged gently on Barbara Ann's reins and slowed

to a stop a few yards behind where Carter was doing the same thing. When she'd met him yesterday, he was a walking, talking, embodiment of her biggest fear—losing someone she loved. But today he was this cowboy who gave her exactly what she'd needed at the end of a weekend that had started off on a very wrong foot.

He looked back at her over his shoulder and tipped his hat.

Her stomach flipped.

"Just a few paces ahead and we can tie off the horses. I brought snacks," he called.

She nodded and followed him over the hill to where it leveled into a small clearing overlooking the ranch and beyond it the main street of town.

A short length of fence was set up—most likely by Sam Callahan and the other ranch owners—that seemed to be there for the sole purpose of making sure you could relax a while without your horse running off.

She hopped down into the overgrown grass and walked Barbara Ann to an open spot on the fence. Carter secured his horse while she did the same with hers. He removed the saddle pack and tossed it over his shoulder.

"Sam said the horses like this spot for grazing, and riders like it for gazing down at the town or up at the stars on a clear night, so I said we should call it Gaze 'n' Graze Hill."

She snorted. "That's the corniest thing I ever heard— but at the same time also kind of cute."

He shook his head. "There you go again with that word. *Cute.* Cute in my uniform. Cute the way I name a hill. I've heard the word so much in the past two days that I'm starting to wonder about that vocabulary of yours."

He nodded in the direction away from the fence, then

pivoted and headed that way without giving her time to come up with some sort of witty retort.

"I have a very good vocabulary, I'll have you know," she said when she caught up to him, then rolled her eyes at her less-than-formidable response. She'd never had to work to impress when it came to wordplay, but Carter Bowen threw her off her game. He made her tongue-tied and nervous and anxious to lob witty comebacks without a second thought. She had the undeniable urge to show him how much of her there was to like because—*ugh*—she was really starting to like him.

Where would that get her, though? She didn't want to think about that, not when she was up here, able to let go of the fear, even if it was only for a short while.

He laid the pack on the ground and unzipped one of three compartments, pulling out a blue-and-white-checked picnic blanket.

"Here," she said, motioning to take it, since he was kneeling. "I can do that."

He relinquished the blanket, and she shook it out, spreading it over the grass.

Next he opened a plastic container filled with sliced apples and another with what looked like warm, grilled sandwiches.

"Damn," he said. "I didn't think to ask. You don't have a peanut allergy, do you?"

She sat down across from him and shook her head. "Carter Bowen, did you make me peanut butter and jelly?" she asked with a grin.

"No, ma'am. Pearl did. You know Pearl at the Meadow Valley Inn?"

Ivy gasped. "Did you bring me Pearl's grilled PB and J with brie? Because if you did, I just might have to kiss you." Her hand flew over her mouth. "I meant because of how much I *love* that sandwich, not because—" She greedily grabbed one of the sandwich halves from the container and tore off a healthy bite. Anything to keep her from saying more incriminating statements about kissing. "Mmm. Delicious," she said around her mouthful of food.

Carter laughed and dropped back onto his ass—the ass she'd had her eye on for much of the trail ride. It wasn't like she had a choice. He led the way. And if she was searching her *limited* vocabulary for a way to describe the view, it was a long way from *cute*.

He handed her a thermos of Pearl's equally delicious raspberry iced tea, then picked up his own half a sandwich from the container and took a bite. He unscrewed the lid from his own tea and took a couple of long swigs.

"You know," he said, resting his elbows on his knees, "you don't have to be embarrassed about wanting to kiss me. Hell, you don't even have to use my great-aunt's cooking as an excuse for wanting to do it."

Her eyes widened, and she stopped herself in the middle of taking another bite. "*Pearl*? Pearl Sweeney is your great-aunt?"

He held his index finger to his lips.

"She is, though I'd appreciate you keeping that between us for right now. When she heard the chief might be looking to hire from the outside, she passed him my name. That was it. Her only involvement. I got the job on my own merits. I *know* I'm good at what I do. But I'm an uninvited guest right now, so until I prove myself to the company—which I know I will—I don't want to give anyone reason to doubt my abilities."

She lowered her sandwich onto the lid of the container.

"But Jessie, Wyatt, and Shane seemed to respect you just fine when you answered my nonemergency alarm."

He laughed, but the smile looked forced. "That's because I'd just written them up for insubordination before we left the station."

"What? Why?" That didn't sound like either of them.

He shrugged. "Because when they saw where the call was coming from, they argued with me about suiting up and taking the truck. 'It's Ivy's place. That girl knows more about fire than we do. By the time we get there, there'll be nothing left to do but paperwork.'"

Ivy winced because they were right about her. But Carter was in the right as their superior. "You did everything by the book like you were supposed to. I get it. No one should take shortcuts in a possible life-or-death situation."

He set his sandwich down and leaned back on his elbows, his long legs stretching out in front of him. His cowboy hat cast a shadow over his eyes. "Anyway," he said. "You can see why I don't want anyone claiming favoritism."

She moved the food out of the way and stretched out next to him on her side. The sun was low enough that she didn't need her sunglasses anymore, so she took them off and tossed them toward her feet. "Why'd you tell me all that, then? Aren't you afraid I'll spill the beans? For all you know, I'm the town gossip."

"Nah," he said. "I know the type, and you're not it. Besides, I needed to tell *someone*. Figured I couldn't do much worse than you."

She scoffed and backhanded him on the shoulder. "I don't know if that's a compliment or an insult. But judging from the sound of your voice, I'm guessing it's the latter."

He rolled onto his side to face her, but the hat was still obscuring his eyes. So she grabbed it and tossed it the same way she did her sunglasses.

"There," she said. "Now I can see those baby blues."

"Are they *cute*?" he asked.

Something in the pit of her belly tightened, and she shook her head.

"Then what?" he asked, his eyes darkening with the same mischief to match his tone.

"Okay," she said. "Before *then what?* I need to ask you something, Mr. Bowen."

"Go ahead, darlin'."

She blew out a breath. "There's something about being up here with you, away from everything at the bottom of the hill. It's like I can forget what happens down there, you know? Like nothing matters except for what's up here."

"The Gazin' and Grazin' Hill," he said with a wink.

She rolled her eyes but laughed. "There's something between us, right? I mean, you brought me here with Pearl's best sandwich and—and I'm not imagining any of it, am I?"

"No," he said simply. "I can't be with a woman who doesn't support what I do. So I know my wooing is going to waste, even if I keep saying that's not what this is. But I can't seem to help myself. Guess I was hoping I'd be able to change your perspective."

"I support what you do," she said. "But I just can't put my heart out there like that. You have to understand." She paused and took a steadying breath. "Wait. No, this isn't where this was supposed to be going. What I meant to say is that maybe up here, for today, I *can* forget what's down there. We both can." She propped herself up and squinted over the top of the hill.

"If I say yes, that I'd like the same thing," he said, "then I get to hear what else is in that vocabulary of yours?"

She lowered herself so she was facing him again and nodded. "You'd get to hear me say how sexy your butt looks in those jeans."

He laughed. "And here I thought we were talking about my eyes."

"Those are pretty sexy, too." She grinned. "I might even find you a little bit charming."

He trailed his fingers down the bare skin of her arm. "Darlin', I find you to be too many things to list."

She batted her lashes, and he laughed again. "Why don't you try," she said.

"Hmm, I should get comfortable. This'll take a minute or two." He rolled onto his back and clasped his hands behind his head. "Smart. Beautiful. A competent rider—"

"I like where this is headed," she interrupted. "Feel free to continue."

"A passion for what you do. Oh, can't forget terrible taste in liquor."

"Hey," she said. "I thought you were supposed to be complimenting me."

He raised his brows. "I said there was too much to list to *describe* you. Never said it was all complimentary." He scrubbed a hand across his jaw. "*And*...headstrong." He held up his hands like he was waiting for some sort of physical retribution, but she simply sat up, crossed her arms, and glared.

It was easier to find a reason to be indignant than to admit to herself how much she liked hearing what he was saying—complimentary or not. Because even his ribbing meant he'd noticed her. He'd paid attention to her. And he'd thought about her as much as she'd thought about him since their walk last night.

"That one *was* a compliment," he said, sitting up so she couldn't escape the depths of those blue eyes. "You know exactly what you want and what you don't, Ivy. I admire the heck out of that. Even if it means you *not* wanting to get involved with a catch like me."

Her gaze softened. "And you don't want to get involved with a mess like me."

"You're not a mess," he said. "But no. We already know we're not right for each other. And despite what you're offering up here on the hill, I think we both deserve better than that."

He grabbed his hat, stood, and dropped it back on his head.

She clamored back to her feet. "Wait. That's it? What about forgetting what's down there while we're up here?"

He dipped his head and kissed her. She didn't have time to think because her body melted into his like she was molten metal and he was made to mold her into shape. Her stomach contracted, and her back arched. His hands slid around her waist, and hers draped over his shoulders. His kiss was everything he had promised and everything she'd hoped—firm and insistent while at the same time careful and considerate. Whatever he asked for right now, she was more than willing to give. She parted her lips, and his tongue slipped past, tangling with hers. He was heat and fire and passion like she hadn't known existed.

Erase it all, she thought. *My fear, my hesitation—heck, even my name.* She knew it wasn't that easy, that a kiss couldn't take away two years of grief and how scared she was to even consider putting her heart at risk again.

But now that she knew what she'd tried to resist, she wanted all she could take before logic stepped back into the picture.

But before she could catch her breath, he backed away and tipped his hat.

"Are you gonna forget that once we get back to town?" he asked. "Because I sure as hell won't."

CHAPTER SIX

Carter Bowen was on fire. Not literally, of course. In the two weeks he'd been in Meadow Valley, the closest he'd gotten to any sort of real flame was the fire at Ivy's shop—the one she'd put out before he'd probably had his gear on.

No gear today, just a very sweaty Meadow Valley Fire Station T-shirt and a pair of basketball shorts. Lieutenant Heinz's crew took over a few hours early so Carter and his team could spend the last of their twenty-four-hour shift doing a scrub down of the rig.

In a hundred-degree heat, because even in the late afternoon, the day was a scorcher, and they needed daylight to see what they were doing. Carter paused from waxing the front of the truck to take a water break.

"You know this rig never sees any action, right?" Shane O'Brien said. "Other than the occasional emergency room transport—and for that we use the ambulance—I think the last fire Meadow Valley saw was two years ago."

He was on top of the rig, checking the ladder hydraulics and making sure there weren't any leaks.

"Not that I owe you an explanation, probie," Carter said, and Shane scowled at the nickname. "But I know the station's history. I'd expect that, having grown up in Meadow Valley, you'd know that while things have been quiet *here* the past eighteen months, we don't service only our own town. Our company has been called for backup more than a few times for forest fires in neighboring jurisdictions. In a rural area like this, debris from low-hanging trees and falling ash can cause issues over time if the upper level isn't cleared out and rinsed every now and then." He took a long swig from his canteen of water. "Plus a good day of work builds character for someone who might have taken a job because he thought he could sit with his feet up and watch ESPN all day."

He'd actually kill to be inside in the air-conditioning checking the Astros score, but there was no way he was going to bond with his team without working with them, and a clean rig was always the safest rig.

"Thanks for the exaggeration," Shane bit back. "I can count how many times *we've* been called for backup on one hand. And just so we're clear, my probationary period ended months ago. I could put myself in the running for your job if I wanted. We all know about your one-month trial period. You mess up and you're out, Lieutenant *Probie*."

Carter's teeth ground together. He'd been the youngest of three, the button pusher, all his life. But it had all been because he looked up to his brothers. He wanted to be like them. This was different. Shane O'Brien had some sort of vendetta, and Carter was the target.

Jessie popped her head out of the driver-side door.

"Mats and underneath the mats are all clean, Lieutenant!" she called. "Gotta admit, it was pretty nasty in there."

Carter did his best to shake off his interaction with Shane. "Let me take a quick look. If all looks good, you're clear to go."

He rounded the rig and climbed inside. The cab was damn near pristine, like no one had ever used it.

"Excellent work, Morris," he said as he hopped out. "I'll see you in forty-eight hours."

She grinned. "Thanks, Lieutenant." Then she gathered up her portion of the cleaning supplies and headed into the garage.

She and a few others on his team had seemed to come around in the past week, even though he'd been extra surly after the way things had ended with Ivy on Sunday. Maybe it started with his team not wanting to poke the bear, as it was, but now they'd fallen into an easy rhythm that felt good. The way he felt about Ivy Serrano, though? There was nothing easy about that.

It was Thursday now, and he was finishing the second of two twenty-four-hour shifts since he'd seen her. He hadn't been able to shake off how much he'd wanted her that evening and how much he still did even after putting four days between them.

It had meant keeping to the station and avoiding any other stops at the Midtown Tavern. But it seemed the more he avoided his attraction, the more he thought about it and wished he hadn't gone from a father who didn't support his life choices to a woman who drove him all kinds of crazy but also couldn't get behind what he did for a living.

He drained his canteen and then finished the rig's waxing. After that he went around the truck, inspecting stations and dismissing his firefighters as they completed their jobs. Until the only one left was Shane O'Brien—who'd decided to take an extended water break.

Carter climbed up to the roof of the truck and found him nestled into a corner, his baseball cap pulled low to cover his closed eyes. But Carter could tell by the rhythm of his breathing that the guy was asleep.

What the hell was it with his guy? It was one thing to push his buttons, but this was a complete disregard for Carter's authority.

He looked down at the small bag of twigs and branches Shane had collected—and at the untouched bucket of soapy water meant to wipe down the roof and ladder.

Carter picked up the bucket and tossed half the contents at the sleeping rookie.

"What the hell?" Shane growled, startling awake.

Carter checked his watch. "I'm off the clock. So is the rest of the team. Except you." He nodded toward the spilled water. "Clean that up and wipe down the rest of the roof. I'll let Lieutenant Heinz know you're not stepping foot off this property until you're done. See you in forty-eight hours."

He gritted his teeth and climbed to the ground before Shane had a chance to be any more insubordinate than he'd already been. Carter needed a shower. And a drink. But that meant hitting the tavern. Except he was *avoiding* the tavern. And right now he wanted to avoid the firehouse as well.

He pulled out his cell phone and called his great-aunt.

"I need a room," he said when she answered.

"Got one ready and waiting. Rough day?"

"Yeah. Does that Everything Store sell liquor?"

She laughed. "And steal business from Casey's place? Kitchen's still open over here, and I might have a few longnecks hiding in the fridge."

He blew out a breath. "You're a lifesaver. Be there in a few." Then he ended the call.

He grabbed his few belongings from the bunkhouse, hoisted his duffel over his shoulder, and headed straight for the front door. He pushed through to find Ivy Serrano heading up the front walkway. Her eyes widened when she saw him.

"Can I help you, Ms. Serrano?" he said with as much formality as he could muster.

Her hair was in two low braids on either side of her head, and she wore a black baseball cap that said SLUG-GERS across the top in yellow, a white tank top under fitted overalls, and a pair of what he guessed used to be white sneakers on which she'd doodled intricate floral designs in vibrant colored marker.

Damn she looked cute.

She hesitated, her hands fidgeting with the bag slung over her shoulder.

"Softball practice was canceled on account of the heat, and I figured since I was free and it looks like you're still in need of that haircut…"

He ran a hand through his hair. The overgrown ends were slick with sweat.

"Ivy," he said, more serious this time. "What are you doing here?"

She shrugged. "You were right. I haven't been able to forget about that kiss." She noticed his duffel. "Are you going somewhere?"

"Decided to take a room at the inn. I need a shower and a cold-as-hell beer."

She worried her bottom lip between her teeth. "I've got a shower. And a six-pack of Coors."

He sighed. Despite having thought about her all week, he had every reason in the world to say no. There was something between them, for sure. But they couldn't be together, not when his job seemed to be growing more complicated, especially after what he'd just done. Not to mention the woman standing in front of him couldn't handle his job to begin with.

He got it. He understood and wouldn't fault her for her grief. But he couldn't be anyone else for her.

No, Ivy. I can't come with you. I can't get deeper into this thing we never should have started because it'll keep getting harder to walk away.

The only problem? He couldn't actually form the word *no*. Not with those big brown eyes fixed on him, those dark lashes batting their way past his defenses—because yes, she batted. And it worked.

"Those are the magic words," he said at last. A free haircut and a beer. He could handle that. "But nothing out of any sort of fashion magazine. Just a trim."

She finally smiled, and he swore it was brighter than the still-blazing sun.

"Deal," she said, then held out her right hand.

He shook it. "And for the record," he said, "I haven't forgotten that kiss either."

They strode off down the street and around the bend. When they got to her porch he texted his aunt.

*Change of plans. I'll still need that room but not until
later this evening.*

Or maybe, if they both threw logic out the window,
not at all.

Carter showered quickly and threw on a clean T-shirt
and jeans. He'd gotten so used to communal living the
past couple of weeks that the quiet of Ivy's house made
him feel odd and out of place. After college he'd moved
straight into a one-bedroom apartment with another probie at the station. It was a tight fit, one of them living in
the bedroom and the other in the living room, but it had
been a necessary inconvenience. After his father decided
he was a colossal disappointment, he couldn't live at
home anymore. So he worked to pay the rent, picked up
any overtime that was offered him, and moved up the
ranks as fast as he could.

And then he left.

It had been a long time since he'd been under a roof
with quiet, space, and permanence.

He padded barefoot into the kitchen, where she was
waiting on a stool at the kitchen island. One frosty
longneck sat on the blue-tiled counter while she sipped
another.

"Evening, Lieutenant," she said, raising her bottle. Her
ball cap hung on the corner of her high-top chair.

"Evening, Ms. Serrano," he said, striding toward the
counter to stand opposite her. "But I'm off the clock."

She nodded. "I know. But the title suits you. You've
got this air of authority that doesn't seem to go away even
when you're off duty."

He blew out a breath and took a healthy swig from his
beer. "I guess it's kind of hard to turn it off sometimes."

He set his beer down and pressed both palms against the counter, shaking his head. "I lost my cool with one of my rookies this afternoon."

She winced. "Shane?"

"How'd you know?" he asked.

She sighed. "Shane's always had a bit of a chip on his shoulder. Wyatt was—and I guess still is—the big brother whose shoes have been hard to fill. He was the starting quarterback our sophomore year. Took the team to state twice. He was as good a student as he was an athlete, and now he's a uniformed town hero in the making. Shane got in with the wrong crowd in high school and sorta disappeared for a few years. Rumor has it that when he turned up in the county jail, his father gave him an ultimatum—clean up his act and get a job or he wouldn't post bail."

"Damn," Carter said. "How long ago was that?"

She raised her brows. "About a year ago."

He whistled. "That explains a lot. Shoot, I'm guessing I fanned the flames pretty good, then."

"Uh-oh." She took another sip of her beer. "What did you do?"

He shrugged. "Caught him sleeping on top of the truck when he was supposed to be scrubbing it down, so I dumped half the bucket of soapy water on him and told him he wasn't leaving until he cleaned up the mess." He scratched the back of his neck. "This sounds kind of crazy, but I think he might have been the internal applicant for lieutenant. It doesn't make any damned sense from an experience standpoint, but now that I know more about his history? I'm nothing more than a reminder to him of not measuring up."

"Oh, Carter," she said, resting a hand over his as she

stifled a laugh. "You've got your work cut out for you, don't you?"

"The thing is," he said, "he and I aren't that different. I'm the youngest of three. I always looked up to my brothers. My father. But when I decided to go down a different path, it was like I lost any chance of filling the shoes I was expected to fill."

She squeezed his hand. "I think maybe you and Shane will be good for each other. You know what it's like to be in his place. Now you get to sort of be the big brother, to show him that the right path can still be his own path."

He flipped his hand over and laced his fingers with hers. "Does this mean you've changed your mind about getting involved with a firefighter?"

She shook her head, nodded, and then groaned.

"What kind of answer is that?" he asked with a laugh.

She slid off her stool and rounded the corner of the island so she was standing right in front of him.

"It's the kind where my heart and my head can't come to an agreement. I felt something with you that first night, Carter, and again up on the hill. I tried to ignore it. Tried to keep my heart safe by staying away, but here we are."

He nodded. "Here we are."

"Something died in me the day we lost Charlie. Loving and losing isn't just about romantic love, you know. No matter which way you slice it, the losing is hard. Too hard. I couldn't take that kind of hurt again."

"I know," he said. "All I can do is promise that if this thing with us turns to something real, I'll do my best not to hurt you."

She pressed her lips together and nodded. "Maybe while we're seeing where this goes, we pretend you have a really boring office job where you sit in a cubicle and crunch numbers at a computer."

He laughed. "Fine. But if I don't get to talk about my passion, you don't get to talk about yours." He wasn't changing who he was, just buying them time for her to be okay with it. Besides, after today, he needed a friendly face. He needed to be with the woman he hadn't stopped thinking about all week.

She scoffed at him imposing this rule on their game, but fair was fair. "But I just opened the shop. This is my fresh start, my future, my—"

He pressed a finger to her lips. "If I have to work in a cubicle, so do you."

She pouted, but there was a smile in her big brown eyes. "Okay. No shoptalk. For now."

She held out her free hand to shake, but instead he slipped both his hands around her wrists and draped her arms around his neck.

"I can think of a better way to seal that deal."

He dipped his head and kissed her, and it was everything he needed after the day he'd had. Her soft lips parted, and he felt her smile against him as he tasted what was far better than a cold beer at the end of a hard day.

"Evening, Lieutenant," she whispered.

"Evening, Ms. Serrano."

He slid his hands behind her thighs and lifted her up. She wrapped her legs around his waist and kissed him harder.

"Can we postpone that haircut?" she asked, her voice breathy and full of a need that matched his own.

"Yes, ma'am," he said, and carried her back down the hall. There were three open doors, and one he could tell just from glancing in was clearly her office or design space. So he strode through the only other door that wasn't the bathroom and carried her toward the bed.

He set her down on her feet. "Wait," he said.

She shook her head and slid her overalls off her shoulders, lifted her fitted tank top over her head, and undid her bra in seconds flat.

"Wow," he said, staring at her breasts. "While this is already way better than a haircut, why are we rushing, Ivy?" Even though he wasn't sure how much time he had with her—how long this would last before she decided she couldn't and *wouldn't* be with him—he wanted to take things slow.

She laughed and lifted his T-shirt up and over his shoulders, then wrapped her arms around his torso and stood on her tiptoes to kiss him again. "Why wait?" she asked. "We're two consenting adults who obviously both want the same thing." She paused and took a step back. "You do want me, don't you?" she asked, the sincerity in her voice too much for him to bear.

"God, Ivy, *yes*. So much it hurts." And likely would hurt for a spell until his body caught up with his brain, but he'd survive. "But I don't want to feel like we're rushing only to get each other out of our systems."

He reached for where she'd tossed his T-shirt on the bed and pulled it back on. For a brief second he wondered if she saw the scarred skin on his left side and simply ignored it or if she was too caught up in the moment to notice. There was also the scar on his right shoulder that had nothing to do with the accident, but she seemed to have missed that one, too. Or maybe it was all a part of their game—of pretending he wasn't fully who he was. That was why he was pumping the brakes. Playing make-believe was fine while they figured out what this was, but he wanted their feelings to catch up with their actions. When and if he and Ivy slept together, he wanted the game to be over.

"I'm sorry," she said, crossing her arms over her chest, and he hated that he'd made her feel self-conscious or guilty. "You're right. I just got caught up, and I—"

He wrapped his hands around her wrists and gently pulled her arms back to her sides.

"You play softball, right?" he said, the corner of his mouth turning up.

She nodded, and he dipped his head down to kiss one breast and then the other. She hummed softly, and he breathed in the scent of lavender and silently swore to himself. Ivy Serrano would eventually be his undoing, but tonight maybe they could simply *be*.

He straightened and grinned when he saw the smile spread across her face. "Well maybe no home run tonight, but I could hit a single or double."

She burst out laughing, then grabbed his right hand and placed it on her left breast, his thumb swiping her raised peak. She sucked in a breath before regaining her composure.

"I think you've already made it to second," she teased. "So what's next?"

He sat down on the bed and patted his knee. She climbed into his lap and wrapped her arms around his neck.

He kissed her and lowered her onto her back, his lips traveling to the line of her jaw, her neck, and the soft skin below. He savored each nibble and taste and watching her react to his touch.

"Who knows?" he asked. "If a good pitch comes along, I might hit a triple."

She pressed her palm over the bulge in his jeans and gave him a soft squeeze.

"Only if my team can, too."

He groaned as she squeezed again, then kissed her once more. "Fair is fair."

"But no home runs," she reaffirmed. "At least, not tonight."

"I predict it'll still be a good game."

"Evening, Lieutenant," she said, echoing her earlier greeting as he slipped a hand beneath the overalls that still hung at her hips. "Thanks for coming over tonight."

He nipped her bottom lip. "Evening, Ms. Serrano. Best night I've had in a long time."

And hopefully the first of many more to come.

CHAPTER SEVEN

Ivy pulled her cap over her eyes and stared at the batter, then glanced at Casey, who was pitching. Her friend gave her a subtle nod, which meant she was sending the ball right over the plate, which in turn would mean a line drive to Ivy, who was covering first base. If she caught the ball, it would be the third out and a win for the Midtown Sluggers. If she didn't, the bases would be loaded, and a grand slam would sink them.

No pressure.

Not like this was the big leagues or anything, but the Main Street Loungers from Quincy—aptly named after the pub who sponsored them—were their biggest rival. The Loungers had creamed them the last time they played each other, and tonight the Sluggers were on their home turf.

Ivy breathed in the fresh scent of the ponderosa pines that rose in the distance. Even in the small residential park, you could see the tree-lined hills that gave Meadow Valley its name. It was more than her grief that had swallowed her up in Boston. It was the city itself. Beautiful as it was and steeped in history, Ivy had longed for the comfort of home—for the place where she and Charlie grew up, where she could feel closer to the brother she still missed.

She wasn't expecting a new reason to solidify Meadow Valley as the place she was meant to be. But there was Carter Bowen, climbing into the bleachers. He said he would come as soon as his shift ended—his boring cubicle office job shift—and there he was. They'd been seeing if this thing between them was real for three full weeks now. She counted the week they avoided each other in there because she'd spent each day thinking about him and wishing they *weren't* avoiding each other.

These days they were very much *not* avoiding each other. Whether it was at her house, his room at the inn, or the afternoon she found him waiting in her office after she closed the shop—he'd snuck back there while she was helping one last customer—they'd pretty much *not* avoided each other all over town.

She smiled at the thought. No one had hit any home runs yet, but they'd been enjoying the game nonetheless.

And now he was here, watching her play softball of all things, and all she could think about was how much brighter Meadow Valley seemed with him around. Others would say it had to do with the incessant sun and lack of rain, but not Ivy. She'd smiled more in the last three weeks than she had in the past two years, and the summer sun had nothing to do with it.

Oof! A burst of pain in her shoulder woke her from her stupor.

"Foul!" she heard the referee call.

She saw Carter bolt up from his seat and then sit back down, like his instinct was to go to her, and despite how much the impact had hurt, her stomach flip-flopped.

"Time out!" Casey called, and she jogged over to first base. "Are you okay?" she asked.

Ivy rolled her shoulder. It would need some ice, but she'd live. "Yeah. I'm fine."

Casey threw her hands in the air, which looked ridiculous, because one was covered by her glove and the other palmed a softball. "Then what the hell was that?" she whisper-shouted. "You could have caught that ball instead of acting as a shield for—I don't know—any stray lightning bugs who might have been in its path."

Ivy groaned. "I know. I'm sorry. I got distracted."

Casey glanced toward the small set of bleachers and then back at Ivy.

"Dreamboat's got you all bent out of shape, doesn't he?" she asked.

"No," Ivy said defensively. "I mean yes. I don't know."

Casey placed her glove on Ivy's shoulder, the one that, thankfully, wasn't throbbing.

"Look, you know there's nothing I want more than to see you smile like you used to. But you know what he does for a living, right? You know where he disappears to every forty-eight hours." Casey cut herself off before saying Charlie's name. Everyone in town pretty much did the same. Unless Ivy got tipsy on apple pie liqueur and toasted her dead brother, everyone played the avoidance game, including herself.

She had lived in the thick of her grief for over a year in Boston with her parents, Charlie's wife, and her niece, Alice. She wanted to leave that grief behind now that she was home and had a soon-to-be-thriving business.

Ivy cleared her throat. "You know how we pretend? Like you just did by not saying—by not saying his name. That's what Carter and I do. As far as I'm concerned, he has a really boring job where he sits in a cubicle and crunches numbers."

Casey's blue eyes softened. "Oh, Ives. Be careful, okay? I like Carter a lot, but I don't want you setting yourself up for heartbreak if you can't handle what he *really* does."

The ref alerted them that their time was up, and Ivy nodded.

"Let's win this damn game, okay?" Casey asked. "Drinks are on me if we do."

Ivy laughed. "I've never paid for a drink at Midtown in my entire life."

Casey shrugged. "Fine. If we lose, I'm starting your first tab."

Ivy narrowed her eyes at her best friend. "You wouldn't."

"Try me," Casey said. "Or catch the damn ball next time, and you'll won't have to see whether or not I'm bluffing." She adjusted her baseball cap and pivoted away, her assured strides carrying her back to the pitcher's mound.

"Make me pay for drinks," Ivy mumbled. "Yeah, right." But when the batter readied himself for the next pitch, Ivy squeezed her eyes shut for a brief moment and pushed everything out of her thoughts except one thing— the game.

When she opened her eyes, Casey was already winding up, so Ivy bent her knees, leaned toward the foul line, and held her mitt open and at the ready.

Again, Casey pitched the ball right over the plate, but this time the batter didn't foul. This time it was a line drive inside first. She barely had time to think before she dove over the plate, arm outstretched. The ball hit her hand hard, and she rolled to the ground, tucking it close to her chest. Nervous as hell to look, she sprang to her knees and glanced down. There it was, the softball that was now the game-ending catch.

She jumped to her feet and held the ball high in the air amid cheers from her team.

"Free drinks for life!" she exclaimed, and Casey barreled toward her, embracing her in a victory hug.

Over her friend's shoulders she saw the small gaggle of Midtown Sluggers supporters cheering in the stands, and among them a gorgeous firefighter cowboy who was striding onto the field with fierce determination.

She pulled out of her friend's embrace, and the two of them stared Carter down.

"I think you're about to get kissed," Casey said with a grin.

"Hell yes, I am."

Ivy jogged toward him, giddy, and jumped into his arms, wrapping her legs around his waist.

"Hell of a catch, Serrano," he said, his deep voice only loud enough for her to hear. And then he kissed her.

"I know," she said when they broke apart. "All I needed was to get the distractions out of my head."

He tilted his head back, and she saw his brows draw together.

"Distractions?" he asked.

She felt heat rush to her cheeks. "I know you said you were coming as soon as your shift ended, but it was the bottom of the seventh, and I figured your shift ran late, and—I don't know. I was really excited to see you. Guess I lost my train of thought."

He lowered her to the ground, then planted a kiss on her left shoulder.

She winced. "There's gonna be one hell of a bruise there by the end of the night."

He nodded. "Come home with me tonight, and I can help you ice it."

She grinned and slid her arms around his waist. "I think that can be arranged. Though I want to know when you're going to stop calling Pearl's inn home and find a more permanent residence."

The corner of his mouth turned up. "You afraid I'm going somewhere?"

Every time you're on a twenty-four-hour shift. Because as much as they pretended out loud, she never really forgot what he did. The only safety was in reminding herself that in her quiet little town, nothing much ever happened. The fire in her shop was the most Meadow Valley had seen in years, and she'd taken care of it with ease. So she convinced herself that it'd be at least a couple years more before something else happened, and other than responding to the station's paramedic services, Carter would be safe.

"Are you?" she finally asked. "Going somewhere?"

He shook his head. "Hope not. But the chief wants to make sure he made the right decision. Fire department is a close-knit team, but most of them are warming up to me. Barring any disasters in the next week, I should be ready to start looking for a real place to call home."

She rolled her eyes. "You make Meadow Valley sound so unwelcoming."

He laughed. "I didn't say the town, just the firehouse.

When you're working in a life-and-death profession, trust is the most important thing and—"

He stopped short, likely noticing her wide eyes and maybe the fact she was holding her breath.

"Shoot," he said. "Ivy, it's just a figure of speech. You know every day I've been on duty has truly been about as boring as a cubicle job."

She bit her lip and nodded. Meadow Valley was safe. *He* was safe. But how long could she keep pretending that the potential for danger wasn't there? How long could she pretend that she wasn't afraid?

"Are you breathing?" he asked, brows raised.

She shook her head. Then she let out a breath.

They weren't going to have this conversation now. Not when things were going so well. Not when she couldn't imagine *not* kissing him again tonight or waking up in his arms tomorrow morning.

"Come on," she said, forcing a smile. "Drinks are on Casey."

They didn't last long at the tavern, even when the celebration moved outside to the tavern's back alley, where Casey's dad had set up a good old-fashioned charcoal barbecue and was grilling burgers and dogs. Not when Ivy knew she could be with Carter in his room. Just the two of them. First, though, they made a quick stop at the inn's kitchen, where Pearl was still cleaning up the remnants of the small restaurant's dinner service.

"Well this is a surprise," she said as Ivy and Carter slipped through the door. She opened her arms—and strode straight for Ivy.

"I heard you won the game!" she said.

Carter laughed. "Even with my own flesh and blood I'm still not the favorite around here."

Pearl gave Ivy another squeeze before releasing her. She waved Carter off.

"As soon as I can shout from the rooftop that my grandnephew is the best lieutenant Meadow Valley could ask for, *then* you'll see some favoritism. Until then it goes to your girl, here."

Your girl. Ivy and Carter spending time together was no secret, but that was the first time anyone had verbalized them as a couple. And Ivy liked the sound of it even more than she'd anticipated.

Carter kissed his great-aunt on the cheek.

"In that case, can we get our star first base player a bag of ice? She took a pretty rough foul ball to the shoulder."

Ivy pulled her T-shirt sleeve over her shoulder, and Pearl gasped when she saw the half-moon purple that had already reared its ugly head.

"Oh, honey. Why didn't you say so in the first place?"

She grabbed a box of gallon-size plastic bags from a shelf over the sink and handed one of the bags to Carter. He headed toward the small ice machine that was next to the combination refrigerator-and-freezer and filled the bag.

"He knows better than I do how to ice a shoulder," Pearl told Ivy. "Did you know he was primed to be the starting quarterback his junior year of high school?"

Ivy's eyes widened as Carter finished at the ice machine and turned to look at her.

He smiled and shrugged, but both movements seemed forced. "Shoulder surgery saw to it that *that* never happened." He let out a bitter laugh. "Turns out a summer of football camp trying to prove myself to the coach combined with my dad putting me on tire changing duty at the shop was the perfect combination for a pretty bad tear in the rotator cuff."

He zipped the bag of ice shut and kissed his aunt again. "Need any help finishing up in here?"

She patted him on the cheek. "You kids head on up. I'm good here. Just need to take out the trash." She nodded toward a door that was propped open into the back alley. "And I'm sorry, sweetheart, if I brought up old wounds."

He shook his head. "You never have to apologize for anything. You're my lifeline, Aunt Pearl. If it weren't for you, I'd have never gotten out of Houston."

"Someday you and your daddy will see eye to eye without expectations or disappointment getting in the way." She sighed. "Now go on before I *do* put you two to work."

She smiled at them both, then busied herself with rolling a trash can toward the kitchen's back door as if they were never there.

Carter turned to Ivy and raised his brows. "Let's go take care of you."

CHAPTER EIGHT

Whoops. When he'd left for his shift yesterday evening, he hadn't bothered to make the bed. Or clean up the clothes strewn over the desk chair. Or hide the pile of leadership manuals he'd been poring over, since he'd had another setback with Shane earlier in the week, and of course Ivy gravitated straight to where they were spread out across the top of the desk.

"Sorry for the mess," he said. "But I made Pearl promise no inn employee would waste any time on my room when I get to live here rent free. I'm just not the best at keeping up with it myself."

She didn't respond, undeterred as she strode toward her destination.

"*How to Make Friends and Influence People*? *The Coaching Habit*?" She closed one book that he'd left open to the last page he'd read. Then she covered her mouth but was unable to stifle her laugh. "*The Leadership Secrets of Santa Claus*?"

He grabbed the book and held it protectively to his chest. "Hey. Don't knock it until you try it. Santa leads one of the biggest teams out there. He's gotta have some good secrets."

He tossed the book back down, set the bag of ice on the nightstand, then quickly neatened the bed and propped the pillows up so she'd be comfortable.

"Come here." He patted the bed, then readied the ice pack in his hands.

She glanced down at herself and tried brushing away the infield dirt from the right side of her body. "I'm filthy," she said. "I don't want to get dirt all over your bed. Got a T-shirt I can borrow?"

He moved to the dresser and opened a drawer. Then he tossed her a gray T that had HOUSTON ASTROS emblazoned on the chest in navy blue letters outlined in orange.

She narrowed her eyes. "I can't wear this in public, you know. And neither should you."

He laughed. "Lucky for you, I'm not planning on us leaving this room tonight. Are you?"

She shook her head. "Nope." Then she sauntered with the balled-up shirt into the bathroom. "Just need a few minutes to freshen up, Lieutenant. Maybe you can read some more about Santa's leadership secrets while you wait."

He crossed his arms defiantly. "Maybe I will."

She closed the door behind her.

He heard her turn the sink faucet on, so he collapsed into the desk chair and did exactly as she'd suggested. *Everything* seemed to be falling into place at the station except for Shane. No matter what method he used to try and connect with the guy, Shane always pushed back.

It had only taken seconds for him to get lost in the

books, so he hadn't heard the faucet being turned off or the bathroom door opened. He didn't even know Ivy was behind him until her hands began massaging his shoulders.

"I think *you're* in need of more TLC than me, mister." She kneaded a knot below his shoulder blade, and he blew out a long breath.

"Good Lord, that feels good," he said.

"Tell me about the books." She worked on all his knots and kinks, the physical manifestation of the pressure he'd felt at the station these last few weeks.

He shook his head, happy she couldn't see the defeat in his eyes.

"I don't get it," he said. "I've tried every approach with that kid. And before you tell me he's a grown man, he's twenty-two. That's barely legal and a kid in my book."

Ivy laughed. "I'm simply here to listen, Lieutenant. Not judge."

"Sorry," he said, scrubbing a hand over his face. "I'm at the end of my rope with him. He couldn't have been serious about going for lieutenant seconds after finishing his probation. But it feels like he has this grudge."

"Some people need someone else to take the blame for their mistakes or shortcomings—or fears. I'm not saying it's right, but it happens."

He spun his chair around to find Ivy standing there in nothing more than his T-shirt and her underwear.

"Well shoot, darlin'. That massage was something, but if I'd have known you were behind me wearing next to nothing, I'd have turned around a lot sooner."

She climbed into his lap, her legs straddling his torso. He slid his hands under the T-shirt and rested his palms on her hips.

"How's his big brother Wyatt doing?" she asked.

Carter shrugged. "Perfect. Best driver engineer I could ask for—should we ever get a real call."

Ivy's throat bobbed as she swallowed, but she didn't change the subject.

"Do you and the captain praise Wyatt for his good work?"

He nodded. "Hell yeah. Chief even singled him out last week to commend him on the CPR training he did for the local mother and toddler group."

Her forehead fell against his. "And what's Shane done to earn anyone's praise?"

Carter groaned. "I swear I've tried, Ivy. I've *tried* to use positive reinforcement with him, but it's like he's determined to buck authority just enough so that he doesn't get let go from the team."

She huffed out a laugh. "Because I'm guessing that dealing with you is a shade or two more bearable than dealing with his father. I'm not condoning his insubordination, but you're right. He's a kid who's still trying to find his place in a very small town that knows he messed up and that puts his brother on a pedestal every which way he turns. To him, you're simply one other person reminding him that he can't measure up, so why should he try?"

"I know how that feels." Carter had realized he was competing with his brothers for his father's approval. But once he chose his own path, his father made it clear that if anyone was keeping score, Carter had lost. Maybe this would be his in with Shane. Maybe it wouldn't. But somehow Ivy made sense of what Carter should have seen on his own.

She cradled his cheeks in her palms and brushed her

lips over his. "You're good at what you do. You don't need to prove yourself to him, Carter."

"To who?" he asked.

She kissed his cheek. "To your father." She kissed the other. "To the chief." She kissed his lips. "To yourself." She lifted his T-shirt over his head. "To me," she added. Then she brushed a kiss over the scar on his shoulder. "Why didn't you tell me about football? About losing your spot on the team because of surgery?"

He slid his hands up her thighs until his thumbs hit the hem of her underwear.

"Because it wouldn't have mattered if I'd been able to play anyway. I'd have gotten kicked off the team because of my attendance eventually."

He let his eyes fall closed as she peppered his chest with kisses. Everything was better with her in his arms, with her warm skin touching his. The pain of the past fell further away each time he kissed her, each morning he woke up next to her, and each day he got closer to calling Meadow Valley his home for good.

"Did your dad know how important it was to you?" she asked.

He shook his head. "There wasn't a point. Either my brothers and I took over the garage or the business would eventually go under when my old man's arthritis wouldn't let him work anymore. He was a very proud, self-made man. And I respect that about him. But he can't get past seeing me as ungrateful for not wanting what he made."

She brushed her fingers through his hair. "It's okay that you chose a different path. What you're doing is something that not many men or women would or could. Be proud of yourself."

He let out a bitter laugh. "For my boring cubicle desk job?"

"No," she said, a slight tremor in her voice. "You risk your life for others. And there's nothing boring about that."

She ran her fingertips over the raised and knotted skin on the left side of his torso.

"I wasn't just talking about Shane when I said people blame others for their own baggage. I've been blaming you, in a way, for my fear of once again losing someone I care about. It's not fair. If you're not ready to be proud of yourself, then know that *I'm* proud of what you've done, of what you continue to do."

He nodded. His throat was tight, and he wasn't sure what it would sound like if he spoke, but he needed to know what this meant. He needed to know where they stood as far as her not being able to deal with his job.

"But can you let go of the fear, Ivy? If you're really proud of me—of how well I do my job—can you accept who I am and what I do, so that this"—he motioned between them—"doesn't have to come to an end?"

A tear slid down her cheek, and she nodded. "I don't want to be afraid," she said. "Because I think I'm falling for you, Carter Bowen."

He grinned and lifted her up. Her legs squeezed tight around his waist, but the vise that seemed to be slowly squeezing his heart for the better part of a decade loosened.

He laid her down gingerly on the bed.

"I'm head over heels and ass over elbow and whatever other phrase you got that says how hard I'm falling for you, darlin'."

He glanced toward the melting bag of ice on the nightstand.

"We forgot about your shoulder."

She tugged him down to her. "Forget about it. I have another one that's in perfectly good condition."

He laughed. Then he lifted the Astros shirt up her torso and over her head. And there she was in nothing other than her underwear—bare and beautiful and falling for him. Everything in his life finally felt like it was clicking into place. She was simply the missing piece he hadn't known he was missing.

"I have a question for you," she added. "Actually, it's more of an observation."

"I'm all ears."

She smiled, and he swore he'd do whatever it took to make her smile the last thing he saw before he went to sleep and the first thing he laid eyes on each morning—for as long as she'd let him.

"I know Midtown won their big game and all, but I think it's *our* turn to hit a home run."

He laughed. "I think that's an excellent observation." Then he brushed a lock of hair out of her eye and stared at her.

"You're so beautiful," he said. "Here..." He kissed each breast. "And *here*." He kissed the skin above her heart. "I didn't plan on you, Ivy Serrano. But I sure am glad your refrigerator cord caught fire—*and* that you were able to put it out so quickly."

He rolled onto his side, and their legs entwined as their lips met, as if this were a choreographed dance they'd learned years ago.

"I sure didn't plan on a cowboy fireman turning my life upside down. I didn't know what it would be like to come home, with my parents in Boston and Charlie gone for good. The past several months have been real hard. And then you showed up."

She kissed him, her breasts warm against his chest. And it was simply right—she and he like this.

"And," she said, "you're wearing too many clothes."

Almost as soon as she had said the words, his jeans and boxer briefs were no more.

He slid her panties to her ankles and over her feet, and she hooked a leg over his.

"I don't want anything between us tonight," she said, wrapping a hand around his hard length.

"But—" He was all for what she was suggesting, but after waiting all this time, he wanted to be careful. Tonight was the start of something bigger than he'd imagined, and he wanted to get everything right.

"I'm on the pill," she said. "Have been for years. And I haven't been— It's only you, Carter. Just *you*."

He knew what she meant on a literal level but wondered if she felt it, too—how hard he was falling for her, how he couldn't fathom it being anyone other than her ever again.

He buried himself inside her, hoping to fill her with all that he was feeling but couldn't yet say.

She arched against him and gasped. He kissed her hard, and she rolled on top of him. He watched her move in a rhythm that was all their own. And he wondered how so much could change in such a short time.

He always thought he was running from a father who couldn't accept his choices, but maybe he was running to her all along.

*   *   *

He woke the next morning before she did, their bodies still tangled and her back against his chest.

He kissed her neck, and she hummed softly, but it was a dreamy hum, one that assured him she was still asleep. Still, it couldn't hurt to check.

"Ivy," he whispered. "You awake?"

She didn't stir.

He knew this was right—that *she* was right. So why deny it any longer.

"Maybe this is too soon, but I'm a man of certainty, and I'm certain that I'm not falling for you, darlin'. I'm not falling because I already fell." He kissed the softball-shaped bruise on her shoulder. "I love you, Ivy."

He wasn't ready to say it to her face, not when a tiny part of him kept whispering that eventually his job would spook her and this would be over. It was better like this, not knowing what she'd say in return. Because if the other shoe dropped, he wanted to be prepared. He could handle her walking away if he never knew that she loved him, too. But if he knew and she still left, that might downright ruin him.

Maybe he risked his life doing what he did for a living, but he realized now that the one thing scarier than walking into a burning building was risking his heart.

CHAPTER NINE

Ivy closed the store at four, since business had been slow. Plus, happy hour at Midtown started at five on Thursdays, and most folks went early to claim their preferred seats, especially those who liked to sit closest to the free appetizers.

"Ow!" Casey said when Ivy accidentally poked her with her hemming pin.

"Sorry," Ivy said with her lips pressed tight around the blunt ends of the remaining pins, so it sounded more like *Srry*.

"I get that you're nervous and all about putting this design on display, but if you poke your very human mannequin one more time, she's quitting. She didn't sign up for acupuncture, *and* she has to get her butt behind the bar soon."

Ivy spit the pins into her palm and sighed.

"Sorry. This is—it's more than the design. It's

symbolic, you know? If I can look at the dress in the store—on an actual mannequin who doesn't complain— it'll mean I'm okay. It'll mean that I can remember the good things about Charlie, about growing up here, and be happy instead of—" She trailed off before finishing. Because she would be a horrible person if she said what came next.

"I know," Casey said with more understanding in her voice. She held out a hand, and Ivy grabbed it, letting her friend give her a reassuring squeeze. "It's okay to be angry."

Leave it to her best friend to know exactly what Ivy was thinking.

"He should have known better," Ivy said softly, the tears pooling in her eyes. "They train to know when the building is safe to enter and when they need to get out. He should have gotten out. He should have thought about his wife and his baby and his family and..."

Ivy hiccupped and sobbed. She'd never said any of this aloud, not to her parents or Charlie's wife. She'd grieved as best she could, but she'd never admitted the ugly part of it, the irrational blame she placed on the brother she'd lost.

"I'm the worst," she said. "You don't need to tell me because I already know."

Casey sat down carefully in Ivy's office chair and patted the top of the desk, for her friend to sit. Ivy nodded and complied.

"Hey," Casey said, taking both of Ivy's hands now. "You know this is normal, right? The anger part? I know you've accepted that Charlie's gone, but I think you skipped right over this part. I should have stayed longer in Boston after the funeral. You kept it together for your parents and Allison, but you didn't get to fall apart with your best friend like you should have."

Ivy choked out a tearful laugh. "You mean like now?" She grabbed a tissue from the box on her desk and blew her nose. Then she grabbed two more to try to dry her tear-stained face. "You had a business to run. I never expected you to stay. I never expected *me* to stay as long as I did, but I couldn't leave until I knew they were all okay..." She paused for a long moment. "Or until I could come back here, knowing home would never be the same." She blew out a long breath. "So, I'm really not the worst?"

Casey smiled sadly and shook her head. "Do you really blame your brother for doing a job not many are cut out to do?"

Ivy shook her head.

"See?" Casey said. "Not the worst. This is actually a really good step, Ives. I think you're finally starting to move past the worst of it."

Ivy worried her bottom lip between her teeth, and Casey's brows furrowed.

Once she said what she was about to say out loud, it would be real. Like *really* real. And real with Carter Bowen still scared her half to death.

"There's something else you're not telling me." Casey narrowed her eyes. "This is about more than Charlie, isn't it? *Spill*," she added. "You have ten more minutes before I turn into a pumpkin and this badass dress changes back to jeans and a T-shirt."

Ivy laughed. Casey always could make her feel better about any situation. Venting her anger was cathartic, as far as taking a productive step past her grief, but it wasn't the only thing she'd been thinking about.

"Did I mention that Carter said he loved me?" she asked softly.

"What?" Casey threw her arms in the air. Then she yelped as a bodice pin scraped along her skin. "Ow!"

"Sorry!" Ivy cried, fumbling to fix the pin.

"Screw the apologies!" Casey said with a grin. "Tell. Me. *Everything*."

Her pulse quickened at having said what *he'd* said out loud. She'd sat on the information all week, not sure what to do with it. Hearing those words from him had been everything—shooting stars, fireworks, and a lifetime supply of fried pickles. She'd wound up exactly where she never wanted to be, except for one minor detail... Ivy loved Carter, too. And the realization solidified how much she had to lose if anything ever happened to him.

Ivy cleared her throat. "I spent the night at the inn with him after the game last week," she started.

"Bow-chica-bow-bow," Casey sang.

She rolled her eyes even though she was grateful for a moment of levity. "Yes. I'm a woman in my mid-twenties who has sex."

Casey waggled her brows. "Yes, but unless you stopped telling your best friend *everything*, you're a woman in her mid-twenties who up until meeting Lieutenant Dreamboat had not had sex in quite some time *and* who was taking things slowly with said Dreamboat."

"Nine months," Ivy admitted. "But who's counting? *Anyway*. If you want your best friend to tell you everything, you're going to need to stop interrupting." She paused, brows raised, and waited. Casey made a motion of zipping her lips, so Ivy went on.

"It was the next morning," she continued. "I was sort of asleep, sort of not. So I'm ninety-nine percent sure I didn't dream it. But he said something along the lines of knowing it was probably too early to say it but that he was a man of certainty and that he was certain he loved me."

Casey stared at her, eyes wide and mouth hanging open.

"You can talk now," Ivy said.

"Phew! Okay, first things first. I think it's reasonable to fall in love with someone in a few weeks. Plus, we're talking you, and you're pretty damn loveable."

"Thank you very much," Ivy said with a grin.

"But the part of the story that's missing is what you said back to him."

Ivy winced.

Casey's eyes narrowed. "Oh my God, Ivy Serrano. Did you pretend you were still sleeping?"

If it was possible for her wince to get bigger, Ivy's did.

"What if I dreamed it?" she asked.

Casey sighed. "You didn't dream it."

"Well, what if he only told me because he thought I was sleeping and didn't *really* want to tell me for *real* for real."

Casey shook her head. "I don't even know what you just said so why don't you tell me this—do you love *him*?"

Ivy sucked in a steadying breath.

"Maybe?"

"*Serrano…*"

"I don't know if I've ever *been* in love before. So how would I know?"

"*Ivy*," Casey said this time, her patience definitely growing thin.

"What if you're wrong and I'm not past the worst of what happened to Charlie? What if I *have* fallen for him

and he—?" She couldn't say it. It was one thing for Casey
to tell her she was moving past Charlie's death. It was a
whole other to be brave enough to risk her heart in an
entirely new and terrifying way.

Casey crossed her arms. "You can be scared, Ives. But
you have to be able to answer the question. So riddle me
this, Batgirl. When you think of your life without him,
how do you feel?"

Ivy's eyes burned with the threat of fresh tears.

Casey laughed. "Oh, honey. It's worse than I thought.
You fell *hard*, didn't you?"

Ivy nodded as the truth took hold. "I love him, Case. I
love Carter Bowen."

"Carter Bowen—who is a firefighter." Casey placed a
hand on Ivy's leg and gave her a soft squeeze. "Can you
handle that?"

Ivy swallowed and placed her hand over her friend's.
"I worked it out in my head. We're not a big city like
Boston. My dad made it to retirement here without any
major injuries. Meadow Valley is safe, which means
Carter is safe, even if he's a firefighter."

"And you'll support him if he has to do something you
don't deem safe?"

Ivy nodded. She could do this if she held on to her
logic—no matter how convoluted—that she couldn't lose
Carter like she lost Charlie. Not here.

"I love him," she said again.

"Then you better finish putting this dress together and
tell him," Casey said.

"I haven't even seen him all week. I think he's been
avoiding me. I went looking for him at Pearl's after his
first shift since that night, and she said he'd decided to
stay at the station for the week—iron some things out

with his unit." It could have been true. He could be working on the situation with Shane. Or he could be taking
extra shifts to keep from running into her.

Casey raised a brow. "Honey, the man's in love with
you and has no idea if you feel the same way. Even the
bravest of the brave get a little gun-shy when it comes to
matters of the heart. Luckily, *you* can fix that."

Ivy grinned. "Okay." Then she grabbed her phone and
hammered out a quick text to Carter.

Meet me at Midtown tonight?

The three dots appeared immediately, and she held
her breath.

Sure. Off at six.

Great. Can't wait to see you.

She waited several seconds, but there was no response
after that. It didn't matter. He was coming, and she
was going to tell him what she should have said that
morning.

Ivy shrugged. "Looks like I'm spilling my heart out at
six o'clock. Wish me luck."

Casey waved her off. "You got this, Ives. Home run.
Or is it a slam dunk?"

Ivy snorted. "Let's go with basketball for this one."

She finished the final pinning and stitching in record
time, fueled by the adrenaline of what she'd been afraid
to admit to herself all week. When she was done, she
and Casey headed to the tavern to celebrate with a drink
and whatever was left of the appetizers while Ivy waited
for Carter.

She tried not to look nervous when the clock hit 6:30
p.m. and he wasn't there, *nor* had she heard from him. At
6:45, she started to worry. And at 7:00 she was near to
panicking. Not that she thought anything had happened to

him. She'd have heard sirens if there had been any sort of emergency. But the kind of panic that said even without telling him how she felt, she'd somehow spooked him. Or maybe he had realized she'd heard what he said and was furious she hadn't reciprocated.

"Hey," Casey said from the other side of the bar. "You *can* call *him*, you know."

"Mmm-hmm," she said, popping a fried pickle into her mouth. Because a stressed-out girl in love needed some comfort food. "Or I could eat my weight in pickles. I think I'm going with option number two." Because wouldn't that be just her luck—to realize she was in love with the guy exactly when he realized he'd made a *huge* mistake saying he loved her?

Casey snagged the basket of fried goodness before Ivy could grab another bite.

"*Hey!*" Ivy said, trying to swipe her prized possession back. But Casey held it over her head. The only way Ivy was getting it back was if she climbed onto the bar and stole it back.

She shrugged. She wasn't above such a move.

Ivy was midclimb when Casey whisper-shouted, "He's here!"

Ivy rolled her eyes. "I want my damn pickles!"

"Ivy?" she heard from behind her. "What are you doing?"

She winced but not before grabbing her food back. Then she slid not-so-gracefully back onto her stool.

She spun to see Carter still in uniform, brows furrowed.

"Just taking back what was stolen from me." She held up her spoils. "Pickle?"

He shook his head, his jaw tight as his confusion morphed to something graver. She forgot her panic and grabbed his hand. "Hey, are you okay? I thought I'd see you at six and was starting to worry."

He climbed onto the stool next to hers.

"Here," Casey said, sliding a mug of beer his way. "No offense, but you look like you need this."

He shook his head. "None taken." And he took a sip.

"I spent the last hour in the chief's office, trying to figure out how to fix things," he said.

Ivy forgot about her fried pickles. "What's broken?"

Carter blew out a breath. "Morale? My team's faith in me? It turns out there have been several complaints turned in about me this week, all pertaining to me not knowing how the station runs and questioning the chief hiring someone based purely on nepotism."

"Nepo-*what*?" Casey asked. When Ivy opened her mouth to answer, she held up her hand. "I know what the word means. I just don't get how it relates, unless Lieutenant Dreamboat is the captain's or chief's long-lost son."

Ivy's eyes widened. "We're calling him Lieutenant Dreamboat to his face now?"

Casey popped a piece of pickle into her mouth. "We are *now*!"

Ivy turned back to Carter. "Okay, so someone found out about you being Pearl's nephew. I really don't get how that's nepotism. Pearl isn't a high-ranking firefighter or anything like that. She put in a good word, and you got the job."

Carter shook his head.

"Turns out I'm not the only one keeping a low profile as far as my Meadow Valley connections. Aunt Pearl is *dating* the chief."

If Ivy had been sipping her beer, this would have been

her first ever spit take, which wasn't the kind of thing a girl wanted to do *before* she and her significant other officially declared those three little words to each other. *Win him over and* then *start embarrassing yourself while eating and drinking.*

"I didn't know Pearl dated. Period," Ivy said.

"Go Pearl," Casey said. "Not only dating but a younger man, too. I want to be her when I grow up."

Carter sighed. "She took it so hard when my uncle passed away. I don't think any of us ever thought of her being with anyone else. Not that she doesn't deserve to be happy. It was just sort of a shock. And of all people..."

"Wait, wait, wait," Ivy said. "Put a pin in the whole nepotism thing for a second. Pearl's husband passed away a decade ago."

Carter nodded.

"Does that mean you were here for the funeral? I mean—I'm retroactively sorry for your loss. But were you here?"

He nodded again, and the set of his jaw loosened as realization set in. "He was my mother's favorite uncle. My brothers and I liked him, too. We drove out with my mom and my grandma for the funeral."

Ivy's eyes widened. "*I* was at that funeral. I mean, the whole town was, because that's small town life for ya, but we were both there."

The corner of his mouth turned up, the first hint of a smile since he walked through the door. Something about it made Ivy's breath catch in her throat.

"You didn't wear black," he said matter-of-factly, and she shook her head. "You had on a blue dress with a sunflower print. And I thought, *What is up with this girl who doesn't know anything about funeral etiquette?*"

She laughed, and her cheeks filled with heat.

"It was the first dress I ever made," she said. And the one that inspired her latest design, the one she hoped to actually finish and display in her shop window. "My mom loved planting flowers, and she taught Charlie and me. Our favorite was the sunflowers. Did you know that when they're young, before they bloom, they actually follow the sun across the sky each day?"

"Heliotropism," Carter said with a self-satisfied grin. "Solar tracking." Her eyes widened, and he shrugged. "I had to take a lab science in college. Botany was the only one that fit my schedule."

He knew about sunflowers. He *saw* her in her first dress.

Her stomach flipped. Every new thing she learned about Carter Bowen made it harder to resist the connection she felt with him.

She nodded. "I thought there was nothing more beautiful, and I wanted to wear something beautiful for Pearl. But it was more than that. I liked the idea of the new buds repositioning themselves each night so they faced east again. I admired their determination—their fierce sense of direction." Direction Ivy wanted so badly now that she was home. She wanted to face the grief and move past it. She wanted to wake up in the morning with the sun shining on her face instead of under the cloud where she'd lived for more than two years. "Pearl loved it, by the way." Ivy cleared her throat. "It's where my *thing* for flowers comes from. Haven't been able to bring myself to plant my own garden, but I add a rose here, a lily there— when it suits the design."

"I have no doubt Aunt Pearl loved it," Carter said. His brows drew together. "But I can't believe that was *you*."

Casey waved a hand between them. "Hell*oo*. Before

you two start talking about nonsense like *meant to be* or *star-crossed lovers* or whatever, can we get back to the *real* story so I can help actual paying customers? What the heck happened with the chief?"

Carter blinked, and the far-off look in his blue eyes that could have swallowed Ivy whole disappeared.

"Someone who knows about Pearl and the chief also knows about me being Pearl's nephew, and there's a petition going around to get me removed as lieutenant. There are quite a few signatures already."

Ivy gasped. "They can't actually *do* that, can they?"

Carter shook his head. "Technically, no. Family members are absolutely allowed to work in the same company."

"Right," Casey said. "Like Wyatt and Shane."

"Oh no," Ivy said. "*Shane.*"

"There's no nepotism clause in the handbook," Carter went on. "But in a job like this, morale is everything. If anyone thinks I got the job because of favoritism from the chief, then they might not trust that I'm up to the task. And if my presence is bringing down the morale of the whole company, then me staying on could be more detrimental than it's worth. Chief won't say who started the petition, but I took a job someone on the inside wanted, and that someone doesn't want me around..."

Casey shook her head. "You really think it was Shane? I mean, the guy carries around resentment like no one's business, but that seems a little over the top even for him."

Ivy winced. "I don't know. He and Carter have been butting heads since the day Carter stepped foot in the station. We were just as shocked when Shane ended up in jail. Maybe this isn't out of character at all."

Carter took another long, slow pull of his beer. "At the end of the day, it doesn't matter who it is if I can't win over the trust of my company."

There was a finality in his voice that made the hair on the back of Ivy's neck stand up.

"So, what does this mean?" she asked.

"It means I'm on leave for the weekend. Captain's taking over my crew. And by the end of next week, I may be out of a job. Leaving Houston for Meadow Valley made sense not simply for the job but also because I had family here. I could find another station in a different city or state, but at my age, a résumé that shows me having already left *two* stations? That doesn't give me a very reliable track record. If I haven't burned a bridge, I could ask for my job back in Houston. But if they say no..." He let out a bitter laugh. "There's always my father's auto shop. I bet he'd love me coming home with my tail between my legs, begging for what I told him I didn't want anymore." He finished his beer in one final gulp, then slapped some bills on the bar.

"Oh you don't—" Casey started, but Carter interrupted.

"It's way less than what I owe you since I got here, but I don't want to fuel the notion that I take handouts. Thanks, anyway," he said. He turned to Ivy. "I'm not gonna be good company tonight." Then he kissed her, his lips lingering on hers even after the kiss ended. "But I sure am happy I got to do that," he finally added. "I'm glad you texted."

Then he stood, pivoted toward the door, and left.

Ivy sat there, dumbfounded, staring at the door for several long moments after it closed behind him. She'd been so scared to lose Carter in the worst way possible that she never had considered him having to leave town.

"You okay?" Casey asked, breaking the silence.

"No," she said, turning to face her friend. "Case, what if he leaves?"

Casey nodded. "What if you go out there and tell him how you feel and see if that makes a difference? Maybe if you let him know you're willing to fight for him, he'll fight for a way to stay. All I know is *not* telling him how you feel will make you always wonder what would have happened if you did."

Ivy's eyes widened. "Are we still talking about me and Carter, or does this have something to do with Boone Murphy's recent engagement?" Ivy had been so wrapped up in everything Carter that she'd forgotten Casey's high school sweetheart was marrying someone else.

Casey rolled her eyes. "You're deflecting, Ives. What this is *about* is not regretting a missed opportunity. If you love the guy, *tell* him. It's as simple as that."

She swallowed the lump in her throat. Casey was right. She *loved* Carter, and he loved her. Once they said it aloud for real, everything would be different, wouldn't it? They could figure this job thing out together.

"I said I was going to tell him, which means I have to go tell him."

Casey nudged her shoulder. "Then get off your ass and go do the thing instead of talking about doing the thing."

She glanced down at Carter's cash on the counter, then back at her friend. "You're okay if I don't make a similar monetary gesture, right? I'll cover your next closing shift for free."

Casey raised her brows. "Yeah, you will. Now *go!*"

Ivy hopped off her stool and bounded toward the door just as she started to smell smoke. She pushed the tavern door open to the blaring sound of sirens filling the street. Along with it came the ringing of the firehouse bell, which meant only one thing.

For the first time in years, there was a real fire in Meadow Valley. And even though he was off duty, amid the ensuing chaos she saw Carter Bowen running across the street, straight toward the firehouse.

CHAPTER TEN

This was bad. He could already smell the smoke, and the air had taken on the type of haze that meant whatever was burning was feeding a fire that was growing.

"Carter!" he heard from behind him, and spun to see Ivy running toward him.

"I have to go, Ivy!" he called back.

She was out of breath when she stopped in front of him. "But you don't," she insisted. "You're—you're off duty. Lieutenant Heinz and his team will take care of whatever's happening."

"Ivy. You don't have to be a firefighter to know that *whatever's happening* probably needs more than one crew. Even when I'm off duty, I'm still on call. And I'm answering the damn call."

She pressed her hands to his chest as the first emergency vehicle pulled out of the station. The engine would be next, which meant he needed to hurry.

"Please," she said, her brown eyes shining. He wasn't sure if it was the threat of tears or because of the smoke in the air.

"Are you asking me *not* to do my job? Because I thought we were past this. I thought you were okay with what I did." Yet he didn't really trust her, did he? Or he'd have said how he felt to her face rather than when she was still asleep.

"And I thought you were done trying to prove yourself. You just told me you were on leave for the weekend, which means you don't *have* to go. I can't—" She swiped underneath one eye. "When you said you might have to go back to Houston, I knew right then that I'd beg you to stay, that I couldn't lose you. And now?" She pressed her lips together and shook her head. "I can't do it, Carter. I can't watch you run head on into a life-threatening situation when there are plenty of others who are prepared to do so. It's selfish of me to ask, and I have no right to do so, but I am begging you, Carter—begging you to stay *safe*."

The chief's voice sounded on his radio. "All available crews report. I repeat, all available crews report."

"I have to go, Ivy," he said firmly. "And you're wrong. I *do* need to prove that I'm what this company needs, that I'm capable of leading my crew into any situation and bringing them all home—safe, myself included. *This* is what I do. We're not tying up horses on the top of a hill and acting like what's down here doesn't exist. I can't pretend for you anymore."

"I love you," she said. It wasn't another plea or a last-ditch effort to get him to stay. He could hear the sincerity in the tremor of her voice. And, God, he *knew* what she'd already lost and how she'd never quite be over it. It was the same for him with Mason. But this was who he was. This was what he did. He couldn't be what she needed if that meant sitting on the sidelines when there were lives at stake.

"I love you, too," he finally said face-to-face, like he should have all along. "And I understand that this is too much for you. But I need you to understand that it's what I'm meant to do."

He kissed her, tasting the salt of her tears on her lips.

"Maybe, after you've had more time, and they haven't shipped me back to Texas..."

She said nothing after his pause, and he wouldn't finish the rest. Because even though he was done pretending for her, maybe he could do it for himself. Maybe he could pretend for tonight that they hadn't said those three words and then followed it up with a kiss that meant good-bye.

He pivoted toward the firehouse and strode up the walkway and inside to where he was met with the type of organized chaos he was meant to control. The chief saw him and nodded, so Carter started barking orders as he jogged into the engine room and suited up just in time to hop on.

All he had to prove was that he was bringing everyone on this crew home safe tonight. Then she'd see.

*   *   *

The street was filled with people by the time Ivy woke from her daze and turned around.

Patrons spilled out of Midtown Tavern, and she started to cross back that way. But then the engine's siren roared as the truck pulled out of the firehouse, around the corner, and onto First Street, causing her to jump back onto the curb. She stared at Wyatt in the driver's seat, then past him to where a pair of bright blue eyes stared back. Carter sat in the passenger seat, his jaw set and determined.

Her stomach roiled, and she thought she might be sick.

When the engine passed, she saw Casey coming toward her, her face pale.

"It's Mrs. Davis's house," she said. "The whole thing is up in flames."

"Oh my God," Ivy said. "Is she still inside?"

Casey shook her head, and for a second Ivy was relieved. But then Casey said, "I don't know. A neighbor called 911, not her." She sniffled. "Jessie called. She's on paramedic duty and said she'll give us an update as soon as she can. This is really bad, Ives."

Ivy hugged her friend. Mrs. Davis lived up the hill from Ivy's childhood home. She was like a second mother to her and Casey. As far as they knew, the woman had never married. At least she never said she had. But she was always adopting rescues from Dr. Murphy, the vet just outside of town, which meant she was never really alone. Today that would mean three cats, two dogs, and a cockatoo.

"I told him not to go," Ivy said, squeezing her friend tighter. "I told him I loved him and that he didn't have to go."

Casey stepped back, her hands still on Ivy's shoulders. "Charlie was in an office building whose roof collapsed. This isn't the same thing. It's Meadow Valley. Tragedies don't happen *in* Meadow Valley."

"It's a *fire*, Case. A fire brought that roof down and trapped my brother. Houses have roofs, too." She was arguing like a petulant child. She *knew* she was. But

Casey didn't get it. *No* one seemed to get it. "He was my best friend, and he left us. Me, my parents, Allison, and the baby. He left us, and for what?"

Casey swiped her thumbs under Ivy's eyes, then crossed her arms. "My sister's on the scene of that very same fire. Am I scared? Hell yes, I'm scared. But there's a reason Jessie's there instead of me. She's *trained* for this, and because of *her* training and Carter's and the whole company's, Mrs. Davis and her home have their best chance."

Ivy swallowed. "I'm sorry. I'm the worst. I know you're worried about Jessie, and—"

"How many people lived that day because Charlie did his job?" Casey interrupted.

Ivy shook her head.

"How many, Ives?"

Ivy squeezed her eyes shut. She'd thought leaving Boston and coming home to start fresh would mean that her grief stayed out east. But it followed her back to Meadow Valley and reared its ugly head without so much as a warning. And it made her forget how good Charlie was at his job—how safe his company was under Charlie's leadership. How even when he lost his own life, he saved so many others.

"Seven," Ivy finally said. "Seven civilians lived because Charlie was an expert firefighter." But even experts can't plan for every contingency. Charlie's company got him out in time so that he didn't have to die alone. His closest buddies rode with him in the ambulance and stayed with him at the hospital until the end. It was the one piece of the story she and her family held on to like a life raft. Charlie wasn't alone.

The sound of sirens clamored in the air once more. This

time it was the ambulance coming back from the opposite direction. It whizzed by them at a speed not normally seen on their quiet little street; then it rounded the corner in the direction of the highway and likely the hospital.

Ivy's stomach sank.

"It's probably Mrs. Davis in there with my sister, but Jessie hasn't sent any updates," Casey said, and for the first time Ivy detected a note of panic in her friend's voice. "There's no way to really get any answers unless…"

"Unless we get as close as we can to Mrs. Davis's house."

Ivy didn't think she had it in her to see the danger into which Carter had walked. But the not knowing felt even worse.

"Let's go," Ivy said.

They headed down the street, following the throng of curious folks who were likely trying to get close enough to marvel at the spectacle. One person who wasn't following the herd, though, was the older woman standing on the front porch of the inn.

Pearl.

She locked eyes with Ivy and gave her a reassuring nod. "I wouldn't have brought my nephew here if I didn't know he was damned good at his job." She stared wistfully down the street, and Ivy suddenly remembered about Pearl and the chief. Pearl had already lost one great love of her life. There was no way the universe would let that happen again or be so cruel as to take her nephew, too. That's what Ivy hoped and what she guessed gave Pearl her stoic strength.

"I'll text you when we get word about any of them," Ivy said.

Pearl nodded again, and Ivy and Casey kept on.

Ivy's heart thudded in time with the rhythm of her feet pounding the concrete. But all she could think about was what Carter had said about life-and-death situations and needing the trust of your team.

Maybe he was good at his job, but who had his back when there was a list of signatures who wanted to send him packing? And how could she let him go, thinking that he couldn't rely on *her*?

She started walking faster until she was in a slow jog and then close to a sprint.

She had Carter Bowen's back. If no one else did, it had to be her. Because though she was terrified for him, she also loved him. He needed to know he wasn't alone in this. She would be there. No matter what.

It was only minutes before she reached the blockade in front of Mrs. Davis's house, but it felt like hours.

"Hey!" Casey called. And Ivy turned around to see her friend halfway up the hill, her hands on her knees as she struggled to catch her breath. "What the hell was that, Flo Jo?" She lumbered the rest of the way until she made it to Ivy's side. Casey slung her hand over Ivy's shoulders and held up a finger while she tried to get her breathing in check. "Seriously," she finally said. "We run bases, not long-distance uphill."

An earsplitting crack followed by a crash cut their conversation short. Both startled and pivoted toward the sound. Half the town stood in front of them, so they could barely see over everyone's head. But they could *feel* the heat, the evidence that not too far away, Mrs. Davis's house burned.

"Screw it," Ivy said and grabbed Casey's hand, tugging her forward. "Excuse us!" she said as she pushed through the crowd. "Coming through! Sorry!" she cried as she stepped on someone's toes. But she wasn't stopping. Not until she made it to the barricade and got some answers. All the while, she held tight to Casey's hand, and Casey did the same with hers.

"Oh my God," Casey said when they got to the front.

Ivy couldn't speak. Her hand flew over her mouth, but no sound escaped.

Mrs. Davis's bright blue bungalow stood there at the top of her driveway like it always had. The front porch—decorated with potted plants and flowers, looked exactly the same. If you only stared at the porch and didn't look up, it was the same house Ivy had known for almost thirty years.

But they did look up, and out of the white-trimmed attic window poured livid orange flames. The place was burning from the top down.

Two firefighters controlled the front of the hose. Actually, one manned the hose while the other held him or her steady by the shoulders. She realized that she'd never seen her father or brother in action, had never truly understood what it meant to work as a team the way they did.

The chief rounded the back of the engine and spoke into his radio. When he finished his conversation, Ivy waved wildly, hoping to get his attention.

"Chief Burnett! Over here!" she cried. She'd known the chief most of her life. He and her father were rookies together. If anyone could ease her mind about what was going on inside Mrs. Davis's house, it was him.

Casey grabbed her arm and yanked it down. "I know how badly you want some information, but I think he's a little busy, Ives."

The chief looked up, though, and strode toward the barricade.

"Who was in the ambulance?" Ivy blurted. "Is Mrs. Davis okay? Is—are all your firefighters safe?"

He scratched the back of his neck.

"Mrs. Davis is being treated for smoke inhalation and some minor burns. Looks like she was going through some old boxes in her attic and dozed off while a scented candle was lit. We're guessing one of the animals knocked it over, and once the drapes caught—"

"The animals!" Ivy said. "Are they out?"

The chief blew out a breath. "It may not look like it, but we have the blaze contained. It's gonna be a while before it's out, though. Lieutenant Bowen and a small team are inside, trying to round up the animals."

Ivy had joked about Carter having to rescue one of Mrs. Davis's cats from a tree. The irony of this situation, though, was far from amusing. It was as dangerous as anything Meadow Valley had ever been.

She nodded and tried to swallow the knot in her throat. "What—what was that sound? Is the structure stable enough for them to be inside?"

"One of the ceiling beams in the attic was torn free." He glanced back toward the house. "We've got every available man and woman on the job. Got another engine from Quincy running a hose with some of our crew from the back and a second and third ambulance at the ready in front of our truck. We assess the situation as best we can, making predictions on what we know about the fire and how we believe it will behave. But there's always risk."

Casey squeezed Ivy's hand and pointed toward the house. "Look!"

A parade of firefighters exited the front door, one carrying Mrs. Davis's cocker spaniel, Lois. Another had a box of kittens. And the third held Butch Catsidy, the

three-legged foster cat she'd had since he was a kitten—
and had kept when no one adopted him. The crowd of
onlookers applauded, but Ivy knew Mrs. Davis's beagle
was still missing. Frederick was old and prone to hiding,
and he was no doubt burrowed somewhere he thought
was safe.

A voice sounded on the chief's radio, and he turned
his back to listen and respond.

Ivy let go of Casey's hand and pulled out her phone
and fired off a quick text to Pearl.

*With the chief. He's outside. Mrs. Davis at the hospital
but will be okay. No word on anyone else yet.*

She couldn't bring herself to say Carter's name. The
not knowing was making it hard to breathe. She started
slipping her phone back into her pocket but then changed
her mind. Even though there was no way he'd see it
now, she hoped with everything she had he'd see it soon.
So she brought up her last text exchange with Carter
and typed.

*I'm here. If you'll let me, I will always be here for you.
I love you.*

She pocketed her phone just as the chief turned back
around.

"They found Frederick," he said.

Ivy breathed out a sigh of relief. But it was short-lived.

"He's under Mrs. Davis's bed. Two of them are trying
to coax him out while another keeps watch on the sound-
ness of the structure." He shook his head. "I wanted
everyone off the second floor by now." He pulled his radio
out again. "Lieutenant, you have two minutes to get your
team out of there, dog or no dog. Do you copy?"

"Copy that, Chief. Two minutes. But we're coming
with the dog. Over."

Ivy's heart lifted. That was Carter's voice. Carter was okay. The team was still okay.

The firefighters on the ground had now moved to the bucket ladder just outside the fiery attic window.

"Who else is inside?" she asked.

"It's just Lieutenant Bowen, O'Brien, and O'Brien."

Carter. Wyatt. Shane.

"The dog is secured, sir. We're coming out. Over," Carter said over the radio.

Ivy choked back a sob. In seconds he'd be out of the building and she'd be able to breathe again.

But instead she heard another screech followed by a crash and then the unmistakable sound of the PASS device, a firefighter's personal alarm that meant he or she was in distress.

Seconds later, one of the firefighters and Frederick ran out the front door, but whoever was carrying the dog set him down on the lawn and ran back inside.

Casey hooked her arm through Ivy's and pulled her close. "He's gonna come out, Ives, okay? This is Meadow Valley. We don't do tragedy here. Plus, you've already had your fill for one lifetime, so this is only going to end with Carter Bowen walking out of that house."

Ivy nodded, but she couldn't speak. Maybe she'd had her share of tragedy, but had she played a role in setting herself up for more? She shook her head, a silent argument with her thoughts. She could let her fear close her off from risk—and also happiness—or she could be here for Carter, believing in him and in what Casey said: This was going to end with Carter Bowen walking out of that house.

"What if that's not how it ends, Case?" she asked, her voice cracking with the reality of the situation.

Casey looked at her, the tears in her best friend's eyes mirroring her own.

"Then you will fall apart, and I will be here to put you back together again. You're not alone in this, okay? You will *never* be alone."

Ivy nodded and held her breath.

"Lieutenant, what's your status? Over," the chief said, somehow maintaining his calm.

"Sir, this is Shane O'Brien. Part of the attic ceiling came down over the stairs. Lieutenant Bowen and my brother—I was already at the bottom with the dog—got knocked down by a burning beam." He went silent for a few seconds. "They're under the beam and neither of them are moving."

Ivy could see the fiery beam through the window. It stretched halfway down the length of the stairs.

The PASS alert ceased, and the chief's radio crackled.

Carter's voice sounded over the radio. "The rest of the ceiling's gonna go, Chief. Don't send anyone else in. O'Brien's got this. Shane?" Carter sounded pained, and Ivy stopped breathing altogether. "Shane can you hear me?"

"Copy that. I hear you, Lieutenant Bowen," Shane said. "But—I can't do this. I can't—"

"I need you to stay calm but act fast. Your brother's unconscious and my arm is broken, and my hand is pinned under the corner of the beam. All you need to do is unpin me, and I can help you carry your brother out."

"This shit isn't supposed to happen here," Shane said. "*Nothing* happens here."

"You can do this, Shane," Carter said. "But it has to be fast. The rest of the ceiling is starting to buckle."

The radios went silent after that. Ivy swore she could

hear her own heartbeat. Her hand was in Casey's again, the two of them squeezing each other tight yet not laying voice to what they were both thinking.

This was Charlie all over again. They got Charlie out but not in time to save him from the internal injuries the paramedics couldn't treat.

The firefighters on the outside still worked tirelessly, and the flames began to retreat. But Ivy knew that did nothing for the internal damage or the safety of the structure. The ceiling was already compromised, and the extra weight of the water would expedite its complete collapse.

A buckling sound came from within the house, and Ivy knew their time was up.

"Come on. Come on. Come on," she chanted.

Then the roof of the house dipped. Less than a second later, it folded in on itself as two figures burst through the front-door opening with a third figure's arms draped over their shoulders.

Shane and Carter ran with the toes of Wyatt's boots scraping across the grass until they were far enough from what once was Mrs. Davis's home and paramedics were able to retrieve Wyatt and get him onto a stretcher. Carter held his right arm against his torso, and when he tore off his hat and mask, she could see an expression wrought with pain as another paramedic escorted him to a third ambulance.

Ivy dropped down to the ground and crawled under the barricade.

"Go get him, Ives!" Casey called after her.

And Ivy ran. She ran past the chief, who called her name, but she didn't stop to listen. She ran past a police car where she recognized Daniela Garcia, who'd graduated high school with Charlie, standing against the bumper. Except she was Deputy Garcia now, and although Ivy didn't think she was breaking any laws by bypassing the barricade, at the moment she didn't care if she had, as long as she made it to Carter.

"You can't be back here, Ivy!" Deputy Garcia yelled. But Ivy still didn't stop.

Not until she was breathless and banging on the already closed back door of the emergency vehicle did she come to a halt.

A paramedic swung the door open, and she climbed inside without being invited. Carter sat on the gurney still in his protective boots and pants, but his jacket had been removed and a ninety-degree splint was affixed to his right arm from shoulder to wrist. A clear tube that led to an IV bag hanging from the ceiling of the vehicle was taped to his left hand.

"Hi," she said, barely holding it together. "All right if I ride along?"

CHAPTER ELEVEN

Carter looked at the paramedic who was closing the door, a younger guy from his team named Ty. "You think you could give us some privacy?" he asked.

The other man hesitated. "With all due respect, Lieutenant—and that's a mighty fine thing you did talking O'Brien through that situation—you know I can't leave you alone back here." He had to give it to the kid for following procedure. He wondered, though, if Ty's name was on that petition.

The ambulance lurched forward, and Ivy fell into the seat meant for the paramedic.

"Guess that means you're staying," Carter told her.

"I can sit here," Ty said, taking a spot on the bench to Carter's right. "And the best I can do about privacy is this." He pulled a pair of wireless earbuds out of his pocket and stuck them in his ears. "Just tap my shoulder if you need something!" he said, already too loud over whatever music he was playing, and Carter laughed.

"Looks like it's just you and me," he said. "Which means that now I can ask you what the hell you were doing so close to the fire. Dammit, Ivy. Don't you know how dangerous that was?"

Her eyes widened. "Me? You're *mad* at me when I came here to show you that I support you no matter what? To tell you that I love you and that you're not alone in this?"

She threw her hands in the air, but with such limited space, she had to keep her arms close to her body. The whole gesture made her look like an exasperated T. rex, and Carter had to bite the inside of his cheek to keep from laughing.

"Are you—laughing?" she said. "I just heard you over the chief's radio say that you were trapped under a burning ceiling beam and that your arm was broken, and you're *laughing*?"

Her voice trembled, and a tear slid quickly down her cheek.

He wasn't laughing anymore.

"Jesus, Ivy," he said. "You heard all that? How long were you out there?"

She sucked in a steadying breath and blew it out slowly.

"Long enough to know that you are really good at your job. Long enough to know that even in the worst situation, you were still in control and knew what to do." She shook her head and pressed her lips together. "I will always be scared when you have to leave that firehouse with sirens blaring. But I also know that you're the best shot your team has at coming home safe whenever you do."

He cupped her cheek in his palm. IV or not, he didn't care. He needed to touch her, and he needed her to know the truth—that as good as he was at his job, he was scared, too, scared that he couldn't guarantee he'd always walk away from a situation like today.

"I can't promise you that'll be the case 100 percent of the time. If we hadn't gone back in for that damn dog, no one on my command would have left in an ambulance. I mean, hell, if Shane wasn't there—if he didn't listen to me?" He dropped his hand and let out a bitter laugh. "You were right," he told her. "The whole month I've been here I've been so hell-bent on proving myself. What if that clouded my judgment? What if—"

"No what ifs," Ivy interrupted. "I heard everything. You listened to the chief's orders. You're alive. Wyatt's alive. And Shane saved you both. I've spent the past four weeks promising myself I wouldn't let you get too close because of what happened to Charlie. Because of *What if?* I never should have told you not to go tonight. And I never will again."

His brows furrowed. "You'll never tell me *not* to go again or you'll never *not* tell me not to go. Either the pain meds are kicking in or there are too many negatives in what you said that I'm not sure if you meant what I think you meant."

This time she was the one to laugh, and the effect of the pain meds paled in comparison to her smile. He could live with being unsure about the future as long as it meant she was in it.

"Just to clarify," he said, "are you saying that if I stay in town, you're not going to turn the other way if you pass me on the street?"

She let out something between a laugh and sob. "If you weren't all busted up, I'd punch you in the shoulder or something."

"Well then, I guess I'm safe from any further *physical*

distress," he said. "But are you gonna break my heart, Ivy Serrano?"

She shook her head, then rested it on his shoulder. "Nah. I love you too much to do that." She tilted her head up, and her brown eyes shimmered in the normally unpleasant fluorescent light.

"That's a relief," he said. "Because I don't think I could walk by you without wanting to do this." His lips swept over hers in a kiss that felt like the start of something new. He couldn't wrap her in his arms, and maybe the bumps in the road made the whole gesture a little clumsy, but she was here. And she was staying. And petition or not, dammit, so was he.

Carter waited outside the chief's office, anxious more about being late for Ivy's fashion show than he was about what would be said behind the office doors. If he was being let go, he was being let go. He was damned good at his job, and he didn't need anyone's approval anymore to know that was true.

Okay, fine, so he needed the chief's approval to *keep* his job but not to know that he did everything he could for this company in the month he was here.

The door swung open, and Chief Burnett popped his head out.

"Come on in, Lieutenant. Sorry to keep you waiting."

Carter stood and brushed nonexistent dust from his uniform pants. His right hand had cramped, so he flexed it, still getting used to the air cast.

He walked inside, expecting to find the chief alone waiting for him, but instead he saw Shane O'Brien standing in front of the chief's desk.

The chief cleared his throat. "Lieutenant Bowen, I

hope you don't mind, but I thought it best for Firefighter O'Brien to speak first."

Carter nodded. "O'Brien," he said. "Heard your brother is being discharged today."

"Yes, sir, Lieutenant. It was a pretty bad concussion, but thanks to you, he's going to be fine."

Carter's brows drew together. The formality from Shane confused him. Not that he'd expected the guy to mouth off, but this was a complete one-eighty from what Carter had seen from him.

"He's going to be fine, O'Brien, because of *you*," Carter said. "Neither of us would be here right now if you hadn't gotten us out of that house before the roof caved in."

Shane's jaw tightened. "With all due respect, Lieutenant, I never wanted to be here. And I made sure everyone knew it. And then I made your life a living hell because I knew I wasn't good enough, and it was your job to remind me of that." He squared his shoulders. "The signatures on the petition were forged. Every one of them but mine. I am not proud of my behavior and need some time to regroup."

Carter opened his mouth to say something, but Shane cut him off.

"I need to figure things out without everything that's been hanging over my head since I was a kid. I'm leaving town, sir. And the company. Effective immediately."

Shane held out his hand to shake but then realized that was Carter's broken arm and dropped it back to his side.

"O'Brien," Carter said. "You don't have to do this."

"It's already done," the chief said. "I tried to talk him out of it, but I think his mind was made up the second he rode away from the Davis fire with his brother in an ambulance."

Shane nodded once, his eyes dark and expression stoic.

"You're a good firefighter, O'Brien," Carter added. "I'd have been proud to keep you on my team."

"Thank you, Lieutenant," he said. He nodded toward the chief. "You too, Chief."

The chief clapped Shane on the shoulder. "You always have a place here if you ever decide to come back."

Shane pressed his lips together but didn't say anything else. Then he strode through the door, closing it behind him.

Carter blew out a long breath. "You think he's going to get into trouble again?"

The chief shook his head. "If you'd have asked me that a month ago, I'd have said yes. But something changed in him since you've been around. And the way you handled things in the Davis fire? We're damn lucky to have you, Lieutenant."

He was staying in Meadow Valley. This was—home.

"Thank you, sir. I feel damn lucky to be here."

After a long moment, Carter turned to head for the door.

"One more thing, Lieutenant," the chief said, stopping him in his tracks. "Your family was notified of your injury, and your father has called your aunt four times in the past two days to check on you. I thought you should know."

Carter swallowed hard but didn't turn back around. "Appreciate the information," he said. "But he knows my number."

"Give him time," the chief said. "Father-son relationships can be a tricky thing."

Carter thought about Shane, who was leaving town

to deal with his own tricky thing, and the weight on his shoulders lifted, if only a fraction of an inch.

"Yes, sir. I suppose they are."

Then he was out the door and down the steps two at a time. When he pushed through the station's front door, Ivy was there on the sidewalk, right where he'd left her on his way in. The sky was overcast, but she was a vision in her bright yellow sundress, brown waves of hair falling over her shoulders.

He only needed one arm to lift her up and press his lips to hers.

"I'm home, darlin'," he said.

"Good," she said through laughter and kisses. "Because I wasn't letting you go without a fight. Now come on. I need to show you something."

She led him down the street to her shop. She bounced on her toes as they slowed in front of the window where a single mannequin stood displaying a dress that could only be described as a field of sunflowers.

"You made that?" he said. "It's like nothing I've ever seen, Ivy. If I didn't know any better, I'd say those were live flowers."

She smiled the biggest, most beautiful smile he'd seen since the fire.

"I made them," she said, and he could hear how proud she was. "It's my version of my and Charlie's garden. I don't think I'd have ever finished it if I hadn't met you, which is why I wanted you to be the first to see it."

She beamed—a ray of sunshine on an otherwise cloudy day.

He stepped closer and wrapped his arm around her waist. "Are you calling me your muse?" he teased, and she laughed.

"I'm calling you my everything, if that's okay," she said, then kissed him.

He smiled against her. "That's about the okayest thing I've ever been called, darlin'. So yeah, I think I'm good with that. As long as you're good with me spending the rest of my days making good on that title."

She kissed him again, and he took that as a yes.

*   *   *

Ivy and Carter tied Ace and Barbara Ann to the fence. She stared at the beautiful, stubborn man she loved and shook her head.

"What would the doctor say if he knew you were on a horse three days after breaking your arm?" she asked. She'd tried to stop him, but he'd threatened to ride off without her if she didn't join him.

He opened and closed his right hand. "Arm's broken," he said. "Thanks to Shane O'Brien, the hand's just fine. Besides, who's snitching on me to the doctor?"

She removed the pack from Barbara Ann's saddle and tossed it on the ground. They'd get to that shortly. Then she wrapped her arms around him and kissed him in the place where they'd kissed for the first time. When they finally parted, he spun her so her back was against his torso, his hands resting on her hips.

From the top of the hill above town, Ivy could see the ruins of Mrs. Davis's home. She could also see the inn where Pearl would give her—and her animals—a place to stay for as long as it took for her to rebuild. She could see the bell above the firehouse, the one that would forever remind her of the day she *didn't* lose the man who held her in his arms right now.

"Can you see that?" he whispered in her ear. "I don't mean the town. I mean what's right in front of you."

Her brows furrowed, and she shifted her gaze from the tapestry of Meadow Valley to a shock of color just a little way down the hill. A sunflower.

She spun to face him. "I don't understand. How did it—I mean, those don't sprout up in a matter of days."

He laughed. "I talked to Sam Callahan, and we thought it might be fun to start a community garden up here between locals and ranch guests. It's public property, so there are permits involved, but I'm sure you can point me in the right direction of who to talk to."

"You want to build me a garden?" she asked, her eyes wide.

"I want to build you everything," he said. "But if the garden's too painful—if the memories are too much..."

She shook her head.

"It *is* painful," she admitted. "But it's also wonderful and thoughtful." She pressed her palms to his chest. "I don't want to forget the painful stuff. And I don't want to wrap myself in a bubble of fire extinguishers and interconnected smoke detectors and—and loneliness to protect myself from getting hurt again. I want to start something new—with this garden and with you. I will always be scared, but I don't have to be alone. *We're* not alone."

"Although fire safety *is* important," he teased. "So don't abandon your extinguishers just to make a statement."

She laughed.

"You know," he said, looking past her and down at the town, "if you need to when things get tough, we can always come here to forget the rest of the world for a little while, pretend it doesn't exist."

She shook her head. "I want to experience it all, the good and the bad. With you."

She gave him a soft kiss and ran her hands through his hair, smiling against him. "Starting with a hilltop haircut," she said. "Are you ready, Lieutenant? Brought all my tools."

He laughed and stepped away. "At the risk of you miscalculating and lopping off my ear, I need to ask you one quick thing before I potentially lose my hearing."

Ivy crossed her arms. "Cut off your ear? Please, Lieutenant. And here I thought you trusted—"

He dropped down to one knee, and Ivy lost the ability to form words.

"I know there's supposed to be a ring and everything, but I'm kind of doing this out of order. It's as simple as the text you sent me the night of the fire. Everything's been so crazy the past few days I didn't even see it until later the next day. I'm here, Ivy. If you'll let me, I will always be here for you. I love you. Say you'll marry me, plant gardens with me, and build a life with me, and *then* I'll let you cut my hair."

She wasn't sure if she was laughing or crying because the tears were flowing, but she was smiling from ear to ear.

She clasped her hands around his neck and kissed him and kissed him and kissed him some more.

"Yes," she said against him, and she felt his smile mirror hers. "Yes. Yes. Yes."

ACKNOWLEDGMENTS

Writing the first draft of a new book is my happy place, and this book was no exception. But making the book all sparkly and pretty—that's the tough stuff, and I wouldn't be able to do it without my wonderful editor, Madeleine Colavita. Thank you for always knowing how to point me in the right direction, for giving me plenty of LOLs and smiley faces in your margin notes, and for wanting to try PB&J with brie. I think we should do this together!

Thank you to the whole Forever team for loving my small-town California ranchers as much as I do. I'm thrilled to keep working with each and every one of you: Amy, Leah, Gabi, and Estelle—who thankfully reminded me that this series needs an animal with personality to rival Lucy the psychic chicken. The addition of Butch Catsidy is thanks to you!

To my fabulous agent, Emily, your guidance, support, and brainstorming phone calls are everything.

Thank you Jen, Chanel, Lia, Megan, and Natalie for cheering me on, inspiring me with your words, and for being the best besties.

To all the readers—thank you for reading, reviewing, and sharing the love of romance.

Dad, thanks for buying all my books but not reading. LOL. Mom, thanks for buying, reading, and sharing with all your friends. And to S and C, thanks for thinking it's cool that your mom is a writer but understanding you're not allowed to read for a few more years. I love you infinity.

ABOUT THE AUTHOR

A librarian for teens by day and a romance writer by night, A.J. Pine can't seem to escape the world of fiction, and she wouldn't have it any other way. When she finds that twenty-fifth hour in the day, she might indulge in a tiny bit of TV to nourish her undying love of vampires, superheroes, and a certain high-functioning sociopathic detective. She hails from the far-off galaxy of the Chicago suburbs.

You can learn more at:
AJPine.com
Twitter @AJ_Pine
Facebook.com/AJPineAuthor

LOOK FOR MORE A.J. PINE BOOKS!

MEADOW VALLEY SERIES—
COMING IN WINTER 2019!

My One and Only Cowboy
Make Mine a Cowboy
Only a Cowboy Will Do

CROSSROADS RANCH SERIES—
AVAILABLE NOW!

Second Chance Cowboy
Tough Luck Cowboy
Hard Loving Cowboy

Looking for more cowboys?
Forever brings the heat with these sexy studs.

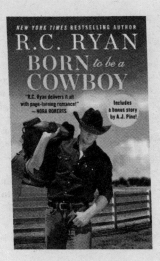

BORN TO BE A COWBOY
by R.C. Ryan

When her aunt disappears not long after her shotgun wedding, Jessie Blair fears the worst. Unable to uncover answers on her own, she hopes lawyer/smooth-talking cowboy Finn Monroe can help solve the mystery—especially since danger seems to lurk around every corner. Finding protection in Finn's arms, Jessie experiences feelings she's never known before. But is love enough, when someone wants them both dead? Includes a bonus novella by A.J. Pine!

Discover bonus content and more on read-forever.com.

CHRISTMAS WITH A COWBOY
by Carolyn Brown

A year ago, cowboy Maverick Callahan fell head-over-heels for an extraordinary woman he met while on vacation—a woman he was convinced he'd never see again. So when she appears on his doorstep like a Christmas miracle, Maverick is determined not to waste his lucky break. Includes a bonus novella by Sara Richardson!

A COWBOY FOR CHRISRMAS
by Sara Richardson

Darla Michaels has come up with the perfect way to save the town from a recent slump in tourism. But planning the first annual Cowboy Christmas Festival means she has to work with Ty Forrester, head of the town's rodeo association and an irresistible bull rider who keeps testing her keep-things-casual policy. Includes a bonus novella by R.C. Ryan!

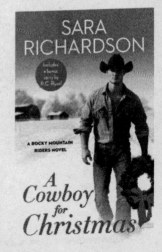

Follow @ReadForeverPub on Twitter and join the conversation using #ReadForever.

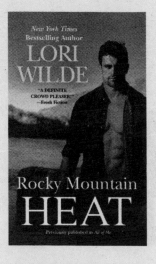

ROCKY MOUNTAIN HEAT
by Lori Wilde

Attorney Jillian Samuels doesn't believe in true love and has never wished for happily ever after. But when a searing betrayal leaves her jobless and heartbroken, a newly inherited cottage in Salvation, Colorado, seems to offer a fresh start. What she finds when she arrives shocks her: the most gorgeous and infuriating man she's ever met is living in her home! (Previously published as *All of Me*)

MY ONE AND ONLY COWBOY
by A.J. Pine

Sam Callahan, co-owner of the Meadow Valley guest ranch, is barely keeping his business in the black. But when a gorgeous blonde barges onto his property insisting he bought the place in a fraudulent sale—and that she's there to prove she still owns half the land—Sam realizes he's got much more to worry about. He could lose everything—including his heart. Includes a bonus novel by Carolyn Brown!

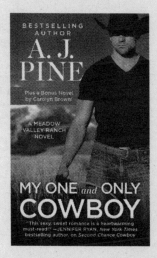

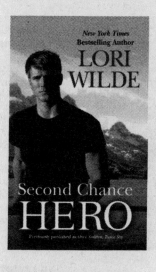

SECOND CHANCE HERO
by Lori Wilde

Tish Gallagher scores the job of a lifetime—too bad it brings her up close and personal with the man she's never stopped loving. Sure, their chemistry was hotter than a Texas summer, but their clashes were legendary, and no amount of longing will change that. (Previously published as *Once Smitten, Twice Shy*)